Liza Marklund is a print and television journalist. She lives in Stockholm with her husband and three children.

# the BOMBER

## LIZA MARKLUND

Translated by Kajsa von Hofsten

POCKET
BOOKS

London · New York · Sydney · Tokyo · Singapore · Toronto · Dublin

First published in Great Britain by Pocket Books, 2002
An imprint of Simon & Schuster UK Ltd
A Viacom Company

1 3 5 7 9 10 8 6 4 2

Simon & Schuster UK Ltd
Africa House
64–78 Kingsway
London WC2B 6AH

www.simonsays.co.uk

Simon & Schuster Australia
Sydney

A CIP catalogue record for this book is available from the British Library

ISBN 0-7434-4084-6

Typeset by M Rules
Printed and bound by
Cox & Wyman Ltd, Reading, Berks.

# the
# BOMBER

# PROLOGUE

The woman who was about to die stepped warily out of the doorway and quickly glanced about her. The stairwell behind her lay in darkness; she hadn't switched on the light on her way down. In her pale coat, she was a ghostly apparition in the shadows of the entryway. She hesitated before stepping out onto the pavement, as if suspecting she was being watched. She took a couple of quick breaths, and for a few moments the white mist of her exhalation hovered around her head like a halo. Then she straightened the strap of her shoulder bag and took a firm grip of the handle of her briefcase. With hunched shoulders, she walked toward Götgatan, taking quick, quiet steps. It was bitterly cold; a biting wind cut through her clothes. She sidestepped an icy patch and for a second was balancing on the curb. Then she hurried away from the streetlight and into the darkness. The sounds of the night were muffled: the sighing of a ventilation system, the yelling of some drunken youths, a faraway siren.

The woman's stride was confident and determined. She exuded assurance and expensive perfume. When her cellphone suddenly rang, she was completely taken aback. Freezing in mid-step, she quickly looked behind her. She bent down to lean the briefcase against her leg. While she rummaged in her handbag, her whole being positively oozed annoyance. She fished out her phone and put it to her ear. Despite the darkness and the shadows, her reaction could not be misjudged. Her irritation turned to surprise, then to anger, and finally, fear.

When she finished the call, the woman stood still for a few seconds, phone in hand. She bent her head, seemingly lost in thought. A police car drove slowly past. The woman looked up at it, watchful, following it with her gaze. She made no attempt to stop it.

Then she appeared to make up her mind. She turned around and started walking back the way she had come, past the dark doorway and up to the crossing at the corner of Katarina Bangata. While waiting for a night bus to drive past, she lifted her head and followed the street with her eyes, past Vintertullstorget and across Sickla Canal. Floating high above it lay the main Olympic arena, Victoria Stadium, where the Summer Olympics would open in seven months' time.

After the bus passed by, the woman crossed Ringvägen and started walking along Katarina Bangata. Her face was expressionless; her hurried steps testified to how cold she felt. She took the footbridge across the canal and entered the Olympic compound via the media village. With sharp and somewhat jerky movements, she hurried toward the stadium. She chose the route along the water's edge, although it was a longer and colder walk: A freezing wind blew in from the sea. But she did not wish to be seen. She repeatedly stumbled in the dense darkness.

When she reached the post office and the pharmacy, she turned up toward the training area and ran the last few hundred yards to the arena. By the time she reached the main entrance, she was out of breath as well as angry. She pulled the door open and stepped into the darkness.

"Tell me what you want, and be quick about it," she said with a cold look at the person who appeared from the shadows.

She saw the raised hammer but had no time to be afraid.

The first blow landed on her left eye.

# EXISTENCE

Just behind the upper fence lay a huge anthill. As a child, I used to study it with utter concentration. I would stand so close that the insects were constantly crawling on my legs. Sometimes I followed a single ant from the grass in front of the house, across the gravel road, along the sandbank, and up to the anthill. There I would steel my gaze so as not to lose sight of the insect, but I always did. Other ants would catch my attention. When they became too numerous, my focus would splinter into so many pieces that I lost patience.

Sometimes I would put a lump of sugar on the hill. The ants loved my gift, and I smiled while they poured over it and pulled it down into the depth of the hill. In the autumn, when days grew colder and the ants slowed down, I would stir the hill with a stick to wake them up again. The grown-ups were angry when they saw what I was doing. They said that I was sabotaging the work of the ants and had ruined their home. To this day, I remember the feeling of injustice. I meant no harm. I just wanted a bit of fun. I wanted to rouse the little creatures.

*My game with the ants haunted me in my dreams. My fascination turned into an unspeakable fear of their crawling. In my adult life, I have never been able to bear seeing more than three insects at a time, of whatever kind. As soon as I'm unable to take them all in, panic starts building up. My phobia came into being the moment I discovered the parallel between myself and the little insects.*

*I was young and still actively searching for answers to my condition, building theories in my mind, trying them out against each other in different problems I would formulate. That life could be arbitrary was not part of my worldview. Something had created me. I was not to be the judge of what that something was: chance, fate, evolution, or possibly God.*

*That life could be without meaning, however, I considered likely, and this filled me with sorrow and rage. If our time on earth had no purpose, then our lives appeared to be an exercise in irony. Someone put us here to study us as we made war, crawled around, suffered, and struggled. At times this Someone would confer a reward on us at random—much like putting a lump of sugar on an anthill—and watch our joy and despair with the same indifference.*

*My certainty grew with the years. In the end, I realized that it makes no difference whether there is a higher meaning to my life or not. Even if there is, I am not supposed to know of it here and now. If there were answers to be found, I would already know what they were, and since I don't, it makes no difference however much I think about it.*

*This has given me some measure of peace of mind.*

## SATURDAY 18 DECEMBER

The sound reached her deep into a bizarre sex dream. She was lying on a glass stretcher in a space shuttle, Thomas on top of and inside her. Three presenters from the radio program *Studio Six* were standing beside them and watching with vacant faces. She was desperate to go to the bathroom.

"You can't go now. We're on our way out into space," Thomas said, and she saw through the panoramic window that he was right.

The second ring tore the cosmos apart and left her thirsty and sweating in the dark. She tried to focus on the ceiling above her in the gloom.

"Answer, for God's sake, before it wakes the kids!" Thomas grunted from among the pillows.

She turned her head to look at the clock: 3:22. Her excitement was gone at a stroke. An arm, heavy with sleep, reached for the phone. It was Jansson, the night editor.

"Victoria Stadium has been blown up. There's one hell

of a fire. The night reporter is there, but we need you for the early edition. How soon can you get there?"

She took a breath, letting the information sink in, and felt the adrenaline course like a wave through her body and into the brain. The Olympic arena, she thought, fire, shit . . . south of the city. The South Bypass or Skanstull Bridge.

"What's it like in town, are the roads okay?" Her voice sounded rougher than she would have wanted.

"The South Bypass is blocked. The exit next to the stadium has collapsed, that much we know. The South Tunnel may be cordoned off, so stick to the streets."

"Who's shooting?"

"Henriksson has gone out, and the freelancers are already there."

Jansson hung up without waiting for her to answer. For a few seconds Annika listened to the hum of the line before she dropped the phone onto the floor.

"What is it now?"

She sighed inwardly before replying.

"Some explosion at the Olympic stadium. I've got to get over there. It'll probably take all day."

She hesitated before adding: "And night."

He mumbled inaudibly.

Carefully she extricated herself from Ellen's sleepy embrace. She breathed in the smells of the child: the sweet skin, the sweat-dampened pajamas, the sour mouth where her thumb was always resting. She kissed her daughter's smooth head. The girl moved sensually, gave a stretch, then curled up into a ball; three years old and utterly self-possessed, even in sleep. With her heavy arm, she dialed the direct number to the taxi switchboard. She got out of the overpowering warmth of the bed and sat down on the floor.

"Could I have a car to 32 Hantverkargatan, please.

Name of Bengtzon. I'm in a hurry . . . To the Olympic stadium . . . Yes, I know it's on fire."

She was dying for a pee.

It was freezing cold outside. She raised the collar and
pulled down her hat to cover her ears. Her toothpaste-
smelling breath was like a cloud around her. The taxi
pulled up at the same moment as the door closed behind
her.

"Hammarby Dock, the Olympic stadium, please,"
Annika said as she landed on the back seat with her big
holdall.

The taxi driver glanced at her in the rearview mirror.

"Bengtzon from *Kvällspressen*, right?" he said with an
uncertain smile. "I often read your articles. I liked your
stuff on Korea; my kids come from there. I've been to
Panmunjom, too, you know. You wrote it just like I saw
it. Soldiers standing there face to face in the DMZ, not
being allowed to talk to each other. That was good stuff."

As always, she listened to the praise without taking it
in. Or resisted taking it in. If she thought she was too
good herself, she might lose it: the magic, whatever it
was that made the writing take off.

"Thanks, I'm glad you liked it. Can you take the South
Tunnel, do you think? Or should we stick to the streets
all the way?"

Like most of his colleagues, he was totally on the ball. If
something happened anywhere in the country at 4 A.M.,
you made two phone calls: one to the police and one to the
local taxi company. After that you'd be guaranteed to have
a story for the first edition. The police could confirm what
had happened, and a taxi driver would almost always be
able to give you some kind of eyewitness account.

"I was on Götgatan the time of the explosion," he said,
doing a U-turn across an unbroken double white line.

"Shit, the streetlights were swaying! 'Jesus,' I said to myself, 'it's the Russians, they're bombing us!' I called in on the radio to ask what's going on. They told me that Victoria Stadium had been blown to shit. One of our boys was down there when it happened, he had a fare to an unlicensed club in those new buildings, you know . . ."

The car rushed toward City Hall while Annika fished out a pen and pencil from her bag.

"How is he doing?"

"Okay, I think. A piece of metal came flying through the side window, missed him by a couple of inches. A few cuts on his face, according to the radio."

They went past the Gamla Stan subway station and were fast approaching Slussen.

"Where did they take him?"

"Who?"

"Your colleague with the shrapnel?"

"Oh, him . . . Brattström's his name . . . South Hospital, I think, it's nearest."

"Got a first name?"

"Dunno, I'll ask on the radio . . ."

His name was Arne. Annika hauled out her cellphone, put the earpiece in her ear, and pressed Menu 1, the speed-dial number for Jansson's place at the news editor's desk in the newsroom. Even before he answered, the man knew it was Annika calling: He recognized her cellphone number on his phone display.

"A taxi driver was hurt, Arne Brattström. They took him to South Hospital," she said. "Perhaps we could visit him and make the first edition . . ."

"Okay," Jansson said. "We'll run a check on him."

He put the phone down and yelled to the night reporter:

"Run a check on an Arne Brattström, and check with

the police whether his next of kin have been informed about his injury. Then call the wife if there is one!"

Back into the phone he said, "We've got an aerial photo. When will you be there?"

"Seven or eight minutes, depending on the police cordons. What are you doing?"

"We've got the incident itself, comments from the police, night reporters calling and talking to people in the houses opposite. One of the reporters is already there, but he'll be going home soon. Then we're doing a recap of earlier Olympic bombs, we've got the guy who was throwing firecrackers in various Stockholm and Gothenburg arenas when Stockholm first applied for the Olympics . . ."

Someone interrupted him. Annika could sense the rush of the newsroom even from the taxi. "I'll be in touch as soon as I've got something," she quickly said before she switched off.

"They seem to have cordoned off the warm-up area," the taxi driver said. "We're best off trying the rear entrance."

The taxi turned into Folkungagatan and sped toward the Värmdö Way. Annika dialed the next number on her cellphone. While listening to the ringing tone, she saw the night's drunken revellers stumbling homeward. There were quite a few of them, more than she would have thought. It was like that these days; the only time she was in town at this time of night was when a crime had been committed somewhere. She had forgotten that the city could be used for anything other than criminal activity or work. The city had another life that was only lived at night.

A tense voice answered at the other end of the line.

"I know that you can't say anything yet," Annika said. "Just tell me when you'll have time to talk. I'll call you back then. Just tell me when."

The man at the other end sighed. "Bengtzon, I really can't say now. I don't know. Call me back later."

Annika looked at her watch. "It's twenty to four. I'm doing a story for the first edition. How about seven thirty?"

"Yeah, fine. Call me at seven thirty."

"Okay, speak to you then."

Now she had a promise, he wouldn't be able to back out. The police hated reporters calling when something big had happened wanting to know everything. Even if the police did have some information, it was difficult to judge what could be made public. By seven thirty she would have her own observations, questions, and theories, and the investigators at the criminal investigation department, Krim, would know what they wanted to tell you. It would work.

"You can see the smoke now," the taxi driver said.

She leaned over the passenger seat and looked up to the right. "Oh yes. Look at that . . ." Thin and black, it trailed up toward the pale half-moon. The taxi left the Värmdö Way and turned onto the South Bypass.

The road had been blocked off several hundred yards from the opening of the tunnel and the arena itself. Some ten vehicles were already parked next to the barriers. The taxi pulled up behind them, and Annika handed over her taxi charge card.

"When are you going back? Do you want me to wait?" the driver asked.

Annika smiled wanly. "No thanks, this is going to take some time." She collected her notepad, pencil, and phone.

"Merry Christmas!" the taxi driver yelled as she shut the door.

My God, she thought, it's a whole week to Christmas. Is this "Merry Christmassing" business starting already? "The same to you!" she said to the rear window of the car.

Annika weaved her way through cars and people and up to the barrier. They weren't police barriers. Good. Those she would have heeded. She jumped over the wooden roadwork barriers and fell into a jog on the other side. She didn't hear the indignant shouts behind her but just stared up at the Olympic complex. She had driven past here many times and never failed to be fascinated by the enormous structure. Victoria Stadium was built into a rock; the hill where there used to be a ski slope had been hollowed out for it. Environmentalists had kicked up a fuss, of course, as they always did as soon as a couple of trees were chopped down. The South Bypass continued straight into the hill and underneath the stadium, but at the moment the tunnel entrance was blocked off by large concrete blocks and several vehicles from the emergency services. Reflections from the rotating lights on their roofs gleamed on the surface of the slippery asphalt. The North Stand normally jutted out like a giant mushroom over the tunnel entrance, but now it was damaged. The bomb must have gone off right there. The normally rounded shape stood jagged and torn against the night sky. She ran on, realizing that she probably wouldn't get much closer than this.

"Hey, where do you think you're going?" a fireman shouted.

"Up there!" she shouted back.

"The area's been sealed off!" he continued shouting.

"Oh yeah," she muttered to herself. "See if you can catch me!"

She continued straight on and to the right as far as she could. She could see that Sickla Canal was frozen. Above the ice-covered canal, there was a concrete platform, some kind of ledge that the roadway rested on before disappearing into the tunnel. She pulled herself up on the railing and jumped down, a drop of about three feet. The holdall bounced on her back as she landed.

She paused for a moment and looked around. She'd only been to the stadium twice before: at a press preview and on a Sunday afternoon last autumn with her friend Anne Snapphane. To her right lay what would become the Olympic Village, the half-finished blocks in Hammarby Docklands where the athletes would be staying during the Olympics. The windows were black holes; it seemed that every pane had been blown out. Straight ahead she could just make out a training facility in the dark. On her left was a thirty-foot-high concrete wall. Above this lay the forecourt in front of the main entrance to the stadium.

She ran along the road, trying to differentiate the sounds she could hear: a faraway siren, distant voices, the hissing of a water cannon or possibly a big fan. The emergency vehicles' lights were flashing across the road. She reached a set of stairs and started running up them to the stadium entrance. At the same moment, a police officer started unrolling blue-and-white tape to block the entrance.

"We're sealing off the area," he told her.

"My photographer's up there," Annika said. "I'm just picking him up." The officer waved her past.

I'd damn well better not be lying, she thought.

The stairs had three equally long landings. As she reached the top, she was forced to catch her breath. The entire forecourt was full of emergency vehicles and people running around. Two of the pillars supporting the North Stand had collapsed, and smashed green stadium seats lay scattered all over the place. A TV crew had just arrived. Annika saw a reporter from another tabloid—*Kvällspressen*'s only serious rival on the market—and three freelance photographers. She turned her head upward and looked into the hole created by the bomb. Five helicopters were circling the area low, at least two from the media.

"Annika!" It was Johan Henriksson, the photographer from *Kvällspressen*, a twenty-three-year-old casual employee who had come from a local newspaper up north in Östersund. He was both talented and ambitious, two qualities of which the latter one was the more important. He came running toward her with two cameras bouncing on his chest and the camera bag dangling on his shoulder.

"What did you get?" Annika asked, pulling out her pad and pencil.

"I got here only half a minute after the fire brigade. I got an ambulance driving off with a taxi driver; he had some cuts. The fire brigade couldn't reach the stand with their hoses. They drove the engines inside the stadium. I've got pictures of the fire from the outside, but I haven't been inside the arena. A couple of minutes ago, the cops started running around like crazy. I think something's happened."

"Or they've found something," Annika said, putting away her pad. Holding her pencil like a baton, she began jogging toward where she remembered the furthermost entrance to be. If her memory didn't fail her, it was to the right, just under the collapsed stand. No one tried to stop her as she crossed the forecourt. There was too much chaos for anyone to notice. She weaved her way through chunks of concrete, twisted reinforcing rods, and green plastic seats. A stairway with four flights led up to the entry door; she was panting by the time she reached the top. The police had already cordoned off the doorway, but that didn't matter. She didn't need to see any more. The door was intact and seemed to be locked. Sticking to their routine, Swedish security companies could never refrain from putting silly little stickers on the doors of all buildings they'd been charged with guarding. Olympic stadium was no exception. Annika took out her pad again and jotted down the name and number of the company.

"Please clear the area! The building could collapse! I repeat . . ." A police car drove slowly across the forecourt below, the loudspeaker droning. People retreated to the training facility and the Olympic Village below. Annika trotted along the outside wall of the arena, which meant she could avoid returning to the forecourt. Instead she followed the ramp that descended gently to the left all the way along the building. There were several entrances, and she wanted to see them all. Not one of them seemed to have been damaged or forced open.

Eventually, Annika was stopped by a policeman. "Excuse me, madam, it's time to go home." The young officer put a hand on her arm.

"Who's the officer in charge?" she asked, holding up her press card.

"He's too busy to talk to you. You have to leave, we're evacuating the entire area."

Noticeably agitated, the officer started pulling her away. Annika wriggled free and stood in front of him. She chanced it: "What have you found inside the stadium?"

The policeman licked his lips. "I'm not sure, and I'm not allowed to tell you anyway."

Bingo! "Who can tell me, and when?"

"I don't know. Try the Krim duty desk. But you have to go now!"

The police sealed off the area all the way beyond the training facility, several hundred yards from the stadium. Annika found Henriksson over by the building that was going to house the restaurants and the cinema. An improvised media center was forming where the sidewalk was at its widest, in front of the post office. Journalists were arriving all the time, many of them walking around smiling, greeting their colleagues. Annika wasn't too keen on the backslapping of fellow journalists, people who would wander about scenes of accidents bragging about the parties they'd been to. She moved aside, pulling the photographer with her.

"Do you have to go to the paper now?" she asked. "The first edition is going to press."

"No, I've sent my rolls along with the other free-lancers. It's cool."

"Great. I have a feeling something's about to happen."

An outside broadcast van from one of the TV companies pulled up alongside them. They wandered off in the other direction, past the bank and the pharmacy down toward the canal. She stopped and stood looking toward the arena. The police vehicles and fire engines were still on the forecourt. What were they doing? The wind from the sea was bitterly cold. Further out on Hammarby Inlet, the sea approach to Stockholm, a channel through the ice glowered like a black wound. She turned her back to the wind and warmed her nose in her gloved hand. Through her fingers she saw two white vehicles on the footbridge from Södermalm. Bloody hell, it was an ambulance! And a doctor's car! She looked at her watch, just gone twenty-five to five. Three hours until she could call her contact. She pushed the earpiece into her ear and tried the Krim duty desk. Busy. She called Jansson, Menu 1.

"What do you want?" Jansson said.

"An ambulance is coming up to the arena," Annika said.

"I've got a deadline in seven minutes."

She heard the clatter of his keyboard. "What are the news agencies saying? Any reports of injuries?"

"They've got the taxi driver, but they haven't talked to him. There's the destruction, comments from the Krim duty desk. They're saying nothing as yet, well, a lot of crap. Nothing important."

"The taxi driver was taken away an hour ago, this is

something different. Aren't they saying anything over the police radio?"

"Nothing interesting."

"Anything scrambled?"

"Nope."

"And the radio news?"

"Nothing so far. There's a special *Rapport* bulletin on TV at six o'clock."

"Yes, I saw their van."

"Keep your eyes open, I'll call you when the front page goes to press."

He hung up. Annika dropped the call but kept the earpiece in her ear.

"Why do you have one of those?" Henriksson asked and pointed at the cord hanging down her cheek.

"Don't you know that your brain is fried by the radiation from cellphones?" she said, smiling. "It's handy. I can run and write and talk on the phone at the same time. And it's quiet; you don't hear when I make a call."

There were tears in her eyes from the cold, so she had to squint to see what was going on over by the stadium. "Have you got a mega telephoto lens?"

"They don't work when it's this dark," Henriksson replied.

"Then take the biggest one you've got and try and see what's going on over there," she said, pointing with her gloved hand.

Henriksson sighed a bit and put his camera bag on the ground. He looked through the lens. "I need a tripod," he mumbled.

The vehicles had driven up a grass slope and parked by the stairs to one of the big entrances. Three men stepped out of the doctor's car and stood talking behind it. A policeman in uniform approached them, and they shook hands. There was no movement in the ambulance.

"They don't seem to be in any hurry," Henriksson said.

Another two men went up to them, one a policeman in uniform, the other he assumed to be a cop in plain clothes. The men were talking and gesticulating with their hands, one of them pointing up toward the gaping bomb hole.

Annika's phone rang. She pressed the answer button. "Yes?"

"What's the ambulance doing?"

"Nothing. Waiting."

"What have we got for the next edition?"

"Have you found the taxi driver at the hospital?"

"Not yet, but we've got people there. He's not married, no partner."

"Have you tried contacting the Olympic boss, Christina Furhage?"

"Can't find her."

"What a disaster for her. She's worked so hard . . . We have to do the whole Olympic angle, too. What happens to the Games now? Can the stand be fixed in time? What does Samaranch say? All that stuff."

"We've looked into it. There are people here working on it."

"I'll do the story on the actual blast, then. It has to be sabotage. Three pieces: the police hunt for the bomber, the scene of the crime this morning, and . . ." She fell silent.

"Bengtzon . . . ?"

"They're opening the back doors of the ambulance. They're taking out the stretcher, wheeling it up to the entrance. Shit, Jansson, there's another victim!"

"Okay. The Police Hunt, I was at the Scene, and the Victim. You've got pages six, seven, eight plus the center spread." The line went dead.

She was on full alert as the ambulance people walked toward the stadium. Henriksson's camera was rattling.

No other journalists had noticed the newly arrived vehicles; the training facility blocked their line of vision.

"Christ, it's cold," Henriksson said when the men had disappeared inside the arena.

"Let's go back to the car and make our calls," Annika said.

They went back toward the media gathering. People were standing around, freezing in the frigid air. The TV people were unrolling their cables, and some reporters were blowing on their ballpoint pens. Why don't they ever learn to use pencils when it's below freezing? Annika thought to herself and smiled. The radio people looked like insects with their sound equipment jutting out their backs. Everyone was waiting. One of the freelancers from *Kvällspressen* had returned from a trip to the newsdesk.

"They're having some kind of press briefing at six o'clock," he said.

"Live on the *Rapport* special bulletin—how convenient," Annika muttered.

Henriksson had parked his car way off, behind the tennis courts and the sports clinic.

"I took the route they first cordoned off to come here," he said apologetically.

They had some way to walk. Annika could feel her feet grow numb from the cold. A light snow had started falling—too bad, when you're planning to take photos in the dark with a telephoto lens. They had to brush the snow off the windshield on Henriksson's Saab.

"This is good," Annika said, looking toward the arena. "We can see both the ambulance and the doctor's car. We've got it all covered from here."

They got in and warmed up the engine. Annika started making her calls. She tried the Krim duty desk again. Busy. She called the emergency services control room and asked who had first raised the alarm, how many calls they had received, if anyone in the apartments nearby had been hurt by flying glass, and whether they had any idea as to the extent of the damage. As usual, the emergency people knew the answers to most of her questions.

She then dialed the number she had found on the sticker on the entrance doors of Victoria Stadium, the one belonging to the security company responsible for guarding the premises. She found herself at an emergency service switchboard in Kungsholmen in west-central Stockholm. She asked if they had received any alarms from the Olympic arena in the early morning hours.

"We treat all incoming alarm calls as confidential," said the man at the other end.

"I understand that," Annika said. "But I'm not asking about an alarm call you've received but about one you probably haven't received."

"Hey," the man said, "are you deaf?"

"Okay," Annika said. "Put it this way: What happens when you get an alarm call?"

"Eh . . . it comes here."

"To the emergency control room?"

"Yeah, where else? It's entered into our computer system and then it comes up on our screens with an action plan telling us what to do."

"So if there were an alarm call from the Olympic stadium, it would appear on your screen?"

"Eh . . . yeah."

"And then it says exactly what steps you should take concerning that alarm call?"

"Eh . . . right."

"So what has your company been doing out at the Olympic stadium tonight? I haven't seen a single one of your cars out here."

No reply from the man.

"Victoria Stadium has been blown up. We can agree

on that, can't we? What's your company supposed to do if the Olympic area catches fire or is damaged in some other way?"

"It comes up on the computer," the man said.

"So what have you been doing?"

The man said nothing.

"You haven't received any alarm whatsoever from the arena, have you?" Annika said.

The man was quiet for a while before he replied.

"I can't comment on the alarm calls we don't get either."

Annika took a deep breath and smiled.

"Thank you," she said.

"You won't write any of what I've said, will you?" the man said anxiously.

"Said?" Annika said. "You haven't said a word. All you've done is refer me to your confidentiality policy."

She switched off. Yes, she had her angle now. She drew a deep breath and stared out through the windshield. One of the fire engines pulled off, but the ambulance and the doctor's car remained. The explosives experts had arrived; their vehicles were dotted around the forecourt. Men in gray overalls were lifting things out of the cars. The fire had been extinguished, so she could hardly make out any smoke.

"How were we tipped off this morning?" she asked.

"Smidig," Henriksson replied.

Every newsroom has a number of more or less professional tipsters who keep an eye on what's happening on their particular newspatch. *Kvällspressen* was no exception. Smidig and Leif were the best police informers; they slept with the police radio on by their beds. As soon as anything happened, big or small, they called the newspapers and told them. Other informers would pore over the records of the different legal institutions and other government authorities.

Annika, lost in thought, slowly let her eyes travel over the facility. Straight ahead lay the ten-floor building where the technical operations of the Games would be conducted. From the roof of this building was a footbridge up to the rock. Strange, who would want to walk there? She followed the footbridge with her eyes.

"Henriksson," she said, "we've got another pic to take."

She looked at her watch. Half past five. They'd make it to the press conference. "If we climb up next to the Olympic flame, at the top of the hill, we should be able to see quite a lot."

"You think so?" the photographer said, unconvinced. "They've built the walls so high no one can sneak in or see inside."

"The actual grounds are probably hidden from view, but maybe you can see the North Stand. That's what we're interested in now."

Henriksson looked at his watch.

"Do we have time? Hasn't the helicopter taken all that? Shouldn't we be watching the ambulance?"

She chewed on her lip.

"The helicopter isn't here right now. Maybe the police ordered it down. We'll ask one of the freelancers to keep an eye on the ambulance. Come on, let's go."

The rest of the journalists had discovered the ambulance, and their questions were buzzing in the air. The *Rapport* team had moved their OB van nearer to the canal to get a better picture of the arena. A frostbitten reporter was rehearsing his stand-up for the six o'clock bulletin. There were no police around. After Annika had given the freelancers instructions, they were on their way too.

It was further to get up the hill than she'd thought. The going was hard—the ground was slippery and stony. They stumbled and cursed in the dark. On top of everything, Henriksson was lugging a large tripod. They didn't encounter any cordons and got up there in time but only to be faced with a seven-foot-high concrete wall.

"I don't believe it," Henriksson groaned.

"Maybe this'll work in our favor," Annika said. "Get up on my shoulders and I'll hoist you up. Then you can climb up on the actual flame. You should be able to see something from there."

The photographer stared at her.

"You want me to stand on the Olympic flame?"

"Yes, why not? It's not alight, and it hasn't been cordoned off. I'm sure you can get on top of it; it's only another yard up from the wall. If it's to hold the eternal flame, it should be able to hold you. Come on, let's go!"

Annika passed up the tripod and the camera bag to him. Henriksson crawled up on the metal frame.

"It's full of little holes!" he shouted.

"Gas holes," Annika said. "Can you see the North Stand?"

He stood up and looked out over the stadium.

"Do you see anything?" Annika shouted.

"You bet I do," the photographer said. He slowly raised his camera and started snapping.

"What?"

He lowered his camera without taking his eyes off the stadium.

"They've lit up part of the stand," he said. "There are about ten people down there walking around picking things up and putting them in little plastic bags. The guys from the doctor's car are there. They're also picking stuff up. They seem to be extremely meticulous about it." He raised his camera again.

Annika felt the hair on her neck stand on end. Shit! Was it really that bad? Henriksson opened up the tripod. After three rolls of film, he had finished. They alternately ran and slid down the hill, shocked, slightly nauseated. What would doctors be picking up and putting in little bags—explosive residue? Hardly.

A couple of minutes before six they were back down with the media scrum. The TV cameras' bluish lights were illuminating the whole scene, making the snowflakes sparkle. *Rapport* had their link in place, and the reporter had powdered his face. A group of police officials, led by the officer-in-charge, headed their way. They lifted the cordon but couldn't get any further. The wall of journalists was solid. There was silence when the officer screwed up his eyes against the camera lights. He glanced at a paper in his hand, raised his eyes, and began talking.

"At 3:17 A.M. an explosive charge went off at Victoria Stadium in Stockholm," he said. "It's not known what kind of explosives were used. The explosion badly damaged the North Stand. It's not clear at the moment whether it will be possible to repair it."

He paused, consulting his papers. The still cameras were clattering, and the TV cameras were rolling. Annika was standing far out to the left so that she could keep an eye on the ambulance while following the press conference.

"The explosion caused a fire, but this is now under control." Another pause.

"A taxi driver was injured as a piece of a reinforcing rod penetrated the side window of his car," the police officer continued. "The man has been taken to South Hospital and is in a stable condition. Some ten buildings on the other side of Sickla Canal have had damage to their windows and facades. These buildings are under construction and not yet occupied. No further personal injuries have been reported."

Another pause. The officer looked very tired and somber as he continued.

"This is sabotage. The explosive device that destroyed the arena was powerful. We are in the process of securing evidence that may lead to the identification of the perpetrator. We are assigning all available resources to the search. That is all for the moment. Thank you."

He turned round and ducked under the cordon. A wave of voices and calls made him stop.

". . . any suspects?"

". . . other victims?"

". . . the doctors at the scene?"

"That is all for the moment," the officer repeated and left. Shoulders hunched, he walked off with determined steps, followed by his colleagues. The media pack dissolved. The *Rapport* reporter entered the camera lights and ran through his piece to the camera, then handed over to the studio. Everyone was punching his or her phone and trying to get his or her pen to work.

"Right," Henriksson said, "that didn't tell us much."

"Time to go," Annika said. They left one of the freelancers behind and walked up toward Henriksson's car.

"Let's go past Vintertullstorget and get some eyewitness stories."

They visited the people who lived closest to the arena. They met families with children, seniors, a couple of drunks, and some club kids. They spoke of the bang that woke them up, if it had, the shock, and how frightening it was.

"That's enough now," Annika said at a quarter to seven. "We've got to pull things together."

They drove back to the office in silence. Annika composed intros and captions in her head. Henriksson mentally leafed through negatives, sorting them through, figuring which shots might work, pushing the film, and dodging the prints.

The snow was coming down heavily now. As a result,

the temperature had risen and made the road surface dangerously slippery. They drove past four cars in a pileup on the West Circular. Henriksson stopped to take some shots.

They arrived at the newsroom just before seven. The atmosphere was composed but charged. Jansson was still there; on weekends the night editor also handled the suburban editions. Normally on a Saturday it was a question of changing the odd story, but they were always ready to change the whole paper around entirely. This was what was happening right now.

"Does it hold?" he asked, standing up the instant he spotted them coming in.

"I think so," Annika said. "There's a dead body on the Olympic stand, in pieces. I'd bet my life on it. Give me half an hour and I'll know for sure."

Jansson rocked to and fro on his feet. "Half an hour—not sooner?"

Annika threw him a glance over her shoulder while wriggling out of her coat. She picked up a copy of the early edition and walked into her office.

"Okay then," he said and went back to his chair.

First she wrote the news article, which was nothing but a supplemented rewrite of the night reporter's work from the first edition. She added quotations from the neighbors and the statement that the fire was under control. After that she set about writing the "I Was There" story, adding descriptions of sounds and other details. Twenty-eight minutes past seven she called her contact.

"I can't say anything yet," he began.

"I know," Annika said. "I'll do the talking and you say nothing, or tell me if I'm wrong . . ."

"I can't do that this time," he interrupted her.

Shit. She took a breath and chose to go on the offensive.

"Listen to what I have to say first," she said. "This is how I see it: Someone died at the Olympic stadium last night. Someone has been blown to bits on that stand. You have people there picking up the pieces as we speak. It's an inside job; all the alarms were disarmed. There must be hundreds of alarms at a stadium like this: burglar alarms, fire alarms, motion-sensor alarms—and they were all disarmed. No doors had been forced open. Someone with a key went inside and switched off the alarms, either the victim or the perpetrator. At this moment you are trying to find out who."

She fell silent and held her breath.

"You can't publish that now," the police officer at the other end said.

Quick release of breath. "What part?"

"The insider theory. We want to keep it secret. The alarms were fully functional but had been disarmed. Someone has died, that's true. We don't know who yet." He sounded completely exhausted.

"When will you find out?"

"Don't know. It could prove difficult to establish the victim's identity visually, if I may put it that way. But we do seem to have certain other leads. That's all I can say."

"Man or woman?"

He hesitated. "Not now," he said and hung up.

Annika darted out to Jansson. "The death has been confirmed, but they still don't know who it is."

"Mincemeat, eh?" Jansson said.

She swallowed and nodded.

Helena Starke woke up with a hangover that was out of this world. As long as she stayed in bed it was all right, but when she got up to get a glass of water she threw up on the mat in the hallway. She stayed panting on all fours for a while before she could make it into the bathroom.

There she filled the toothbrush glass with water and gulped it down. Dear God, she was never going to drink again. She lifted her gaze to meet her bloodshot eyes among the toothpaste specks in the mirror. Christ, would she never learn? She opened the bathroom cabinet and fumbled with the Tylenol container. She swallowed three with a great deal of water and prayed she'd keep them down.

Helena staggered out into the kitchen and sat down by the table. The seat was cold against her naked thighs. How much did she drink last night? The brandy bottle stood on the worktop, empty. She leaned her cheek against the tabletop and searched for memories of the night before. The restaurant, the music, people's faces— it was all one big flashback. Christ, she couldn't even remember how she got home! Christina was with her, wasn't she? They left the restaurant together, didn't they?

She groaned, stood up, and filled a jug with water that she took with her to the bedroom. On her way to the bedroom, she scrambled together the hall mat and threw it in the laundry basket in the wardrobe; she nearly threw up again from the stench.

The clock radio by the bed said five to nine. She groaned. The older she got, the earlier she woke up, especially if she'd been drinking. In years gone by she'd been able to sleep it off for a whole day. Not any more. Now she woke early, sick as a dog, and then spent the rest of the day sweating in bed. She'd drift off for short periods, but she couldn't sleep. Mustering all her energy, Helena reached for the jug. She piled the pillows up against the headboard and settled herself against them. Then she saw her clothes from last night folded up in a neat pile on the chest of drawers by the window, and a shiver went up her spine. Who the hell had put them there like that? Probably she did. That was the scariest thing about having blackouts when you drank: You went around like a zombie, doing normal things without having a clue. She shuddered and switched on the radio. She might as well listen to the news while waiting for the Tylenol to kick in.

The main news this morning made her throw up again. She also knew that there would be no more rest for Helena Starke today.

After flushing her vomit down the toilet, she picked up the phone and called Christina.

The news agency TT ran Annika's information at 9:34 A.M. So, *Kvällspressen* had been first with the report of a victim at the Olympic blast. Their headlines ran: OLYMPIC BLAST KILLS ONE and THE HUNT IS ON FOR THE BOMBER.

The first one was a gamble, but Jansson argued it would hold. Henriksson's picture from the Olympic flame dominated most of the center spread. It was a striking image: the illuminated circle beyond the hole made by the bomb, the men bent forward, the falling snowflakes. It was extremely nasty without being macabre. No blood, no body, only the knowledge of what the men were doing. They had already sold the picture to Reuters. TV2's *Rapport* quoted *Kvällspressen*, while the radio news program *Eko* pretended the story was theirs.

When the city edition had gone to press, the crime reporters and news editors gathered in Annika's office. Boxes with her ring binders and files with cuttings of her old articles were still piled up in the corners. The couch had been inherited, but the desk was new. For two months now Annika had been crime editor; the office had been hers for as long.

"There are of course a number of things we have to go through and parcel out among ourselves," she said, putting her feet on the desk. Tiredness had hit like a rock to the back of the head when the paper went to press and she came to a halt. She leaned back and reached for her coffee mug.

"One: who is the corpse on the stand? Tomorrow's major splash, which could become several. Two: the hunt for the killer. Three: the Olympic angle. Four: How could it happen? Five: the taxi driver; no one has talked to him yet. Maybe he saw or heard something."

She looked up at the people in the room, reading their reactions to what she had said. Jansson was half asleep; he was going home soon. The news editor Ingvar Johansson looked at her with an expressionless face. The reporter Nils Langeby, the oldest on the crime desk at 53, was, as usual, unable to hide his hostility toward her. The reporter Patrik Nilsson was listening attentively, not to say rapturously. The third reporter, Berit Hamrin, calmly paid attention. The only one not there from the crime desk was the combined secretary and research assistant, Eva-Britt Qvist.

"I think the way we approach these things is disgusting," Nils said.

Annika sighed. Here we go again. "What approach would you suggest?"

"We're far too focused on this type of sensationalist violence. What about all the environmental crime we never write about? Or crime in schools."

"It's true that we should improve our coverage of that type of . . ."

"We damned well should! This desk is sinking into a shit hole of women's sob stories and bombs and biker wars."

Annika drew a deep breath and counted to three

before replying. "You've brought up an important point, Nils, but this is maybe not the right time to discuss it . . ."

"Why not? Am I incapable of determining when I can raise a subject for discussion?" He raised himself up in the chair.

"Environmental and school crime is your beat, Nils," Annika said calmly. "You work full time on those two issues. Do you feel we're tearing you away from your patch when we pull you in on a day like this?"

"Yes, I do!" the man roared.

She looked at the furious man in front of her. How the hell was she going to deal with this? If she didn't call him in, he'd be pissed off for not having a part in the Bomber story. If she did give him an assignment, he'd first refuse and then screw it up. But if she kept him on standby, he'd argue that he was being cold-shouldered.

She was interrupted when the editor-in-chief, Anders Schyman, walked in the room. Everybody, including Annika, said hello and sat up straighter in their chairs.

"Congratulations, Annika! And thanks, Jansson, for a great job this morning," the editor said. "We beat the others. Outstanding! The center-spread picture was fantastic, and we were the only ones to have it. How did you do it, Annika?" He sat down on a box in the corner.

Annika told the story. She got some applause, cheers even. Standing on the Olympic flame and all! This would be a classic at the Press Club.

"What are we doing now?"

Annika put her feet on the floor and leaned over the desk, ticking off items on a list while talking. "Patrik, you take the hunt for the murderer, the forensic evidence, and all contacts with the officers on duty and the people in charge of the investigation. It's likely they'll hold a press conference this afternoon. Find out when and get the pics ready now. I'm sure we'll all have a reason to be there."

Patrik nodded.

"Berit, you take the victim angle, who is it and why? Then there's the old Olympic bomber, the Tiger, he was called. He's got to be a suspect, even if his bombs were firecrackers compared with this. What's he doing these days, and where was he last night? I'll try and get hold of him, since I interviewed him at the time. Nils, you do the Olympic security aspects. How the hell could something like this happen just seven months away from the Olympic Games? How has the security situation looked up to now?"

"That's just background. You could get an intern to do that. I'm a reporter," Nils Langeby said.

"It's not background," Anders Schyman said. "I think it's one of the most important and wide-ranging questions you can ask on a day like this. Get to the bottom of this type of action from a social and global perspective. How will this damage sports as a whole? That'll be one of today's most important stories, Nils."

The reporter didn't know how to react, whether to be honored to be assigned one of the most important jobs or to resent being told off. He chose, as always, the most self-important option. "Naturally, it all depends on how you do it," he said.

Annika looked gratefully at Anders Schyman. "Perhaps the night shift can do the Olympic angle. What's up with the taxi driver?" she said.

Ingvar Johansson nodded. "Our people are taking him to a hotel in town as we speak. He lives in the south suburbs, but the rest of the media could find him there. We'll keep him hidden at the Royal Viking until tomorrow. Janet Ullberg can hunt down Christina

Furhage. A picture of her in front of the bomb damage would be just the thing. We've got students from the School of Journalism manning the phones for *Ring and Sing* . . ."

The paper often held phone-in polls for major news stories. It made people feel like they were part of the process. Schyman liked that.

"What's the question?" he asked, reaching for a paper.

" 'Should the Olympics be canceled? Call in tonight, between 5 and 7 P.M.' It's obvious that this is an attack by the Tiger or some group that doesn't want Sweden to host the Games."

Annika hesitated for a moment.

"Of course we should cover that angle, but I'm not so sure that's what's going on here."

"Why not?" Ingvar Johansson asked. "We can't dismiss it. Besides the victim, the terrorist angle's got to be tomorrow's big thing."

"I think we should be careful not to beat the terrorist drum too loudly," Annika said, cursing her promise not to say anything about the insider lead. "As long as we don't even know the identity of the victim, we can't speculate about what or who the bomb was directed against."

"Of course we can," Ingvar Johansson objected. "We'll have to get the police to comment on the theory, but that won't be too difficult. They're not in a position to confirm or deny anything at the moment."

Anders Schyman broke in. "We shouldn't settle on anything at the moment. Or toss anything out. Let's keep our options open and get on with things before we decide on tomorrow's stories. Anything else?"

"Not with what we've got right now. Once the victim has been identified, I suppose we'll have to approach the members of the family."

"In the nicest way possible," Anders Schyman advised unnecessarily. "I don't want people pissed off at us for intruding on their grief."

Annika smiled faintly. "I'll do it myself."

When the meeting was over, Annika called home. Kalle, her five-year-old, answered the phone.

"Hi, darling, how are you?"

"Fine. We're going to McDonald's, and you know, Ellen spilled orange juice all over *101 Dalmatians*. I think that was really silly, 'cause now we won't be able to watch that again . . ." The boy fell silent and a sob was heard.

"That's a shame, yes. But how could she spill juice on it? What was it doing on the kitchen table?"

"No, it was on the floor in the TV room, and Ellen kicked over my glass. She was going to the bathroom."

"But why did you put your juice on the floor in the TV room? I've told you not to bring your breakfast into the TV room. You know that!" Annika felt the anger rising. Christ, every time she left the house unexpectedly something got broken. Nobody ever stuck by the rules.

"It wasn't my fault!" the boy wailed. "It was Ellen! Ellen ruined the videotape!" He was crying loudly now. He dropped the phone and ran off.

"Kalle, hello! Kalle!" Why the hell did this have to happen now? She had meant to call the kids to salve her conscience. Thomas picked up the phone.

"Christ, Annika, what did you say to him?"

She sighed. She was getting a headache. "Why were they having breakfast in the TV room?"

"They weren't," Thomas said. Annika could tell he was struggling to keep calm. "Kalle was allowed to bring his juice in, nothing else. Not smart, considering the consequences, but I'm going to bribe them with lunch at McDonald's and a new video. Don't imagine everything depends on you all the time. You just concentrate on your stories. How's it going?" He was making peace.

She swallowed. "A really nasty death. Murder, suicide, or an accident, maybe. We don't know yet."

"Yeah, I heard. You'll be late, I guess?"

"That's just the beginning of it."

"I love you," he said.

Unexpectedly, she felt tears welling up. "I love you, too," she whispered.

Her contact had worked through the night and gone home, so she had to rely on the normal police channels. Nothing further had happened during the morning; the body still hadn't been identified, the fire-fighting operation was done, and the forensic investigation was in progress. She decided to go back to the arena with a new photographer, a casual called Ulf Olsson.

"I've got the wrong clothes for this assignment," Ulf said in the elevator down to the garage.

Annika looked at the man. "How do you mean?" He was dressed in a dark gray woollen coat, ordinary shoes, and a suit.

"I'm dressed to take pictures of a first-night audience at the theater. You could've told me earlier we were going to a murder scene. You must've known for hours."

The freelancer was looking at her imperiously. Her headache was worse. Now this.

"Don't fucking tell me what I should have done! You're a photographer. You photograph what we need pictures of. This is a bit more important than a first night. If you don't want to shoot mincemeat in your Armani suit, keep some overalls in your camera bag!" She kicked the door open to the garage. Fucking amateurs!

"I don't like the way you're talking to me," the man whimpered behind her.

Furious, Annika turned on her heel. "Grow up," she
hissed. "Besides, there's nothing stopping you from finding out for yourself what's going on. Do you think I'm
some fucking valet service for your wardrobe?"

Ulf swallowed hard, clenching his fists. "I think you're
being really unfair," he sniveled.

"For God's sake," Annika groaned, "stop whining!
Get in the car and drive to the stadium, or do you want
me to drive?"

The photographer usually drove when a team went
out on an assignment, even if it was in the newspaper's
car. In many places, a newspaper's cars were in fact the
photographers' company cars. But the fuss made over
the expense of this perk meant that *Kvallspressen* had
given up the practice.

So now Annika got the wheel and drove out onto the
West Circular. Neither Annika nor Ulf said a word
during the drive out to Hammarby Dock. Annika took
the road past Hammarby industrial estate. She planned
to get into the complex from the back, but it was no use.
The entire Olympic Village had been cordoned off.
Annika felt frustrated. Ulf Olsson was relieved. He
wouldn't have to get his shoes dirty by sneaking about
around the back of the stadium.

"We have to have a shot of the stand in daylight,"
Annika said, making a U-turn at the plastic tape on
Lumavägen. "I know someone at a TV company that has
its offices out here. If we're lucky, someone'll let us on the
roof."

She fished out her phone and called her friend Anne
Snapphane, who produced talk shows for women on one
of the cable channels.

"I'm editing. What do you want?" Anne hissed. "Who
is it?"

Five minutes later, they were on the roof of the old

lamp factory in Hammarby South Dock. The view of the lacerated stadium was fantastic. Olsson used a telephoto lens and shot one roll. That was enough.

Not a word was spoken on the drive back.


"The press conference starts at two!" Patrik yelled when she walked back into the office. "I've got the photos sorted."

Annika waved a reply and went into her office. She hung up her things, threw the holdall on the desk, switched batteries in her phone, and put the old one in the charger.

Annika thought about her outburst against the photographer. Why did she react so strongly? Why did she feel bad about it? She hesitated for a moment, then punched the speed dial number to the editor.

"Of course I've got a minute for you, Annika," he said.

She walked through the open-plan cubicles toward Anders Schyman's corner office. Activity on the floor was almost at zero. Ingvar Johansson was eating a salad with the phone pressed to his ear. The picture editor, Pelle Oscarsson, was absentmindedly flipping through pictures in Photoshop. One of the sub-editors was arranging the following day's pages on his computer.

As Annika closed the office door behind her, the opening chimes of the lunchtime *Eko* news peeled from the editor's radio. *Eko* focused on the terrorist angle: that the police were hunting for a group with something against the Olympic Games. And that was as far as they got.

"The terrorist theory doesn't hold water," Annika said. "The police think it was an inside job."

Anders Schyman whistled. "Why?"

"No doors had been forced and all alarms had been disarmed. Either the victim disarmed them or the Bomber. Either would mean the perpetrator's on the inside."

"Not necessarily—the alarms could have been broken," Schyman said.

"They weren't," Annika said. "They were fully functional, but disarmed."

"Someone could've forgotten to prime them," the editor persisted. Annika gave it a moment's thought and nodded. That could be the case.

They sat down on the comfortable couches along the wall, half listening to the radio. Annika looked out over the Russian Embassy. The day was fading even before it had properly arrived; a gray haze made the windows look dirty. Someone, at long last, had put a few Christmas decorations up in the editor's office—some red poinsettias and two Christmas candelabra.

"I lost my rag with Ulf Olsson today," Annika said in a low voice.

Schyman waited.

"He complained about having the wrong clothes for the Hammarby Dock assignment and blamed it on me, saying I should have warned him earlier that we would be going there." She fell silent.

Anders Schyman watched her for a moment before replying. "You don't decide which photographer goes on which assignment, the picture editor does. And reporters and photographers should be dressed to tackle any kind of assignment, at any time. That's part of the job."

"I swore at him," Annika said.

"That wasn't very clever," the editor said. "If I were you, I'd apologize. Throw him a bone. Give him some advice. And find out how we're handling the sabotage hypothesis. We mustn't fall in the terrorist trap if it's wrong."

Schyman stood up, indicating that they were done. Annika was relieved, partly because she'd had support for her attitude to the Olympic coverage, partly because she'd got herself to tell her superior about the outburst. People got angry with each other every day at the paper, but she was a woman and new as an editor, so she had to be prepared to take some stick.

She picked up a large holdall with the company logo and took it to the photo room. Ulf Olsson was alone in the room, reading a magazine.

"I want to apologize for swearing at you," Annika said. "Here you are, it's a bag to fill with winter clothes. Put some long underwear, warm shoes, a hat, and gloves in it, and put it in your locker or in the trunk of your car."

The man gave her a glum look. "You should have told me earlier that we were going . . ."

"You'll have to take that up with the picture editor or the editor. Have you developed the pictures?"

"No, I was . . ."

"Well, then do it."

She left the room, feeling his glare on her back. On the way back to her office, it struck her that she hadn't eaten all day, not even breakfast. She passed by the cafeteria and bought a meatball sandwich and a Diet Coke.

The news of the explosion at the Olympic stadium had by now broken worldwide. All the major TV companies and international newpapers had sent correspondents to the 2 P.M. press conference at the police headquarters: CNN, Sky News, BBC, the Nordic TV companies; *Le Monde*, the *European*, the *Times*, *Die Zeit*, and many more. The TV companies' cellphone units were blocking most of the driveway up to the entrance.

Annika arrived with four others from her paper: reporters Patrik and Berit, plus two photographers. The room was packed with people and equipment. Annika and the other reporters stood on chairs at the back, while the photographers elbowed their way further forward.

As always, the TV people had parked themselves right at the front of the podium, blocking everyone else's view. People were tripping over their endless miles of cable coiling all over the floor, and everyone would have to make allowances for them having to put their questions first. Their camera lights glared across the room in all directions, although most were directed at the podium where the police officials would soon address the nation. Several of the TV companies were transmitting live, including CNN, Sky, and the Swedish *Rapport*. The reporters were rehearsing their stand-ups, scrawling in their scripts; the still photographers were loading their cameras; radio reporters were twiddling the knobs of their DAT recorders, mumbling "testing, testing, one-two . . ." The murmur of voices sounded like a waterfall. The heat was already unbearable. Annika groaned, dropping her coat and scarf in a heap on the floor.

When the police officials walked in through a side door next to the podium, the murmur subsided and was replaced by the snapping of cameras. Four men stepped onto the podium: the Stockholm police press officer, the Chief District Prosecutor Kjell Lindström, a Krim investigator whose name Annika couldn't remember, and, finally, Evert Danielsson from the Olympic Secretariat. They took their time to get seated at the table, then sipped from the mandatory glasses of water.

The press officer opened with the established facts: An explosion had taken place, leaving one person dead; the extent of the resulting damage was reiterated; and the forensic investigation was in progress. He already seemed tired and careworn. What would he look like once this has been going on for a couple of days? Annika mused.

Then the Chief District Prosecutor took over. "We haven't as yet been able to identify the victim at the arena. Progress has been hampered by the state of the body. We

do, however, have some leads that could assist in estab-
lishing the identity of the victim. The explosive residues
have been sent to London for analysis. We haven't had
any definite results from them yet, but we can say at this
point that the explosive is probably civilian-made. The
explosives used were not from a military source."

Kjell Lindström drank more water. The cameras were
clattering.

"We are also looking for the man who was convicted
of two bomb attacks against sports arenas seven years
ago. This man is not under suspicion at the moment, but
will be brought in for questioning."

The chief prosecutor looked down at his papers for a
moment, seemingly hesitant. When he resumed, he
looked straight into *Rapport*'s camera:

"A person wearing dark clothes was seen near the
arena just before the explosion. We appeal to the public
to contact us with any information that may be relevant
to the bombing of Victoria Stadium. The police want to
talk to anyone who was in the area between midnight
and 3:20 A.M. Information that might appear irrelevant to
the general public may provide the police with vital
clues."

He rattled off a couple of telephone numbers that
would soon appear on the *Rapport* news.

When the chief prosecutor was done, Evert
Danielsson of the Olympic Secretariat cleared his throat.

"Well, this is a tragedy," he said nervously. "Both for
Sweden as the host nation of the Olympic Games and for
the world of sports as a whole. The Games symbolize
competition on equal terms regardless of race, religious
creed, politics, or sex. It makes it all the more lamentable
that anyone would target this global symbol, the arena of
the Olympic championships themselves, and commit an
act of terrorism."

Annika craned her neck to see above the CNN camera. She watched the reaction to Danielsson's Olympic lament on the faces of the police officers and the prosecutor. As might have been expected, they flinched as, right in front of their eyes, the head of the Olympic Secretariat produced both a motive and a method: The explosion was an act of terrorism directed at the Games themselves. Yet they still didn't know who the victim was. Or did they? Didn't the head of the Secretariat know what had already been confirmed to Annika, that the attack had probably been staged by someone on the inside?

The prosecutor interrupted, trying to silence Danielsson, who went on regardless. "I appeal," he continued, "to everybody who thinks he or she may have seen something to contact the police. It is of the utmost importance to apprehend the perpetrator of . . . What?" Bewildered, he looked at the chief prosecutor, who must have pinched or kicked him out of sight of the reporters.

"I just want to point out," Kjell Lindström said while leaning toward the microphones, "that at the present time, we can in no way identify a motive." He glared sideways at Evert Danielsson. "There is nothing, I repeat, nothing, which indicates that this is an act of terrorism directed at the Olympic Games. There have been no threats delivered to either the facilities or the Secretariat. As matters stand, we remain open to various lines of enquiry and motives."

He sat back in his chair. "Any questions?"

The TV reporters were prepared and raring to go. As soon as the reporters got the floor, they would shout out their questions. A face-off it's called, from the ice-hockey term. The first few questions were about facts that were already known but which had been said too slowly or in a too complicated manner for a segment of

90 seconds. That was why TV reporters always asked the same things all over again, hoping to get a straighter and simpler answer.

"Do you have any suspects?"

"Do you have any leads?"

"Has the victim been identified?"

"Could it be an act of terrorism?"

Annika sighed. The only reason for going to this kind of press conference was to study the behavior of the investigators. Everything they said was reported in other media, but to observe the facial expressions of those who weren't on camera was often more rewarding than the usually predictable answers. Now, for example, she could see just how angry Kjell Lindström was with Evert Danielsson for shooting his mouth off about "acts of terrorism." If there was one thing the Swedish police were extremely keen to steer clear of, it was for the world to put the taint of terrorism on Stockholm and the Olympic Games. The terrorist angle was probably totally off the mark. For once, though, they actually had released some new information. Annika scribbled some questions in her notepad. There was the bit about a person wearing dark clothes having been seen near the arena—when and where? If there was a witness, who was it and what was he or she doing there? The explosives had been sent to London for analysis—why? Why wasn't the forensic lab in Linköping dealing with it? And when were the results of the analysis expected? How did they know the explosives were civilian-made? What were the implications for the investigation? Did it narrow it down or widen its reach? How easy are civilian-made explosives to come by? How long would it take to repair the North Stand? Is the arena insured, and if so, by whom? And who was the victim? Did they know? And what were the lines of enquiry Kjell Lindström had been talking about that might help them in the investigation? She sighed again. This could become a very long, drawn-out story.

Chief District Prosecutor Kjell Lindström strode down the corridor leading from the conference room. His face was pale and taut. He gripped the handle of his briefcase so tight his knuckles were white. He felt sure that unless he managed to keep his hands in check, he would strangle Evert Danielsson. Behind him followed the rest of the participants in the press conference, plus three uniformed cops who had been standing in the background. One of them pulled the door closed, shutting out the last of the persistent reporters.

"I don't see why it should be so controversial to say what everyone is thinking," the director said from behind him. "It's perfectly obvious to everyone that it's a terrorist attack. The Olympic Secretariat believes it's important to quickly establish an opinion, a force that can withstand any attempt to sabotage the Games . . ."

The prosecutor spun around to face Evert Danielsson, inches from his face.

"Read my lips: There is no suspicion whatsoever of a terrorist act. Okay? The last thing the police need right now is a big fucking debate about terrorist control. That would place demands on the security of arenas and public buildings that we just don't have the resources for. . . . Do you know how many arenas are connected with the Games in one way or another? Yes, of course you do. Don't you remember what happened when the Tiger was doing his thing? He let off a couple of charges and every frigging reporter in the country went sniffing around unprotected arenas in the middle of the night. Then they wrote sensationalist stories about the shitty security."

"How can you be so sure it's not a terrorist attack?" Danielsson said, somewhat intimidated.

Lindström sighed and resumed. "Believe me, we have our reasons."

"Such as?" the director persevered.

The prosecutor stopped again. Calmly, he said, "It was an inside job. Someone in the Olympic organization did it. Okay? One of your lot, mate. That's why it's extremely unfortunate for you to go mouthing off about terrorist attacks. Do you understand what I'm saying?"

Evert Danielsson turned pale. "That's not possible."

Kjell Lindström started walking again. "Oh, yes, it is. And if you would follow the investigators up to the Serious Crimes Division, you can tell them exactly who in your organization has access to all entry cards, keys, and security codes for Victoria Stadium."

The moment Annika entered the newsroom after the press conference, Ingvar Johansson waved to her from behind the office modem computer.

"Come and see if you can make any sense of this," he called.

Annika passed by her office and dumped her bag, coat, scarf, and mittens. Her sweater felt sticky in the armpits, and suddenly she was conscious of not having had a shower that morning. She pulled the jacket tighter around her, hoping she didn't smell.

Janet Ullberg, a young freelance reporter, and Ingvar Johansson were both leaning over one of the newsroom computers that had a fast modem installed.

"Janet hasn't been able to get hold of Christina Furhage all day," he said while typing something. "We've got a number that's supposed to work, but there's no answer. According to the Olympic Secretariat, she's in town, probably at home. So we wanted to look up her address and go and knock on her door. But when we enter her data, nothing happens. She's not in there."

He pointed to the information on the screen. No Christina Furhage—"*The name does not exist for the given data.*" Annika squeezed in behind Janet and sat down on the chair in front of the keyboard.

"Of course she's here, everybody is," Annika said. "You've done a too narrow search, that's all."

"I don't get it," Janet said in a faint voice. "What are you doing?"

Annika explained while typing away. "The Public Register, the government department for citizen information—people's births, deaths, marriages, and addresses—usually goes under the name of the PubReg. It's not even state owned anymore; they sold it to some Anglo-French company. Anyway, here you can find every person in the country—their identity numbers, addresses, previous addresses, and places of birth of Swedes and immigrants who've been given identity numbers. Before, you'd be able to find family ties as well—children and spouses—but that was stopped a couple of years ago. Now, using the modem, we log in to something called the Info Market, look . . . You can choose from a number of databases, the National Vehicle Register and the Register of Limited Companies, for example, but we want the PubReg. Look here—you type " 'pubreg" up here where the prompt is . . ."

"I'll go back to my desk. Call me when you're done," Ingvar Johansson said and left in the direction of the newsdesk.

". . . and, hey, presto! We're in. Here we can choose between a number of different functions, things we want to enquire about. See? Use F2 if you have the personal number and want to know whose it is, F3 if you have a birth date but not the four ID digits, F4 and F5 are off limits—family ties—but we can use F7 and F8. To find out where a person lives you hit F8, name enquiry. Voilà!"

Annika pressed the command and a document appeared on the screen.

"So, we're looking for Christina Furhage, living somewhere in Sweden," she said, typing in the necessary data: sex, first and second names. She left the fields for approximate date of birth, county code, and postal code empty. The computer did its thinking, and after a few seconds, three lines appeared on the screen.

"Okay, one at a time," Annika said, pointing at the screen with her pen. "Look here: 'Furhage, Eleonora Christina, born 1912 in Kalix, hist.' That means the data is historical. The old lady is probably dead. Dead people stay in the register for about a year. It can also mean that she has changed her name; she could have married an old geezer from the home. If you want to check that, you highlight her name and press F7, for historical data, but we won't do that now."

She moved her pen down to the bottom line.

" 'Furhage, Sofia Christina, born 1993 in Kalix.' A kid. Presumably a relative of the first one. Unusual surnames often pop up in the same place."

She moved the pen again. "This will be our Christina."

Annika typed a "v" in front of the line and gave the command.

"My God . . . !" she said, leaning closer toward the screen as if she didn't believe her own eyes. A very rare piece of information appeared.

"What?" Janet said.

"The woman is off the record," Annika said. She typed "command p" and went over to the printer. With the printout in her hand, she walked over to Ingvar Johansson.

"Have we ever written anything about Christina Furhage having bodyguards? That she's received death threats or anything like that?"

Ingvar Johansson leaned back in his chair and considered her question. "Not that I know of. Why?"

Annika held out the computer printout. "Christina Furhage must have received some serious threats. No one but the director of the local tax office knows where she lives. You know, there are only about a hundred people in Sweden who have this protection."

She handed the paper to Ingvar Johansson. He looked at it blankly.

"What do you mean? Her personal data isn't protected. Her name is here."

"Right, but check the address: 'c/o loc dir Tyresö'."

"What are you talking about?" Ingvar Johansson said.

Annika sat down.

"There are different levels of protection the authorities can use when people are at risk," she explained. "The lowest protection is when you have a security flag in the Public Register. That's not too unusual; there are about five thousand people whose personal info is classified. That's when it says 'protected data' on the screen."

"Yeah, I know all that. But it doesn't say that here," Ingvar Johansson said.

Annika pretended not to hear. "To have a security flag against your data, there has to be some form of tangible threat. The decision to classify data is made by the director of the local tax office in the area where the person is officially living."

Annika tapped her pen on the printout. "This, on the other hand, is really unusual. This level of protection is much tighter and a lot harder to get than being merely flagged. You're invisible in the Public Register. Furhage simply isn't listed in the register, except like this, with a reference to the director of the local tax office in Tyresö outside Stockholm. He's the only civil servant in the entire country who knows where she lives."

Ingvar Johansson gave her a skeptical look. "How do you know all this?"

"You remember my work on the Paradise Foundation—articles on people living underground in Sweden?"

"Of course, I do. So what?"

"The only other time I've come across this was when I was searching for people the government had done their best to hide deep down."

"But Christina Furhage isn't hidden, is she?"

"We haven't found her, have we? What telephone number do we have for her?"

They searched the newspaper's contacts book, which could be found on all the computers in the newsroom. Under the name Christina Furhage, title Olympic Boss, there was a GSM cellphone number. Annika dialed the number and got connected to an automated answering service.

"Her phone's not on," she said. She called directory enquiries to find out in whose name the subscription was. The number was ex-directory.

Ingvar Johansson sighed. "It's too dark anyway for my picture of Furhage in front of the arena," he said. "We'll save it till tomorrow."

"We still have to find the woman," Annika said. "It's obvious that she'll have to comment on what's happened."

She stood up and started toward her room.

"What are you going to do now?" Ingvar Johansson asked.

"I'm calling the Olympic Secretariat. They've got to know what the hell is going on here."

Annika dropped into her chair with a thud and leaned her forehead on the desk. Out of the corner of her eye she saw a cinnamon bun that had been sitting there since the day before. She took a bite. It was stale, but she mixed it in her mouth with the dregs of the Diet Coke she'd had at lunch. Having collected the crumbs with her fingers, she dialed the switchboard of the Olympic Secretariat. Busy. She tried once again, this time changing the last digit from nought to one, an old trick to bypass the switchboard and get straight on to someone's desk. Sometimes you had to try a hundred times, but sooner or later you'd end up on the desk of some poor bastard working late. Not so this time: Amazingly, she was successful at the first attempt. The director of the Secretariat himself, Evert Danielsson, answered.

Annika deliberated for half a second before she decided to skip the small talk. She'd try to beat him up a bit. "We want a comment from Christina Furhage," said Annika, "and we want it now."

Danielsson groaned. "You've called ten times already today. We have promised to pass on your questions."

"We want to talk to her ourselves. Surely you must appreciate she can't hide on a day like this? How would that look? They're *her* Games, for Christ's sake! She's never been afraid to talk before. Why is she hiding? Come on, give her to us now."

Danielsson breathed down the phone for several seconds. "We don't know where she is," he said in a low voice.

Annika felt her pulse quicken. She switched on the tape recorder next to her phone. "Haven't you been able to reach her either?" she said slowly.

Danielsson swallowed. "No," he said, "not all day. We haven't been able to reach her husband either. But you won't write about this, will you?"

"I can't tell," Annika said. "Where could she be?"

"We thought she was at home."

"And where is that?" Annika asked, thinking about what she'd found on the computer.

"Here in town. But no one's answering the door."

Annika breathed in. Why was he telling her this? He sounded desperate; Annika pressed on and quickly asked:

"Who's been threatening Christina Furhage?"

The man gasped. "What? What do you mean?"

"Come off it!" Annika said. "If you want me to not write about it, you'll have to tell me what's really going on here."

"How did . . . ? Who said . . . ?"

"She's off the record on the Public Register. Which means the threat against her is so serious that a court of law would issue a restraining order against the assailant. Has this happened?"

"My God," Danielsson said. "Who told you this?"

Annika groaned inwardly. "It's in the Public Register. If you know the language, all you have to do is to read the screen. Has a restraining order been issued against someone who's threatened Christina Furhage?"

"I can't talk any longer," the man said stiffly, and hung up.

Annika listened for a few seconds to the hum of the line before she sighed and put the phone down.

Evert Danielsson stared at the woman standing in the doorway. "How long have you been there?"

"What are you doing in here?" Helena Starke replied, crossing her arms.

The director got up from Christina Furhage's chair, looking around distractedly, as if not having noticed until now that he was sitting at the Managing Director's desk. "Well, I was . . . checking Christina's diary to see if she'd made a note of where she was going or something . . . but I can't find it."

The woman looked hard at Evert Danielsson. He met her gaze.

"You look like shit," he said before he could stop himself.

"What a truly sexist comment," she said with a disgusted look, walking up to Christina Furhage's desk. "Since you asked, I got drunk as a skunk last night and threw up on the doormat this morning. If you say that was unusually unladylike, you're dead.

"Christina is spending the day with her family," Helena Starke said while pulling out the second drawer of the Olympic boss's desk with practised movements. "That means she's working from home rather than here at the office," she explained.

The director saw Helena Starke pull out a thick diary, opening it near the end. She leafed through it, the paper rustling.

"Nothing. Saturday, December 18 is completely empty."

"Maybe she's doing her Christmas cleaning," Evert Danielsson said, and now both he and Helena Starke smiled. The thought of Christina in a housecoat with a feather duster in her hand was funny.

"Who called?" Helena Starke asked, putting the diary away in the drawer. The director noted that she pushed it firmly shut and turned a key in the upper right-hand corner of the drawer unit.

"Some journalist from *Kvällspressen*. A woman. I don't recall her name."

Helena put the key in her jeans pocket. "Why did you tell her we haven't been able to reach Christina?"

"What was I supposed to say? That she has no comment? That she's hiding? That would make it even worse." Danielsson flung his hands out to the sides in a gesture of helplessness.

"The question is . . ." the woman said, coming so close that he could smell the stale alcohol on her breath. "The question is: where *is* Christina? Why hasn't she come in?

Wherever she is, has to be in a place where she hasn't been getting any news whatsoever, right? Where the hell could that be? Any ideas?"

"Her country cottage?"

Helena looked at him with pity. "Please . . . And that terrorist bullshit you came out with at the press conference wasn't very smart, was it? What do you think Christina will say about that?"

Evert Danielsson lost his temper now; the overwhelming feeling of failure felt stiflingly unjust. "But that's what we agreed on. You were there when we discussed it. It wasn't only my view. On the contrary, we were going to seize the initiative and direct public opinion straight away. We all agreed on that."

Helena turned away and started walking toward the door.

"It got a bit embarrassing when the police denied it all with such emphasis. On TV you appeared hysterical and paranoid—not particularly becoming."

She turned around in the doorway and put a hand on the doorpost. "Are you staying in here or can I lock up?"

The director left Christina Furhage's room without a word.


The evening news meeting took place around the large conference table in the editor's office. TV1's *Aktuellt* news would start in fifteen minutes. Everybody except the night editor Jansson was present.

"He'll be here," Annika said. "He's just . . ."

"He/she is just" is the code for delays caused by general disturbances or other b.s.—reporters who don't know what they're supposed to do or readers on the phone who simply have to state their opinions at that very moment. It can also mean you've gone to the toilet or to get coffee.

The participants around the table were preparing or waiting. Annika went through her list of points to be presented during the meeting. She didn't have a long list like Ingvar Johansson, the news editor, who was handing out slips of paper with the different jobs in progress to the people around the table. The picture editor, Pelle Oscarsson, was on his cellphone. The editor was rocking to and fro on his feet, staring unseeing at the muted TV.

"Sorry," the night editor said as he hurtled into the room, coffee mug in one hand and the dummies for all the pages of the paper in the other. He was barely awake and was into his second mug. Naturally, he spilled some coffee on the floor as he shut the door. Anders Schyman noticed and sighed.

"Okay," he said, pulling out a chair and sitting down at the table. "Let's begin with the Bomber. What have we got?"

Annika didn't wait for Ingvar Johansson but started talking straight away. She knew the news editor liked to go through the whole lot, including her patch. She wasn't going to sit around and wait for that.

"The way I see it, there'll be four stories from us on the crime desk," she said. "We won't be able to escape the terrorist angle. Evert Danielsson himself brought it up at the press conference, but the police want it toned down. That in itself could be a story. The fact is that we have discovered that Christina Furhage has been on the receiving end of some kind of intimidation. She is off the PubReg, and her address is care of the Tyresö local tax office. Furthermore, no one knows her whereabouts, not even her closest colleagues at the Olympic Secretariat. I'll take care of that one."

"What headline did you have in mind?" Jansson asked.

"Something like 'Olympic boss living under threat'

and then a pull-quote from Danielsson, 'This is a terrorist attack'."

Jansson nodded approval.

"Then we have the main story, which has to be really thorough. We could put it together with graphics and captions around a big photo of the devastation. Patrik will take care of that. We've got daylight pictures of the stadium, both aerial and from the roof of the lamp factory, haven't we, Pelle?"

The picture editor nodded. "Yes. I think the helicopter pictures are better. The rooftop pictures are a bit under-exposed, unfortunately; they're simply too dark. I've tried to brighten them up on the Mac, but they're a bit out of focus, so I think we should go for the aerial shots."

Jansson wrote something on his dummy page. Annika felt the anger surge within her like fire, fucking Armani photographer who couldn't even set the focus or the right aperture!

"Who took the rooftop pictures?" Anders Schyman asked.

"Olsson," Annika responded curtly.

The editor made some notes. "What else?"

"Who's the victim? Man, woman, young, old? The pathologist's report, the forensic investigation, what are the lines of enquiry the Chief District Prosecutor mentioned at the press conference? Berit and I are looking into this."

"What have we got so far?" Schyman said.

Annika sighed. "Not much, I'm afraid. We'll continue our digging during the evening. I'm sure we'll find something."

The editor nodded and Annika continued. "Then there's the mysterious murder, the hunt for the Bomber, the leads, the theories, the evidence. Who was the man outside the arena just before the explosion? Who was the witness who saw him? Patrik is doing that. We haven't been able to locate the Tiger; neither have the police. According to Lindström, he's not a suspect, but that's bullshit. They may put out a nationwide alert for him this evening or during the night; you'll have to keep an eye on that. And then, of course, there's the Olympic angle, and you've got all that covered, Ingvar . . ."

The news editor cleared his throat. "Right. The security surrounding the Olympic Games—we've talked to Samaranch at the IOC in Lausanne. He has full confidence in Stockholm as host for the Games and fully believes that the Swedish police will apprehend the perpetrator very soon, blah blah. . . . Then he says that this in no way jeopardizes the Games, which I think we should emphasize. Then we've got the 'what now' stuff, Janet has done that. The stand will be rebuilt immediately. The work will start as soon as the police technicians have left the place and is estimated to be done in seven or eight weeks. Then there's the injured taxi driver; we're alone on that one, so we'll blow it up. We're doing a color piece with a retrospective of infamous Olympic attacks, the Tiger among others, unless we get hold of him during the night. Then I suppose we'll do a separate piece on him."

"His home telephone number's in the contacts book," Annika said. "I've left a message on his answerphone; it's possible he'll be in touch."

"Okay. Nils Langeby is working on world reactions; that will be an additional tie-in. And then we've got the vox pop on the attack, the *Ring and Sing* has just begun."

He stopped speaking and leafed through his papers.

"Anything else?" the editor said.

"There's Henriksson's pictures from the Olympic flame," Annika said. "We ran them in the early editions this morning, but they haven't been printed nationwide. He shot several rolls, so maybe we could do a variation on that to accompany the story about the victim in tomorrow's paper—a bit of recycling?"

Pelle Oscarsson nodded. "Yep, there are plenty of pics. I'm sure we could find one that isn't all that similar."

"*Aktuellt* is on," Ingvar Johansson said, turning up the TV with the remote.

They all turned their attention to the TV to see what Swedish Television had cooked up. They opened with footage from the police press conference, then went back to the morning when the arena was still on fire. After this, interviews followed with all the obvious people: Chief District Prosecutor Lindström, Evert Danielsson from the Olympic Secretariat, a Krim investigator, and an old lady who lived next to the arena and who woke up from the explosion.

"They've got nothing new," Ingvar Johansson stated and switched to CNN.

The meeting resumed and Ingvar Johansson ran through the rest of the contents of tomorrow's paper. They kept the TV on low while CNN ran their Breaking News. A CNN reporter appeared at regular intervals doing stand-ups from outside the cordons around the Olympic Village. They had another reporter in front of the police headquarters and a third one at the International Olympic Committee's headquarters in Lausanne. The live broadcasts were interspersed with recorded segments about the Olympics and various acts of violence that had hit the Games throughout the years. They had comments from internationally known celebrities and a condemnation of the attack by a White House press spokesperson.

Annika realized she wasn't listening to what Ingvar Johansson was saying. When he got to the soft-news pages, she made her excuses and left the meeting. She went back to the cafeteria and ordered a prawn pasta and a low-alcohol beer. While the microwave was humming behind the counter, she sat down and stared into the darkness. If she strained her eyes and focused hard, she could see the windows of the building opposite. When she relaxed, all she saw was her own reflection in the window.

Having finished her meal, she assembled the members of her own little desk, Patrik and Berit, and compared notes with them in her office.

"I'll do the terrorist story," Annika said. "Have you got anything on the victim, Berit?"

"A little," the reporter said, leafing through her notes. "The technicians have found some stuff inside the arena they believe belonged to the victim. It was pretty badly damaged, but they've established that there's a briefcase, a Filofax, and a cellphone."

She fell silent and noticed that both Annika's and Patrik's eyes were wide open.

"Christ!" Annika exclaimed. "That must mean they know who the victim is."

"Possibly," Berit said, "but they're not saying a word. It took me two hours just to get this from them."

"But that's great," Annika said. "Fantastic! You've done really well. Really! I haven't heard this anywhere else."

She leaned back in her chair, laughing and clapping her hands. Patrik smiled. Annika turned to him: "And how are you getting on?"

"I've done the blast itself. You can look at it for yourself; it's on the server. I've matched it to the picture of the arena, like you said. But I don't have much on the actual hunt for the murderer, I'm afraid. The police have done door-to-door interviews around the Docklands during the day, but not many people have moved into the apartments of the Olympic Village yet, so the place is quite empty."

"Who is the dark man, and who is the witness?"

"I haven't been able to get anything on that," Patrik said.

Suddenly Annika remembered something her driver had said in the car on the way out to the stadium early that morning. "There's an unlicensed club out there," she said, straightening up in her chair. "The injured driver had a fare there when the bomb went off. There must've been people there, both guests and staff. That's where we'll find our witness. Have we talked to them?"

Patrik and Berit looked at each other.

"We've got to go to the docks and talk to them," Annika said.

"An unlicensed club?" Berit was skeptical. "How keen will they be to talk to us?"

"What the hell," Annika said, "you never know. Let them speak anonymously or off the record—they can just tell you if they saw something or know anything."

"Sounds like a good idea," Patrik said. "It could be productive."

"Have the police talked to them?"

"I don't know. I didn't ask," Patrik said.

"Okay," Annika said. "I'll call the police. You get out there and try to find the club. Call the injured driver. We've got him hidden away at the Royal Viking. Ask him exactly where the club is. They won't be open tonight, I presume; the place is probably inside the police cordons. Still, talk to the driver and see if he had a name for the customer he drove there. Maybe it was he who recommended the club because he knows someone there, you never know."

"I'll go right now," Patrik said. He picked up his jacket and was gone.

Berit sighed. "I can't really believe it was a terrorist attack," she said. "Why? To put a stop to the Games? Then why start now, it's a little late in the day."

Annika doodled on her pad. "One thing I *do* know," she said. "The police better catch this Bomber person, otherwise this country will have a hangover it hasn't seen since Olof Palme was killed."

Berit nodded, picked up her things, and went out to her desk.

Annika called her contact, but he wasn't available. She e-mailed an official police communication about the illegal club to Patrik. Then she went and picked up a copy of the Government's official yearbook and looked up the name of the director of the local tax office in Tyresö. It gave his name and the year of his birth. His name was much too common to be easily found in the phone directory, so Annika had to Reg him first. This way she got his home address, then information found him quick as a flash.

He answered on the fourth ring and sounded quite drunk. It was Saturday night after all. Annika switched on her tape recorder.

"I can't say a word about Christina Furhage," the tax director said, sounding like he was about to hang up on her straight away.

"Naturally," Annika said calmly. "I'd just like to ask a few general questions about people being off record and about threat scenarios."

A group of people burst out laughing simultaneously in the background. She must have called in the middle of a dinner party or a Christmas drinks party.

"You'll have to call me at the office on Monday," the tax director said.

"But the paper will have gone to print long before then," Annika said in a silky voice. "The readers have a right to a comment tomorrow. What reason shall I give for you not answering?"

The man breathed silently down the line. Annika

could feel him debating with himself. He understood that she was alluding to his intoxication. She wouldn't ever write anything like that in the paper; you just don't. But if an official was awkward, she didn't hesitate to use a few tricks to get her way.

"What do you want to know?" he said icily.

Annika smiled. "What does it take for a person to be off record?" she asked.

She knew that already, but the man's words when describing it would be a recapitulation of Christina's case.

The man sighed, giving it some thought. "Well, there has to be a threat. A real threat," he said. "Not just a telephone call, but something more, something serious."

"Like a death threat?" Annika said.

"For example. Though there has to be more, something to make a court issue a restraining order."

"An incident? Some kind of violent act?" Annika asked.

"You could put it that way."

"Would someone be made off record for less than what you've described to me?"

"No, they wouldn't," the man said firmly. "If the threat were of a less serious nature, it would suffice to have a security flag in the Public Register."

"How many people have you approved for going off record during your time in Tyresö?"

He pondered the question then said, "Uh . . . three."

"Christina Furhage, her husband, and her daughter," Annika declared.

"I didn't say that," the tax director said.

"Can you comment on Christina Furhage being off record?" she swiftly continued.

"No, I cannot," the man said in a surly tone.

"What kind of death threat was directed at Christina Furhage?"

"I can't comment on that."

"What was the act of violence behind your decision to grant her off-record status?"

"I can't say anything more on the matter. We'll end the interview here," the man said and hung up.

Annika smiled happily. She was home and dry now. Without saying a word about Christina, the man had confirmed it all.

After another couple of verifying calls, she wrote her copy on the threat scenario, keeping the terrorist theory at a reasonable level. Just after 11 P.M. she was done. Patrik still hadn't returned. That boded well.

She gave her copy to Jansson, who was now in full owing out by the desk, ruffling his hair and continually speaking on the phone.

She decided to walk home, despite the cold and the dark, despite her empty head. Her legs were aching; they always did when she was exhausted. A brisk walk was the best remedy, then she wouldn't have to take a painkiller when she got home. She quickly put on her coat and pulled the hat over her ears before she had time to change her mind.

"I'm on my cellphone," was all she said to Jansson on her way out. He waved to her without looking up from the phone.

The temperature had really shifted up and down today; now it was just below freezing again and large snowflakes were slowly falling. They were nearly hanging still in the air, wavering back and forth on their way to the ground. The snow wrapped all sounds and deadened them. Annika didn't hear the 57 bus until it drove past right next to her.

She took the stairs down to the Rålambshov Park. The path across the wide lawn was muddy and cut up by prams and bicycles; she slipped and nearly fell, swearing to herself. A startled hare leapt away from her into the shadows. Amazing that there were so many animals in the middle of the city. Once Thomas had been chased by a badger on their own street on his way home from the pub. She laughed out loud in the dark at the memory.

The wind was stronger here than up among the buildings, so she pulled her scarf tighter around her neck. The snowflakes were wilder and wet her hair. She hadn't seen her kids all day. She hadn't called back since the morning; it would only have been painful. Usually she felt okay working in the week, since all the kids in Sweden were at daycare centers then and her conscience could rest. But on a Saturday like today, the last one before Christmas, you were supposed to be at home making toffee and baking saffron buns. Annika sighed, and the snowflakes whirled around her. The problem was that when she did organize a baking session or some other big activity it was never much fun. At first both children thought it was great and would quarrel about who would stand next to her. By the time they'd fought over the dough and messed up the whole kitchen, her patience would be giving out. It would be worse if she'd had a hard time at work; she'd end up blowing her top. It had ended that way on more occasions than she cared to think of. The kids would sulk in front of the TV, while she finished the baking at lightning speed. Then Thomas would put them to bed while she cleaned the kitchen. She let out another sigh. Maybe this time it would have been different. No one would have burned their fingers on the sticky toffee and they could all have eaten freshly baked saffron buns together in front of the fire.

When she reached the footpath along the water by Norr Mälarstrand, she quickened her pace. The pain in her legs was already easing and she was forcing herself to keep a steady, resolute stride. Her breathing increased and the heart found a new, more intense rhythm.

She used to think it was more fun to be at work than to be at home. As a reporter she would see quick results, get everyone's appreciation, and have a picture byline several times a week. She had full command of her beat and knew exactly what was expected of her in different situations; she could swing things and make demands. At home the demands were more numerous, harder, and less explicit. She was never sufficiently happy, horny, calm, efficient, parental, or rested. The apartment was always more or less in a mess, the laundry basket always on the verge of overflowing. Thomas was very good with the kids, almost better than she was, but he never, ever wiped the cooker or the worktop, hardly ever put the dirty dishes in the dishwasher, and always left clothes and unopened letters lying in mounds on the bedroom floor. It was as if he thought the dirty dishes found their own way into the dishwasher and the bills paid themselves.

But it wasn't as much fun to go to work anymore, not for the past eight weeks since she became an editor. She hadn't had the faintest idea of how strong the reactions to her promotion would be. The decision hadn't even been particularly controversial. In practice she'd been running the crime desk alongside her job as a reporter for the past year. Now she was paid for it; that's how she saw it. But Nils Langeby had hit the roof, of course. He considered the job his. He was 53, Annika only 32. She had also been astounded by how people felt they had a right to openly discuss her and criticize her over all kinds of matters. Suddenly people would comment and question her dress, something they'd never done before. They would say things about her character and abilities that were completely insulting. She hadn't realized that she became public property when she put on the editor's hat. Now she knew.

She quickened her pace further. She longed to be at home. She looked up at the houses on the other side of the street. The windows gave out a warm, welcoming glow over the water. Nearly all of them were decorated with Christmas lights or Christmas candelabra. It looked beautiful and safe. She left the bank and turned into John Ericssonsgatan, up toward Hantverkargatan.

The apartment was quiet and dark. Carefully she wriggled out of her boots and coat and tiptoed into the children's room. They were sleeping in their little pajamas, Ellen's with Barbie on them and Kalle's with Batman. She sniffed them slightly, as Ellen moved in her sleep.

Thomas was in bed but not yet asleep. A reading lamp cast a discreet light over his side of the bed. He was reading *The Economist*.

"Exhausted?" he asked, after she had pulled off her clothes and kissed him on his hair.

"So-so," she answered from inside the walk-in closet where she was pushing her clothes into the laundry basket. "This explosion has turned into a nasty business."

She was naked when she came out of the closet and crept in beside him.

"You're freezing cold," he said.

All of a sudden Annika noticed how cold her thighs were. "I walked home."

"The paper didn't pay for a taxi? You've worked for twenty hours, a whole Saturday!"

A feeling of irritation immediately hit her. "Of course the paper would have paid for a taxi. I wanted to walk." She was almost shouting. "Don't be so bloody critical!"

He put the magazine on the floor and switched off the lamp, demonstratively turning his back.

Annika sighed. "Come on, Thomas, don't sulk."

"You're away the whole Saturday and then, when you finally come home, you swear and shout at me," he said wearily. "Are we just here to take shit from you?"

She could feel the tears welling up in her eyes, tears of fatigue and inadequacy. "I'm sorry," she whispered. "I didn't mean to fly off the handle at you. It's just that they're at me all day at work, and it's really hard. And then I feel guilty for not being at home with you and the kids. I'm so scared you'll think I'm letting you down, but the paper won't allow me to let them down, and so I'm caught in the middle of some crossfire . . ."

She started crying for real now. She could hear him sighing on the other side of his back. After a few moments, he turned around and took her in his arms.

"There, there, damn it. Come on, darling, you'll be all right. You're better than the whole lot of them. . . . Shit, you're cold as ice! I hope you don't catch cold, just before Christmas."

She laughed through her tears and cuddled up in his arms. Silence fell over them in a warm and safe mutual understanding. She leaned her head back onto her pillow and blinked. Up there in the dark, the ceiling was floating. Suddenly she remembered the image from the morning and the dream she was woken up from by the telephone.

"I dreamed of you this morning," she whispered.

"I hope it was a dirty dream," he mumbled, half asleep.

She laughed quietly. "And how! In a space shuttle, no less. And the men from *Studio Six* were watching."

"They're just envious," Thomas said and went to sleep.

# LOVE

I was an adult and had already gained a certain position in life when it first hit me. For a few short moments, it lifted my sense of universal loneliness. Our souls really did merge in a way I hadn't experienced before. It's interesting to have taken part in it, I won't say more than that, and since then I have met with this sensation on several occasions. Looking back on it, however, most of my impressions can be summed up as indifferent and almost resigned. I say this without bitterness or disappointment; it's simply a statement. It's only now, this last year, that I have started to waver in my opinion. The woman I have found and come to love is perhaps capable of changing it all.

But deep down I know this isn't so. Love is banal. It fills you with the same chemical intoxication as a long-sought success or the dizzying experience of high speed. Your mind is oblivious to everything except your own enjoyment, your existence is distorted, and an irrational state of possibility and happiness is created. Despite the varying subjects, the magic has never been long lasting. In the long run, it breeds nothing but weariness and aversion.

*The most beautiful love is always impossible to attain. It has to die when it's most alive; as for the rose, its only chance is to be cut down at its prime. A dried or preserved plant can give pleasure for many years. A love that is hastily crushed at its moment of strongest passion has the ability to hold people spellbound for centuries.*

*The myth of love is a fairy tale, as unreal and unrealistic as a continuous orgasm.*

*Love shouldn't be mistaken for true devotion. That's something completely different. Love doesn't "ripen"; it only fades and, at the best of times, is replaced by warmth and tolerance, though mostly by unspoken demands and bitterness. This goes for all types of love: that between the sexes, between generations, and in the workplace. How many times haven't I come across bitter wives with fingers scoured to the bone and sexually frustrated husbands? Emotionally handicapped parents and neglected children? Misunderstood managers and employees who long ago stopped being glad they had a job and instead were only making demands?*

*It is possible to love your job. That love has for me always been truer than that between people. The genuine delight in succeeding with something I had set my mind on outshines all other experiences I've ever had. To me, it's self-evident that devotion to your task can be just as strong as to a person who doesn't deserve it.*

*The thought that my beloved perhaps does deserve it fills me with dread and insecurity.*

# SUNDAY 19 DECEMBER

Sunday has always been the tabloids' day of big sales. People have both the time and the inclination to read something reasonably undemanding, and they are relaxed enough to do crossword puzzles and try out various quizzes on one another. For years, most Sunday papers have also invested in bulky supplements with extra reading. The TS, *Tidningsstatistik*, the body that authenticates and publishes newspaper publication figures in Sweden, therefore separates the Sunday edition from the rest of the week's sales when compiling the statistics.

Nothing ever sells as much as a really good piece of news, however. If, in addition, it happens on a Saturday, there's potential for huge sales. That this was the case this Sunday, Anders Schyman immediately saw when he had in his hands the tabloids that were delivered to his house in the fashionable leafy suburb of Saltsjöbaden. He brought the papers with him to the breakfast table, where his wife was pouring out the coffee.

"Looking good?" his wife asked but only got a grunt in reply from the editor-in-chief. This was the magic moment of the day. His nerves were taut and he focused completely on the papers, putting his and the rival's on the breakfast table, comparing the two front pages. Jansson had done it again, he noted and smiled. Both papers had gone for the terrorist angle, but *Kvällspressen* had a scoop with the death threat against the Managing Director Christina Furhage. *Kvällspressen* had a better lead story, better celebs in the masthead, and a more dramatic picture of the stadium. He smiled even wider and relaxed.

"Fine," he said to his wife and reached for the coffee. "Very good, actually."

The cartoon voices from the children's morning TV were the first thing Annika heard. The high-pitched howls and special effects leaked in under the bedroom door. She put the pillow over her head to block out the noise. This was one of the few drawbacks of having children: The affected C-movie actors who supplied the Swedish voices to *Darkwing Duck* were more than she could take on a Sunday morning. Thomas as usual didn't notice. He slept on with his half of the duvet crumpled up between his legs.

She lay still for a moment to see how she was feeling. She was tired, and the pain in her legs wasn't completely gone. She immediately started thinking about the Bomber and realized she must have been dreaming about the attack. It was always like that when a big story broke—she would enter a long tunnel and wouldn't appear again until after the story was finished with. Sometimes she had to force herself to stop and breathe, both for her own and the kids' sake. Thomas didn't like it when she became swallowed up by her work.

"It's just a job," he would say. "You're always writing as if it were a matter of life and death."

But it almost always was, Annika mused, at least in her particular line of work.

She sighed, tossed the pillow and the duvet to the side, and got up. She stood there swaying for a moment, more tired than she'd thought at first. The woman reflected in the window looked a hundred years old. She let out another sigh and walked out into the kitchen.

The kids had already eaten. The plates were still on the table, standing in pools of various spilled dairy products. Nowadays, Kalle could take out yogurt and cereals himself. After burning himself on the toaster, he had stopped serving Ellen toasted rye bread with peanut butter and jam, which otherwise was a big favorite.

She put the kettle on and went in to the children. The cries of joy rose to meet her before she was through the door.

"Mommy!"

Four hungry arms and eyes rushed toward her, wet mouths kissing and bubbling and hugging and assuring her, "Mommy, Mommy, we've missed you so much! Mommy, where were you all day yesterday? Were you working all day, Mommy? You didn't come home, Mommy, we were already in bed . . ."

She held them both in her arms, squatting in the doorway to the TV room.

"We got a new film yesterday, Mommy. *You're Crazy, Mardie!* it's called. It was really scary, the horrible man hit Mia. Do you want to see my drawing, Mommy? It's for you!"

They wriggled free from her hold and ran off in different directions. Kalle came back first, with the cover for the film based on Astrid Lindgren's book about her childhood friend.

"The head teacher was really horrible. He spanked Mia for taking his wallet," Kalle said earnestly.

"I know, that was really bad of him," Annika said, stroking the boy's hair. "It was like that at school in the past. Terrible, isn't it?"

"Is it like that at school now?" he asked with concern.

"No, not anymore," Annika said and kissed him on the cheek. "No one could ever hurt my little boy."

A terrific howl came out of the children's room, "My drawing's gone. Kalle has taken it!"

The boy stiffened.

"I have not!" he shouted back. "You've lost it yourself. You did!"

The howl in the background turned into loud crying. "It's Kalle. He took my drawing!"

"Little brat! I never did!"

Annika put the boy down, stood up, and took him by the hand.

"That's enough now," she said firmly. "Come on, let's go and look for the drawing. It's probably somewhere on the desk. And don't call your sister a brat. I don't want to hear that word."

"Brat! Brat!" Kalle yelled.

The loud crying became a howl again. "Mommy, Kalle's being horrid! He's calling me a brat!"

"Be quiet now, both of you!" Annika said, raising her voice. "You're waking Daddy up."

As she entered the room with the boy, Ellen's clenched fist was in the air to hit her brother. Annika caught it before it landed, feeling her patience giving out.

"Stop it now!" she shouted. "Stop it, both of you!"

"What's the row?" Thomas was standing in the bedroom doorway. "Christ, can't I have one single morning of sleep?"

"See, you've woken Daddy up," Annika shouted.

"You're louder than the two of them together," Thomas said and slammed the door shut.

Annika felt the tears well up again. Damn, damn, damn. Why didn't she ever learn? She sank to the floor, heavy as a rock.

"Mommy. Are you sad, Mommy?"

"No, I'm not sad. I'm just a bit out of sorts. It's because I worked so late yesterday." She forced a smile and reached out for the two of them. Kalle looked at her earnestly.

"You mustn't work so much," he said. "You get too tired."

She gave him a hug. "You're so wise," she said. "Shall we look for that drawing now?"

It had fallen behind the radiator. Annika blew away the dust and expressed her admiration gushingly. Ellen beamed with delight.

"I'll put it up on the wall in the bedroom. But Daddy has to wake up before I do that."

The kettle was boiling away in the kitchen; half of it was steam on the windows. She put more water in and opened the window slightly to get rid of the mist.

"Do you want more breakfast?"

They did, and now they had toasted rye bread with butter. Their twitter rose and fell while Annika ploughed through the morning papers and listened to the radio news. There was nothing new in the papers, but the radio quoted both of the tabloids: her report about the death threat against Furhage, as well as the competition's interview with IOC president Samaranch. Oh well, Annika thought to herself, they beat us with Lausanne. Too bad, but that was not her headache.

She had another piece of rye bread.

Helena Starke unlocked the door and switched off the alarm. Occasionally, when she got to the Olympic Secretariat the alarm was disarmed: The careless bastard who had left last the evening before would have forgotten to switch it on. This time she knew it had been done properly. She was last to leave the night before, or rather, early this morning.

She went straight to Christina's door and unlocked it. The voicemail indicator was flashing; Helena felt her pulse quicken. Someone had called during the night. She quickly lifted the receiver and dialed Christina's password. There were two messages, one from each of the two tabloids. She swore and threw the phone down. Damn those hyenas! They must have figured out Christina's direct number. With a sigh, she sank into her boss's executive chair, swiveling back and forth. She still hadn't quite recovered from the hangover—there was a bitter taste in her mouth and her head was buzzing. If only she could remember what Christina had said the night before last. Her memory had cleared enough for her to remember that Christina had been with her in the apartment. She had been quite angry, hadn't she? Helena shuddered and got up from the chair.

When she heard someone entering through the front door, she quickly pushed the chair in and walked around to the other side of the desk.

It was Evert Danielsson. He had dark rings round his eyes and a tense line around his mouth.

"Have you heard anything?" he asked.

Helena shrugged. "About what? They haven't caught the Bomber, Christina hasn't been in touch, and you've certainly succeeded in planting the terrorist theory everywhere. I assume you've seen the morning papers?"

The line round Danielsson's mouth tightened. I see, it's his own big mouth he's worried about, Helena thought, feeling contempt rise within her. It wasn't the incident itself and its consequences that worried him but his own skin. How selfish, and how sad.

"The board is meeting today at 4 P.M.," she said and left the room. "You'll have to give a full report on the situation before we can make a decision on what to do after this . . ."

"Since when are you on the board?" Evert Danielsson said coolly.

Helena Starke froze, stopping short for a moment, but then pretended she hadn't heard his comment.

"And I suppose it's time to summon the big guns. If nothing else, they have to be informed. They'll be pissed if we don't, and we need them now more than ever before."

Evert Danielsson watched the woman while she locked Christina's door. She was right about the big guns. The captains of industry, the royalty, the church, and others on the representative Honorary Board had to be summoned as soon as possible. They needed greasing and polishing up, so that they could shine outwardly. "We need them more than ever before." How true.

"Will you see to that?" Evert Danielsson said.

Helena Starke gave a short nod and disappeared along the corridor.

Ingvar Johansson was at his desk talking on the phone when Annika arrived at the paper. She was the first reporter to turn up; the others would show around ten. Ingvar Johansson first pointed at the fresh papers lying in piles alongside the wall, then at the couch next to the newsdesk. Annika draped her coat over the back of the couch, picked up the early edition and a plastic mug of coffee, then sat down to read while Ingvar Johansson finished his call. His voice rose and fell like a song in the background while Annika checked what they had got together since she left last night. Her own story on the terrorist angle and the threat against Christina Furhage were on pages six and seven, the two heaviest and most important news pages. The picture editor had found a picture in the archive of Furhage walking at the head of a group of men, all dressed in dark suits and overcoats. She was dressed in a white tailored suit and a short, pale coat, standing out as a figure of light in front of all the men. The woman looked stern and strained, an excellent image of an innocent person under threat. On page seven was a photo of Evert Danielsson emerging from the press conference. A good picture of a hard-pressed man. Annika noted that it was taken by Ulf Olsson.

On the next spread were Berit's stories on the victim and the police finds at the scene of the crime. Jansson had picked another of Henriksson's pictures from the Olympic flame to accompany them. It worked just as well today. And there was the injured taxi driver Arne Brattström's account of the explosion.

On the spread of pages ten and eleven, she found the biggest surprises so far; Patrik had been hard at it all night, getting two stories together. " 'I saw the mysterious man outside the arena,' the secret police witness tells his story" and "The Tiger wanted by the police."

Well done! Annika thought. He had found a guy who worked at the illegal club, a bartender who told of how on his way to work he saw someone hurrying across the forecourt in front of the arena's main entrance. But this had been about one in the morning, not just before the explosion as the police had said.

"I saw a person in a black anorak with the hood up, dark trousers, and heavy shoes," the bartender was quoted as saying.

Now we have an image of our Bomber, at least until we find a better one, thought Annika.

Predictably, the police had pulled out all the stops to get hold of the Tiger. Also on the spread were the meager police theories on the murder and the attack so far.

Pages eleven and twelve were dedicated to the Olympics, the consequences for the Games, and future security issues. The retrospective of past attacks on the Olympics was also here. The following spread was given over to a display ad for the last few days of Christmas shopping, pages sixteen and seventeen were the vox pop, plus Nils Langeby's compilation of world reactions.

Then the pages flickered past up to the center spread: celebrities coming clean about their various maladies, a sick child to be pitied, a trade union scandal, an unknown pop star caught drunk-driving, and a group of drag queens protesting against cutbacks in the national health sector.

Patrik's main story about the actual attack took pride of place on the center spread. Sequence of events, places and arrows, everything concise and succinct, laid out around the helicopter photo.

She looked up and saw that Ingvar Johansson had finished his call. He must have been watching her for a while.

"This is good stuff, don't you think?" Annika said, waving the paper in the air before putting it on the couch.

"It's not bad," Ingvar Johansson said, turning round. "But that's all history. Tomorrow's paper is all that matters now."

Damn killjoy, Annika thought. Tabloid news editors lived far too much in the future and not enough in the past, in her opinion. If you got something wrong, you didn't give a shit because that was already yesterday's news. If you did something good, you never got enough credit for it. That was a pity. She thought they could gain from reflecting on what they had done, both good and bad.

"What have you got for tomorrow?" he said, his back turned to her.

What the hell is wrong now? she thought wearily. Why is he doing this? I must have pissed him off and now he's punishing me. What could it be? Is he annoyed because I stole the show at the news conference yesterday?

"How am I supposed to know what's up, I only just walked through the damn door!" she exclaimed, surprised at how angry she sounded. She quickly got up and grabbed her coat and bag. Her arms full, she started walking toward her office.

"There's a police press conference at half past ten," Ingvar Johansson called after her.

She looked at her watch at the same time as she fumbled for the door to her office. Fifty minutes left; she had time for a few phone calls.

She began with the cellphone number that was said to be Christina Furhage's. The Olympic boss hadn't made a single comment anywhere, which meant that not even the Secretariat could get hold of her. Something was very wrong with her complete silence, that much Annika knew.

To her great surprise, she got a ringing signal. The phone was on. She quickly cleared her throat while listening to the beeping signals. After the fifth one, she got the automated answering service again, but at least she knew now that the phone was working and was in use. She made a mental note of the number.

Patrik and Berit appeared simultaneously in the doorway.

"Are you busy?"

"Christ, no! Come inside and let's have a quick look at things." She got up, walked around her desk and sat down on the old couch.

"Great work yesterday, both of you," she said. "We're alone with the stuff about what was found at the crime scene, and no one else had anything on the bartender at the illegal club."

"Though our rival's interview with Samaranch was much better, unfortunately," Berit said. "Did you read it? Apparently he was furious and threatened to cancel the Games unless the Bomber was apprehended."

"Yes, so I heard," Annika said. "It's a shame we had nothing on that. But I wonder—did he really say that? If he really wants to cancel the Games, why hasn't he gone public with it? He's said to all the other media and in the press release that the Games will go ahead, at all costs."

"Has the competition got a monopoly on what Samaranch's really thinking?" Berit said.

Annika opened the paper at the page with the interview in the other paper. "Their Rome correspondent wrote it. He's good," Annika said. "I think it's correct, but Samaranch will still make an official denial this afternoon."

"Why this afternoon?" Patrik asked.

"Because by then CNN will have mentioned it and put together a special item on it," Annika said and smiled, " 'The Olympics at stake' will be the headline, and there'll be some grandiose music in a minor key . . ."

Berit smiled. "I heard there's another press conference soon," she said.

"Yes," Annika replied, "they're probably going to announce who the victim is, and I wonder if it's not the Olympic boss herself."

"Furhage?" Patrik said. "What makes you think that?"

"Think about it," Annika said. "Either she's hiding, or something is seriously wrong. No one can get hold of her, not even her closest colleagues. There isn't a place on earth where the attack hasn't been reported. She couldn't have missed it. Either she doesn't want to make herself known—that means she's hiding—or she can't, probably because she's sick, dead, or has been kidnapped."

"I've thought about that," Berit said. "I actually asked the investigators about it yesterday when I talked to them about the finds at the scene, but they denied it categorically."

"That doesn't mean anything," Annika mused. "Furhage is a story today too, whatever happens. We have to follow up that death threat: What was it exactly? If she *is* the victim, we'll have to focus on her life story. Do we have an obit for her?"

"Not for her," Berit said. "Christina Furhage wasn't exactly about to peg out."

"Let's ask for pics and cuttings before we set off for the police headquarters. Did either one of you talk to Eva-Britt yesterday?"

Both Berit and Patrik shook their heads. Annika went over to her desk and dialed the secretary's home number. When Eva-Britt Qvist answered, Annika asked her if she could come into the office.

"I know it's the last Sunday before Christmas, but it would be great if you could come in all the same," she said. "The rest of us are going to a press conference at police headquarters, and it would be really helpful if you could collect all the stuff we have on Christina Furhage while we're there, both pics and copy."

"I've just put some dough aside to rise," Eva-Britt Qvist said.

"Oh, that's a shame," Annika said. "But big things are happening here today, and the rest of us are a bit out of it. Patrik was here until half past four this morning, I worked from a quarter past three in the morning until eleven at night yesterday, Berit about the same. And we need help with what is really your job, looking things up in databases and compiling material . . ."

"I'm sorry, I've already said I can't," Eva-Britt Qvist said. "I do have a family."

Annika swallowed the first response that came into her mind. Instead she spoke very deliberately: "Yes, I know what it's like when you have to change your plans. It's awful to disappoint your children and partner. Naturally, you'll be paid overtime or you'll get time off in lieu whenever you want. Between Christmas and New Year, or the next school holiday, whatever. But it would be really great if you could have the material ready by the time we get back from the press conference."

"I told you, I'm in the middle of baking! I can't come in!"

Annika took a deep breath. "Okay, then we'll do it this way instead, if that's what you prefer. I order you to come in. I expect you to be here in fifteen minutes."

"What about my buns?!"

"Ask your family to mould them," Annika said and hung up. To her annoyance, she noticed that her hand was shaking.

She hated this. She would never dream of doing what Eva-Britt Qvist had just done if a superior called her and asked her to do overtime. If you worked at a newspaper and something big happened, you had to be prepared to come in, that's just the way it was. If you wanted a nine-to-five job, Monday to Friday, you should join the accounts office of a phone company or something like that. Other people could check the databases—she or Berit or one of the newsroom reporters. But in a situation like this, everyone was hard-pressed. And everyone wanted to celebrate Christmas. It made sense to distribute the workload as fairly as possible and let everyone do their bit, even if it was Sunday. She couldn't climb down and let Eva-Britt off the hook because that would make her life as a manager hell. The kind of disrespect the crime-desk secretary had just shown her would not be rewarded with days off. She wished she could just fire the bitch.

"Eva-Britt's coming in," she said to the others, thinking she saw the shadow of a smile on Berit's face.

They took two cars to the press conference. Annika and Berit in one, together with the photographer Johan Henriksson, and Patrik in the other with Ulf Olsson. The media pack was, if possible, even more hysterical today. Henriksson had to park on Kungsholm's Square half a mile away; both Bergsgatan and Agnegatan, the streets running alongside the police headquarters, were solid with OB vans and Volvos with large media logos on them. Annika enjoyed the short walk. The air was clear and fresh after the previous day's snowfall, the top floors of the buildings aglow in the sharp sunlight. The snow crunched under their shoes.

"I live over there," she said, pointing at the newly renovated nineteenth-century apartment building further up on Hantverkargatan.

"Do you rent or own?" Berit asked.

"Secure tenancy," Annika said.

"How did you get hold of an apartment there?" Henriksson said, thinking of his sublet in the outer southern suburbs.

"Stubbornness," Annika replied. "I got a short lease in the house eight years ago. A small two-bedroom apartment with no mod cons at the back of the block. There was a communal bathroom in the basement of the adjoining house. The house was scheduled for a renovation and I was given a six-month lease. But then the recession came and the owner went bust. No one wanted to buy the place, and after five years I got tenancy rights. By then there were almost four of us in that small apartment: me, Thomas, Kalle, and Ellen on the way. When the building was finally renovated, we got a four-bedroom apartment at the front of the building. Not bad, eh?"

"Jackpot," Berit said.

"What's your rent?" Henriksson asked.

"Ask me something else, like how nice the wood paneling is or how high the ceilings are," Annika said.

"Goddamn yuppie," Henriksson exclaimed, and Annika laughed out loud.

The group from *Kvällspressen* was late and barely managed to get inside the press conference room. Annika ended up in the doorway and could hardly see anything. She craned her neck and saw reporters doing their best to show everybody else how extremely important and focused on their job they were. Henriksson and Olsson elbowed their way to the front, arriving there at the same time as the press conference participants filed into the room. There were fewer of them than the day before. Annika could only see the Chief District Prosecutor Kjell Lindström and the police press officer. Evert Danielsson wasn't there, nor was the Krim investigator. Above the head of a woman from one of the morning papers, Annika saw the press officer clear his throat and begin to speak. He summed up the situation and went through already known facts, that the Tiger was wanted for questioning by the police and that the forensic investigation was underway. He talked for ten minutes and then Kjell Lindström leaned forward, with the entire press corps doing the same. Everybody had an idea of what was coming.

"The identification procedure of the victim at the stadium is now more or less complete," the prosecutor said, as all of the reporters craned their necks.

"The family has been informed, which is why we have decided to make it public, although there is some work still to be carried out. . . . The deceased is Christina Furhage, Managing Director of SOCOG, the Stockholm Organizing Committee of the Olympic Games."

Annika's reaction was almost physical: yes! I knew it! I knew it! When the excited voices at the press conference were reaching fever pitch, she was already on her way out of the building. She pushed the earpiece into her ear and dialed the number she had memorized. Without a sound, her phone called the other handset, and then the number was ringing. She stopped in the small lobby between the reception area and the front doors, took a deep breath, closed her eyes, and focused all her energy on communicating a telepathic message: please, somebody, pick up, pick up! Three rings, four rings, and there was a click! Someone was answering! Christ, who could it be?

Annika screwed up her eyes even tighter and began talking quietly and slowly. "Good afternoon. My name is Annika Bengtzon and I'm from *Kvällspressen*. To whom am I speaking?"

"I'm Bertil Milander," someone said in a faint voice.

Bertil Milander, Bertil Milander, surely that was Christina Furhage's husband? Wasn't that his name? To be on the safe side, Annika continued as slowly as before: "Is this Bertil Milander, Christina Furhage's husband?"

The man at the other end sighed. "Yes, that's right."

Annika's heart was pounding. This was the most unpleasant call a reporter could ever make—to the house of a person whose next of kin had just died. There was an ongoing debate within the press corps whether these calls should be made at all. Annika felt it was better to call than not, if for no other reason than to tell people what the paper was doing.

"Let me begin by saying how deeply saddened I am by the tragedy that has struck you and your family. The police have just announced that it was your wife Christina who died in the explosion at Victoria Stadium," she began.

The man said nothing.

"By the way, isn't this Christina's cellphone?" she heard herself ask.

"No, it's the family's," the man said in surprise.

"The reason I'm calling is to tell you that we will be writing about your wife in tomorrow's paper."

"You already have," the man said.

"Yes, we have been covering the bomb attack, the event itself."

"Weren't you the ones with that photo? The photo where . . ."

His voice cracked as he started sobbing. Annika put her hand over her mouth and stared up at the ceiling. God, the man had seen Henriksson's picture of the doctors picking up the pieces of his wife. God almighty! She soundlessly drew a breath.

"Yes, that was us," she said calmly. "I regret we couldn't warn you we would run that picture, but we have only now found out that your wife was the victim. I couldn't call any sooner. I apologize if the picture caused you suffering. That's why I believe it's vital to talk to you now. We will continue writing about this tomorrow."

The man was crying.

"If there's anything you want to say, I'm here," Annika said. "If you have any complaints or want us to write, or not write, about something in particular, we want you to tell us. Mr. Milander?"

He blew his nose.

"I'm still here," he said.

Annika looked up and through the glass wall saw the phalanx of media beginning to leave the building. Quickly she pushed the door open and went outside to stand next to the steps. Through the earpiece she heard two signals announce that someone was trying to get through to the other phone.

"I understand how completely awful this must be for

you," she said. "I can't even begin to understand what it must be like. But this is a world event, one of the worst crimes ever committed in this country. Your wife was a prominent figure and a role model to the women of Sweden. That's why it's our duty to cover the event. And that's why I appeal to you to talk to us, to give us a chance to be respectful. Just tell me how you want it. We could make things even worse by writing the wrong things and unintentionally hurt you."

The call-waiting signal again. The man was wavering.

"I'll give you my own and my editor's direct numbers, and then you can call when you feel ready . . ."

"Come here," the man cut in. "I want to talk."

Annika closed her eyes and was ashamed of the exultation she felt inside. She had an interview with the victim's husband! She took the secret address, jotting it down on the back of a taxi receipt she found in her pocket. Before she had time to consider the ethics of it, she quickly added:

"Your phone will be ringing without interruption from now on. Don't hesitate to switch it off if you feel it's too much for you."

She had got hold of him. It would be best if no one else did.

She pushed inside the building to find her colleagues. The first one she bumped into was Berit.

"I got hold of the family," she said. "I'll take Henriksson and go there now. You do Furhage's last hours and Patrik the hunt for the murderer. How does that sound?"

"Fine," Berit said. "Henriksson is somewhere at the back. He dragged Kjell Lindström out to get a picture of him. It's probably quicker to go around . . ."

Annika rushed out and, sure enough, found Henriksson on Bergsgatan, the street around the corner from police headquarters. He was perched on a paper recycling container with Lindström below him and the steel-mesh corridor leading to the police station's security lodge in the background. She greeted Lindström and then pulled the young photographer along with her.

"Come along, Henriksson, you're getting the center spread again tomorrow," she told him.

Helena Starke wiped her mouth on the back of her hand. She noticed it was smeared but didn't smell the vomit. All her senses were shut off, disengaged, gone. Smell, sight, hearing, taste were no more. She groaned and leaned further over the toilet. Was it really dark in here or had she gone blind? Her brain wasn't working; she couldn't think. There were no thoughts left. Everything she was had been grilled to charcoal and died. She felt the salty tears running down her face, but she didn't feel she was crying. There was nothing but an echo in her body. Her body was a void, filled only with a roaring noise: Christina is dead, Christina is dead, Christina is dead, Christina is dead . . .

Someone knocked on the door.

*"Helena! How are you? Do you need any help?"*

She groaned and sank to the floor, curling up under the washbasin. Christina is dead, Christina . . .

*"Open the door, Helena! Are you ill?"*

Christina is dead, Christina is dead . . .

*"Get this door open, someone!"*

Something hit her, something that hurt. It was the light from the fluorescents in the corridor.

*"Christ, help her up! What happened?"*

They would never understand, she mused, noticing that she still could think. They would never understand. Never ever.

She observed how someone was lifting her up. She heard someone screaming, then realized it was herself.

The building was a burnt ochre color and was built in Art-Nouveau style. It was situated in Upper Öster-malm, on one of those tranquil streets where all the cars were shiny and the ladies had little white dogs on a leash. The entrance was magnificent, of course: marble floors, paneled doors with faceted glass panes, beech-wood and brass in the elevator, marbled walls in a warm yellow tone. Facing the courtyard was a large ornamental stained-glass window with a floral pattern. The floor from the street door and all the way up the stairs was covered with a deep-pile runner carpet in green. Annika thought she recognized it from the Grand Hotel.

The apartment of the Furhage-Milander family was on the top floor.

"Let's tread very softly now," Annika whispered to Henriksson before she rang the doorbell. Five chimes sounded somewhere inside.

The door immediately opened, as if the man had been standing waiting behind it. Annika didn't recognize him; she had never seen him, even in a photo. Christina never brought her husband along anywhere. Bertil Milander was gray in the face and had dark shadows under his eyes. He was unshaven.

"Come in," was all he said.

He turned around and went straight into what looked like a large drawing room. His back was stooped under the brown jacket, and Annika was struck by how old he seemed. They took off their coats, then the photographer hung a Leica on his shoulder, leaving the camera bag by the shoe rack. Annika's feet sank into the thick carpets—this home would cost a fortune to insure.

The man had sat down on a couch, while Annika and the photographer ended up on another couch opposite him. Annika had taken out a pad and a pen.

"We're here to listen," she calmly began. "If there is anything you want to say, anything you want us to write, we'll take it into consideration."

Bertil Milander was looking down on his clasped hands. Then he began to cry quietly. Henriksson moistened his lips.

"Tell us about Christina," Annika urged him.

The man pulled a monogrammed handkerchief from his pocket and blew his nose. He painstakingly wiped his nose before putting the handkerchief away. He gave a deep sigh and began:

"Christina was the most remarkable person I've ever met. She was absolutely formidable. There was nothing she couldn't do. Sharing one's life with such a woman was . . ."

He pulled out the handkerchief and blew his nose again.

". . . a fresh adventure every day. She organized everything to do with the household. Food, cleaning, parties, laundry, finances, the responsibility for our daughter, she took care of everything . . ."

He stopped short and contemplated what he had said. It looked like he suddenly was struck by the meaning of his words. From now on it was all down to him.

He looked down at his handkerchief.

"Would you like to tell me how you met?" Annika asked, only to fill the silence. He didn't seem to have heard her.

"Stockholm would never have gotten the Olympics without her. She wrapped Samaranch around her little finger. She built up the entire campaign organization. It was such a success. Once she had secured the Games for Stockholm, they wanted to remove her and put someone else in charge, but naturally that was impossible. No one but she could do the job, and they soon realized that."

Annika noted down what the man was saying with a feeling of mounting confusion. She had often come across people in shock after traffic accidents and at crime scenes and knew that they could react in very peculiar ways, often quite irrationally, but Bertil Milander didn't sound like a bereaved husband. He sounded like a bereaved employee.

"How old is your daughter?"

"She was selected as 'Woman of the Year' by that American magazine, what's it called again . . . ? Woman of the year. She was woman of the year. Woman of the whole of Sweden. Woman of the whole world."

Bertil Milander blew his nose again. Annika put her pen down and stared into her notepad. This didn't feel right. The man didn't know what he was doing or saying. He didn't seem to understand what she and the photographer were doing there.

"When did you hear about Christina's death?" Annika ventured.

Bertil Milander looked up.

"She never came home," he said. "She went to the Secretariat's Christmas party and never came home again."

"Were you worried when she didn't come home? Was she away often? She must have traveled quite a lot?"

The man straightened up on the couch and looked at Annika as if seeing her for the first time.

"Why do you ask that?" he said. "What do you mean?"

Annika deliberated for a second. This did not feel

right. The man was in shock. His reactions were confused, he was rambling, and he didn't know what he was doing. But there was one question she had to ask.

"A threat had been made against the family," she said. "What was the nature of this threat?"

The man stared at her with his mouth open. He didn't seem to have heard her.

"The threat," Annika repeated. "Could you say anything about the threat against the family?"

He gave Annika a reproachful look.

"Christina did all she could," he said. "She's not a bad person. It wasn't her fault."

Annika felt a cold shiver run down her back. This was definitely not right. She collected her pad and pen.

"Thank you so much for seeing us under these circumstances," she said and started getting up from the couch. "We'll be . . ."

A slamming door made her jump and spin around. An emaciated-looking young woman with tousled hair and a sullen look came and stood behind the couch.

"Who are you? What are you doing here?" the woman said.

Christina's daughter, Annika thought. She collected herself. She said they were from *Kvällspressen*.

"Hyenas," the woman said contemptuously. "Did you smell blood, is that why you came here? To get at the remains of the body? Suck out the best parts while you can?" She walked around the couch and came closer to Annika, who forced herself to remain seated and look calm.

"I'm so sorry about your mother's death . . ."

"Well, I'm not!" the daughter screamed. "I'm glad she's dead. Glad!" She burst into tears and left the room running. Bertil Milander showed no reaction; he was looking down at his hands twiddling the handkerchief.

"Is it okay to take a picture?" Henriksson said. It woke Bertil Milander up.

"Yes, yes, of course it is," he said, getting to his feet. "Right here?"

"Maybe if you could walk over to the window, that'll give us a bit more light."

Bertil Milander posed next to the beautiful, high windows. It would make a good picture. The thin daylight filtered through the mullioned window, the expensive blue curtains framing the portrait.

While the photographer shot his roll, Annika quickly went after the young woman into the room next door. It was a library, tastefully decorated with English period furniture and thousands of books. The woman was sitting in a burgundy leather armchair.

"I'm sorry if you feel we're intruding," Annika said. "It's not our intention to cause you any pain. On the contrary, we just want to tell you what we're doing."

The woman didn't reply. She didn't seem to notice Annika's presence.

"You and your father are welcome to call us if there's anything you wish to bring up, if you feel we're not telling the truth, or if there's anything you want to add or tell us."

No reaction.

"I'll give my phone number to your father," Annika said and left the room. Carefully, she closed the beautiful twin doors behind her.

Henriksson and Bertil Milander were standing in the hallway. Annika went up to them, pulled out a business card from her wallet, and added the editor's direct number to her own.

"Just call, if there's anything," she said. "I always have my phone on. Thank you for your trouble."

Bertil Milander took the card without looking at it. He put it on a gilt table next to the front door.

"My grief over her is endless," and Annika knew she had just gotten her headline for the center-spread photo.

The editor let out a sigh when he heard the knock at the door. He had hoped to get to the bottom of at least one of the piles of paper on his desk, but since he arrived at the paper an hour ago he hadn't had a quiet second.

"Come in," he said. He tried to relax. After all, he prided himself on his open-door policy.

It was Nils Langeby, and Anders Schyman's heart sank a bit further toward his shoes.

"Nils. What can I do for you?" he said without getting up from behind his desk.

Nils Langeby poised himself in the middle of the floor of the corner office, wringing his hands in a theatrical gesture.

"I'm worried about the crime desk," he began. "It's a complete mess."

Anders Schyman looked up at the reporter, stifling a sigh.

"How do you mean?"

"We're going to miss out on things; things are hanging in the air. Everyone feels insecure after the changes. What will become of our crime coverage?"

The editor pointed at a chair on the other side of his desk and Nils Langeby sat down.

"All change, even change that means improvement, brings some turbulence," Schyman said. "It's quite natural for the crime desk to be a bit unsettled. You've been without a chief for a long time and have just gotten a new one."

"Exactly, and that's what I feel is the problem. I don't think Annika Bengtzon is up to scratch."

Schyman gave it some thought.

"You don't think so? I feel exactly the opposite. I think she's a formidable reporter and a good organizer. She knows how to prioritize and delegate. And she doesn't balk at doing difficult and uncomfortable things. She's driven and knowledgeable. Just look at today's paper for an example of that. What's your problem with her, Nils?"

Nils Langeby leaned forward in a confidential gesture.

"People don't trust her. She thinks she's a big shot. She steps on people's toes and doesn't know how to behave properly."

"What do you mean, Nils?"

The reporter threw his hands out to the side.

"Well, I haven't been affected personally, but one hears things . . ."

"So you're here because you're concerned for your colleagues?"

"Yes. And because we're losing our coverage of crimes against the environment and in the school system."

"But I thought those particular areas were your responsibility?"

"Yes, but . . ."

"Has Annika tried to take them away from you?"

"No, not at all."

"So if we fail to get stories in those particular areas, it's really your responsibility, isn't it? It doesn't really have anything to do with Annika Bengtzon, does it?"

A look of confusion spread on Nils Langeby's face.

"I think you're a good reporter, Nils," the editor went on calmly. "It's people like you, with your weight of experience that this paper needs. You'll be continuing to supply us with headlines for a long time to come, I hope. I have full confidence in you, just as I have full confidence in Annika Bengtzon as crime desk editor. That's why my job here gets better and better every day. People grow and learn to work together for the benefit of the paper."

Nils Langeby was listening intently. He grew taller with each word. This was what he wanted to hear. The editor believed in him. He would go on producing head-line copy and he would be a force to be reckoned with. When he left the room, he felt cheerful and in good heart. He was actually whistling to himself on his way out of the newsroom.

"Hiya, Nisse, what have you got cooking today?" he heard someone call from behind him.

It was Ingvar Johansson, the news editor. Nils Langeby stopped short and thought for a moment. He hadn't planned to work at all today, and he hadn't been called in. But the editor's words made him feel the meas-ure of his responsibility.

"Well, quite a lot," he therefore replied. "The terrorist attack, the terrorist angle. That's what I'm working on today . . ."

"Great, it would be good if you could write it up straight away, so we have it ready for when the subs come in. Everyone else will have their hands full with Furhage."

"Furhage?" Nils Langeby said. "What about her?"

Ingvar Johansson looked up at the reporter.

"Didn't you hear? The mincemeat at the stadium, it was the Olympic boss."

"Yeah, right. Well, my sources tell me it was a terrorist attack, a clear as day terrorist attack."

"Police sources?" Ingvar Johansson sounded surprised.

"Impeccable police sources," Nils Langeby said, thrusting his chest out. He took off his leather jacket, started rolling up his shirt sleeves, and walked off toward his room along the corridor that overlooked the parking lot.

"I'll fucking show you, bitch!"

Anders Schyman barely had time to lift the first piece of paper from the top of the highest pile before there was another knock at the door. This time it was the photographer Ulf Olsson who wanted a heart-to-heart. He had just returned from the press conference at police headquarters and wanted to tell the editor in all confidentiality how he had been treated by the crime editor Annika Bengtzon the previous day.

"I'm not used to people criticizing me on account of my clothes," the photographer said, adding that he had been wearing an Armani suit at the time.

"Tell me what happened," Schyman said.

"Annika Bengtzon expressed her disapproval of my wearing a designer suit. I don't think I should have to take that. I've never been treated like that at other jobs."

Anders Schyman contemplated the man for a few seconds before replying.

"I don't know what went on between you and Annika Bengtzon," he said. "Nor do I know where you've worked previously or what the dress code was there. As far as I'm concerned—and I know that goes for Annika Bengtzon, too—you can wear Armani as much as you like. You can wear it down a coal mine if you want. But don't blame anyone but yourself if you've got the wrong clothes for a job. I and all the rest of the senior editors of this paper take it for granted that everyone here is reasonably up to date on what's happening in the world when they come to work. If there's been a murder or a bomb attack, just assume you'll be covering it. I suggest you get a big bag with long johns and maybe a tracksuit and keep it in the car . . ."

"I've already got a bag," the photographer said morosely. "Annika Bengtzon gave one to me."

Anders Schyman gave the man a detached look.

"Anything else I can do for you?" he said. The photographer got up and left.

The editor sighed heavily when the door closed. Jesus.

Sometimes he felt like a grade school principal. Bunch of children. He longed to go home to his wife and a large whisky.

Annika and Johan Henriksson pulled up at McDonald's on Sveavägen and bought two Big Mac meals, which they ate in the car on their way back to the paper.

"I hate doing that," Henriksson said when he had put away the last of his French fries.

"Visiting bereaved families? Yeah, I guess that's about as bad as it gets," Annika said, wiping ketchup off her fingers.

"I can't help it, but I feel like a parasite sitting there," Henriksson said. "Like I'm only there to revel in their misfortune. Gloat because it looks good in the paper."

Annika wiped her mouth and pondered his words for a moment.

"Yes," she said, "it's easy to have that feeling. But sometimes people just want to talk. You mustn't think people are stupid just because they're in a state of shock. Sure, you have to show respect. It's not certain you'll write about the family just because you listen to and talk to them."

"But people who've just lost someone don't always know what they're doing."

"How can you be so sure?" Annika said. "Who are you to decide that someone shouldn't get the chance to talk? Who are we to judge what's best for a particular person in a particular situation? You, me, or that person? We're always arguing about this in the papers and no one has the right answer."

"I still think it's horrible," he said sulkily.

Annika smiled faintly.

"Of course it is. Facing a person who's just met with the worst possible misfortune is one of the hardest things that can happen to you, that's a fact. You can't do many interviews like that in a month. But you get used to it too. Think of people in the caring professions or in the church; they work with tragedies daily."

"They don't have to parade them on the front page," Henriksson said.

"Christ, will you stop carping!" Annika exclaimed, suddenly all steamed up. "It's not as if it's a punishment being on the front page! It shows you're important, that you count. Should we ignore all victims and members of family? Think of the fuss the victims' families kicked up after the *Estonia* ferry disaster. They felt they were getting far too little attention from the media, saying the papers only wrote about the faulty bow doors—and they were right. There was a time when it was taboo to even talk to an *Estonia* victim's family member. If you did, the entire morality mob from the current affairs programs would come after you full force."

"All right, Annika. No need to shout," Henriksson said.

"I'll shout if I fucking want to," Annika said.

They were quiet for the rest of the journey to the paper. In the elevator up to the newsroom, Henriksson gave a conciliatory smile and said:

"I think we got a really good picture of Mr. Milander by the window."

"That's nice," Annika said. "We'll have to see if we use it."

She opened the elevator door and quickly walked out without waiting for a reply.

Eva-Britt Qvist was busy compiling background material on Christina Furhage when Annika walked past on her way to her room. The secretary was surrounded by files full of old cuttings and computer printouts by the mile.

"There's no end to how much has been written about

this woman," she said, trying hard to sound curt. "But I think I've found most of it now."

"Do you think you could prioritize the stuff, then hand it over to someone else to continue with?" Annika said.

"You have a way of presenting orders in the guise of questions," Eva-Britt said.

Annika couldn't be bothered even to answer but went into her office and hung up her coat and scarf. She got a cup of coffee and went over to Pelle Oscarsson, pulled up a chair, and looked at his computer screen. It was filled with stamp-sized pictures, all from the paper's archives, all depicting Christina Furhage.

"We've published more than six hundred in-house pictures of this woman," Pelle Oscarsson said. "We must have photographed her on average once a week over the last eight years. That's more than the King."

Annika gave a lopsided grin; yes, perhaps that was possible. Everything Christina Furhage had done over the past few years had attracted attention, and the woman had enjoyed it. Annika studied the photos: Christina Furhage at the inauguration of the Olympic arena; Christina Furhage briefing the Prime Minister; Christina Furhage meeting the popular singer Lill-Babs; Christina Furhage embracing Samaranch; Christina Furhage showing off her new autumn wardrobe in the Sunday supplement.

Pelle Oscarsson clicked and a new set of images appeared on the screen: Christina Furhage greeting the U.S. President, attending a Royal Theater gala premiere, having tea with the Queen, speaking at a women and leadership conference . . .

"Is there a single picture of her at home or with her family?" Annika wondered aloud.

The picture editor thought for a moment. "I don't

think so," he said, taken aback. "Now that you mention it, there isn't one single personal picture of her. They're all official."

"I think we'll be all right, though," Annika said as the photos flashed by.

"We should use this one on the front page," Pelle said, clicking on a portrait taken in the newspaper's own studio. In a couple of seconds, the picture covered the entire screen, and Annika saw that the picture editor was right in his choice. It was a brilliant portrait of Christina Furhage. The woman was professionally made-up, her hair was shiny and styled, the lighting was warm and soft, smoothing out the lines in her face, she was wearing an expensive, close-fitting tailored suit, and had assumed a dignified, relaxed pose in an elegant antique armchair.

"How old was she?" Annika wondered.

"Sixty-two," the picture editor replied. "We did a piece on her last birthday."

"Wow," Annika said. "She looks fifteen years younger."

"Plastic surgery, healthy lifestyle, good genes . . ." Pelle said.

"Or all of them," Annika replied.

Anders Schyman walked past with an empty, dirty coffee mug in his hand. He looked tired, his hair was tousled, and he had loosened his tie.

"How are you doing?" he stopped and asked.

"We've been to see Furhage's family."

"Anything we can use?"

Annika hesitated. "Yes, I think so. Some. Henriksson took a picture of the husband, who was quite confused."

"We'll have to look at it carefully," he said and continued walking in the direction of the cafeteria.

"What pics do we use for the news stories?" Pelle Oscarsson asked while clicking the portrait away.

Annika swallowed the last of her coffee.

"We'll have to run through that with the others as soon as they arrive," she said.

She threw her plastic cup in Eva-Britt Qvist's wastepaper basket, went into her office, and shut the door behind her. It was telephone time. She started off with her contact; he was on the day shift today. She dialed his direct number, past the police headquarters' switchboard. She got lucky—he answered on the first ring.

"How did you figure that out, about her being off-record?" he wondered.

"When did you figure out it was Furhage?" Annika retorted without answering the question.

The man let out a sigh.

"Almost straightaway. It was her stuff at the stadium. But the actual identification took a bit longer, of course. You don't really want to make a mistake . . ."

Annika waited in silence, but he didn't continue. So she said:

"What next?"

"Checking, checking, checking. At least we know it wasn't the Tiger."

"How do you know?" Annika said in surprise.

"I can't tell you that, but it wasn't him. It was someone on the inside, just like you thought yesterday."

"I have to write that story today, you know that, don't you?" she said.

He sighed again.

"Yeah, I guessed as much," he said. "Thanks for keeping it under wraps for twenty-four hours, though."

"Give and take," Annika said.

"So what do you want?" he asked.

"Why was she off-record?"

"There was a threat, a written one, three or four years back. A kind of violent incident, too, but not very serious."

"What kind of violent incident?"

"I don't want to go into that. The person in question was never prosecuted. Christina didn't want to 'ruin' them, as she's supposed to have put it. 'Everyone deserves a second chance,' she is also reported to have said. She was content with moving and asking for—and getting—herself and her family classified as off-record."

"How magnanimous of her," Annika said.

"Absolutely."

"Did the threat have anything to do with the Olympics?"

"Not in the least."

"Was it someone she knew—a member of the family?"

The policeman hesitated.

"Yes, you could say that. The attacker had purely personal motives. That's why we don't want to make it public; it's too close to her. There is absolutely nothing that points to the bomb attack on the arena being a terrorist act. We believe it was aimed at Christina personally, but that doesn't mean the perpetrator was someone close to her."

"Will you question the person who threatened her?"

"We already have."

Annika blinked.

"You're not exactly sitting around doing nothing, from what you're saying. What did that give you?"

"We can't comment on that one. But I can say this: There is today no one person who's under more suspicion than anyone else."

"And who is 'anyone else'?"

"That you can figure out for yourself. Anyone who's ever had contact with her. That must be about four or five thousand people. We can rule out quite a few of them, but I don't intend to tell you who."

"There must be a lot of people with entry cards," Annika coaxed him.

"Who are you thinking of?"

"The Olympic Secretariat, the members of the IOC, the caretakers at the arena, people from all the contractors building the facilities, electricians, builders, foundry workers, transport firms, architects, security firms, the TV sports people . . ."

He remained silent.

"Am I wrong?" she asked.

"Not really. All the groups you mentioned have, have had, or will get entry cards, that's correct."

"But?"

"You won't get into the arena in the middle of the night with just an entry card," he said.

Annika racked her brains.

"The security codes! They've only been given to a small group of people!"

"Yes, but you'll have to keep that under your hat for the time being."

"Okay. For how long? Who has access to the security codes?"

The man laughed.

"You're incorrigible!" he said. "We're working on that right now."

"Couldn't the alarms at the arena have been disarmed?"

"And the doors unlocked? Come on, Bengtzon!"

She heard two voices in the background, then her contact covered the handset and said something. He removed his hand and said:

"I've got to go now."

"One more thing!" Annika said.

"What?"

"What was Christina Furhage doing at the stadium in the middle of the night?"

"That, my dear, is one hell of a good question. Speak to you later."

They hung up and Annika tried phoning home. No answer. She called Anne Snapphane, but she only got the fax machine. She called Berit until the automated answering service switched on. The phone-freak Patrik answered, however. He always did. It was one of his little quirks. Once he had answered while in the shower.

"I'm at the Olympic Secretariat," he yelled down the phone, another of his quirks. Despite his fondness for the phone, he didn't quite trust it, so he always had to shout to make sure his voice would be heard.

"What's Berit doing?" Annika asked, noticing that she too raised her voice.

"She's here with me, doing Furhage's last night," Patrik shouted. "I'm doing the Secretariat in shock."

"Where are you just now?" Annika forced herself to lower her voice.

"In some corridor. People are really upset," he roared.

Annika could imagine the Secretariat staff listening to the yelling tabloid reporter from behind their half-open office doors.

"Okay," Annika said. "We'll have to concoct something about the police hunt for the Bomber. When will you be back?"

"In about an hour," he shouted.

"Good, see you then," Annika said and hung up. She couldn't help smiling.

Evert Danielsson closed his door to shut out the noise of some reporter shouting into his phone in the corridor. In an hour, the board of directors would meet, the operational, active board of experts that Christina had called "her orchestra." The board was the real board, as opposed to the Honorary Board, or the Host Committee, as it was also called, which mostly posed for the camera. All decisions were officially made by the Honorary

Board, but that was just a formality. The big guns there could be compared with the members of parliament in a one-party state, while the board was the executive committee of the ruling party.

The director was nervous. He was well aware of the series of mistakes he'd made since the bombing. He should have convened the board of directors yesterday, for one. Now the chairman of the board had done that instead, one day late, and that was a major slip. Instead of convening the board, he'd gone ahead and briefed the media on a number of issues that he really had no authority to talk about. On one hand, the talk of terrorist acts; on the other, the details about the reconstruction of the North Stand. He knew that question should have been discussed by the board first. There had been a brief strategy meeting the day before, a meeting which with hindsight had taken on an increasingly panicky appearance. The informal management group had decided to seize the initiative and not to hesitate, nor attempt a coverup. They would grasp the nettle immediately. Awaiting Christina's reappearance, they'd decided to use Danielsson as a spokesman, instead of the press people, to lend weight to the message.

But the management group had no executive powers. Only the board could make any real decisions. That's where you found the real heavyweights: the government representative being the Minister for Trade and Industry; a leading councillor of the Stockholm City Council; the managing directors of the various firms involved; an IOC expert; two representatives of the sponsors; and a lawyer specializing in international law. The chairman of the board was also a government man, Hans Bjällra, the Stockholm County Governor. The management group might be fast and efficient, but its importance was pitiful compared with the board of directors. The group was composed of a core of people who were responsible for the day-to-day administration of the project: the financial manager; himself and Christina; Helena Starke and the communications director; a couple of the deputy managing directors; and finally Doris from the budget department. Between them they dealt with practical matters swiftly and easily. Christina saw to it that the board endorsed their decisions after the event. It could be anything from money and budget matters to policymaking on various environmental issues, infrastructure, the design of arenas, legal obstacles, and all sorts of campaigns.

The difference now was that Christina wasn't there to sweep up after them. He knew he wouldn't be let off the hook. The director of the Secretariat put his elbows on the desk and rested his head in his hands. He couldn't stop a deep sob from traveling the whole length of his body. Damn! Damn! He had worked so hard these past few years! He really didn't deserve this. The tears fell in drips between his fingers and onto the papers on his desk, forming transparent little globules that blurred the writing and graphs. He didn't care.

Annika turned on her computer and sat down to write. She began with the information gleaned from her police source. The things she learned from her unofficial channels, her "deep throats," she kept strictly to herself. She never recorded these conversations—there was always a risk that the tape would be left in the machine and someone else would find it. Instead she took notes, and then immediately typed them out, saving her text on a disk. These disks she kept under lock and key in a drawer of her desk. The handwritten notes she tore up and threw away. She never imparted any part of these conversations to people in handovers or at news conferences. The only one who, if necessary, got to hear her confidential information was the editor-in-chief, Anders Schyman.

She had no illusions about why this information was given to her especially. It wasn't because she was better or more important than any other reporter. She *was* dependable, and that together with her clout at *Kvällspressen's* news conferences made her the right person to give information the police wanted publicized. There were a lot of reasons to leak information like this, but for the police, as for all other organizations, one thing was paramount: They wanted their version of events to be presented by the mass media. Especially when it came to the dramatic kind of events the police were usually concerned with, TV and newspapers had a tendency to rush ahead and jump to conclusions. A controlled leak gave the police a chance to stop the worst blunders at least.

In some journalistic circles, it was considered unethical not to report everything you knew at all times. You were always a reporter, first and foremost a reporter, nothing else but a reporter. This meant that you didn't hesitate to expose your neighbors, friends of your children, or your mother-in-law. Santa Claus himself if you got something on him. Talking to a police officer or a politician off the record just wasn't an option. Annika thought this was bullshit. She was first and foremost a human being, then a mother, then a wife, and after that an employee of *Kvällspressen.* She didn't at all feel she was a reporter in the sense of being a special correspondent of God or some other higher power. Her experience had also taught her that the reporters with the loftiest and noblest principles were the biggest bastards. That was why she was happy to let people speculate on her sources and be sniffy about her working methods. As for herself, she felt her work was important and that was good enough for her.

Once she had locked the disk away in her drawer, she wrote a short piece about her visit to Bertil Milander's house. She kept it to the point and made it dignified, stressing that Milander himself had invited the paper, and she included his praise of his wife. She didn't mention the daughter at all. She filed her copy into the list of stories held on the newsroom server.

She got to her feet and restlessly stretched her legs in her glass cage. Her office lay between two newsroom landscapes, news and sports, with glass walls either side. The only daylight came in indirectly from beyond the two offices. To make it feel less like a fish tank and to shut out people's stares, her predecessor had put up blue curtains of some obscure material. It must have been at least five years since anyone had washed, aired, or paid any attention to these pieces of fabric. They may once have looked stylish, but now they were simply sad. Annika wished someone would do something about them. One thing she knew for certain, it wouldn't be her.

She went out to Eva-Britt Qvist's desk, which was right outside her office. The crime-desk secretary had obviously gone home and she hadn't told her. The research material lay in piles on the desk, marked with yellow Post-it notes. Annika perched herself on the desk and started browsing through the material at random, full of curiosity. Christ, so much had been written about the woman. She picked up the printout that lay on top of the pile marked "Outlines" and started reading. It was a long interview from one of the main Sunday broadsheets, a warm and intelligent piece that actually gave a taste of the person Christina Furhage was. The questions were sharp and to the point, and Furhage's answers clever and succinct. The conversation, however, exclusively turned on the relatively impersonal subjects of Olympic economics and organization theory; femininity and career opportunities; and the importance of sport for the national identity. Annika skimmed the text. Christina Furhage consistently managed to avoid saying anything that was the least bit personal.

But then this was taken from one of the broadsheets. They didn't care much for the personal, only the public. They only touched on that which was masculine, politically correct, and clean, avoiding anything that was emotional, interesting, or feminine. She put the printout to the side and leafed through the pile to look for an interview from the tabloid supplements. Sure enough, they were there, with the obligatory fact box on the person: Name: Christina Furhage; family: husband and one child; residence: house in Tyresö; income: high; smokes: no; drinks: yes, wine and coffee; best personal quality: that's for others to judge; worst personal quality: for others to judge . . . Annika leafed on. The answers in the boxes were the same for the four years since she was put off the records. Never any mention of her husband's or child's name, and she always said she lived in the house in Tyresö. She found a six-year-old article in a Sunday supplement where she gave Bertil and Lena as her family. So that was the name of the daughter. Her surname was probably Milander.

She left the pile of profiles and started on the thinnest pile, marked "Conflicts." There didn't seem to have been many of these. The first piece was about a dispute over a sponsor that had backed out. It had nothing to do with Christina Furhage; her name was mentioned in one place, thus the "hit" in the computer search. The next article was about a demonstration against the effects of the building of the Olympic stadium on the environment. Annika was getting annoyed. This had nothing to do with Christina Furhage personally. Eva-Britt had done a lousy job. She was supposed to weed out stuff like this.

That was the whole point of having a research assistant on the crime desk. She was supposed to compile background material to save time for the reporters in tight situations. Annika picked up the whole pile of conflicts and leafed through it: demonstrations, protests, a think piece . . . Annika stopped. What was this? She fished out a small piece from the bottom and dropped the rest of the pile. "Olympic Supremo Fires Secretary for Love Affair" was the headline.

Annika immediately knew who had carried the story: It was *Kvällspressen*, of course. The story was seven years old. A young woman was forced to leave her job at the newly established Olympic Secretariat because of an affair with one of her superiors. "It's humiliating and outdated," the woman had said to the reporter from *Kvällspressen*. Christina Furhage declared that the woman had not been fired but that her contract had simply expired. It had nothing to do with any love affair. End of story. The article didn't name either the woman or her superior. No one else had run the story. Annika wasn't surprised: It was extremely thin. This was the only conflict involving Christina Furhage that had been reported in the media. She must have been a brilliant boss and administrator, Annika concluded. For a moment she contemplated the mass of media coverage over the years about conflicts in her own workplace, and this wasn't even such a bad place.

"Anything interesting?" Berit asked from behind her. Annika stood up.

"You're back, good. No, nothing special. Well, maybe. Furhage let a young woman employee go because she'd had a relationship with her boss. It's worth keeping in mind . . . What have you found?"

"Quite a lot. Shall we go through it quickly?"

"Let's wait for Patrik," Annika said.

"I'm here," he called from the picture desk. "I'm just . . ." He walked away to attend to whatever he needed to do.

"Let's go into my office," Annika said.

Berit went to her desk and hung up her things. In Annika's office, she sat on the old couch, balancing her notes and a cup of coffee from the coffee machine.

"I've tried to piece together Christina Furhage's last hours. The Secretariat had a Christmas party at a restaurant in west-central Stockholm on Friday evening. Christina stayed until midnight. I went over there and talked to the waiters. I also spoke to Evert Danielsson, the director of the Secretariat."

"Good." Annika said. "So what were her movements?"

Berit looked at her notes. "Furhage arrived late at the restaurant, after 10 P.M. The others had already eaten—a Basque Christmas dinner, as a matter of fact. She left with a colleague, Helena Starke, just before midnight. No one saw her after that."

"The explosion was at 3:17 A.M., which leaves more than three hours unaccounted for," Annika said. "What does Helena Starke say?"

"Don't know, she's ex-directory. She lives in South Island, but I haven't had time to go there yet."

"Starke's good; we have to talk to her," Annika said. "What else? What was Furhage doing before she went to the Christmas party?"

"Danielsson thinks she was at the office, but he isn't sure. Apparently she put in hugely long hours at the office, like fourteen, fifteen hours a day."

"Superwoman," Annika muttered, remembering Christina's husband's ovation for all the work she did at home too.

"Who does The Furhage Story?" Berit asked.

"One of the masters of style over at the features department. I went to see the family—that didn't produce much. Tricky lot . . ."

"How do you mean?"

Annika thought a second. "Bertil, her husband, was old and gray. He was quite confused. He seemed to feel admiration for his wife rather than love. The daughter came in screaming and crying, saying she was glad her mother was dead."

"Really . . ."

"How's it going?" Patrik said as he came through the door.

"Fine. What about you?" Annika asked.

"Well, this will be great," he said, sitting down next to Berit. "So far the police have found one hundred and twenty-seven pieces of Christina Furhage."

Both Berit and Annika grimaced.

"That's disgusting! You can't use that!" Annika exclaimed.

The young reporter smiled, unruffled.

"They've found blood and teeth all the way over to the main entrance. That's several hundred meters."

"You're making me want to puke. Have you got anything worse?" Annika said.

"They still don't know what the Bomber used to blow her up. Or they're not saying."

"So what will your story be?"

"I've talked to an all-right cop about the hunt for the killer. I can do that."

"Okay," Annika said. "I've got some stuff on that, too. What have you got?"

Patrik leaned forward, his eyes shining.

"The police are looking for Christina Furhage's laptop. They know she had a laptop computer with her on the Friday night; a girl from the Secretariat saw it. But it's gone, it wasn't among the debris at the arena. They believe the murderer must have taken it."

"Couldn't it have been blown up?" Berit asked.

"Impossible, at least according to my source," Patrik said. "The computer is gone, and that's their best lead, so far."

"Anything else?" Annika said.

"They're considering asking Interpol to help catch the Tiger."

"It wasn't the Tiger," Annika said. "It was an inside job. The police are sure of that."

"How do they know?" Patrik said with surprise.

Annika thought about her promise not to say anything about the security codes. "Trust me, I've got a reliable source. What else?"

"I've talked to the staff at the Olympic Secretariat. They're on the verge of a collective breakdown. Christina Furhage seems to have been a Christ figure to them. Everyone's in tears, including Evert Danielsson. I heard him through his door. I don't know how they're going to get by without her. She seems to have had all the good qualities a person can have."

"Why do you sound so surprised?" Berit said. "Isn't it possible for a middle-aged woman to be liked and appreciated?"

"Sure, but to that extent . . ."

"Christina Furhage had an outstanding career, and she handled her job as Olympic supremo excellently. When a woman succeeds in running a project like this from start to finish, you can bet your life she's something out of the ordinary. Twenty-eight simultaneous world championships, that's what the Olympics is."

"Are her achievements so remarkable just because she was a woman?" Patrik said teasingly, and that really made Berit hot under the collar.

"Oh, please, will you grow up!"

Patrik got to his feet. "What the hell do you mean by that?" he exclaimed.

Annika wanted to back up her female colleague. "Patrik, you're a man and you aren't affected by the oppression of women. Of course, it's more difficult for a woman than for a man to hold down a position like hers, just as it would be more difficult for someone who was deaf and dumb than for someone with his faculties intact. Being a woman is tantamount to being a walking handicap. Do you have anything more?"

Patrik was bemused. "What do you mean, 'a walking handicap'?"

The atmosphere was getting a little tense. Annika let it drop. "Do you have anything else?"

He leafed through his notes.

"The hunt for the Bomber, the Olympic Secretariat in shock . . . No, that's all I've got."

"Okay, Berit does Christina Furhage's last day. I do the family and add to your story on the hunt for the killer. Finished?"

They parted without saying anything more. The strain is beginning to show on us, Annika thought. She switched on the radio for the news at a quarter to six. Their top story was naturally the followup on the news that one of Sweden's most powerful and well-known women, Christina Furhage, was dead. They started off with commentaries on her life and work and continued with the effects this would have on the Games and sports in general. As might have been expected, Samaranch retracted his earlier statement he had made in a rival paper. After eleven minutes, they mentioned the fact that Furhage had been murdered. That's how they did it at *Dagens Eko*, first everything that was nice and general and impersonal, then—to the extent that they mentioned it at all—the unpleasant and upsetting. If they covered a murder, they almost always put their focus on some legal subtlety, never on the victim, the families, or the perpetrator. They would, however, run seventeen stories on the piece of equipment with which the perpetrator's brain had been examined; that was science and therefore superior information. Annika let out a sigh. In passing, they also mentioned her own story from yesterday's paper about the threat and Furhage being off-record, but it was an aside. She turned off the radio and collected the material she needed for the news meeting in the editor's office. She had a sinking feeling. Ingvar Johansson had been strange all day, short-tempered and offhand. She realized she must have done something wrong but had no idea what. There was no sign of him now.

Anders Schyman was on the phone; it sounded like he was talking to a child on the other end. Picture Pelle had already taken a seat at the conference table with his long lists. She opted to go over to the window and stare at her own reflection. If she put her hand against the glass to block out the light from the room and stood really close, she could make out the world beyond. There was a dense darkness. The yellow lights of the Russian Embassy were golden specks floating in a sea of blackness. Even this little morsel of Russia was gloomy and ominous-looking. She shuddered from the cold coming in through the window.

"*Alles gut?*" chirped Jansson, who had just woken up, spilling a bit more coffee on the editor's carpet. "My last night with you lot, then I've got three shifts off. Where the hell's Ingvar Johansson?"

"Right here. Shall we get started?"

Annika sat down and noted that Ingvar took hold of the reins today. So that was it, she had talked too much at yesterday's meeting.

"Right, let's set the ball rolling," Anders Schyman said, putting the phone down. "What have we got, and what's the page lead?"

Ingvar Johansson handed out copies of his list and started talking as he did so: "I think we should lead with Nils Langeby's stuff, that the police are sure it was a terrorist attack. They're chasing a foreign terrorist group."

Annika was stunned. She couldn't believe what she was hearing.

"What are you talking about?" she exclaimed. "Is Nils here today? I didn't even know. Who called him in?"

"I don't know," Ingvar Johansson said, irritated. "I assumed you did: You're his boss."

"But where on earth did he get that about a terrorist attack from?" Annika said, barely able to keep her voice steady.

"Why should he have to divulge his sources? You never do," Ingvar Johansson said.

Annika felt the blood surge into her face. Everyone around the table was looking at her. Suddenly it hit her that they were all men, except for her.

"We have to synchronize our stories," she said in a strained voice. "My information is the exact opposite: It wasn't a terrorist act. The attack was aimed at Christina personally."

"In what way?" Ingvar Johansson said, and Annika knew she was done for. She could either disclose what she knew, and then both Jansson and Ingvar Johansson would demand she write about the security codes. The news editor who'd keep a juicy angle like that under wraps didn't exist. Or she could keep quiet, and that she couldn't do because then they'd walk all over her. She quickly chose a third way out.

"I'll call and talk to my source again," she said.

Anders Schyman gave her a questioning look. "We'll

sit tight and wait before we decide on the terrorist lead," he said. "Let's go on."

Annika didn't say anything but waited for Ingvar Johansson to continue. Which he did more than willingly.

"We'll do a whole pull-out: Christina Furhage in memoriam. Her life in words and images. We have lots of tributes: the King, the White House, the Cabinet, Samaranch, a whole bunch of sportsmen and women, TV personalities. Everyone wants to pay tribute to her. It'll be really potent, really strong . . ."

"What happened to the sports supplement?" Anders Schyman said softly.

Ingvar Johansson was at a loss.

"Well, we'll make use of those pages for the memorial pull-out, sixteen pages in four-color print, and then add two pages to the regular sports section."

"Four-color?" Anders Schyman said doubtfully. "That means lifting a lot of color pages from the actual paper to the pull-out. It will leave the paper virtually gray, won't it?"

Ingvar Johansson was blushing by now.

"Well, er, yes, I suppose . . ."

"How come I wasn't informed of this?" Anders Schyman said calmly. "I've been here more or less the whole day. You could have come in at any time and discussed it."

The news editor looked like he wished a hole would open up in the conference room floor.

"I don't have an answer to that. It all went so fast."

"That's a shame," Schyman said. "Because we're not having a four-color pull-out on Christina Furhage. She wasn't a popular favorite in that way. She was an elite business executive, enormously admired by some, true, but neither royalty, nor elected by the people, nor a TV personality. We'll put the memorial pages inside the paper, forget about the pull-out, and increase the number of pages instead. Because I don't suppose sports will have started on a pull-out?"

Ingvar Johansson was staring down at the table.

"What else have we got?"

No one said a word. Annika waited in silence. This was extremely unpleasant.

"Bengtzon?"

She straightened her back and looked at her papers.

"We can do quite a substantial bit on the hunt for the killer. Patrik has found out that Furhage's laptop is missing and I've also got a good source for the insider theory . . ."

She fell silent, but no one said anything so she continued: "Berit is doing Furhage's last hours. I've met her family."

"Oh, yes, how was it?" Schyman asked.

Annika paused, thinking, then said:

"The husband was mildly confused, that has to be said. The daughter was totally unhinged. I'm not mentioning her. The question is: Should we publish anything at all? We could be in for a lot of criticism for even approaching the husband."

"Did you trick him into talking?" Anders Schyman said.

"Absolutely not," Annika replied.

"Was he reluctant in any way?"

"No, not at all. He asked us to come, so that he could tell us about Christina. I've written the copy, and it's on the server. He didn't say much, though."

"Do we have a picture?" Schyman wondered.

"Henriksson got a great photo," Pelle Oscarsson said. "The man is standing by the window, tears glistening in his eyelashes. It's a beauty."

Schyman gave the picture editor an expressionless look.

"Okay. I want to see that picture before it goes off to print."

"Sure," Pelle Oscarsson said.

"Well, then," Schyman said. "There's another issue I'd like to discuss, so we might as well do it right away."

He pulled his fingers through his hair, leaving it standing on end, then reached for his coffee, but changed his mind. For some reason this gave Annika the creeps. Had she made any more mistakes?

"There's a killer on the loose," the editor said, quoting a famous 1970s rock song. "I want each and every one of us to be aware of this when we publish pictures and interviews with people who were close to Christina Furhage. The majority of all murders are committed by someone close to the victim. That seems to be the case here, too: The Bomber could be someone who wanted revenge on Christina personally."

He fell silent and let his gaze travel around the table. No one said anything.

"Well, you must know what I'm getting at," he said. "I'm thinking of the Bergsjö murder, you remember? The little girl who was murdered in the basement. Everyone pitied the weeping mother while the father was the main suspect. Then the mother turned out to be the killer."

He raised his hand against the immediate protests.

"Yes, I know, we can't be police detectives and it's not our job to judge, but I do think we should bear it in mind with this case."

"Statistics say it should be her husband," Annika said dryly. "Husbands and partners are responsible for almost all murders of women."

"Could that be the case here?"

Annika paused and considered the question.

"Bertil Milander is a stooped old man. It's difficult to imagine him running about in sport arenas with his arms full of explosives. But he may not have done it himself. He could have hired someone to do it."

"Any other possible suspects? What about the people at the Secretariat?"

"Evert Danielsson, the director," Annika said. "The deputy managing directors of the different divisions: accreditation, transport, arenas, events, the Olympic Village. There are quite a few of them. There's the chairman of the board, Hans Bjällra. Among the members of the board, there are both local politicians and cabinet ministers . . ."

Schyman sighed.

"Okay, it's pointless to lose sleep over that. What have we got for the rest of the paper?"

Ingvar Johansson ran through the rest of his list: a pop singer who'd been given planning permission to build a winter garden despite protests from the neighbors, a cat that had survived five thousand spins in a tumble-dryer, a sensational derby victory, and all-time high audience figures for Channel 1's Saturday programming.

They ended the meeting soon afterwards, Annika hurrying away to her office. She closed the door behind her, feeling dizzy. Partly because she'd forgotten about dinner, partly because she could feel the power struggles in the news conferences were grinding her down. She held on to the desk while walking toward the chair. She'd just sat down when there was a knock at the door and the editor-in-chief walked in.

"What did your source say?" Schyman asked.

"It was an act by a single perpetrator," Annika said and pulled out the bottom drawer. If her memory served her right, there was a cinnamon bun there.

"Directed at Furhage personally?"

The bun was moldy.

"Yep, not at the Games. They are convinced of it

because someone had used the security codes to disarm the alarm system to get in the stadium. The codes were only distributed to a very narrow circle of people. The threat against her had nothing to do with the Olympics. It came from someone close to her."

The editor gave a whistle.

"How much of this can you write about?"

She pulled a face.

"None of it, really. It's difficult to say anything about serious threats against her immediate family. The family would have to comment, and they don't want to do that; I asked today. The security codes I promised to keep quiet about. The codes and Patrik's missing laptop are essentially all the police have to go on."

"That's what they say to you," Schyman said. "It's not clear they're telling you everything."

Annika looked down.

"I'm going off to Langeby to find out what the hell he's up to. Don't go anywhere, I'll be back."

He got up and closed the door carefully behind him. Annika stayed in her chair, her head almost empty and her stomach emptier than that. She had to eat something before she fainted.

Thomas didn't come home with the kids until half past six. All three of them were soaked through, exhausted and supremely happy. Ellen almost fell asleep on the sled on the way home from the park, but one more song and a snowball fight soon made her shriek with laughter again. Now they all fell in a big heap on the floor inside the front door and helped each other off with their wet clothes. The kids took hold of one foot each to help Thomas off with his boots. When they didn't succeed, they both pulled in opposite directions until he pretended to split in two. Then he put them in a hot bath and let them splash around while he cooked semolina pudding for them. That was real Sunday-night food: white porridge with lots of cinnamon and sugar, plus ham sandwiches. He took the opportunity to wash Ellen's long hair, using the last of Annika's conditioner because the girl so easily got knots in her hair and it hurt her to comb it out. They ate in their towel bathrobes, and then they all crept into the big double bed and read *Bamse*. Ellen fell asleep after two pages, but Kalle listened wide-eyed to the end of the story.

"Why is Burr's daddy so mean all the time?" he asked afterwards. "Is it because he doesn't have a job?"

Thomas thought about it. He ought to be able to answer that, manager at the Association of Local Authorities that he was.

"You don't get mean and unkind just because you don't have a job," he said. "But you can become unemployed if you're really nasty and mean. Nobody wants to work with someone like that, do they?"

The boy gave that some thought.

"Mommy sometimes says I'm mean to Ellen. Do you think I'll get a job?"

Thomas lifted the boy into his arms and blew softly in his wet hair, rocking him slowly back and forth, feeling his damp warmth through the bathrobe.

"You're a wonderful little boy, and you're going to get any job you want when you grow up. But both Mommy and I get sad when you and Ellen quarrel, and you can be such a tease, you know. You don't have to tease people and quarrel with them. You and Ellen love each other, you're sister and brother. That's why it's nicer for everyone if we can all be friends."

They boy nestled up in a little ball, put his thumb in his mouth, and said: "I love you, Daddy."

The words filled Thomas with a great and powerful

sense of warmth. "I love you, too, my little boy. Do you want to go to sleep in my bed?"

Kalle nodded, and Thomas pulled off his damp bathrobe and put the pajamas on him. He carried Ellen to her bed and put on her nightie. He watched her lying in her little bed for a few moments; he never tired of looking at her. She was the spitting image of Annika, but she had his blond hair. Kalle looked just like he had at that age. They were truly two miracles. It sounded banal, but it was an inescapable fact.

He put out the lamp and closed the door quietly. This weekend the children had barely laid eyes on Annika. He had to admit that it got to him when she worked this much. She became engrossed in her work in an unhealthy way. She got completely absorbed, and everything else in the world came second. She lost her temper with the children and thought only about her stories.

He went into the TV room, grabbed the remote, and sat down on the couch. The bomb attack and Christina Furhage's death was undeniably a big thing. All the channels, including Sky, BBC, and CNN, had nonstop coverage of it. On Channel 2, there was a commemorative program about the Olympic supremo; a load of people in a studio discussing the Olympics and Christina's achievements, interspersed with an interview with the deceased that Britt-Marie Mattsson had conducted a year before. Christina Furhage was actually extremely clever and funny. He watched with fascination for a while. Then he called Annika to see if she was on her way home.

Berit stuck her head through the door.

"Do you have a minute?"

Annika waved her in. The phone started ringing. She glanced at the display and continued writing.

"Aren't you going to get it?" Berit wondered.

"It's Thomas," Annika replied. "Asking me when I'll be leaving—trying to sound sweet. If I don't answer he'll be happy because he'll think I've already left."

The phone on the desk stopped ringing, and instead the cellphone started playing a melody that sounded familiar to Berit. Annika ignored that too and let the answering service take it.

"I can't get hold of this Helena Starke woman," Berit said. "She's not listed, and I've asked her neighbors to ring her doorbell and put notes in her letterbox asking her to call us and all sorts of things like that, but she hasn't been in touch. I don't have time to go there myself. I have to write up my Christina Furhage story . . ."

"Why?" Annika said with surprise and stopped writing. "I thought the features department was taking care of that?"

Berit smiled a lopsided grin

"Yes, but the master of style developed a migraine when he heard the pull-out had been spiked. So I now have three hours to write a puff piece."

"Oh, I'm sorry. Don't despair," Annika said. "I'll pass by Starke's on my way home. South Island, wasn't it?"

Berit gave her the address. When the door closed behind her, Annika tried calling her police contact again, in vain. She groaned quietly. She'd have to write the story now; she just couldn't sit on this information any longer. It would have to be a technical somersault, since the words "security codes" couldn't be mentioned, but the essentials would be there.

She managed better than she'd expected. The angle was that the act was an inside job. She couldn't mention that the arena's alarms were not primed and nothing had been broken into. She quoted sources other than the police in connection with the entry card and the possibility of getting access to the arena in the middle of the night. She also wrote that the police were closing in on a small group of people who, theoretically speaking, could possibly have committed the act. Together with Patrik's stuff, it made two great stories. After that, she wrote up a separate piece about the police having already interviewed the person who threatened Christina Furhage a couple of years back. She was almost done when Anders Schyman returned.

"Why did I ever become an editor!" he exclaimed and sat down on the couch.

"What do we do? Splash the news of an international terrorist organization on the front page, or expose the Olympic Secretariat?" Annika asked.

"I think Nils Langeby is losing it," Schyman said. "He maintains his story is accurate but refuses to divulge a single source or say exactly what they've said."

"So what do we do?" Annika said.

"We do the insider job, of course. But let me read it first."

"I've got it right here." Annika clicked on the document, and the editor got up and walked over to her desk.

"Do you want to sit down?"

"No, no, you sit . . ."

He glanced through the text.

"Crystal clear," he said and prepared to leave. "I'll talk to Jansson."

"What else did Langeby say?" Annika quietly asked.

He stopped and gave her a serious look.

"I think Nils Langeby is going to become a real problem for both of us," he said, leaving the room.

Helena Starke lived in a brown 1920s apartment block on Ringvägen. Naturally, the street door had a code lock and Annika didn't have the code. She pushed the phone earpiece into her ear and called information, asking for numbers for some of the residents at 139 Ringvägen.

"We can't just hand out numbers like that," the operator said tartly.

Annika let out a sigh. Sometimes it worked to ask for numbers in that way but not always.

"Okay, I'm looking for an Andersson at 139 Ringvägen."

"Would that be Arne Andersson or Petra Andersson?"

"Both," Annika replied quickly and jotted down the numbers on her pad. "Thank you!"

She called the first number. No answer, maybe he'd gone to bed. It was nearly half past ten. Petra was at home, and she sounded somewhat put out.

"I'm so sorry," Annika said, "but I'm visiting a friend who lives next door to you. I've been buzzing, but there's no answer. I know she's there. I'm getting a bit worried . . ."

"Which neighbor?" Petra asked.

"Helena Starke," Annika said. Petra laughed. It wasn't a friendly laugh.

"So you're visiting Starke at half past ten at night? Good luck, girl!" she said and gave Annika the code.

You hear so many strange things, Annika thought while walking inside. Helena Starke lived on the fourth floor. She rang the doorbell twice, but no one answered the door. She looked around the hallway, trying to figure out which direction Helena Starke's apartment faced and how big it could be. She went down on the street again and started counting. Starke ought to have at least three windows facing the street, and the light was on in two. She was probably at home. Annika returned inside and went back up in the elevator. She pushed the doorbell for a long time, then she opened the letterbox and said:

"Helena Starke? My name is Annika Bengtzon. I'm

from *Kvällspressen*. I know you're there. Won't you open the door?"

She waited in silence for a while, then she heard the door-chain rattle on the other side. The door opened slightly and she caught a glimpse of a woman with eyes swollen from weeping.

"What do you want?" Helena Starke said quietly.

"I'm sorry to bother you like this, but we've been trying to get hold of you all day."

"I know. I've had fifteen notes through my letterbox from you and all the others."

"Could I come in for a moment?"

"Why?"

"We'll be writing about Christina Furhage's death in tomorrow's paper, and I was wondering if I could ask you a couple of questions."

"What about?"

Annika sighed.

"I'll be happy to explain, but I'd rather not do it out here."

Starke opened the door and let her in the apartment. It was extremely untidy. The air was heavy, and Annika thought she could smell vomit. They went into the kitchen, where the dishes were piled high, and on one of the burners stood an empty bottle of brandy. Helena Starke herself was dressed only in a T-shirt and panties. Her hair was in disarray and her face was all swollen.

"Christina's death is a terrible loss," she said. "There wouldn't have been any Stockholm Olympics if it weren't for her."

Annika took out a pad and pen and took notes. How come everyone kept saying the same things about Christina Furhage? she wondered.

"What was she like as a person?" Annika asked out loud.

"Extraordinary," Helena Starke said, staring down at the floor. "She was a great role model for the rest of us. Driven, intelligent, tough, funny . . . everything. She could do anything."

"If I've understood it correctly, you were the last one to see her alive?"

"Except for the murderer, yes. We left the Christmas party together. Christina was tired and I was pretty drunk."

"Where did you go?"

Helena Starke stiffened.

"What do you mean 'go'? We said goodbye by the subway. I went home and Christina took a taxi."

Annika raised her eyebrows. She hadn't heard anything about Christina Furhage getting in a taxi after midnight. Then there would be someone who had seen the woman after Helena Starke. The taxi driver.

"Did Christina have any enemies within the Olympic organization?"

Helena Starke gave a sob.

"Who would that be?"

"That's what I'm asking you. You work at the Secretariat, don't you?"

"I was Christina's PA," the woman said.

"Meaning you were her secretary?"

"No, she had three secretaries. I was her right hand, you could say. I think it's time for you to go now."

Annika collected her stuff in silence. Before she left, she turned around and asked:

"Christina fired a young woman from the Secretariat for having an affair with one of her superiors. How did the rest of the personnel react to that?"

Helena Starke stared at her.

"I think you should go now."

"This is my card. I'll leave it here. Call me if there's

anything you want to add or correct," Annika reeled off her usual spiel and put the card on a table in the hall. She saw a note with a telephone number by the phone on the table, and she quickly jotted it down. Helena Starke didn't follow her to the door. Annika quietly closed it behind her.

# HUMANITY

I have always liked walking. I love the light and the wind, the stars and the sea. I have walked for so long that my body would eventually start walking by itself, barely touching the ground, dissolving into the elements around me and becoming an invisible, jubilant cheer. At other times, my legs would help me focus on life. Instead of dissolving into the environment, they would contract it into a single darkening point. I have walked along the streets, concentrating on my body, letting the thrust from the heels travel up through my limbs. With every step the question would echo: What am I? Where am I? What makes me be me?

In the days when the question was important to me, I was living in a town where the wind never stopped blowing. Wherever I walked, I had the wind against me. The gusting winds were so strong that I would sometimes be breathless. While the dampness crept into my bones, I would go over my flesh and my blood, bit by bit, trying to determine where my essence was situated. Not in my heels and not in the fingertips, neither in my knees, nor in my womb or stomach. My

*conclusion after these long walks can hardly be considered
controversial. My essence of being is somewhere behind my
eyes, above the neck but below the top of my head, diagonally
above my mouth and ears. That is where the part that is really
me sits. That is where I live. That is my home.*

*My house at the time was cramped and dark, but I remem-
ber it as being immense, impossible to fill or conquer. I was so
busy trying to understand what I was. In bed at night I would
close my eyes and try to feel whether I was a man or a woman.
How should I know? My sex throbbed in a way that could not
be put down to anything other than lust. Had I not known
what it looked like, I couldn't have described it in any other
way than as heavy, deep, and pulsating. Man or woman, white
or black? My mind could not define me any closer than as
human.*

*When I opened my eyes, they would be hit by the electro-
magnetic radiation that we call light. They would interpret
colors in a way which I could never be certain I shared with
other people. What I called red and experienced as warm and
pulsating might be seen differently by others. We have learned
and agreed on common names, but perhaps our perception is
wholly individual.*

*We can never know.*

## MONDAY 20 DECEMBER

Thomas left the house before Annika and the children woke up. He had a lot of work to get off his hands before the holiday, and today he was doing the nursery run early. They would take turns doing it during the week, preferably collecting them already by three. Partly because the children were tired and weary but also to get the house ready for Christmas. Annika had hung up an electric Star of Bethlehem made of copper and put out the Christmas candelabra, but that was all. They hadn't started with the Christmas shopping, either for food or presents, nor had they marinated the gravlax, glazed the ham, or chosen a Christmas tree, not to mention cleaning the house—they were six months behind on that. Annika wanted to hire a Polish cleaning woman, the one Anne Snapphane used, but Thomas refused. He couldn't be a manager at the Association of Local Authorities and hire workers off the books. She understood that, but she still didn't clean herself.

He stepped out and braved the slush. The holidays

were ill-timed this year: Christmas Eve fell on a Friday and the days up to New Year's Eve were all normal working days. He should be pleased, being on the employers' side. Nonetheless he sighed again, wholly on behalf of himself, as he crossed Hantverkargatan to catch the 48 bus from the stop on the other side of Kungsholm's Square. He felt a dull pain in his lower back as he lengthened his strides; he often did when he'd slept in a funny position. Kalle had still been in their bed this morning, lying diagonally with his feet against Thomas's back. Thomas turned his torso from side to side, like a boxer, to bring some life into his stiff muscles.

The bus took an age to arrive. Thomas was completely soaked and frozen by the time it pulled up in the slush. He hated taking the bus, but the alternatives were even worse. The subway was just around the corner, but it was the blue Hjulsta line, which was halfway down to hell. It took longer getting through the tunnels down to the actual trains than walking all the way to T-Centralen. Then you had to change trains after only one stop. After that, new tunnels, escalators and walkways, and elevators that always reeked of urine. After that, another train to Slussen, steamed-up carriages, and a hundred elbows from Metro-reading commuters. Going by car was out of the question. He had kept his Toyota in the city at first, but when the monthly parking tickets began exceeding the daycare fees, Annika had had a fit and he'd deregistered it. Now the car was rusting away under a tarpaulin at his parents' house in Vaxholm. He wanted to buy a house outside the city, but Annika refused point blank. She loved their exorbitantly expensive rented apartment.

The bus was chock-full of people, and he had to jostle with the strollers and baby buggies by the middle doors. But already by City Hall the bus was emptying out and by the next stop he found a seat, at the back on top of the wheels, but a seat nonetheless. He pulled up his legs and glanced furtively at the government department buildings at Rosenbad as the bus drove past. He couldn't help wondering what it would be like to work there. And why not—his career, rising from accountant with the social services in Vaxholm to middle manager at the Association of Local Authorities, had been positively meteoric for that profession. That he'd been helped along by Annika and her work was something he did not admit even to himself. If things continued at this pace, he might have a job in the parliament or one of the government departments before he turned forty.

The bus rumbled on past Strömsborg and the House of Nobility. He felt impatient and restless but didn't want to admit that it was because of Annika. He had barely exchanged a word with her over the weekend. Last night he had thought she was on her way home when she didn't answer the phone at the paper. He had made toasted sandwiches and tea for her return. It took her several hours. He had finished his toast, the tea had a film on it, and he had read both *Time* magazine and *Newsweek* from cover to cover before he heard her keys in the door. When at last she tumbled through the double doors, she had had the phone earpiece in her ear and was talking to someone at the paper.

"Hello there, you've worked late," he said as he walked toward her.

"I'll call you back on another phone," she said, switched off the phone, and walked past him with a pat on the cheek. She'd walked straight over to her desk, let her coat drop in a heap by her feet, and called the paper again. She had been talking about some taxi journey that had to be checked with the police, and he had felt his irritation grow to the size of a nuclear bomb. When she'd hung up, she'd just stood there, holding on to the desk as if dizzy.

"I'm sorry I'm so late," she'd said quietly, without looking up. "I had to go to South Island for an interview on my way back."

He hadn't replied, had just stood there with his arms hanging down, looking at her back. She had been swaying slightly, looking absolutely done in.

"You'll work yourself to death," he'd said, in a drier tone of voice than he'd intended.

"I know," she'd said, putting her coat on the desk and going to the bathroom. He had gone into the bedroom, pulling the bedspread down while listening to the running water and the brushing of teeth. When she came to bed, he'd pretended to be asleep. She didn't notice. She had kissed him on the neck and stroked his hair, then she'd fallen fast asleep in two seconds. He had lain awake for a long time, listening to the cars in the street and her soft breathing.

He got off the bus at Slussen to walk the few blocks up to his office on Hornsgatan. A damp wind was blowing from the bay, and an early street vendor had already assembled his stall, selling straw Santas in front of the underground station.

"Some glogg for the early bird, sir?" said the hawker, holding out a steaming cup of alcohol-free mulled wine to Thomas as he passed.

"Well, why not?" Thomas said and fished out some money from his pocket. "And give me a gingerbread heart too, the biggest one you have."

"Can I ride too, Mom?" Kalle said and placed himself at the back of the stroller so it nearly overturned. Annika caught hold of it at the last moment.

"No, I think we'll leave the stroller at home today since it's so slushy outside."

"But I want to go in it, Mom," Ellen said.

Annika went back to the elevator, gently shoved her out, and closed the doors. She crouched on the carpet in the stairwell and gave Ellen a hug. The stiff beaver nylon of her snowsuit felt cold against her cheek.

"We'll take the bus today, and I'll carry you. Would you like that?"

The girl nodded and put her arms around her neck, hugging her tight.

"I want to be with you today, Mom."

"I know, but you can't. I have to go to work. But on Friday we'll all be together. Do you know what day that is?"

"Christmas Eve, Christmas Eve!" Kalle shouted.

Annika laughed. "That's right. And do you know how many days it is until then?"

"Three weeks," Ellen said and held up three fingers.

"Dimwit," Kalle said. "It's four days."

"Don't call people dimwits, but you're right, it's four days. Where are your mittens, Ellen? Did we forget them? No, here they are . . ."

Outside on the pavement, the slushy snow had turned to water. A thin drizzle was falling and the world was an absolute even gray. She carried the girl on her left arm and held Kalle's hand with the other. Her bag bounced on her back with each step she took.

"You smell nice, Mom," Ellen said.

She walked up Scheelegatan and took the 40 bus from outside Indian Curry House, rode two stops, and got off by the white 1980s palace where Radio Stockholm was housed. The children's daycare center was on the third floor. Kalle had been coming here since he was fifteen months old, Ellen since she was just over a year old. When talking to other parents, she realized they'd been lucky; the staff were long-serving and competent, and the manager was committed.

The hallway was full of people and noise, and the grit and the snow had collected in a mound inside the front door. There were screaming children and admonishing parents everywhere.

"Is it okay for me to join in the morning assembly today?" Annika asked and one of the staff nodded.

Her two children sat at the same table during meals. Despite all their fighting at home, they were good friends at daycare. Kalle protected his little sister. Annika sat with Ellen on her lap during the breakfast and had coffee and a sandwich.

"We're going on a trip on Wednesday so the kids need to bring a packed lunch," one of the staff said, and Annika nodded.

After breakfast, they gathered in a room filled with cushions where they held roll call and sang some songs. Quite a few children had already started their Christmas holidays. Those that were still there sang the old classics "I'm a Little Rabbit," "Fabian the Pirate," and "In a House at the Edge of the Wood." Then they talked a bit about Christmas and finished with a Christmas song.

"Now I have to go," Annika said as they all filed out. Ellen started crying, and Kalle clung to her arm.

"I want to stay with you, Mommy," Ellen wailed.

"Daddy is picking you up early today, after the afternoon snack," Annika said cheerfully while trying to free herself of the children's arms. "Won't that be fun? Then you can go home and do some Christmas stuff, maybe go and buy a Christmas tree. Would you like that?"

"Yes!" Kalle said, Ellen joining in like a little echo.

"See you tonight," she said, quickly shutting the door on the children's little noses. She paused for a moment outside the door, listening for any reaction inside. She heard nothing. With a sigh she opened the front door.

She caught the 56 bus outside the Trygg-Hansa building

and didn't reach work until half past ten. The newsroom was full of babbling people. For some reason she could never get used to this. To her the normal state of the newsroom was when it was one big empty room with only a few people sitting quietly in front of flickering computer screens with some telephones ringing continuously for background noise. That was what it was like at the weekends and at night, but now there were close to ninety people here. She grabbed a copy of all the papers and started toward her own room.

"Nice job, Annika!" someone shouted, she couldn't tell who. She waved her hand above her head in acknowledgement.

Eva-Britt Qvist was clattering on her computer.

"Nils Langeby has taken paid leave today," she said without looking up.

Still sulking, in other words. Annika hung up her coat, went to get a cup of coffee, and walked past her pigeon-hole. It was jammed. She groaned loudly and looked around for a bin to dump her coffee in; she'd never be able to take both the mail and the coffee without spilling it.

"Why this loud groaning?" she heard Anders Schyman say behind her, and she gave an embarrassed smile.

"Oh, it's just all this mail. Opening it is such a waste of time. We get more than a hundred press releases and letters every day. It takes forever to go through it all."

"But there's no reason you should sit there opening letters," Schyman said in surprise. "I thought Eva-Britt did that."

"No, I began doing it when the last chief went to New York and I've just kept on doing it."

"It was Eva-Britt's job before he became foreign correspondent. It makes more sense for her to take care of the mail, unless you want to control it. Do you want me to have a word with her?"

"Thanks, it would be a great relief."

Anders Schyman picked up the whole pile of letters and dumped it in Eva-Britt Qvist's pigeonhole.

"I'll speak to her right away."

Annika went over to Ingvar Johansson who, as always, sat with the phone glued to his ear. He was wearing the same clothes as the day before and the day before that. Annika wondered if he got undressed before he went to bed.

"The police are pissed at you. Your piece about the security codes," he said when he'd hung up.

Annika stiffened. Fear pounded like a fist in her stomach and roared in her forehead.

"What? Why? Have I made a mistake?"

"No, but you've blown their best lead sky high. They say you'd promised not to mention the codes."

She felt the panic rising in her veins like a seething poison.

"But I didn't write about the codes! I didn't even mention the word!"

She threw away the coffee and frantically looked at a paper. "The Bomber Was Close to Christina, Suspect Taken in for Questioning" was the front-page headline. Inside she found the big black headline: "The Solution Lies in the Security Codes."

"What the fuck!" she shouted. "Who wrote this headline?"

"Hey, don't get hysterical," Ingvar Johansson said to her.

She felt her field of vision fill with something red and warm, her gaze landing on the smug man in the office chair. She could see how pleased he was behind the nonchalant face he had on.

"Who approved this?" she asked. "Did you?"

"I have nothing to do with the inside-page headlines,

don't you know that?" he said and turned around to continue working. But she wasn't letting him off the hook that easily. She grabbed the back of his chair and swiveled it around so that his legs hit the desk drawer.

"Don't be an asshole," she said, making a hissing sound. "It doesn't matter if I'm screwed, don't you see? But it will damage the paper. It will hurt you, Ingvar Johansson, and Anders Schyman—and your daughter who works in the mail room in the summer. I'm going to find out who wrote this headline and on whose initiative it was done. Don't you worry. Who called?"

His smug grin was gone, replaced by an expression of distaste.

"Don't make such a big deal of it," he said. "That was the police press officer."

She looked at him with surprise. The police press officer had no idea of what promises she had made. He was probably pissed off with the story being leaked. And that headline *was* completely unnecessary. But she was not going to treat Ingvar Johansson to a rebuke for her having betrayed a confidence.

She turned on her heel and walked away, not noticing the way people were staring at her. Scenes like this were commonplace at the paper and people always found it interesting to listen in. Bosses fighting was always great entertainment. Now they were wondering what had made the crime editor blow up. They would open the paper on pages six and seven and look at Annika's piece but not see anything out of the ordinary, and with that the fight would be forgotten.

But Annika didn't forget. She placed Ingvar Johansson's deed on top of all the others in a pile of shit that was growing taller by the day. Any day now she feared the shit would hit the proverbial fan, and then no one in the newsroom would escape without getting it on their faces.

"Do you want your personal mail, or do you want me to handle that as well?" Eva-Britt Qvist was standing in the doorway with a couple of letters in her hand.

"What? No, put them here, thanks . . ."

The crime-desk secretary walked up to Annika's desk on clattering heels and threw down the letters.

"Here you are. And if you want me to start making coffee for you, you can tell me straight to my face instead of sending the editor-in-chief."

Surprised, Annika looked at her. The other woman's face was dark with contempt. Before Annika had a chance to reply, she turned around and stormed out.

Christ almighty, Annika thought, tell me this isn't happening! She's pissed off because she thinks I went behind her back and ordered her to start opening the mail. Oh, Lord, give me strength!

And the pile of shit grew a bit taller.

Evert Danielsson stared at his bookcase, his mind a blank. He had a strange feeling of being hollow. He gripped the desk tightly with both hands, trying to keep it, or himself, in place. It wouldn't work, he knew that. It was only a matter of time before the board would issue a press release. They didn't want to wait until a new assignment had been arranged for him; they wanted to show their strength and decisiveness without Christina at the helm. Deep down he knew that he hadn't been quite up to all aspects of the job during these years, but with Christina right above him, he'd been sheltered. Now that she wasn't there any longer he had nothing to hold on to. He was finished, and he knew it.

Some things he had learned in this time, however. What happened to people who were no longer wanted, for example. Often you didn't even have to make a decision to remove people because they would leave of their own accord. There were many ways of freezing someone out, and he was familiar with most of them, even if he hadn't personally made use of them very often. When the decision was made, by whoever it may be, the staff would be informed. The internal reaction was almost always positive: A person who was made to leave had seldom managed to retain any popularity. Then the public would be informed, and if the person was known, the media was turned loose. That was where the story could move in either of two directions. Either the media would side with the ousted person and let him or her have a good public cry, or they would gloat and crow, "It serves you right!"

The first category was composed of mainly women, unless they were too highly placed. In the second category, you found mostly men from the private sector who were given enormous golden handshakes. He suspected he would end up with the latter. In his favor was the fact that he'd been fired, that he'd been made the scapegoat for Christina Furhage's death. It might be possible to steer things in that direction. Evert Danielsson felt that, even without quite being able to formulate the words in his empty mind.

There was a knock on the door, and his secretary popped her head in. Her eyes were a bit swollen and her hair was disheveled.

"I've written the press release. Hans Bjällra is here to go through it with you. Can he come in?"

Evert Danielsson looked at his secretary. She had stayed loyal to him for many years. She was close to sixty and would never get a new job. Because that's how things went when someone left, their assistants went with them. No one wanted to take on someone else's underlings. It didn't work. There would never be any real loyalty.

"Yes, of course, show him in."

The chairman of the board came in, tall and dressed in a black suit. He was in mourning after Christina's death, the bastard—everyone knew he couldn't stand her.

"I think we should keep this as brief and civilized as possible," Bjällra said and sat down on the couch, uninvited.

Evert Danielsson nodded energetically. "Yes. Clean and dignified . . ."

"I'm glad we agree on that. The press release will say that you're leaving your post as director of SOCOG, the Stockholm Organizing Committee of the Olympic Games. The reason being that after the tragic death of Christina Furhage you will be given another assignment. What this will be is not clear at the moment, but the matter will be worked out in cooperation with you. Nothing about being fired or about your severance package. The board has agreed to keep quiet about that. What do you think?"

Evert Danielsson let the words sink in. It was a lot better than he'd dared hope. It almost sounded like a promotion. He let go of the desk with his hands.

"Yes, well, I think it sounds very good," he said.

"There are a few things I'd like to talk to you about," Annika said to Eva-Britt. "Could you come into my office for a second?"

"I'm really very busy."

"Now," Annika said and walked into her room, leaving the door open. She heard Eva-Britt demonstratively punch the keys on her computer for a few seconds. Then she came and stood in the doorway with her arms crossed over her chest. Annika sat down behind her desk and pointed at the chair opposite.

"Shut the door and take a seat."

Eva-Britt sat down without closing the door. Annika sighed, got up, and closed the door. She noticed that she was shaking slightly; confrontations always were unpleasant.

"What's the matter, Eva-Britt?"

"Why? What do you mean?"

"You seem so . . . angry and upset. Has anything happened?"

Annika forced herself to sound calm and gentle, and the woman squirmed in her seat.

"I don't know what you're talking about."

Annika leaned forward and noted how Eva-Britt crossed both her legs and her arms in an unconscious defensive posture.

"You've been so hostile to me this past week. And we really fell out yesterday . . ."

"So is this some kind of ticking off for me not being nice enough to you?"

Annika felt anger rising within. She struggled to keep calm. She couldn't keep blowing her top.

"No, it's about you not doing what you're supposed to do. You didn't prioritize the material yesterday, you didn't write a handover report, you went home without saying a word. I didn't know that handling the mail used to be in your job description. It wasn't me, but Schyman himself, who suggested you start doing that again. You have to cooperate with the rest of us, otherwise this desk won't function properly."

The woman looked at her coolly. "This desk was functioning perfectly well long before you joined it."

The conversation wasn't going anywhere. Annika rose to her feet.

"Okay, let's forget about this for now. I have to make a call. By the way, have you looked everywhere and been through absolutely everything there is about Christina Furhage. Archives, books, pictures, articles, databases . . . ?"

"Every nook and cranny," Eva-Britt Qvist said and left the room.

Annika remained standing with a bitter taste in her mouth. That hadn't gone very well. She wasn't a good boss. She was a useless team leader who couldn't get the staff to go along with her. She sat down and beat her head against the keyboard. What was it she was going to do now? First things first. The police press officer, of course. She raised her head, took the phone and dialed his direct number.

"Surely you must understand that when you publish practically everything we know, you make our job more difficult," the press officer said. "Some things shouldn't be made public. They might obstruct the investigation."

"Then why do you tell us everything?" Annika said innocently.

The press officer sighed. "Some things we need to make known, but it's not the idea that it should all be in the papers."

"Please!" Annika said. "Then who decides what should be made public, and whose responsibility is it? It can't be me or my colleagues who should have to sit and guess what's best for the investigation? It would be unprofessional of us to even try."

"Yes, of course, that's not what I meant. But the security codes. It was a great shame it got in the paper."

"Yes. I'm really sorry about that. They're not mentioned anywhere in the text. The wrong words got in the headline. I'm sorry if this has caused any problems. That's why I think we should have an even closer dialogue in the future."

The press officer laughed. "Well, Bengtzon, you certainly know how to twist someone's words. If we were to get any closer to you, we'd have to give you an office next to the superintendent's."

"Not a bad idea," Annika said, smiling. She was off the hook. "So, what's happening today?"

The press officer turned serious. "Right now there's nothing I can tell you."

"Come on, it's seventeen hours to deadline; we're not publishing until tomorrow morning. There must be something you can tell me."

"Well, seeing as it's in the open, I may as well tell you now. We're looking at people with access to the security codes. The murderer is among them, we're sure of that."

"So the alarms at the stadium were primed that night?"

"Yes."

"How many people are involved?"

"Enough to keep us more than busy. Now I've got to take another call here . . ."

"Just one more thing," Annika added quickly. "Did Christina Furhage take a taxi after midnight the night she died?"

The police press officer breathed down the phone. Annika heard another phone ringing.

"Why do you ask?"

"I was given that information. Is it correct?"

"Christina Furhage had a private chauffeur. He took her to the restaurant where the Christmas party was held. After that she dismissed him. He was actually at the party. Christina Furhage had a company charge card with Taxi Stockholm, but as far as we know she didn't use it."

"Couldn't she have paid cash? And where did she go?"

The press officer remained silent for a moment, and then said: "That's the kind of thing that shouldn't be made public, for the sake of the investigation. And for Christina Furhage's."

They hung up. Annika was more puzzled than ever. Several things didn't make sense. First, the security codes. If there were that many people with access to them, then why was it so damaging for that information to be disclosed? What was the dark secret of the perfect Christina Furhage's private life? Was Helena Starke lying about the taxi? She called her contact, but no one answered. If anyone had a reason to be angry, it was him.

She called reception and asked whether Berit and Patrik had said when they would come in today. About two, they had both said when they left last night.

She put her feet on the desk and started going through the pile of papers. The "highbrow" broadsheet had found an interesting passage in one of the legal briefs that regulated the franchise between SOCOG, i.e., the Stockholm Olympics, and the IOC, the International Olympic Committee. There were numerous legal agreements between SOCOG and the IOC, not just concerning the rights to the Games themselves but also for international, national, and local sponsorship. The paper had found a clause that gave the main sponsor the right to pull out if the Olympic stadium wasn't ready for use on the first of January the year the Games were being held. Annika couldn't be bothered to read the whole story. If she remembered correctly, there were several thousand clauses. She thought they were irrelevant. The writer of the story hadn't been able to reach the main sponsor for their view. Big deal.

The rival had talked to several of the people working for Christina, among them her private chauffeur, but not to Helena Starke. The chauffeur recounted how he'd driven Christina to the restaurant and that she was as happy and nice as always, not at all worried or tense, only focused and attentive as always. He mourned her enormously because she had been such a considerate employer and nice person.

"She'll be growing wings next," Annika muttered to herself.

For the rest, there was nothing new in the papers. It took forever to go through them, they were all packed with advertising. November and December are the best months financially for Swedish daily newspapers, January and July the worst.

She went to the ladies' room to pee out the coffee and wash the printing ink off her hands. She caught sight of her own face in the mirror, not a very pleasant experience. She hadn't had the energy to wash her hair that morning but had put it up with a clip at the back. Now it lay flat and lank, separated into brown furrows. There were dark rings under her eyes and light red spots from stress on her cheeks. She rummaged through her pockets for some foundation to cover the spots but found nothing.

Eva-Britt Qvist had gone to lunch, her computer switched off. She logged out as soon as she left her desk, terrified someone would send rogue messages on the office intranet from her computer. Annika went into her own office and smeared some moisturizer on the rash, then took a stroll round the newsroom. What did she need to find out? What was the next thing to check? She walked over to the shelves holding the reference books and looked up the Olympic supremo in the National Encyclopedia. Christina Furhage née Faltin, the only child of a good but poor family, partly raised by relatives in the far north of Sweden. Career in banking. Driving force behind the efforts to win the Olympic Games for Stockholm, MD for SOCOG. Married to business executive Bertil Milander. That was it.

Annika looked up. The information that Christina's maiden name was Faltin was new to her. Then where did she get the name Furhage from? She looked at the preceding entry: Carl Furhage, born at the end of the previous century to a landed gentry family in the northern city of

Härnösand. Official in the forestry industry. Third marriage to Dorotea Adelcrona. Had made his place in history
and the National Encyclopedia by instituting a generous
scholarship for young men who wanted to study forestry.
Died in the 1960s.

Annika slammed the book shut. She quickly went
over to the computer terminal and typed the names
"Carl" and "Furhage." Seven hits. Since they computerized the archive in the early 1990s, they had written
about the man on seven occasions. Annika chose F6 for
"show" and gave a whistle. Not a bad sum of money—a
quarter of a million kronor was handed out every year.
Carl Furhage wasn't mentioned in any other context.

She logged out, picked up her entry card, and walked
out through a fire door next to the sports desk. A steep
staircase took her two floors down; she went through
another door that called for both entry card and a code.
On the other side lay a long corridor with worn linoleum
on the floor and hissing pipes in the ceiling. At the far
end of the corridor was the paper's archive, with double
steel fireproof doors. She went inside and greeted the
staff who sat hunched over their computer terminals.
The steely gray filing cabinets, with everything written in
*Kvällspressen* and in its sister "highbrow" broadsheet
since the 19th century, filled the enormous room. She
started walking slowly between the cabinets. She
reached the biography section and read A-Ac, Ad-Af,
Ag-Ak, skipped a couple of rows of cabinets and found
Fu. She pulled out a large box with surprising ease. She
leafed her way up to Furhage, Christina, but there was
no Carl. She sighed. She'd drawn a blank.

"If you're looking for the cuttings on Christina
Furhage, most of them have already been picked out,"
someone said behind her.

It was the head archivist, a competent little man with

firm opinions on how to do his job. The correct heading to file a story under was one of his favorite peeves.

Annika smiled. "I'm actually looking for another Furhage, a Director Carl Furhage."

"Have we written about him?"

"Oh, yes, he instituted a large scholarship. He must have been loaded."

"Is he dead?"

"Yes, he died in the 1960s."

"Then you may not find him under his name. The cuttings will still be there, but they could be filed under another subject field. What do you think we should start with?"

"No idea. Scholarships, perhaps?"

The archivist looked doubtful. "There are quite a lot. Do you need it today?"

Annika gave a sigh and started walking back. "Not really, it was just a hunch. Thanks anyway . . ."

"Could he have been photographed?"

Annika stopped short. "Yes, I guess so. Some special occasion or something like that. Why do you ask?"

"Then he'll be in the picture archive."

Annika went straight over to the other end of the room, past the sports archive and the reference section. She found the right box and leafed through it to Furhage. The envelopes with pictures of Christina filled almost an entire box, but on one flat little C5 envelope, frayed at the edges, she read: Furhage, Carl, director. The dust whirled when she pulled it out. She sat down on the floor and emptied the contents of the envelope onto the floor. Inside were four pictures. Two were little black and white portrait photos of a stern-looking man with thin hair and a firm chin: Carl Furhage, 50 years old, and Carl Furhage, 70 years old. The third was a wedding photo of an aging Carl and an old woman, Dorotea Adelcrona.

The fourth was the largest of the photos. It was upside down. Annika turned it over and felt her heart do a somersault. The caption was taped to the picture. "Director Carl Furhage, 60 today, with his wife Christina and son Olof." Annika read the caption twice before believing her eyes. It was definitely Christina Furhage. A very young Christina. She must have been barely twenty years old. She was very slim and had her hair put up in an unbecoming frumpy hairdo, dressed in a dark suit with a skirt down to below the knees. She looked shyly into the camera, attempting a smile. On her lap was an adorable little boy of two with blond curls. The boy wore a light sweater and short trousers with suspenders. He was holding an apple in his hands. Carl Furhage was standing behind the couch with a determined look, a protective hand resting on his young wife's shoulder. The picture was extremely stiff and contrived, breathing turn of the century rather than the '50s, which was when it must have been taken. She hadn't read a word about Christina being married before or about her having a son. She had *two* children! Annika let the picture drop to her lap. She didn't know how or why, but somehow this was of vital importance; she felt it inside. A child couldn't disappear. This boy exists somewhere and was sure to have a thing or two to tell about his mom Christina.

She put the pictures back in the envelope, got to her feet and went over to the head archivist.

"I'd like to take this with me," she said.

"Sure, just sign this," he said without looking up.

Annika signed for the picture envelope and walked back through the corridor to her room. She had a feeling this would be a long afternoon.

The press release about Evert Danielsson's resignation was sent to the news agency TT at 11:30 A.M. After that, the Olympic Secretariat's press department faxed it first to all major newspapers, the morning broadsheets, and TV, then the radio, the evening tabloids, and the bigger local newspapers in descending order of importance. Danielsson wasn't a major player in the Olympics so the editors around the country didn't exactly fall on the information. Forty minutes after the release reached TT at Kungsholm's Square, a brief item was added to their news schedule about the head of the Olympic Secretariat leaving his current post to deal with the repercussions of Christina Furhage's death.

Evert Danielsson sat in his office while the fax machines rustled in the background. He would keep his office until his new assignment had been sorted out. His initial happiness at the wording of the press release was gone. Reality had set in. The anguish was beating like a hammer inside his forehead. He couldn't focus long enough to read a whole sentence in a report or a newspaper. He was waiting for the wolves to set upon him, for the frenzy to begin. He was fair game now; the mob would soon be snapping at his legs. But to his surprise, the phone wasn't ringing.

Somewhere inside him he'd expected the situation to be similar to the one after Christina's death, when all the telephones in the office had been ringing throughout the day. They didn't. One hour after the release had gone out, the "highbrow" broadsheet called for a comment. He heard his voice sound completely normal as he said he saw this more as a promotion and that someone had to bring order in the chaos that Christina Furhage's death had caused. The reporter had been satisfied with that. His secretary came in, had a little cry, and asked if she could get him anything. Coffee? A cookie? Maybe a salad? He said no, thank you, he wouldn't be able to get it down. He gripped the desk and sat waiting for the next call.

Annika was on her way down to the canteen to get something to eat when Ingvar Johansson came walking toward her with a paper in his hand.

"Isn't this one of your guys?" he said, handing her a press release from the Olympic Secretariat. She took it and read it.

" 'One of my guys' is putting it a bit strongly," she said. "He's answered the phone when I've called. Why, do you think we should do something with it?"

"I don't know, I thought it might be good for you to know."

"Sure. Anything else going on?"

"Not in your line of business," he said and walked off.

Asshole, Annika thought. She walked over to the cafeteria instead of the canteen. She wasn't really hungry anyway. She bought a pasta salad and a Christmas *must*, the special Swedish Christmas soft drink, and brought it back to her room. Annika ate the salad in four minutes flat, went back to the cafeteria, and bought another three bottles of *must*. She was into the second one when she dialed the Olympic Secretariat and asked to speak to Evert Danielsson. He sounded distant. He said that he really saw the change as a promotion.

"So what will you be doing?" Annika asked.

"That isn't quite decided yet," Evert Danielsson replied.

"So how do you know it's a promotion?"

The man at the other end went quiet.

"Well, eh, I don't see it as being fired," he finally said.

"Well, have you been?" Annika said.

Evert Danielsson reflected.

"It depends on how you look at it," he said.

"I see. Did you resign?"

"No, I did not."

"So whose was the decision that you should change jobs? The board's?"

"Yes, they need someone to bring order in the chaos after . . ."

"Couldn't you have done that in your capacity as head of the Secretariat?"

"Well, yes, of course."

"By the way, did you know that Christina Furhage had a son?"

"A son?" he said, confused. "No, she had a daughter, Lena."

"Well, she had a son as well. Do you know where he is?"

"I haven't got a clue. A son, you say? Never heard of him."

Annika paused and thought for a moment. "Okay," she resumed, "do you know which of the bosses at the Secretariat had an affair with a woman who had to leave seven years ago?"

Evert Danielsson felt his chin drop.

"Where did you get that information?" he said when he'd collected himself.

"From a news item in the paper. Do you know who it was?"

"Yes, I do. Why?"

"What happened?"

He thought for a moment, and then said: "What do you really want?"

"I don't know," Annika said, and Evert Danielsson thought she sounded perfectly sincere.

"I guess I just want to know how it all hangs together."

Annika was surprised, to say the least, when Evert

Danielsson asked her to come over to the Secretariat so they could have a chat.

Berit and Patrik still hadn't arrived when Annika set out for Hammarby Dock.

"I'm on my cellphone," she said to Ingvar Johansson, who gave a curt nod.

She took a taxi and paid with her card. The weather was awful. All the snow had been washed away by the rain and left the ground in a state somewhere between mudhole and lake. Hammarby Dock was a sad part of town, with its empty, half-finished Olympic Village, gloomy offices, and busted stadium. The mud was flowing freely as the shrubs and flowerbeds planted last summer hadn't yet taken root. Annika jumped across the worst puddles but still got mud on her pant legs.

The reception area of SOCOG was spacious, but the offices inside were remarkably small and plain, Annika thought. She compared them with the only other administrative complex she was familar with, the Association of Local Authorities where Thomas worked. Their premises were nicer and more practical. The Secretariat was almost spartan: white walls, plastic floor, strip lights everywhere in the ceiling, white chipboard bookshelves, desks that could be from IKEA.

Evert Danielsson's office was halfway down a long corridor. It wasn't much bigger than the office clerks', something Annika found a bit odd. A sagging couch, a desk, and some bookcases, that was all. She had thought the head of a secretariat would have mahogany furniture and a window office.

"What makes you think Christina had a son?" Evert Danielsson said and invited her to sit on the couch.

"Thanks," Annika said, sitting down. "I have a picture of him."

She pulled off her coat but decided not to take out a pad and pen. Instead she took a closer look at the man in front of her. He was sitting at his desk, holding on to the desk firmly with one hand—it looked a bit strange. He was around fifty, with a good head of steely gray hair and quite a pleasant face. But his eyes were tired, and he had a cheerless line around his mouth.

"I have to say I find that highly unlikely," he said.

Annika pulled out a scan of the Furhage family photograph from her bag. She had returned the original to the archive since it wasn't allowed to leave the building, but nowadays you could scan a picture and have a paper copy within a minute. She handed the picture to Evert Danielsson who looked at it with obvious surprise.

"Well, I'll be damned . . ." he said. "I had no idea."

"Of the husband or the child?"

"Either, actually. Christina didn't talk about her private life."

Annika waited in silence for the man to continue. She didn't quite understand why he had asked her to come there. He was fidgeting in his chair. Then he said:

"You were asking about the secretary who got fired."

"Yes, I found a short piece about it in the archive. But there was no mention of her being a secretary or about being fired. All it said was she had worked here and had to go."

Evert Danielsson nodded. "That's how Christina wanted it. But Sara was an excellent secretary. She would doubtless have done well if it hadn't been for . . ."

The man fell silent.

"There is a rule within the Olympic organization saying that employees in the same workplace are not allowed to have a relationship," he continued. "Christina was adamant about it. She said it had a disruptive effect, disturbed people's focus, divided their loyalty. It subjected the others in the team to unnecessary stress; it made them play favorites."

"Who was the man?" Annika asked.

Evert Danielsson sighed heavily.

"It was me."

Annika felt herself raising her eyebrows.

"And whose rule was it?"

"Christina's. It applied to everyone."

"Still?"

Evert Danielsson let go of his desk.

"I don't know, actually. But one thing I *do* know. It's completely irrelevant to me now."

He covered his face with his hands. He was crying again. Annika waited in silence while the man collected himself.

"I really loved Sara, but I was married," he finally said, lowering one hand onto his lap and gripping the desk with the other. His eyes were dry but slightly red.

"You're not now?"

He gave a short laugh.

"Oh no. Someone told my wife about Sara, and Sara dropped me when I couldn't see to it that she could keep her job. I lost my wife and kids and lover at the same time."

He fell silent for a while and then went on, almost as if speaking to himself:

"Sometimes I wonder if she seduced me to forward her career. When it was clear I was dragging her down, she dumped me like a hot brick."

He gave another quick, bitter little laugh.

"So maybe she wasn't all that terrific, after all," Annika ventured.

He looked up.

"No, perhaps not. But what are you going to do with this? Are you going to write about it?"

"Not at the moment," Annika said. "Maybe never. Would you mind if I did?"

"I don't know, it would depend on what you wrote. What are you after, really?"

"Why did you ask me to come here?"

He sighed.

"There's so much that comes to the surface on a day like this. Thoughts and feelings. It's chaotic. I've been here since the beginning, there's so much I could tell . . ."

Annika waited. The man stared at the floor, lost in his own thoughts.

"Was Christina a good boss?" she asked in the end.

"She was a prerequisite for my being in this post," Evert Danielsson said, letting go of the desk. "Now she's not here any longer, and I'm finished. I think it's time for me to go home now."

He rose and Annika followed. She put her coat back on, hung her bag over her shoulder, shook his hand, and thanked him for seeing her.

"By the way, where was Christina's office?"

"Didn't you see it? Right behind the entrance. I'll walk you out and I can show you."

He put on his coat, wrapped a scarf around his neck, picked up his briefcase, and looked pensively at his desk.

"Today I don't need to bring a single paper with me."

He switched out the lights and left the office with his empty briefcase, conscientiously locking the door behind him. He popped his head in next door and said:

"I'm off now. If anyone calls you can refer them to the press release."

They walked side by side down the white corridor.

"Christina had several offices," he said. "You could call this her everyday office. Two of her secretaries were based here."

"And Helena Starke?" Annika queried.

"Her enforcer, you mean. Right, her office is next to Christina's," Evert Danielsson said, rounding the corner. "Here it is."

The door was locked, and the man sighed. "I don't have the key," he said. "Well, it's nothing special, a corner office with windows facing in two directions, a large desk with two computers, a couch and chairs and a coffee table . . ."

"You'd expect something grander," Annika said and recalled an archive picture from a magnificent palatial room with a period desk, dark wooden panel walls, and chandeliers.

"Well, this is where she did the spadework. Then she had her office downtown, just behind Rosenbad. That's where she had her third secretary, where all meetings and negotiations took place and where she received the press and various guests. . . . Do you want a ride somewhere?"

"No, thanks, I'm going to say hello to a friend over at the old lamp factory," Annika said.

"You can't walk there in this mud," Evert Danielsson said. "I'll drop you over there."

He had a brand new company car, a Volvo—naturally. Volvo was one of the main sponsors. He unlocked the central locking, beep-beep, with a remote control, caressing the car roof before opening the door. Annika got in on the passenger side, put on the seat belt, and said:

"Who do you think blew her up?"

Evert Danielsson started up the car and revved it twice, carefully put it in reverse, and stroked the wheel.

"Well," he said, "one thing I know for sure. There were a lot of people with a reason for doing it."

Annika bounced. "What do you mean by that?"

The man didn't reply but drove in silence the five hundred meters to the old factory building. He stopped outside the gates.

"I want to know if you write anything about me."

Annika gave him her card and asked him to call her if there was anything he wanted to tell her, thanked him for the ride, and got out.

"One thing I know for sure," she told him, "this story keeps getting more and more complex."

She went up to the TV company where Anne Snapphane worked. Anne was still editing and seemed relieved to have a break.

"I'll be done soon," she said. "Do you want some glogg?"

"Nonalcoholic," Annika said. "Is there a phone I could use?"

"Take the one on my desk. I'm just . . ."

Annika went over to Anne Snapphane's desk and threw her coat on top of it. She started by calling Berit.

"I've talked to the limo driver, Christina's chauffeur," Berit said. "The rival already did that yesterday, but he had some new stuff to tell me. He confirmed that Christina had her laptop with her—she left it behind, so they had to go back and get it. He hadn't worked long for Christina, only about two months. She had a hell of a turnover of drivers."

"You don't say," Annika said.

She heard Berit turning over the pages on a pad.

"He also said that she was extremely worried about being followed. He was never allowed to drive straight from the Secretariat to her house. He also had to check the car carefully every day. Christina was scared of bombs."

"Well done!"

"What else was there . . . Oh, yes, he'd been given express orders never to let the daughter, Lena, anywhere near the car. Weird, eh?"

Annika sighed lightly.

"Christina seems to have been a bit paranoid. But it'll

make for one hell of a story, Christina afraid of being blown up. The bit about the daughter we'll have to leave out."

"Absolutely. I'm chasing the police for a comment right now."

"What's Patrik doing?"

"He hasn't showed up yet. He worked almost right through last night. Where are you?"

"At my friend Anne Snapphane's. I've had a little chat with Evert Danielsson. He's out."

"Booted out?"

"Well, not quite. He wasn't quite sure himself. It's not really anything to write about. I mean, who cares? He's not going to cry on our shoulders, but he isn't going to blast anyone either. Doesn't seem capable."

"So what did he say?"

"Not much. He was the guy who had an affair at the Secretariat. We talked about that, mostly. And he hinted that Christina had a lot of enemies."

"Well, well, it's all coming out now," Berit said. "What else are we doing?"

"Christina was married before and had a son. I'll see what I can find on that."

"A son? But I wrote her life history last night. I didn't know she had a son."

"She's hidden him well. I wonder if there are any other secrets in her closet . . ."

They hung up and Annika fished out her pad. On the back of it she had noted Helena Starke's telephone number. She dialed the number, starting 702, which they often did on Ringvägen, and hoped for the best.

Helena Starke had had another lousy night, waking up repeatedly from ghastly nightmares. When at last she'd gotten out of bed and looked out the window, she nearly went straight back to bed again. It was raining, a gray drizzle that killed all the colors in the street outside. The stench from the closet had become unbearable, so she had put on a pair of jeans and gone down to the laundry room to book a time. Things are very organized in Sweden. Needless to say, there wasn't a single slot available before the new year. So she quickly emptied one of the running machines, threw the dripping load in a basket and went and collected her mat. She shoved it into the machine, poured in too much washing powder, and hurried away. She took a long shower to finally get rid of the smell of vomit from her hair and then scrubbed the closet and the floor in the hallway. She considered collecting the mat but refrained; it was better to wait until tonight and let the old bags downstairs rant and rave first.

She went into the kitchen to have a cigarette. Christina didn't like her smoking, but that didn't matter anymore. Nothing mattered anymore. She stood by the kitchen table in the dark, having had the second deep drag on the cigarette when the phone on the windowsill rang.

It was the woman from last night, the bitch from *Kvällspressen*.

"I don't know if I want to talk to you," Helena Starke said.

"You don't have to, of course . . . Are you smoking?"

"So what if I am? Yes, I'm smoking. What's it to you?"

"Nothing. Why do they call you Christina's enforcer?"

Helena didn't know what to say.

"What the hell do you want from me?"

"Nothing really. It's Christina I'm interested in. Why wouldn't she acknowledge her son? Was she ashamed of him?"

Helena Starke's head was spinning. She sat down and

put out the cigarette. How could she know about Christina's son?

"He died," she said. "The boy died."

"Died? When?"

"When he was . . . five."

"Really? That's terrible. Five, just like Kalle."

"Who?"

"My son, he's five. How awful! What did he die of?"

"Malignant melanoma, skin cancer. Christina never got over it. She didn't ever want to talk about him."

"I'm so sorry I . . . Sorry, I had no idea . . ."

"Anything else?" Helena Starke said, trying to sound as cold as possible.

"Yes, quite a lot, actually. Do you have a moment?"

"No, I'm doing my laundry."

"Laundry?"

"Yeah, what's so strange about that?"

"No, it's just that I . . . I mean . . . Well, you knew Christina really well, you were so close to her." Annika pushed it. "It must be difficult to think about doing ordinary stuff like laundry so soon after . . ."

"Yes, I knew her well!" Helena Starke shouted, and the tears started running. "I knew her best of all!"

"Apart from her family, perhaps."

"Right, her fucking family! That senile old man and her crazy daughter. You know she's a pyromaniac? Cuckoo bird. Spent most of her teens in a psychiatric ward. Set fire to anything she could lay her hands on. That special home in Botkyrka that burned down six years ago, do you remember? That was her, Lena. Talk about nutcase, you couldn't have her in the house."

She cried straight into the phone, loud and uncontrolled, hearing how awful she sounded, like some strange trapped animal. She put the receiver down and let her arms drop onto the kitchen table, her forehead landing among the breadcrumbs, and then she cried and cried and cried until everything was black out there and everything inside her had run out.

Annika could hardly believe what she had just heard. For a long while, she sat with the receiver held out from her ear, listening to the silence after Helena Starke's unbearable scream.

"What's up? Why are you sitting like that?" Anne Snapphane said, placing a coffee mug full of glogg and a stack of ginger biscuits on the desk next to Annika.

"Bizarre . . ." Annika said, putting the phone down.

Anne Snapphane stopped nibbling at her biscuit.

"You look wretched. What happened?"

"I just spoke to a woman who knew Christina Furhage. It was kind of over the top."

"How so?"

"She started crying loudly, really howling. I always feel awful when I go too far."

Anne Snapphane nodded sympathetically and pointed at the mug and the stack of biscuits.

"Come with me to the editing suite and I'll show you the beginning of our New Year's show. *Things We Remember—That They'd Rather Forget* is the title. It's about celebrity scandals. Delicious!"

Annika left her coat but hung her bag on her shoulder and followed Anne, balancing the glogg and the biscuits. The TV offices were empty of people. The season's productions were finished, and they wouldn't start on the next until after the holidays.

"Do you know what you're doing next season?" Annika asked while they stepped down the spiral staircase to the editing suite.

Anne Snapphane pulled a wry face. "What do you think? Fat chance. I'm hoping to get away from *Women's*

*Sofa.* I've done it backwards and forwards a million times now. He cheated on me with my best friend, my best friend cheated on me with my son, my son cheated on me with my dog . . . Count me out . . ."

"So what do you want to do instead?"

"Anything. I might go to Malaysia with this new show in the spring. People living on a desert island for as long as possible without being voted out by the audience. Sounds like fun, doesn't it?"

"Sounds damn boring to me," Annika said.

Anne Snapphane looked at her with mock scorn and continued down another corridor.

"Luckily you're not head of the program. I think it'll be great. People love that shit. Here we are."

They stepped into a room filled with TV monitors, Digibeta players, keyboards, consoles, and cables. The room was considerably larger than the little cubicles they called editing suites at the state television newsroom. There was even a couch, two armchairs, and a coffee table in the corner. The editor was sitting on a swivel chair in front of the main console—a young guy who handled the technical side of putting together the program—staring at a screen where images were rushing past. Annika greeted him and then went and sat down in one of the armchairs.

"Run the opening sequence," Anne said and sat down on the couch.

The editor reached out for a large Digibeta tape and fed it into one of the players. The screen on the largest monitor flickered and a countdown clock appeared. Then the show started and the well-known presenter stepped out on the studio floor. The audience cheered. He presented the program that would feature a politician who had thrown up in the head waiter's booth at the famous Café Opera, the most talked about divorces of the year, TV gaffes we remember, and other important items.

"Okay, you can turn down the volume," Anne said. "What do you think? Isn't it good?"

Annika nodded and took a sip from her mug. The glogg was pretty strong. "Do you know someone called Helena Starke?"

Anne let her cookie drop and thought about it.

"Starke . . . it sounds really familiar. What does she do?"

"She works at the Olympic Secretariat with Christina Furhage. Lives in South Island, around forty, short black hair . . ."

"Helena Starke, now I know! Sure. She's a lesbian activist. Butch dyke type."

Annika looked at her friend with skepticism in her eyes.

"Come on, what do you mean 'butch dyke'?"

"She's active in the National Swedish Association for Sexual Liberation—writes articles and stuff like that. She's trying to make lesbians look less soft. Complains about 'vanilla sex,' for example."

"How do you know this?"

It was Anne Snapphane's turn to look skeptical.

"What do you think I do all day? There isn't a single activist in this country I don't have the private phone number of. How do you think we make these programs?"

Annika raised her eyebrows apologetically and finished her glogg.

"Has Starke been on your show?"

"Nope, no way would she come on. Come to think of it, we've asked her a couple of times. She says she stands for her sexuality but won't have it exploited by the media."

"Sensible woman," Annika said.

"Luckily for me, not everyone thinks like she does, or there wouldn't be a *Women's Sofa* program. More glogg?"

"No, I've got to get back to the snake pit. They'll all be wondering what happened to the little rabbit."

Anders Schyman's afternoon had been tedious. He'd been in a meeting with two guys from the marketing department: a circulation analyst and a number-cruncher. Two economists whose job it was to interfere with everything that wasn't their business. They had both rejected his pitch for more investigative social journalism. The analyst had gone over his overhead transparencies and pointed at various charts, columns, and figures comparing the three largest evening tabloids, day by day.

"Here, for example, the rival sold exactly 43,512 copies more than *Kvällspressen*," he said, pointing at a date at the beginning of December. "The kind of serious news we had on that particular day didn't stand a chance against the competition."

The number-cruncher got in on the act.

"That whole focus on heavy pieces in early December hasn't worked very well. We're hardly increasing our circulation at all compared with last year. And you've been using resources that were allocated for other items."

Anders Schyman had been pensively twirling a pen while the economists talked. When they had finished, he answered circumspectly:

"Yes, you've got a point, of course. I mean, yes, in retrospect we can see that the lead in question wasn't particularly spectacular, but what was the alternative? The defense budget being overspent wasn't exactly the scoop of the decade, but we were the only ones to have it and got credit for it in other media. The rival had a special pull-out with Christmas gift bargains that day. And that TV celebrity who came clean about his eating disorder. From a circulation perspective, it would have been hard to beat that day with anything."

The editor got up and walked over to the window facing the Russian Embassy. It really was completely gray out there.

"There was a lot going on early December. Remember?" he went on. "That plane crashed coming in to Bromma Airport, the soccer star who got caught drunk driving and his club threw him out, a TV star was convicted of rape. Our circulation figures in December last year were enormous. And this year we're up. Even with investigative news stories, we've been reaching and improving upon last year. Losing the race against the rival on one particular day doesn't mean that our scrutiny of the powers that be is misguided. I think it's too early to draw that conclusion."

"Our financial health is based on successful sales on particular days," the number-cruncher remarked dryly.

"Well, superficially, yes. But look at the bigger picture," Anders Schyman said and turned to face the two men. He must have given this speech nineteen times. "We have to concentrate on building up our credibility with the readers. It's been neglected for a long time. We'll have big-selling front pages with blondes and car crashes, but we have to stick to our long-term investment in quality."

"Well," the number-cruncher said, "it's really a matter of what kind of resources we invest."

"Or how we invest them," Schyman countered. "Juggling the budget within the limits prescribed—I have the board's full endorsement to allocate resources. At my discretion."

"And that is something that could well be worth looking at again," the number-cruncher said.

Anders Schyman sighed. "Do we have to talk about that again?" It seemed like the bean counters sat in his office every month and went on about this.

"I think we should," said the number-cruncher, waving his transparencies in the air. "We have the formula for a successful tabloid right here. It's in our data."

A business degree and six months in the sales department and these jerks thought they had invented the business. The numbers were good; he just wasn't doing it according to the right theory.

"Well, I disagree. Why do you think I'm sitting here? Why don't they just put a computer in this office and save my salary? If all that matters is the formula? Tabloids and front pages aren't made by analyzing computer breakdowns of circulation figures. They're made with your heart. With experience. I wish you guys would concentrate on marketing. When are our circulation figures at their highest? How come? Could we change distribution? Should we change our printing schedule? Can we save time printing via satellite in other cities? You know about that stuff. Leave the editing to me."

"We've already been through all that," the number-cruncher replied shortly.

"Then do it again, and better," said Schyman.

He'd let out a sigh when the men closed the door behind them. This kind of discussion could be quite rewarding, sometimes. It wouldn't have been possible ten years ago. In those days there was a sharp dividing line between the marketing department and the editors. Now he saw it as his job to at least build a few bridges between the Numbers and the Words. The marketing people mustn't think that they could start dictating the editorial content. But he needed them. He was sure about that. He knew that the circulation statistics for separate issues were extremely important; he spent many hours every week going over the figures with the circulation analyst. But that didn't mean the number-crunchers should try to do his job.

A tabloid's circulation is an extremely sensitive mechanism affected by a near infinite number of factors. Every morning around 4 A.M., analysts come in to calculate the number of copies to be sent to the thousands of outlets around the country. All the basic variables would already be in the computer: the season, the day of the week, holidays. If it was going to rain, for example, the copies were moved from the beach kiosks to the IKEA stores. People did their weekly shopping on Thursdays and would buy the paper then. So, more papers to the supermarkets on Thursdays. And if it was the Christmas holidays and people were on the roads, they would increase the number of copies along the highways.

A big event in a small place would generate localized stories and increase local sales. It was then up to the analysts to figure it out; not just add ten percent across the board. For a kiosk in the sticks that normally sold ten copies, ten percent would mean one extra copy. There you would have to increase the circulation by four hundred percent.

The last factor of the circulation breakdown was what was going on the front page. It was of marginal importance, unless the King got married or there was a plane crash.

Besides the circulation breakdown, other variables were involved. If a big story broke up north, the analyst might have to make a quick decision to get extra planes to deliver the papers. This was obviously a financial question: How much the air delivery would cost compared with the revenue of the extra newspapers sold. But a disappointed reader who went to the rival instead was also worth taking into consideration. Usually they put on the extra plane.

Schyman sat down in front of his computer and logged into the TT news agency's database. He quickly scrolled through the menu of cable copy that had been filed over the past twenty-four hours. There were a couple of hundred items, covering sports, domestic, and international news. All Swedish newsdesks rely on this wire copy. Their selection of both domestic and international news is governed by what TT puts out.

Anders Schyman thought back to another of the number-cruncher's lectures. The demographics were lousy. He presented the Reader, a standardized profile of the *Kvällspressen* readership. The Swedish stalwart, the Man in a Cap, 54 years of age, blue-collar guy, who had been buying the paper since he was in his twenties. All tabloids had their loyal readers, those who would, the paper liked to think, go through fire and water to get hold of their copies. They were called elephant hides and were, in the case of *Kvällspressen*, a dying breed. Anders Schyman was painfully aware of that.

The next category was called Loyal Readers, a group of people who would buy the paper several times a week. If these Loyal Readers stopped buying the paper just one time a week, it would have a disastrous effect on the circulation. That's how the crisis started a couple of years ago. Now they were working toward finding a new readership. Anders Schyman was sure they were succeeding, but these new readers had not yet supplanted the Man in a Cap. But it was only a matter of time. He needed senior staff with a new way of thinking. They couldn't go on relying on men over 45 to make the paper. Anders Schyman knew this, and he was clear how he would go about making the changes that had to be made.

Annika was feeling a bit dizzy from the mulled wine when she reached the paper. Not a very pleasant feeling. She concentrated on walking in a straight line. She didn't talk to anyone on the way to her office. Eva-Britt Qvist's chair was empty. She had already gone home, even though her

working hours were until 5 P.M. Annika threw her coat and
scarf on the couch and went and collected two mugs of
coffee. Why had she drunk that damned glogg?

She started by calling her contact. Busy signal. She
hung up and started writing down what she had found
out about Christina's children, that the son had died and
the daughter was a pyromaniac. She finished her first
mug of coffee and brought the other one with her to the
computer terminal where she ran a search of the
archives. Yes, a children's home in Botkyrka had burned
down six years before. A fourteen-year-old girl had
started the fire. Nobody was hurt but the building had
been completely destroyed. So far the details of Helena
Starke's outburst tallied.

She went back to her office and called her contact
again. This time the call went through.

"I know you have a right to be angry with me about
the security codes," was the first thing she said to him.

The man sighed. "What do you mean, 'angry'? Are
you serious? You blew our best lead sky-high, and you
ask me if I'm angry? I was fucking furious. Mostly with
myself for talking about it in the first place."

Annika closed her eyes and felt her heart sink deep into
her shoes. It was pointless to try and find excuses about
editors writing headlines they shouldn't have. The only
thing that would work here was to go on the offensive.

"Oh, please," Annika said in as reproachful a tone of
voice as she could muster. "Who revealed what exactly?
I had the whole story and sat on it for twenty-four hours.
Just like you asked. I think you're being unfair."

"Unfair? This is a murder investigation, for Christ's
sake! What's fair got to do with it?"

"It wouldn't have taken a total genius to figure out
that there were security codes involved. You shouldn't
have let me write anything at all," Annika said dryly.

The man exhaled slowly. She had him.

"Okay, give me your apologies and let's be done with it."

Annika took a breath. "I'm sorry that the words 'security codes' got in the headline. As you may have noticed, they were nowhere in the actual text. The editor wrote the headline sometime in the early morning. He was only trying to do a good job. He didn't know."

"Damned editors," the police officer said. "Well, what is it you want now?"

Annika smiled.

"Have you questioned Christina's daughter, Lena Milander?"

"About what?"

"About what she was doing last Friday night?"

"Why do you ask?"

"I've found out about her pyromania."

"Fire fixation," the man corrected her. "Pyromania is an extremely rare condition. It's very precise. A pyromaniac has to meet five distinct criteria that largely have to do with a person having a pathological fascination with, and being excited by, both fire and everything connected with fire, like fire brigades, fire extinguishers . . ."

"All right, fire fixation, then. Have you?"

"Yes, we've checked her out."

"And?"

"That's all I can say."

Annika fell silent. She wondered whether she should say anything about the son that died but decided not to. A dead five-year-old had nothing to do with this.

"So what's happened with the security codes?"

"Do you think I should tell you?"

"Come off it," Annika said.

The man paused.

"We're working on it," was all he said.

"Do you have a suspect?"

"No, not at this stage."

"Any leads?"

"Yes, of course, what the hell do you think we do up here?"

"Okay," Annika said and looked at her notes. "How about this: You're still looking into the security codes—I can write that now that it's out in the open, can't I? That you've had several people in for questioning without finding a particular suspect but that you're working on several leads at the moment."

"That sounds about right," her contact said.

Annika hung up with a taste of bitter disappointment in her mouth. The idiot who had written that headline had ruined years of work for her. What she had found out now was nothing, *nada*, the usual bullshit. Now she had to rely on her colleagues and their sources.

At that moment Berit and Patrik popped their heads in the door.

"Are you busy?"

"No, come right in. Take a seat, just chuck my clothes on the floor. They're so dirty, it won't make any difference."

"Where have you been?" Berit asked and hung Annika's coat on a hook.

"In the mud outside the Olympic Secretariat. I hope you've had better luck than I have today," she said cheerlessly and gave them a brief outline of the conversation with her contact.

"Accident at work," Berit comforted her. "Shit happens."

Annika sighed. "Well, let's get started. What have you got today, Berit?"

"I've told you about my interview with the chauffeur; he's quite good. And I've been making calls about that taxi tip off. It's odd. No one wants to say anything about where Christina disappeared to after the Christmas party. We don't know what she was doing between midnight and 3:17."

"Right, so you have two things: Christina was afraid of being blown up, according to her private chauffeur, and her missing hours. Patrik?"

"I just got here, but I've made a couple of calls. Interpol is putting out an alert for the Tiger during the evening."

"Really?" Annika said. "Global?"

"I think so. Zone two, they said."

"That's Europe," Berit and Annika said simultaneously, and laughed.

"Any particular country?"

"Don't know," Patrik answered.

"Okay, so you can deal with stuff that comes in this evening," Annika said. "Unfortunately I don't have much that's worth writing about, but I've discovered a couple of things."

She told them about Christina Furhage's first husband, the wealthy old forestry official, about her dead son and pyromaniac of a daughter, Evert Danielsson's devastating love affair at work and his uncertain future, about Helena Starke's unexpected outburst, and the fact that she was a militant lesbian.

"Why are you poking about in all that?" Patrik said skeptically.

Annika gave him a look of mild indulgence.

"Because, dear boy, this type of general research into the human nature sometimes produces something. Cause and effect. An understanding of the individual and her impact on society. As you'll learn when you've been around here as long as I have."

Patrik looked like he didn't believe her.

"Whatever. I just want to get my copy onto the front page," he said.

Annika smiled slightly.

"Great. Shall we pack it in?"

Berit and Patrik left. She listened to *Eko* before she went into the evening news conference, the handover that the rank and file called the Six Session. The radio news pursued the morning broadsheet's discovery of the legal technicality and then went to town on the parliamentary elections in India. Annika switched off.

She went past the kitchen and drank a big glass of water before joining the meeting. The dizziness from the glogg had thankfully worn off.

The editor was alone in his office when she entered. He seemed to be in a good mood.

"Good news?" Annika asked him.

"Hell, no. Numbers aren't good enough. I've just had a meeting with the marketing people, that always cheers me up. How are you doing?"

"The headline with the security codes in today's paper was unnecessary. I want to bring that up at the meeting. It's a bit of a catastrophe for me. Then I've found some skeletons in Furhage's closet. I can tell you about it afterwards if you have a minute . . ."

Ingvar Johansson, Pelle Oscarsson, and Spike, the other night editor, entered at the same time. They were loud and noisy, laughing among themselves in the way men among equals do. Annika sat silently waiting for them to sit down.

"There's something I want to say," Anders Schyman said briskly, pulling out a chair and sitting down. "I know that no one in this room had anything to do with it, but I want to deal with it officially. It's about the headline on pages six and seven in today's paper. 'The Solution Lies in the Security Codes.' We weren't supposed to mention the codes. There could have been no doubt about that after yesterday's discussion. Still the headline ended up in the paper. A big fuck-up. I'll be calling Jansson straight after this meeting to find out how the hell it could happen."

Annika felt her cheeks go redder and redder while the editor was speaking. She struggled to look unmoved, but without great success. It was clear to everyone in the room whose brief he was holding and whose side he was on.

"It's amazing to me that I should even have to say this. I thought it was clear that we act in accordance with the decisions made in these meetings and with the directives I give. There are certain times we know of things that we don't write about. I decide when this is so. Annika's deal with her contact was to not mention the codes, which she didn't. Even so, it ended up like this. How was that possible?"

No one replied. Annika stared down at the table. To her annoyance, she felt the tears welling up, but she swallowed hard and forced them back.

"Right," Schyman said, "since no one seems to have an explanation for this, I think we should learn from it and make sure it never happens again. Agreed?"

The men mumbled inaudibly. Annika swallowed again.

"Let's go through today's list," the editor said. "Annika, what do you have at the crime desk?"

Ingvar Johansson's lips tightened as she straightened up and cleared her throat.

"Berit has two stories: She's met the chauffeur who told her Christina was afraid of being blown up, and she's looking into Christina's last hours. Patrik says Interpol will put out an international wanted alert of the Tiger tonight. He'll have to write something about the hunt for the killer during the night. I'll get the cold shoulder from my sources from now on. I met Evert Danielsson,

Furhage's nearest subordinate, who's been shown the door . . ."

She fell silent and looked down at the table.

"Sounds promising, but we're not leading with the blast tomorrow," Schyman said, thinking of the number-cruncher. According to their calculations, no story sold for more than two, at the most three days, regardless of its significance. "We're into the fourth day and it's time to change the track. What have we got to lead with instead?"

"Should we really let go of the terrorist angle already?" Spike said. "I think we've lost that part of the story completely."

"How?" the editor asked.

"All the other papers have had accounts of the different terrorist attacks against Olympic facilities over the years, looking at which terrorist groups could be behind this. We haven't even touched on that."

"I know you haven't been in the last few days, but surely you get the paper in the northern suburbs," Schyman said patiently.

Spike swallowed the bitter pill. Once again the editor felt he was addressing a bunch of recalcitrant children.

"We did the list of past Olympic attacks in both the Saturday and Sunday papers. We deliberately refrained from unethical speculation on different terrorist groups. We've had our own stuff, which has been unrivaled. All we can hope for is that today's moronic headline hasn't put a stop to that in the future. Instead of barking up the terrorist tree, we've been leading the news, and that's something to be proud of. Our sources tell us that this was not an attack on the Olympics, neither the event itself nor the arenas. According to our information, this was a private attack on Christina Furhage, and we have confidence in ourselves. That's why we won't be doing any lists of possible terrorist groups tomorrow either. But what should we lead with, Mr. News Editor?"

Ingvar Johansson instantly put on an air of importance and started going through his voluminous list. Annika had to admit he was efficient and usually had sound judgement. While he talked, she could feel Spike's hostile gaze on her. She was relieved when the meeting ended and the men left the room.

"So what have you found out today?" Schyman asked her.

Annika told him what she knew and showed the picture of the young Christina, her first husband, and young son.

"The deeper I dig into her past, the darker it gets," she said.

"Where's it going?" the editor asked.

She hesitated. "What I have so far can't be published. I'm sure there's an explanation for it all somewhere in her closet."

"What makes you think the truth can't be published?"

Annika blushed. "I don't know. I just want to find out how it's all connected and be one step ahead. Then I can ask the police the right questions that will give us the answers before anyone else."

The editor smiled. "Great," he said. "I'm really pleased with the work you've done these past few days. You don't give up, that's a good quality, and you're not afraid of confrontation if need be. That's even better."

Annika cast down her eyes and blushed even more. "Thanks."

"Now I'm going to call Jansson and ask what happened with that fucking headline."

She walked over to her office and suddenly realized she was starving. She went over to Berit and asked if she'd like to go to the staff canteen. She did, so they picked up their coupons and set off. They were serving Christmas ham with potatoes and apple sauce tonight.

"Christ, it's all starting now," Berit said. "They won't change the menu until after New Year's Eve."

They skipped the ham and chose the salad bar instead. The big canteen was almost empty, and they took a table in the corner.

"What do you think Christina did after midnight?" Berit said and bit into a piece of carrot.

Annika thought about it while shoveling sweet corn into her mouth.

"She left the restaurant in the middle of the night, together with a well-known lesbian. Did they go somewhere together?"

"Helena Starke was drunk as a skunk. Maybe Christina helped her home?"

"How? On the night bus?"

Annika shook her head and continued her reasoning: "She had both a taxi charge card, money, and approximately two and a half thousand employees who could see to it that a colleague got home in a car. Why should she, the MD of the Olympic Games, Woman of the Year, drag a plastered lesbian down to the subway? It's not logical."

The thought hit them both at the same time.

"Unless . . ."

"Is that possible . . . ?"

They started laughing. The thought of Christina Furhage being gay seemed far-fetched.

"Maybe they went to register their partnership," Berit said, and Annika smiled.

"No, really. Could they have been having a relationship?"

They chewed on their lettuce leaves and thought about it.

"Why not," Annika said. "Helena Starke said she knew Christina best of all."

"Doesn't mean they slept together."

"True," Annika said. "But it *could* mean that."

One of the busboys approached their table.

"Excuse me, but is either of you Annika Bengtzon?"

"I am," Annika said.

"They want you in the newsroom. They're saying the Bomber has struck again."

They were already sitting in the editor's office when Annika returned. No one looked up as she entered, with some corn still wedged between her teeth and her bag slung over her shoulder. The men were planning a strategy to squeeze as much as possible out of the terrorist angle.

"We're lagging hopelessly behind," Spike said louder than called for. Annika still got it. She had heard fragments of what had happened on her way up from the canteen. She sat down at the far corner of the table, the chair making a clattering noise when she wedged in her legs.

"Sorry," she said, and the word hung in the air. She'd be apologizing for more than scraping her chair. She'd have to eat some. An hour before she'd sat at this very table and insisted that the Bomber was after Christina Furhage personally, that there was no connection to the Olympics at all, and then bang! Another blast, at another Olympic facility.

"Do we have anyone there?"

"Patrik Nilsson has gone over," Spike said with authority. "He should be at Sätra Hall in ten minutes."

"Sätra Hall?" Annika said in surprise. "I thought an Olympic arena had been blown up."

Spike gave her a supercilious look.

"Sätra Hall *is* an Olympic arena."

"For what? A training room for the shot-putters?"

Spike averted his gaze.

"They're holding some events there. Don't know what."

"The question is how we should proceed," Anders Schyman interspersed. "We'll have to recap what other media have been doing on the terrorist angle. Make it sound like we've been in on it all along. Who'll do that?"

"Janet Ullman has the night shift. We can call her in early," Ingvar Johansson said.

Annika felt a giddiness grip her and pull her down to the floor and up the wall. Nightmare, nightmare. How could she have been so wrong? Had the police really been lying to her all along? She had staked her entire professional reputation on the paper covering the story along her lines. Could she really stay on as a chief after this?

"We have to go around and check security at all the other facilities," Spike said. "We'll need to call in some extras, the second night team, the second evening team . . ."

The men turned their chests toward each other and their backs against Annika where she was sitting in the corner. The voices dissolved in a cacophony; she leaned back and struggled to get air. She was finished, she knew she was finished. How the hell could she stay at the paper after this?

The meeting was brief and to the point; everyone was in total agreement. They all wanted to get to work and deal with the terrorist attack. Only Annika remained in the corner. She didn't know how she could leave it without falling to pieces. She had a lump the size of a brick in her throat.

Anders Schyman went to his desk and made a call. Annika could hear his voice rising and falling. Then he came over and sat down next to her.

"Annika," he said, trying to catch her eye. "Don't worry, okay? It's all right."

She turned away and blinked away the tears.

"Everybody can be wrong," the editor continued in a low voice. "That's the oldest truth of them all. I was wrong, too. I reasoned just like you. Now we have to rethink. We just have to make the best of it, right? We need you here for that. Annika . . ."

She drew a deep breath and stared down at her lap.

"Yes, of course, you're right," she said. "But I feel like such an idiot. I was so sure I was right . . ."

"Well, maybe you are," Schyman said circumspectly. "It does seem improbable, I admit, but Christina Furhage could have a personal connection with Sätra Hall."

Annika couldn't help laughing. "Hardly," she said and smiled.

The editor put his hand on her shoulder and stood up.

"Don't let it get you down. You've been right about everything else on this."

She pulled a face and got to her feet, too.

"How did we find out about the explosion? Did Leif call it in?"

"Yes, he or Smidig in Norrköping. One of them."

Schyman sat down with a heavy sigh on the chair behind his desk.

"Will you go out there tonight?" he asked.

Annika pushed the chair in and shook her head.

"There's no point. Patrik and Janet will have to deal with it tonight. I'll get started on it tomorrow instead."

"When all this blows over, I think you should take a holiday. This weekend you must have collected more than a week off in overtime."

Annika smiled wanly. "Yes, thank you, I think I will."

"Go home and get some sleep."

The editor picked up the phone. Their talk was over. She picked up her bag and left the room.

The newsroom was on the boil, the way it always was

when something really big had happened. Everything seemed calm enough on the surface, but you could see the tension in the watchful eyes of the senior editors and in the straight backs of the sub-editors. The words flying in the air were clipped and concise, reporters and photographers were purposefully moving to the phones or toward the exits. Even the receptionists were pulled into the flow, their tone of voice deepening and the fingers dancing more resolutely over the switchboard. Annika usually enjoyed the feeling, but now she felt uncomfortable crossing the floor.

Berit came to her rescue.

"Annika! Come and listen to this!"

Berit had brought her salad with her from the canteen and was sitting in the radio room, the booth next door to the crime desk, which had access to all the Stockholm police channels and one of the national channels. One of the walls was covered with loudspeakers and their respective switches and volume controls. Berit had switched on the ones for the South Stockholm and City police districts, those dealing with the explosion at Sätra Hall.

Annika could only hear crackling noise and blips. "What?" she said. "What's happened?"

"I'm not quite sure. The police arrived there about a minute ago. They started calling to the control room for a scrambled channel."

At that moment, the babbling resumed. The Stockholm police had two secure channels that were scrambled. You could hear that someone was talking, but the words were completely unintelligible. It sounded like Donald Duck talking backwards. These scrambled channels were rarely used, and then mainly by the drugs squad. The County Police Division might sometimes use them during big operations where they suspected that

the criminals had access to police radio. A third reason
for using them was when the information was so sensitive that they wanted it kept secret.

"Can't we get a descrambler?" Annika said. "We
could miss out on big stuff this way."

The chatter died out while the blips and noise from
the other channels continued. Annika's eyes traveled
along the loudspeakers. The eight police districts in
Stockholm County used two different radio systems,
System 70 and System 80.

System 70 had channels from 70 megahertz and
upwards, and System 80 was called that because it came
into use in the 1980s. They were supposed to have transferred over to System 80 already ten years ago, but they
hadn't managed it yet.

Annika and Berit listened expectantly to the noise and
the electronic tones for a minute, and then a male voice
on Channel 2 South dispersed the electronic mist:

"This is 2110."

The call was from a police car from the southern
suburb of Skärholmen.

The response came after a second: "Yes, 2110. We read
you."

"We need an ambulance to the address in question, a
bag car, really . . ."

The noise took over for a moment. Annika and Berit
looked at each other in silence. "Bag car" was another
phrase for hearse. The "address" had to be Sätra Hall
because nothing else was happening in the south suburbs at that moment. The police often used that kind of
language when they didn't want to spell things out over
the radio. They'd say "the place" or "the address" and
suspects were often called "the subject."

The control room replied: "2110, ambulance or bag
car? Over."

Annika and Berit both leaned forward. The answer was crucial.

"Ambulance, over."

"One dead, but not quite as badly smashed up as Furhage," Annika said.

Berit nodded.

"The head is still attached to the body, but the person's dead," she commented.

For a police officer to be authorized to pronounce someone dead, the head has to be severed from the body. It was a pretty reliable indicator of someone's demise. This was obviously not the case here, even if it was evident that the victim was dead. Otherwise the police officer wouldn't have talked of a hearse, the "bag car." Annika went out to the desk.

"There's a victim," she said.

Everyone around the desk where the paper was edited during the night stopped whatever he or she was doing and looked up.

"What makes you think that?" Spike said woodenly.

"The police radio," Annika replied. "I'll call Patrik."

She turned around and went to her office. Patrik answered on the first signal, as always; he must have been holding the cellphone in his hand.

"What's it like?" Annika asked.

"Shit, the place is crawling with cop cars!" the reporter roared.

"Can you get past the cordons?" Annika said, forcing herself not to raise the level of her voice above normal.

"Not a chance in hell," Patrik bellowed. "They've cordoned off the entire complex and grounds around it."

"Any reports of casualties?"

"What?"

"Any reports of casualties?!"

"Why are you shouting? No, no casualties, there are no ambulances or hearses here."

"There's one on its way. We heard it over the radio. Stay put and report to Spike. I'm going home now."

"What?" he roared down the line.

"I'm going home now. You report to Spike!" Annika yelled back.

"Okay!"

Annika hung up and then saw Berit in the doorway, grinning.

"You don't have to tell me who you were talking to," she said.

She came home to the apartment on Hantverkargatan just after eight. She'd taken a taxi and had been seized with a severe dizziness in the backseat. The driver was angry because of something the paper had written and was going on about the responsibility of reporters and the autocratic ways of politicians. That was the problem with the company charge card. Half the drivers felt obliged to sound off as soon as they knew they had someone from the paper on board.

"Talk to one of the editors. I'm just the cleaner," Annika had said, closing her eyes and leaning her head back. The dizziness turned into a feeling of sickness as the car weaved its way through traffic on Norr Mälarstrand.

"Are you not feeling well?" Thomas asked when he appeared in the hallway with a dish towel in his hand.

She sighed heavily. "I'm just a bit dizzy," she said and pushed the hair away from her face with both hands. Her hair felt greasy—she had to wash it in the morning. "Any food left?"

"Didn't you eat at work?"

"Half a salad. A news break got in the way."

"It's on the table—fillet of pork and roast potatoes."

Thomas flipped the dish towel onto his shoulder and started walking back to the kitchen.

"Are the kids asleep?"

"An hour ago. They were wiped out. Ellen might have caught something. Was she tired this morning?"

Annika tried to remember. "Not particularly. A bit clingy, perhaps. I had to carry her to the bus."

"You know, I can't take any time off work right now," Thomas said. "If she gets ill, you'll have to stay home with her."

Annika felt anger surge up within.

"But I can't stay at home right now, surely you know that. There's been another Olympic killing tonight, didn't you hear the news?"

Thomas turned around.

"Shit! No, I only heard the afternoon *Eko*. They said nothing about a murder."

Annika entered the kitchen; it looked like a bomb site. But a plate of food was waiting for her on the table. Thomas had put potatoes, meat, gravy, sautéed mushrooms, and iceberg lettuce on her plate. Next to the plate was a beer, which a couple of hours ago would have been ice cold. She put the plate in the microwave and set it for three minutes.

"You won't be able to eat the lettuce," Thomas said.

"I've been wrong all along," Annika said. "I've made the paper suppress anything about terrorism because I've been getting the opposite information from the police. It seems I've been well and truly conned. There's been another explosion at Sätra Hall tonight."

Thomas sat down at the table, throwing the dish towel on the worktop.

"That place? It barely has stands, you couldn't have any Olympic events there."

Annika poured a glass of water and removed the towel.

"Don't put that on here. It's filthy. Every damn arena in town seems to have been taken over by the Olympics. There are about a hundred facilities associated with the Games one way or another: arenas or training facilities or warm-up tracks."

The microwave beeped. Annika took out the plate and sat down opposite her husband. She ate in silence, greedily.

"So how was your day?" she asked, opening the tepid beer.

Thomas sighed and stretched his back.

"Well, I had hoped to finish off getting ready for the advisory committee on the 27th, but I didn't manage it. The phone never stops ringing. The regional question's coming on, and I'm happy about that, but it seems some days all I do is sit in meetings and talk on the phone."

"I'll do the nursery run tomorrow. Maybe you can get some of the work out of the way," Annika said, suddenly feeling a pang of guilt. She chewed the fillet; the microwave had made it tough.

"I was going to look at one of the interim reports now. One of my guys has been working on it for months. It's probably totally unreadable. It usually is when someone spends too long working on it. Hundred percent jargon."

Annika smiled feebly. Sometimes she was over-whelmed by these feelings of guilt. Not only was she a useless boss and a terrible reporter, but she was also a bad wife and an even worse mother to boot.

"You sit down and read, honey. I'll clear up here."

He leaned across the table and gave her a kiss.

"I love you," he said. "The Christmas ham is in the oven. Take it out when it reaches 167 degrees."

Annika's eyes opened wide.

"You found the cooking thermometer!" she exclaimed. "Where was it?"

"In the bathroom, next to the family thermometer. I took Ellen's temperature when we came home, and there it was. I think Kalle put it there. Logical, really. He denies putting it there, of course."

Annika pulled Thomas close and kissed him with her mouth wide open.

"I love you, too," she said.

# HAPPINESS

Far up in the forest, beyond the barn and the bogs, lay the lake, Långtjärn. In my earliest childhood, it came to represent the edge of the world for me, presumably because the grown-ups' land ended there. I often heard it used as a symbolic terminal point, and I pictured the lake as a bottomless pit of darkness and fear.

On the day when at last I had been given permission to go there on my own, all such thoughts vanished. Långtjärn was an absolutely wonderful place. The little lake lay wedged in the virgin forest, barely a mile long and a few hundred yards wide, with glittering water and beaches covered in pine needles. It felt like the innocence of dawn; this was what the world must have looked like before the arrival of humans.

Once there must have been fish in the lake. A small, dilapidated log cabin stood next to the stream. It had been used as a fishing and hunting cabin and was surprisingly ambitious in its construction. There was only the one room, but it had an open fire on the far end, planed floorboards, and a little window facing the lake. The furnishing was sparse: two bunks fixed to the wall, two rough-hewn stools, and a small table.

Thinking back, my happiest moments in life have been spent in that little cabin. Every now and again, I've returned to the peace and tranquillity of the lake; its shimmering surface changing with the seasons. I have lit a fire in the fireplace and looked out over the surface, filled with a sense of absolute harmony. It now shows traces of the ravagings of people: The wood surrounding the road leading to the lake has been felled, but they've spared the trees lining it.

It's possible these words may be seen as provocative and, as such, be interpreted as ingratitude or nonchalance, but nothing could be further off the mark. I'm highly satisfied with the success I've had, but this should not be confused with happiness. Society's fixation with success and hedonism is the opposite of true happiness. We have all become addicts of happiness; constantly striving for more, higher and farther, will never make us satisfied with our lives.

In reality, success and prosperity are far less interesting than failure and destitution. Real success creates a feeling whose exultation borders on the erotic. But it's a banal trip to the stars. A proper failure has considerably more nuance and depth. Prosperity breeds, at best, tolerance and generosity but more often envy and indifference.

The secret of happiness in life is to be satisfied with what one has, to stop climbing and find one's inner peace.

Sadly, I've rarely done so myself. Except in the cabin by the lake.

# TUESDAY 21 DECEMBER

The smell of newly baked glazed ham was still in the air when Annika woke up—one of the few blessings of having a busted extractor fan in the kitchen. She loved the taste of newly baked ham, but really hot—just out of the oven, the juices still trickling. She took a deep breath and threw the duvet aside. Ellen moved in her sleep next to her. Annika kissed the girl's forehead and caressed her plump little legs. Today she had to see to it that she left for work in time, so she'd be able to finish everything off before she had to pick the kids up at three.

She got in the shower and emptied her bladder straight into the floor drain. The pungent smell rose with the steam and hit her straight in the face, making her instinctively turn her head away. She washed her head with dandruff shampoo and swore when she realized they were out of conditioner. Now her hair would look like wood shavings until she washed it again.

She got out of the shower, dried herself and the floor where the water had seeped out, applied a good amount of antiperspirant under her arms, and smeared her cheeks with moisturizer. The rash wasn't quite gone, so she put some cortisone cream on as a precaution. A little mascara and a daub of eye shadow and she was good to go.

Annika tiptoed into the bedroom and opened the door to the walk-in wardrobe. The squeak made Thomas turn in his sleep. He had been up reading his report until long after she'd gone to bed. The main report on the regional question, which was Thomas's responsibility, was supposed to be ready in January. His staff still hadn't produced the interim reports it would be based on, so the pressure on Thomas was mounting. She knew that he suffered from stress just as much as she did, only his deadlines were further away than hers.

She felt a bit Christmassy and put on a red stretch top, red jacket, and black trousers. She finished just in time to catch *Rapport*'s first news of the day at six thirty.

The footage from Sätra Hall wasn't very dramatic. The TV crew hadn't been allowed inside the cordons; they only had pictures of the usual blue-and-white tape flapping in the night wind. The voice-over announced that the explosion had occurred inside one of the changing rooms in the old part of the building. The fire brigade had found the remains of a man there.

There was a dispute between the police and firefighters' unions as to who should handle the remains of bodies they came across in their work. The fire department refused, saying it was not their responsibility; the police said the same. *Rapport* spent a large chunk of the program reporting on the standoff and announced they would return to the subject later on with a studio debate.

After that, a reporter walked around an empty arena somewhere in the suburbs, shouting "Hello!" There was no reply, and the reporter considered this a scandalous state of affairs.

"How is the police handling the security?" was the predictable rhetorical question. The exhausted police press officer was interviewed, saying it was impossible to watch all parts of every facility all the time.

"So how will you manage during the Games?" the reporter asked insinuatingly.

The press officer sighed, and Annika knew that the police now were faced with exactly the debate they had wanted to avoid most of all. The discussion of Olympic security would naturally grow louder the longer it took for the Bomber to be apprehended. Samaranch appeared, telling the Reuters reporter the Games were not in jeopardy.

The transmission ended with an analysis of a meeting of the Bank of Sweden, *Riksbanken*, later in the day. What would happen to the interest rate? They wouldn't change it, guessed the reporter. So it will go up or down for sure, Annika mused. She switched off the TV and went to get the morning paper from inside the front door. There was no mention of the victim's name; one reporter had been walking around shouting, "Hello!" in some other arena in some other suburb; Samaranch and the police press officer said the same things they had said on TV a second ago. None of the papers had time to get together any plans showing where the bomb had detonated; she wouldn't get that info until she reached the office and could get her hands on the evening papers.

Annika ate some strawberry yogurt and corn flakes, blow-dried her hair straight, and put on lots of warm clothes. The weather had changed during the night; it was snowing and a hard wind was blowing. Her original plan had been to catch the 55 bus to the paper, but she quickly revised it when the first squall hit her face, smearing her mascara. She quickly jumped into a taxi. The seven o'clock *Eko* started just as she landed on the back seat. Even the lofty *Eko* desk had been out "helloing" during the night; the police press officer sounded tired and strained; Samaranch was getting repetitive. She turned a deaf ear and stared out at the houses they passed along Norr Mälarstrand, one of the most high-priced addresses in Sweden. She couldn't understand why. The houses were wholly unremarkable: The short sides of the buildings faced the water and some had balconies—that was it. But the heavy traffic in the street below must make it impossible to sit outside and enjoy the view. When they arrived, she paid with a Visa card, hoping the paper would reimburse her.

During the week, Annika always grabbed a copy of the paper from the big stand in the main entrance. She would normally have time to leaf through it to the middle before the elevator landed her on the fourth floor, but not today. The paper was so full of ads that it was almost impossible to get through it at all.

Spike had just gone home, so she was happy about that. Ingvar Johansson had just come in and was absorbed in one of the morning papers, the first mug of coffee in his hand. She picked up a copy of the rival and some coffee and went into her office without saying hello.

Both of the papers had the name and a photo of the latest victim. He was a thirty-nine-year-old builder from Farsta by the name of Stefan Bjurling. Married with three children. For fifteen years he had worked for one of the hundreds of subcontractors engaged by SOCOG, the Stockholm Organizing Committee of the Olympic Games. Patrik had spoken to his employer.

"Stefan was the best supervisor you could wish for on a building site," the victim's boss said. "He had a great sense of responsibility, always finished on time, didn't stop working until everything was done. There was no messing around if you were on Stefan's team, that's for sure." He sounded like a great guy: hugely popular, wonderful sense of humor, cheerful temperament. "He was a great workmate, fun to work with, always upbeat," said another colleague.

Annika was angry, cursing whoever had killed this man and ruined the life of his family. Three small children had lost their father. She could only imagine something of how Ellen and Kalle would react if Thomas died suddenly. What would *she* do? How *do* people survive tragedies like this?

And what a shitty way to die, she thought, feeling sick when she read the preliminary police account of the killing. The explosive charge had probably been tied to the back of the victim, level with the kidneys. The man had been tied, hands and feet, to a chair before the explosion. What type of explosives had been used and how the charge had been detonated wasn't established, but the killer had probably used some kind of timer or delay mechanism.

Christ, Annika said to herself, wondering if they shouldn't have spared the readers the most graphic details.

She pictured the man sitting there with the bomb ticking on his back, struggling to get free. What do you think about right then? Do you see your life flashing past? Did this man think of his children? His wife? Or just of the ropes around his wrists? The bomber wasn't just nuts; he was a sadist to boot. She shuddered, despite the dry electric heat of the room.

She leafed past Janet Ullberg's description of yet another empty arena at midnight and skimmed through the ads. One thing was certain: There were enough toys in the world.

She went out and fetched another cup of coffee and looked into the photographers' office on her way back. Johan Henriksson was working the morning shift and was reading the morning broadsheet *Svenska Dagbladet*.

"Nasty murder, don't you think?" Annika said, sitting down in an armchair opposite him.

The photographer shook his head. "Yeah, he seems like a real head case. I never heard anything like it."

"Do you want to go and have a peek?" Annika said teasingly.

"It's too dark," Henriksson said. "You won't see a thing."

"No, not on the outside, but maybe we can get inside. They may have removed the cordons now."

"Not likely, they'll barely have swept the guy up yet."

"The builders should be coming out there now in the morning. His workmates . . ."

"We've already talked to them."

Annoyed, Annika got to her feet.

"Forget it, I'll just have to wait for a photographer who can be bothered to get off his ass . . ."

"Hey . . ." Henriksson said, "of course I'll go with you. Just trying to be practical."

Annika stopped short and tried to smile. "Okay, sorry I lost my temper. My last photographer copped a real attitude."

"Sure. Don't worry." Henriksson said and went to pick up his camera bag.

Annika finished her coffee and went over to Ingvar Johansson.

"Do you know if the morning team needs Henriksson, or can I have him? I want to try to get inside Sätra Hall."

"The morning team won't get a word in the paper unless World War Three breaks out. That's how packed the paper is," Ingvar Johansson said and closed the rival paper. "We've got sixteen extra pages for the suburban edition, every column chock-a-block with ads. *And* they've sent out a team to cover the snarl-up the snowstorm is causing. Beats me where they think they're going to publish that."

"You know where to reach us," Annika said and went to put on her coat.

They took one of the paper's cars. Annika drove. The state of the roads really was appalling; the cars on the West Circular were crawling along at thirty miles an hour.

"I'm surprised there are pile-ups. You can't go fast enough," Henriksson said.

At least it was finally growing light—always a good thing. Annika drove south along the combined E4/E20 and the traffic eased up somewhat. She could drive at forty. She turned off at the Segeltorp/Sätra exit and slowly drove down past Bredäng. On the right hand, she dimly glimpsed row upon row of yellow, brick, terraced houses, while on the left were some drab tin buildings— some kind of warehouses or small factories.

"I think you missed our turning," Henriksson said at the same time as they saw Sätra Hall flicker past in the sleet on the right-hand side.

"Shit!" Annika said. "We'll have to go all the way to Sätra and turn around."

She shuddered as she saw the gray tower blocks. The top floors were invisible through the snowfall. She had been up in one of them once, when Thomas was buying Kalle's first bicycle. Thomas believed in buying second-hand. It was cheaper and environmentally friendly. They had bought the most popular buy-and-sell magazine and pored over the ads. Once Thomas found a suitable bicycle, he became nervous that it might be stolen. He wouldn't pay until he had seen with his own eyes both the receipt and the child who had outgrown it. The family had lived in one of these houses.

"Cordoned off," Henriksson pointed out.

Annika didn't reply but turned the car around. She drove back and parked between the snowdrifts in a deserted car park on the other side of the road.

She stood looking at the building. It was built of red-wood. The sides were shaped somewhat like a standard UFO, and the slightly curved roof rose into a steep arch in the middle.

"Have you ever been here before?" she asked Henriksson.

"Never."

"Bring the cameras and let's see if we can get in," she said.

They trudged through the snow around to the back side of the facility. If Annika's calculations were right, they were at the furthest point from the main entrance.

"This looks like some kind of goods entrance," she said and tramped on toward the middle of the short end. The door was locked. They trudged on through the snow, around the corner, and along the side of the building. Halfway down were two doors that looked like balcony doors; Annika guessed they were emergency exits. The first was locked, but the second was not. There were no cordons in sight. Annika felt a giddy sensation of joy in her stomach.

"Welcome," she mumbled and pulled the door open.

"Can we walk in just like that?" Henriksson said.

"Of course, we can," Annika said. "Just put one leg in front of the other in a repeated and controlled falling movement."

"But aren't we trespassing or something?" Henriksson said worriedly.

"That remains to be seen, but I don't think so. This is a public sports facility, owned by the City of Stockholm. It's open to the public and the door was unlocked. It shouldn't be a problem."

Henriksson entered, a skeptical expression on his face. Annika shut the door behind them.

They came in at the top of the small stand of the arena. Annika looked around; inside, it was a beautiful building. Seven wooden arches supported the entire structure. The oddly shaped UFO top turned out to be a row of glass panes high up under the ceiling. A banked running track dominated the arena, and at the far end on the right were the pole vault supports and pit. On the opposite far end of the track was a row of what looked like offices.

"There are lights on over there," Henriksson said, pointing at the Secretariat at the far left end.

"Let's go," Annika said.

They followed the wall and reached what had to be the main entrance. They heard someone crying in a room next to them. Henriksson stopped.

"Christ, I don't want to do this," he said.

Annika paid no attention to him but walked over to the office where the crying was coming from. The door was open, so she knocked softly on the frame and waited for a reply. When none came, she pushed the door open and looked inside. The room looked like a building site: Electric cables were jutting out from the walls, there was a big hole in the floor, and boards and a power drill were on a workbench. A young, blonde woman sat crying on a plastic chair in the middle of the mess.

"Excuse me," Annika said. "I'm from *Kvällspressen*. Can I help you at all?"

The woman went on crying as if she hadn't heard Annika.

"Do you want me to get someone to come and help you?" Annika asked.

The woman didn't look up but continued bawling, her face hidden in her hands. Annika waited in silence in the doorway, then she turned around and was about to close the door behind her when the woman spoke.

"Can you believe someone could be so evil?"

Annika stopped short and turned around to face the woman again.

"No," she said. "It's beyond comprehension."

"I'm Beata Ekesjö. I work here," the woman said and blew her nose on a piece of toilet paper. She wiped her hands on another piece and then held out her hand to Annika who took it without batting an eyelid. Handshakes were important. She could still remember the first time she'd shaken hands with someone who was HIV-positive, a young woman who had been infected at the birth of her second child. The mother had been given blood by the Swedish health service and got the virus in the bargain. Her soft, warm handshake had been burning in Annika's hand all the way back to the paper. On another occasion, she'd been introduced to the president of a hang-around club of Hell's Angels. When Annika held out her hand, the president had stared hard at her while slowly licking his right hand from the wrist to the finger tips.

"People are so fucking stupid," he had said, holding out his saliva-sticky fist. Annika shook it without a moment's hesitation. The memory flashed before her now she was holding the crying woman's hand, feeling the remnants of tears and snot between her fingers.

"I'm Annika Bengtzon," she said.

"You've written about Christina Furhage," Beata Ekesjö said. "You wrote in *Kvällspressen* about Christina Furhage."

"That's right," Annika said.

"Christina Furhage is the most fantastic woman," Beata Ekesjö said. "That's why it's such a shame it had to happen."

"Oh, yes, absolutely," Annika said, waiting.

The woman blew her nose again and pushed her flaxen hair behind her ears. Annika noted that she was a natural blonde—no highlights with the roots showing like Anne Snapphane's. She looked around thirty, same as Annika.

"I knew Christina," Beata Ekesjö said in a low voice, looking down at the toilet roll on her lap. "I worked with

her. She was my role model in life. That's why it's such a
tragedy it had to happen."

Annika started fidgeting. This was leading nowhere.

"Do you believe in fate?" the woman suddenly asked,
looking up at Annika.

Annika noticed that Henriksson was standing right
behind her.

"No," Annika replied. "Not if you mean in the sense
of everything being predestined. I think we shape our
own fates."

"Why do you think that?" the woman said with interest, straightening up.

"The future is determined by the decisions we make.
Every day we make vital choices. Shall I cross the street
now, or wait until that car has gone past? If we make the
wrong decision, our lives might end. It's all up to us."

"So you don't believe there's someone watching over
us?" Beata said open-eyed.

"A God, you mean? I believe there's a purpose to our
existence, if that's what you mean. But whatever that is,
we're not meant to find out, because in that case we
*would* have known about it, right?"

The woman stood up and seemed to be reflecting on
this. She was short, no more than five-foot three, and
slender like a teenager.

"Why are you here in this room right now?" Annika
finally asked.

The woman sighed and stared at the wall with the
exposed cables.

"I work here," she said and blinked away some new
tears.

"Did you work with Stefan Bjurling?"

She nodded, and the tears began rolling down her
cheeks again.

"Evil, evil, evil," she mumbled while rocking from

side to side with her face in her hands. Annika picked up the toilet roll from the floor where the woman had put it and pulled off a good length.

"Here you go," she said.

The woman turned so violently that Annika took a step backwards, stepping on Henriksson's foot.

"If fate doesn't exist, then who decided that Christina and Stefan had to die?" she said, her eyes glowing.

"A human being," Annika calmly replied. "Someone killed both of them. I wouldn't be surprised if it was the same person."

"I was here when it went off," Beata said, turning away again. "I asked him to stay behind and check the changing rooms. Does that make me guilty?"

Annika didn't answer but took a closer look at the woman. She didn't seem to fit in here. What was she talking about, and what was she doing here?

"If it wasn't fate that put Stefan in the way of the bomb, then it was my fault, right?" she said.

"What makes you think it was your fault?" Annika asked. At the same moment, she heard voices behind her. A police officer in uniform came in through the main entrance followed by eight or nine builders.

"Can I take your picture?" Henriksson quickly asked.

Beata Ekesjö smoothed down her hair.

"Yes," she said. "And I want you to write about this. It's important it gets out. Write what I have said."

She stared straight at the photographer. He took a few pictures without a flash.

"Thanks for talking to us," Annika said quickly, shaking Beata's hand and then hurrying toward the police officer. He might have something, unlike poor, confused Beata.

The group of men was entering the arena when Annika caught up with them. She introduced herself and Henriksson. The cop was furious.

"How the hell did you get in here? Didn't you see the cordons?"

Annika calmly met his angry gaze. "You were sloppy last night, officer. You hadn't cordoned off the south side of the arena or the emergency exits."

"It's all the same because you're out of here," the officer said, grabbing Annika by the arm.

At the same moment, Henriksson snapped him, this time with a flash. The officer was startled and let go of Annika.

"What are you doing now?" Annika said, taking up a pen and pad from her bag. "Questioning, a forensic investigation?"

"Yes, and you're leaving this minute."

Annika sighed and gestured imploringly with her pad and pen.

"Oh, come on! We need each other. Let us have five minutes with the guys and get a picture of them inside the arena, and then we'll be happy."

The officer gritted his teeth, turned around, and pushed his way through the workers to the entrance. He was probably going off to get his colleague. Annika saw she had to work fast.

"Okay, can we get a group picture?" she said and the men hesitantly slouched over to the small stand.

"I'm sorry, maybe you think we're pushy, but we're only trying to do our job. It's obviously important that Stefan's murderer is apprehended, and hopefully we can help," Annika said while Henriksson started taking pictures.

"We'd like to express our sympathy for the loss of a workmate. It must be terrible to lose a colleague in this manner."

The men said nothing.

"Is there anything anyone would like to tell us about Stefan?" she wondered.

The photographer arranged the group so that they sat on the stand, everyone turned toward him with a full view of the arena behind them. It would make a suggestive picture.

The men hesitated. No one wanted to say anything. They were all restrained, serious, dry-eyed; they were probably in some kind of shock.

"Stefan was our boss," a man in worn overalls eventually said. "He was a good man."

The others muttered in agreement.

"What kind of work are you doing here?" Annika asked.

"We're fixing up the building, changing stuff for the Olympics: security, electricity, plumbing . . . Same at all the Games sites."

"Stefan was your most senior boss?"

The men in the group started muttering again.

"Not really, he was our immediate boss," the man in the overalls said. "It's she, the blonde, who's the project manager."

Annika raised her eyebrows. "Beata Ekesjö?" she said in surprise. "Is she the boss here?"

A few of the men gave a little laugh and glanced furtively at each other in mutual understanding: Yes, Beata was the boss. The sniggering was cheerless and sounded like snorting.

Poor cow, Annika thought. She can't be having an easy time with these guys.

For want of anything else to say, Annika then went on to ask if they'd known Christina Furhage. Now all the men were nodding appreciatively.

"Now, there was a woman and a half," said the man in overalls. "The way I see it, no one could have pulled this off except her."

"Why do you think so?" Annika asked.

"She went around all the building sites and talked to the workers. No one could understand how she found the time to do it, but she insisted on meeting everyone and finding out how everything worked."

The man fell silent. Annika tapped pensively with her pen against the pad.

"Will you go on working today?"

"We're talking to the police, but then I guess we'll go home. And we're holding a minute's silence for Stefan," said the man in overalls.

The police officer returned together with two colleagues. They looked pretty uptight and were heading straight for the little group.

"Thanks a lot," Annika said in a hushed voice and picked up Henriksson's bag that was next to her. Then she abruptly turned on her heel and started walking along the side of the building toward the open emergency exit. She heard the photographer jogging behind her.

"Hey, you!" the policeman called out.

"Thanks a million, we won't bother you any more now," Annika called back, waving her hand but not slowing down.

She held the door open for Henriksson and then let go of it with a bang.

The photographer was silent while Annika drove back to the paper. It was still snowing, but they had full daylight now. The traffic was even heavier, Christmas shoppers having added to the usual flow. There were only three days left now.

"Where are you spending Christmas?" Annika said to break the silence.

"Are you going to use any of that stuff?" was Henriksson's reply.

Annika looked at him in surprise. "Why?"

"Can you really use it when you just marched in like that?"

Annika gave a sigh. "I'll talk to Schyman and explain what happened. I think we'll run a picture of the guys and let them say something about their minute's silence for Stefan Bjurling. It won't be much more than a caption. In the story next to it, I can quote what the police have said and that the questioning of the builders continues, as does the forensic investigation, blah, blah, blah—you know."

"What about the woman?"

Annika chewed on her lip. "I'm not using her. She was too unbalanced. She didn't have anything useful. I thought she wasn't all there. All that crap about fate."

"I didn't hear all of it," Henriksson said. "Did she talk about evil and guilt all the time?"

Annika scratched her nose.

"More or less . . . That's why I won't use her. She *was* in the building when the bomb went off, but she had nothing to say about that. You heard her. I don't want to expose her, even though she wanted it. I don't think she's capable of judging what's best for her."

"But you said it isn't up to us to decide who can cope with being written about in the paper," Henriksson retorted.

"True, but it *is* up to us to judge whether a person is sound enough of mind to understand who we are and what we are saying. That woman was just too unhinged. She's not going in the paper. But I can say something about the project manager being in the building when the explosion took place and that she is completely devastated by Stefan's death and blames herself for it. But I don't think the paper should publish her name and picture."

They drove in silence the rest of the way. Annika

dropped Henriksson outside the main entrance before parking the car in the multistorey car park.

Bertil Milander sat in front of the TV in his magnificent Art-Nouveau library, feeling his heart thumping in his chest. There was a murmur and trickle in his veins; his breath filled the room. He could feel he was falling asleep. The sound on the TV had been turned down to a soft whisper and reached him intermittently above the clamor of his body. Right now there were some women talking and laughing on TV, but he couldn't hear what they were saying. Some signs appeared at regular intervals on the screen, showing flags and telephone numbers next to different currencies. He didn't understand what it was all about. The sedatives were blurring everything. Now and then he gave a little sob.

"Christina," he muttered and cried some more.

He must have nodded off, but suddenly he was wide awake. He recognized the smell and knew it meant danger. The warning signal had been so deeply ingrained in him that it reached him even through his drug-induced sleep. He struggled to get up from the leather couch. His blood pressure was low, which made him slightly dizzy. He got to his feet and held on to the back of the couch and tried to locate the smell. It came from the drawing room. He walked carefully, holding on to the bookcases until he could feel his blood pressure catching up.

His daughter was crouching in front of the tiled stove, feeding it with a rectangular piece of stiff paper.

"What are you doing?" Bertil Milander asked, confused.

The old stove didn't draw well and some of the smoke was puffing into the room.

"I'm clearing up," said his daughter Lena.

The man went up to the young woman and sat down next to her on the floor.

"Are you making a fire?" he asked warily.

His daughter looked at him. "I'm using the stove. Not on the parquet floor this time."

"Why?" he said.

Lena Milander stared into the flames, which quickly died out. She took another page and fed the fire with it. The flames engulfed it and embraced it. For a few seconds it lay flat in the fire, then it quickly rolled up and disappeared. Christina Furhage's smiling eyes dissolved forever.

"Don't you want any memories of Mom?" Bertil asked.

"I'll always remember her," Lena replied.

She tore another three pages from the photo album and tossed them into the fire.

Eva-Britt Qvist looked up when Annika walked past on the way to her room. Annika gave her a friendly greeting, but Eva-Britt immediately cut her off.

"You're back from the press conference already?" she said triumphantly.

Annika realized that Qvist wanted her to say "which press conference?" and then the secretary would have a chance to make it known that she was the one who had to take care of *everything* on the crime desk.

"I didn't go," she said, smiling even wider, and then walked into her room and shut the door. There, now you can sit there and wonder where I've been, she thought.

She phoned up Berit's cellphone. The signal went through, but then the voice mail took the call. Berit always had her phone at the bottom of her bag and never managed to find it in time. Annika waited thirty seconds and tried again. This time Berit answered straight away.

"I'm at a press conference at police headquarters," the reporter said. "You were out on a job. I came here with Ulf Olsson."

Thank you, darling! Annika thought.

"What's going on?"

"Some good stuff. I'll be back soon."

They switched off. Annika leaned back in her chair and put her feet on the desk. She found a half-melted chocolate bar in the pencil tray of the top drawer and broke it into smaller pieces. The chocolate was partly crystallized but edible.

She couldn't help thinking, even though she probably wouldn't dare say it out loud in the newsroom: The link between the two murders and the Olympics was extremely weak. Perhaps they were two personally motivated murders of two individuals. Sätra Hall was as far from an Olympic arena as you could get. But there had to be a lot of common denominators for Christina Furhage and Stefan Bjurling. The link could of course be the Olympic Games but not necessarily. Somewhere in their past there was something that tied them to the same person who became their killer. Annika was sure of that. Money, love, sex, power, envy, injustice, family, friends, neighbors, schools, childcare, transport—their lives could have intersected a thousand different ways. Already at the building site this morning there were at least ten people who had met both Stefan Bjurling and Christina Furhage. The victims didn't even have to know each other.

She called her contact.

He gave a deep sigh. "I thought you and I had finished talking to each other."

"Right, and see where that landed you. You enjoying this security debate? 'Hello! Hello, is anybody there?' " she said, imitating the reporter on radio that morning.

He sighed again and Annika waited.

"I can't talk to you anymore."

"Okay, fine," Annika swiftly replied. "I know you're busy. I'm sure you're all frantically searching for links between Stefan Bjurling and Christina Furhage. Perhaps you've found the right one. How many people had access to the security codes *and* knew Stefan?"

"What we're trying to do is answer the questions about security."

"I don't think so," Annika said. "You're quite happy the focus has been moved from the investigation to an irrelevant debate about arena security."

"Bullshit," her contact said. "At the end of the day, security is always the first responsibility of the police."

"I'm not talking of the entire police force, I'm talking about you and your friends who are trying to solve these murders. It's all down to you, isn't it? If you succeed, the whole debate is finished."

"If?"

"When. That's why I think you ought to start talking to me again. The only way to get anywhere is through communication. We've got to keep talking."

"Is that what you were doing in Sätra Hall this morning—communicating?"

Shit, he'd heard about that.

"Among other things," Annika said.

"I've got to go," he said.

Annika drew a breath and then said: "Christina Furhage had another child, a son."

"I know. Bye!"

He was still pissed. Annika hung up. Berit stepped through the door.

"Awful weather," she said, shaking snowflakes out of her hair.

"Have they caught anyone?" Annika asked facetiously and offered Berit some chocolate. She looked at it with alarm and declined.

"No, but they think it's the same person. They maintain there's no threat to the Games."

"What makes them think that?"

Berit picked up her pad and started leafing through it.

"They say there have been no threats to any people associated with the Games. No threats against any Olympic building. The threats that have been made have all been personal and had no connection to arenas or Olympic events."

"They're talking about the threat to Furhage. Had Stefan Bjurling received any threats?"

"I'm hoping to find out this afternoon—I'm meeting his wife."

Annika raised an eyebrow. "Really? Was she okay with that?"

"Yes, she had no objections to seeing me. We'll see what that leads to. She may be too shaky to say anything we could put in the paper."

"Still, it's great. Anything else?"

Berit turned over the pages.

"Yes, they'll soon have a preliminary analysis of the explosives from the first murder. They were hoping to issue a press release by noon. They thought it'd be ready for the press conference, but it was held up by something in London."

"Why was the stuff sent to London in the first place?" Annika asked.

Berit smiled. "The equipment at the lab in Linköping was out of order, as simple as that."

"Did they say why they're still ignoring the terrorist angle?"

"Didn't say."

"You know what," Annika said. "I think they're close to solving the murders."

"But you don't know who they're looking at?"

"No," said Annika.

Berit got up. "Well, I'm hungry. What about you?"

They went to the cafeteria, where Berit had lasagne

and Annika chicken salad. As their food arrived, Patrik came in. His hair was in disarray and he looked like he'd slept in the clothes he was wearing.

"Good morning," Annika said. "Great job last night. How did you get all those quotes from Bjurling's work-mates?"

The young man grinned, embarrassed, and said: "I just called them at home and woke them up."

Annika smiled.

They talked about Christmas neurosis, buying presents, and the stress of the season. Berit had bought all her presents before the beginning of December; neither Patrik nor Annika had even started.

"I was hoping to get some shopping done today," Annika said.

"I'll buy chocolates for my mother on the plane," Patrik said.

He was spending Christmas with his parents in Småland, in southern Sweden. Berit's two grown-up children were visiting her. She had a daughter in the U.S.A. and a son in Malmö.

"We've worked our butts off these past few days. Why don't we organize it so that we can all have some time off the next few days?" Annika suggested.

"Cool. I'd love to have Thursday off," Patrik said. "I could catch an earlier flight."

"I'd like to get some cleaning done tomorrow; Yvonne and her family are arriving on Thursday."

"Perfect!" said Annika. "I'll leave early today and early-ish on Thursday."

They moved to Annika's office to run over what had to be done. Patrik went off to get a copy of the rival.

Annika and Berit took their usual places, Berit on the couch, Annika with her feet on the desk. A second later Patrik came rushing in like a hurricane.

"They got the test back. They know what blew up Furhage!"

He waved the police press release in the air.

"Okay," said Berit. "What does it say?"

Patrik read in silence for a couple of seconds. "It was dynamite," he said, disappointedly.

"What kind of dynamite?" Annika asked and reached for the press release. Patrik pulled it away.

"Hang on, hang on. This is what it says: "The analysis of the explosives used at the detonation at Victoria Stadium, Stockholm, at 3:17 on blah-blah . . . when the MD for SOCOG, Christina Furhage, was killed, has now been completed. The substance used was a gelatinous explosive mixture containing nitroglycerine, as well as nitroglycol. It is marketed under the trade name Minex and is available in a number of weights and forms. The charge in question is estimated to have been approximately fifty pounds made up of fifteen plastic-wrapped cartridges, 50 x 550 millimeters in size . . . ' "

"Fifty pounds, that's a lot of explosives," said Annika.

"Especially when it's above ground," Berit said. "I'm not surprised the blast was felt all the way to South Island."

Patrik continued, demanding attention: " 'The batch in question was manufactured in Poland, sometime in the past three years. It is characterized by its high power, high density, and high V of D, velocity of detonation. It's soft in consistency and has a relatively mild smell. The substance is characterized by its low sensitivity . . . ' What the hell does that mean?"

"Something to do with safety," Berit said. "It's a safe explosive."

"How do you know that?" Annika was impressed.

Berit shrugged. "I'm good at crosswords, too."

" 'It has a high energy level, the volume of detonation

gas being slightly above average, the power is 115 percent of ANFO and the density approximately 1.45 grams per cubic centimeter. The velocity of detonation is 5,500–6,000 m/s.' "

"Okay, what does *that* mean?" Annika wondered.

"Take it easy. Just technical stuff. I'm coming to the important part. 'Minex is one of the most widely used dynamite brands in Sweden. The general agent in Nora has sold it to more than a hundred building projects in the last three years. Including some Olympic sites. It has not been possible to ascertain to this point which lot the charge in question originated from.' "

"So it was common building dynamite," Berit said.

"What do you *build* with dynamite?" Annika asked.

"They use it for all kinds of things. You blast to prepare for roads; in mines, in opencast mining, you make gravel out of rock with the help of dynamite, you make the ground level for building . . . We hired a blaster when we installed a new septic tank at our country cottage. It's done every day."

"I guess so," Annika remembered. "They were blasting away like crazy when they built that new housing development next to us."

"Listen, there's more here: 'The charge was initiated with the help of electric detonators. The firing switch of the device was a timer connected to a car battery.' "

Patrik put the paper down and looked at his colleagues.

"Well," he said, "we're really talking premeditation here."

They sat in silence for a while, digesting the information. Annika took her feet off the desk and shook herself.

"This is a creepy one," she said. "So, who's doing what? Berit, you've got the victim's family; Patrik, can you do the analysis and the police hunt?"

Both of the reporters nodded and Annika went on:

"I've written a column on the builders who came to their workplace and held a minute's silence for their dead colleague. That will show how much they're mourning their friend."

"What was it like out there?" Berit wanted to know.

"Well, there was a woman who just cried and cried. She was rambling on about guilt and punishment and evil—it was a bit spooky. I've left her out completely because it didn't seem right to expose her."

"I'm sure you're right," Berit said.

"Have we forgotten anything? Was there anything else?"

The reporters both shook their heads and went out to their telephones and computers. Annika filed her copy on the server, put her coat on and left. It was only half past one, but she wasn't going to sit around any longer.

The snow was still falling as Annika walked to the bus stop. Since the temperature was hovering around the freezing point, the snowflakes turned into a grayish brown slush the instant they reached the sidewalk. But the snow was managing to stick in other places, forming a fairly white cover on the grassy slope outside the Russian Embassy.

She sat down heavily on the bench by the bus stop. There was no one else there, which made her think that she'd just missed a bus. On top of that, she'd sat on something wet, a puddle or a snow patch. She sat on a glove.

They were spending Christmas in town. Thomas's parents would be with them on Christmas Eve. She had hardly any contact with her own family. Her father was dead and her mother still lived in Hälleforsnäs, the small town where Annika grew up. Her sister lived in Flen nearby and worked part time at the checkout at the Right

Price. They hardly ever saw each other. She didn't mind; they had very little in common any more, apart from the time they'd shared growing up in the dying industrial community. Though Annika sometimes wondered whether they really ever had been in the same place all that time. Their experiences of the small town were utterly different.

The bus was nearly empty. Annika took a seat at the very back and went into Hötorget in the city center. She went to the PUB department store and bought toys on her Visa card for 3,218 kronor, trying to comfort herself with the bonus points she would earn. She bought a cookbook on sauces and a shirt for Thomas and a woollen scarf for his mother. Thomas would have to buy something for his father—he usually only wanted brandy anyway. She was back in the apartment at two thirty. After a moment's hesitation, she hid the gifts at the back of the big walk-in closet. True, last year Kalle had found all the presents there, but she didn't have the energy to think of another place at the moment.

She went out in the slush again and on a sudden impulse walked over to a nearby antiques shop. They had the most amazing collection of diamanté jewelry, necklaces, and earrings, big like those on 1940s film stars. She went in and bought a classic gold-plate brooch with garnets for Anne Snapphane. The neat gentleman behind the counter wrapped it in shiny gold-colored paper and tied a glittering blue ribbon around the little parcel.

The children joyously rushed toward her when she stepped into the daycare center. Her guilty conscience stabbed her like a knife in the heart. This was what a real mother should do every day, right . . . ?

They went to the Co-op supermarket and bought marzipan, cream, treacle, chopped almonds, gingerbread

dough, and cooking chocolate. The children were twit-
tering like little birds:

"What are we making, Mommy? What will it be? Will
we get candy today, Mommy?"

Annika laughed and hugged them both while they
stood in the checkout queue.

"Yes, you'll get candy today—we're making our own,
won't that be fun?"

"I like Liquorice Cats," Kalle said.

When they arrived home, she put big aprons on the
kids. She made a conscious decision to ignore the out-
come and let them enjoy themselves. First, she melted
the chocolate in the microwave to a creamy sauce, in
which they rolled little balls of marzipan. The marzipan
balls that survived were few in number and not pretty.
Her mother-in-law would surely turn up her nose at
them, but the kids were having fun, especially Kalle. She
had planned to make toffee as well, but she realized the
kids couldn't help because the mixture was far too hot.
Instead she started the oven and set about the gingerbread dough. Ellen was blissfully happy. She rolled out
dough and cut out little figures and ate the dough
between them. In the end, she was so stuffed she couldn't
move. They made enough for a couple of baking trays,
and they were quite acceptable.

"You're so clever!" she said to the children. "Look
how well you've done, all this yummy gingerbread."

Kalle swelled with pride and had a biscuit and a glass
of milk, even though he was quite full himself.

She placed the children in front of a video while she
cleared up the kitchen. That took forty-five minutes. She
joined the children on the couch when the film was at its
scariest, the scene when Simba's father died. When the
kitchen was clean, there was still some time to spare
before *The Lion King* ended, so she took the opportunity

to call Anne Snapphane. Anne lived alone with her little daughter on the top floor of a house in Lidingö. The girl, Miranda, lived with her father every other week. They were both there when Annika called.

"I haven't had the energy to start the Christmas shit yet," Anne groaned. "How come you always manage and I don't?"

Annika could hear the music of *The Hunchback of Notre Dame*. They were watching Disney in Lidingö, too.

"I'm the one who never manages," she said. "Your house is always spotless. I get a guilty conscience just visiting you."

"All I say is Tonia from Poland," Anne said. "Are you okay otherwise?"

Annika sighed. "I'm having a hard time at work. The same bunch of people always trying to put me down."

"It's fucking awful when you first become a manager. I thought I was going to die during my first six months as a producer. My heart hurt every day. There's always some bitter and twisted little bastard out to spoil you."

Annika chewed on her lip.

"Sometimes I wonder if it's worth it. This is what I should be doing: baking with the kids and sitting with them when there's something scary on TV . . ."

"You'd go crazy within a week," Anne said.

"I know. But the kids still matter most, you can't get away from that. The woman who was murdered, Christina Furhage, she had a son who died when he was five. She never got over it. Do you really think her work and success could erase that memory? Could make up for that?"

"That's terrible," Anne said. "What did he die of?"

"Malignant melanoma, skin cancer. Pretty gruesome, eh?"

"No, Miranda, get down from there! . . . How old did you say he was?"

"Five. Just like Kalle."

"And died from malignant melanoma? Who told you that? It's not possible."

Annika was lost. "What do you mean?"

"He couldn't have died from malignant melanoma if he was only five years old. That's just impossible."

"How do you know?" Annika said in amazement.

"Annika, we talked about it, remember. I had all my moles removed. I don't have a single one left on my body. I did all that research into skin cancer at the time. Do you think that I, of all people, would be mistaken about a thing like that? Annie, please . . ."

Annika felt confusion mounting within. Could she have misunderstood what Helena Starke said to her?

"Well, refresh my memory. Why couldn't he have had malignant melanoma?" she asked.

"Because the malignant, the fatal, variety of melanoma never appears before puberty. But he may have entered puberty very early. That's called . . ."

Annika racked her brains. Anne Snapphane was sure to be right. She was a full-blooded hypochondriac; there wasn't a disease she hadn't been through. Countless times she'd had herself rushed in an ambulance to the Accident & Emergency Department at Danderyd Hospital; even more times she'd visited the city's various emergency departments, public as well as private. She knew everything about all forms of cancer, could list the differences between the symptoms of MS and familial amyloidosis. She wouldn't be mistaken. Consequently, Helena Starke was wrong, or she lied.

"Annika . . . ?"

"Listen, I've got to go. I'll talk to you later."

She hung up and felt a thrill run along her spine. This was crucial, she could feel it was. Christina Furhage's son did not die from malignant melanoma. Maybe he died under altogether different circumstances. Did he suffer from another disease, was there an accident, or was he killed? Maybe he didn't die at all. Maybe he was still alive.

She got up and restlessly paced around the kitchen, adrenaline pumping. Shit, shit, she knew she was on to something! Then she froze. Her contact! He knew Christina had a son, he'd said so just before ringing off. The police were on the case! Yes, yes, that was it!

"Mommy, *The Lion King* has ended."

They entered the kitchen in a small procession, Kalle first and Ellen one step behind. Annika resolutely pushed the thoughts of Christina Furhage to the back of her mind.

"Was it good? Are you hungry? No, no more gingerbread now. Pasta? What about a pizza?"

She called La Solo on the other side of the street and ordered one *capricciosa*, one with meat and garlic, and one calzone with pork. Thomas wouldn't like it, but that couldn't be helped. If he wanted elk casserole again today, he could've come home at two in the afternoon and started making it.

Evert Danielsson turned off the Sollentuna road and into the OK garage in Helenelund that had a good service department and a big do-it-yourself car wash. He came here once a week to pamper his car. His secretary had booked him in for three hours, starting at 7 P.M. You didn't have to book, but he didn't like to take chances because it might be difficult to get three uninterrupted hours without prebooking.

He first went into the shop and picked out the things he needed: a spray bottle of degreasing agent, car shampoo without wax, two bottles of Turtle Original Wax, and a pack of cloths. He paid at the checkout: 31.50 for the degreaser, 29.50 for the shampoo and 188 kronor for two bottles of wax. The three hours in the car wash cost 64 kronor an hour for members. All in all it came to less than 500 kronor for a full evening. Evert Danielsson smiled at the checkout girl and paid with his company card.

He went outside and drove the car into his usual spot, pulled the door to, took out his folding chair and placed his little portable stereo on the bench in the corner. He picked a CD with arias from famous operas: *Aida, The Magic Flute, Carmen* and *Madame Butterfly*.

While the Queen of the Night advanced to F sharp three octaves above middle C, he started hosing down the car. The sludge of mud, sand, and ice was running down the drain in little rivulets. He proceeded to spray degreaser all over the car. While he waited for the agent to work, he sat down on the folding chair and listened to *La Traviata*. He didn't necessarily have to listen to opera in the car wash; sometimes he'd play old R&B, like Muddy Waters, or Hank Williams. Sometimes he even ventured into contemporary music: He liked Rebecka Törnqvist and some songs by Eva Dahlgren.

He let his thoughts wander freely but soon ended up on the one subject that occupied most of his existence at the moment. His career. He had spent the day trying to put a structure to what his job could look like, prioritizing the most urgent tasks. Somewhere he felt a certain relief at Christina being gone. Whoever blew her up might actually have done the world a big favor.

When the piece ended, he changed CDs and put on some piano music by Eric Satie. The melancholy notes filled the hall as he grabbed the hose and started washing the car. He didn't much enjoy the splashing about with water; it was the final phase he looked forward to: waxing and polishing the paintwork until it sparkled and gleamed. He passed his hand over the car roof. He felt sure everything would turn out all right.

Thomas put the children to bed just after half past seven. Annika had read a story to them about a girl who goes to daycare and her mother. In the book, the mother tells the daycare nurses about her boss who no one would obey, and they all think it's hilarious.

"It's okay to bully bosses everywhere, even in children's books," Annika said.

"I guess it is," Thomas said, opening the paper on the business pages.

"I mean, look at this," Annika said and held out a glossy women's magazine. "Answer all these questions to find out what your work situation is really like. Take question fourteen: 'What's your boss like?' The alternatives are: weak, incompetent, pretentious, useless, and arrogant. What kind of attitude is that? And look here, on the next page they give you advice on how to become a boss yourself. The moral is that everyone who becomes a boss is an idiot and that everyone who isn't a boss wants to be one. That's not how it is."

"Of course not," Thomas said, turning over the page.

"But the whole of society rests on these myths!"

"You used to be quite a fault-finder with your bosses at the paper, have you forgotten?"

Annika put the magazine on her lap and gave Thomas a reproachful look.

"Oh, come on, they were the wrong people in the wrong positions."

"See . . . ?" Thomas said and continued reading his paper.

Annika sat thinking while the weatherman talked about the holiday weather. Everywhere in the country would have a white Christmas Eve, but on Christmas

Day rain would approach from the west, which could mean showers on the west coast by late Christmas Eve.

"You had a hard time in your job before you began to find your feet, didn't you?" Annika said.

Thomas put down the paper, switched off the TV with the remote, and reached out his arms to Annika.

"Come here, sugar," he said.

There was a deafening silence with the TV turned off. Annika left her armchair and went over to Thomas on the couch, leaning her back against his chest, her feet on the coffee table. Thomas put his arms around her and caressed her shoulders, blew on her neck and kissed the hollow by her collarbone. She felt a tingle down below, maybe they'd have the energy to make love tonight.

Right then, Annika's cellphone rang, the tinny tones traveling from her bag and into the TV room.

"Don't answer it," Thomas said and nibbled on Annika's ear lobe, but it was too late. Annika had already lost the mood and was sitting upright on the couch.

"I just want to see who it is," she mumbled and got up.

"You've got to change that ring," Thomas said from behind. "What is that tune it's playing now?"

Annika didn't recognize the number on the display. She decided to answer.

"Annika Bengtzon? Hello, this is Beata Ekesjö, we met this morning in Sätra Hall. You said I could call you . . ."

Annika groaned inwardly, damned business cards. "Sure," she said shortly, "what's it about?"

"Well, I was wondering what you're going to write about me in the paper tomorrow."

"Why do you ask?" Annika said and sat down on the seat in the hallway.

"I was just wondering. It's important it comes out right."

Annika sighed. "Can you be a bit more precise?" she said and looked at her watch.

"I could tell you more about myself, how I do my work and things like that. I've got a lovely house, you're welcome to come and have a look."

Annika heard Thomas switch the TV back on.

"As things stand now, I don't think that's going to happen. As I'm sure you appreciate, there's limited space in the paper. You may not be quoted at all."

There was a few seconds' silence.

"Are you saying you're not going to write about me at all?"

"Not this time."

"But . . . you talked to me! And the photographer took my picture."

"We talk to a lot of people we never write about," Annika said, trying hard to sound reasonably nice. "Thanks again for giving us your time this morning, but we won't be publishing any parts of our conversation."

This time the silence was longer at the other end of the line.

"I want you to write what I said this morning," the woman said in a low voice.

"I'm sorry," Annika said.

Beata Ekesjö exhaled. "Oh well, thanks anyway."

"Thanks. Goodbye," Annika said and switched off. She hurried back to Thomas on the couch, took the remote from his hand, and turned the TV off.

"Where were we?" she said.

"Who was it?"

"A woman I met this morning. About my age. Seems a bit loopy. She's the project manager for the building work at Sätra Hall."

"She must have a pretty tough job. At least statistically speaking," Thomas said. "Younger women in male-dominated workplaces have the hardest time of anyone."

"Is that so? Has that been statistically established?" Annika said with mock earnestness.

"Yes it has, actually, smartass!" Thomas shot back. "I read it in a report that just came in. Surveys show that it's women who take traditionally male jobs who have the hardest time in the labor market. They're bullied, threatened, and are subjected to sexual harassment more often than all other men and women. A survey at the Nautical Department at Chalmers University of Technology showed that four out of five female applicants had been harassed because of their gender," Thomas reeled off.

"How do you remember all this?" Annika was interested now.

Thomas smiled. "It's the same as you remembering the details of Berit Hamrin's stories. There are more examples, the army being one of them. Many women quit the military, despite having joined voluntarily. One of the main reasons they give is problems with male colleagues. Female managers actually have worse health, especially if they're hassled by colleagues."

"That's something we should write about," Annika said, trying to get up.

"Yes, you should. But not just now, because right now I'm going to give you a massage. Off with your sweater, that's it. And then this, take it off . . ."

Annika protested feebly as Thomas took her bra off. "The neighbors will see . . ."

Thomas got up and turned off the light. The only light in the room was coming from the swaying street lights far below. The snow was still falling, snowflakes as big as the palm of a hand. Annika reached out and pulled her husband toward her. They went about it slowly, staying on the couch, licking each other's clothes off.

"You drive me crazy," Thomas mumbled.

They moved down on the floor and started making love, infinitely slow at first, then hard and loud. Annika screamed when she came. Thomas a little less loud. Afterwards, Thomas fetched a duvet, and they moved back onto the couch, wrapping their limbs around each other. Exhausted and relaxed, they lay in the dark, listening to the evening sounds of the city. Far below a bus shrieked to a halt, the neighbor's TV was on, someone bawled and cursed down in the street.

"Christ, I'm looking forward to some time off!" Annika said.

Thomas kissed her. "You're the best," he said.

## LIES

I had my assurance from the start. The world was a stage, set
to deceive me, and the people around me were all part of the
drama. The object was to make me believe it was all for real: the
land, the forest, the fields, the farmer's tractor, the village, the
village shop, and the mailman. The world beyond the distant
Furu Hill was a blurred set piece. I was constantly listening for
false tones of voices, patiently waiting for people to give themselves away. When I left a room, I would quickly turn around
just as I reached the door to get a glimpse of the people inside as
they really were. It never worked. In the winter, I would climb
the snow heap outside the drawing room window and peer
inside. When I wasn't present, people took off their masks,
leaning their tired heads in their hands and resting. They
talked in low tones, sincerely at last—artlessly, intimately,
earnestly, and truly. When I was on my way in, they all had to
step into their uncomfortable bodies again, these frames that
didn't fit them, with their embittered faces and false tongues.

I was absolutely certain that it would all be revealed to me
on the day I turned ten. Then all the people would come to me

*in the morning with their real bodies, dressing me in white.
Their faces would be peaceful and true. I would be carried in a
procession to the barn in the thicket on the other side of the
road. And there the Director would be waiting by the entrance.
He would take me by the hand and lead me into the Kingdom
of Enlightenment.*

*He would explain everything to me.*

*Sometimes I would find my way to the old barn. I can't say
exactly how old I was, but I had short legs, the woolly drawers
itched, and my thick oilskin trousers made it difficult to walk.
Once, I got stuck in the snow, up to my waist.*

*The barn was deep in the thicket, in what remained of a
meadow. The roof had fallen in, the gray timbered walls were a
shimmering silver glimpsed between the brush. One part of the
gable end was sticking up like a signal to heaven.*

*The square entrance was on the farther short side; on my
way around the building, I would stroke the rough walls. The
hole was positioned a bit from the ground; it was difficult to get
up.*

*Inside, time stood still: dust in the air, slanting rays of light.
The double feeling of sheltering walls and open sky was intox-
icating. The floor also had begun collapsing. I had to be careful
as I moved around.*

*Down there, under the floor, lay the stage entrance. I knew
that. Somewhere below the rotten planks, Truth lay waiting.
Once I screwed up courage and crawled down to examine the
ground and find the way to the light. But all I found was hay
and dead rats.*

# WEDNESDAY 22 DECEMBER

It was Annika's turn to do the nursery run, so she could stay in bed for a while after Thomas had left. Only two days remained until Christmas Eve. She was in the home stretch. It was amazing how little was required for her to win back her courage to face life. After an hour in town, some gingerbread baking, and a good fuck, she was ready to face the vultures afresh. For once, she'd had a whole night without any kids in the bed, but now they were awake and came rushing into the bedroom. She scooped them up and romped about in bed with them for so long they were late leaving for daycare. Ellen had invented the "Meatball Game," which consisted of tickling each other's toes while screaming "meatballs, meatballs!" Kalle liked playing airplane, with Annika lying on her back and balancing him on her feet high above. The plane would crash at regular intervals amid shouts of joy. Finally, they built a house with all the pillows, the duvet, and Thomas's big pajamas. Then they quickly ate their strawberry yogurt with honey puffs and made sandwiches for lunch. They just made it in time for morning assembly. Annika didn't hang around.

It was still snowing. The dirty sludge lay in drifts along the side of the road. Ever since the City Council had been divided into smaller district councils, all ploughing had ceased. She wished she had the energy to be politically active.

She was lucky with the bus. She picked up the paper by the entrance and took the elevator upstairs. Annika greeted the postboys outside the newsroom entrance.When she saw one of them dragging in the second lot of the day's mail, she felt gratitude toward Schyman. Things *had* been easier since Eva-Britt Qvist had resumed her mail-opening job.

She picked up a copy of the rival tabloid by the newsdesk and grabbed a coffee on the way to her office. Eva-Britt was in her usual place and said a surly "hello." Everything was normal, in other words.

Berit had done a fantastic job on the wife of Stefan Bjurling. The story was the center spread with one single picture of the woman and her three children sitting on the family leather couch in the suburban terraced house. "Life Must Go On," was the headline. The woman, who was thirty-seven and called Eva, looked collected and serious. The children, who were eleven, eight, and six years old, were looking wide-eyed straight into the camera.

"Evil appears in many shapes here on earth," Eva said in the piece. "It would be foolish to think we're exempt from it here in Sweden just because we haven't had a war since 1809. Violence crops up where you least expect it."

She had been making pancakes when the police had rung the doorbell to bring her the news of her husband's death.

"You simply can't break down when you have three

kids," Eva was quoted. "Now we have to make the best of it and get on with our lives."

Annika studied the picture for a long while. A feeling of something being wrong nagged her. Wasn't this woman a bit too calm and collected? Why didn't she express any feelings of grief and despair? Oh, well, the text was good and the picture worked. It was a good piece. She pushed away her feeling of unease.

As usual, Patrik had done a solid job with the technical analysis and the police hunt. The hypothesis that the same person lay behind the two bombings was still valid, even though the explosives hadn't been exactly the same. "The blasting action was considerably smaller this time," the police press officer said. "Preliminary lab reports seem to suggest the explosive agent was either of a different kind or that a different configuration was used."

At the next meeting of the senior editors she would recommend they gave Patrik a permanent contract.

Her own piece with Johan Henriksson's photo of the builders in Sätra Hall had been given a whole page. It was okay.

She leafed on, leaving the Bomber behind and reaching the WAK section, short for Women and Knowledge. Within the office, these pages were of course never referred to as anything other than the "wank" pages. Today, the wank pages had employed the reliable trick of writing about some new American pseudo-psychological book, spicing it up with examples of some well-known Swedish women. The title of the book was *The Ideal Woman*, written by a woman with a hyphenated name and very thin nose, the kind you only get by surgically removing half of it. Apart from a small photo of the author, the story was accompanied by a five-column photo of Christina Furhage. The readers were told of a book that AT LAST gave all women a chance to become a truly IDEAL WOMAN. Next to this was a small piece outlining the main facts about Christina Furhage. Annika realized that the myth of the murdered Olympic supremo was germinating. Christina Furhage, it said, was a woman who had succeeded at everything. She had a fantastic career, a beautiful home, a happy marriage, and a gifted daughter. Furthermore, she had taken good care of herself; she was slim and fit and looked fifteen years younger than her age. Annika got a stale taste in her mouth, and it wasn't only from the cooling coffee. This was not quite right. Christina's first marriage had gone to pot, her first child had died or disappeared some way or another, her second child was a pyromaniac, and she herself was blasted to smithereens in a deserted sports stadium by someone who hated her. That was the reality. And this person also hated Stefan Bjurling, she could swear to it.

She was about to go for a second mug of coffee when the phone rang.

"Come here," a man said. "I'll tell you everything." He was crying. It was Evert Danielsson.

Annika bagged a pen and a pad and called a taxi.


Helena Starke woke up on the kitchen floor. At first she didn't know where she was. Her mouth felt like sandpaper. She was cold and her hip hurt. The skin on her face felt tight after all the tears.

She sat up laboriously, leaning her back against a cupboard and looking at the falling snow through the dirty window. She was breathing slowly and consciously, forcing air into her lungs. They also felt like sandpaper—she wasn't used to smoking. Funny, she thought, life feels completely new. My brain is empty, the sky is white, and my heart is calm. I've reached the bottom.

A sense of peace rose within her. She sat on the kitchen

floor for a long time, watching the wet snow gather on the windowpane. Memories of the past days hovered like gray ghosts at the back of her mind. She thought she must be quite hungry. As far as she could remember, she hadn't eaten for ages, only drunk a bit of water and one beer.

The conversation with the newswoman last Monday had broken down all barriers. For the first time in her life, Helena Starke had felt deep and genuine grief. The hours that had passed since then had made her realize that she actually had loved someone—for the first time in her life. The realization that she was capable of loving had slowly dawned on her during the long hours of last night, making her grief all the more profound. She had loved someone and now she was dead. Her disorientation and feelings of loss had developed into a massive self-pity, which she understood she would have to learn to accept. She was the classic widow-in-mourning, with the difference that she never would receive any support or understanding from the world around her. These expressions of sympathy were reserved for the established institution of heterosexual relationships.

She struggled to her feet. She really was stiff. She had been sitting at the kitchen table, chain-smoking one cigarette after another, lighting one on the stub of the other. In the small hours of the morning, she hadn't been able to sit upright on the chair any longer, so she had moved down on the floor. She must have dropped off finally.

She grabbed a glass from the worktop, rinsed it under the tap, filled it with water, and took a sip. She felt her stomach turn. She remembered what Christina used to say, almost hearing her voice inside her head: *You have to eat, Helena. Take care of yourself.*

She knew she'd been important to Christina, perhaps *the* most important person in the Olympic supremo's life. But she knew Christina's darker sides. She had no illusions what that might mean. People simply weren't important to Christina.

She opened the fridge and found—miracle of miracles—a small pot of yogurt only two days past its eat-by date. She took a spoon, sat down at the table, and started eating. It was vanilla, her favorite. She looked out at the sludge; it really was dreary. As the traffic rumbled on as usual in the busy street below, she wondered how she could stand it here. All at once she realized she didn't have to anymore. She was worth more than this. She had plenty of money in the bank and could go anywhere she liked in the world. She put down the spoon on the table and wiped the last of the yogurt from the pot with her finger.

It was time to move on.

Restaurant Sorbet lay on the eighth floor in the old lamp factory in Hammarby Dock. They served Swedish and Indian food. The owners of the establishment weren't fussy about opening hours. They let Evert Danielsson come in and served him coffee, although they didn't open for another fifty minutes.

Annika found the head of the Secretariat behind a trellis on the right-hand side of the room. His face was completely gray.

"What's happened?" Annika asked and sat down opposite him. She pulled off her scarf, gloves, and coat and threw them on the chair next to her with her bag.

Evert Danielsson looked down on his hands. As was his custom, he was holding on firmly to the table.

"They lied to me," he said in a strained voice.

"Who?"

He looked up.

"The board," he said.

"About what?" Annika asked.

The man gave a sob.

"The board. Hans Bjällra. They all lied. They said I would get another assignment, that I would be handling practical matters after Christina's death. But they lied to me!"

Embarrassed, Annika looked around. She didn't have time to nanny bureaucrats.

"Now tell me what's happened," she said gruffly, gaining the desired effect: The man pulled himself together.

"Hans Bjällra, the chairman of the board, promised me I'd be involved in the formulation of my new assignment, but that won't happen now. When I came into the office today, a letter was waiting for me. It had been couriered over early in the morning . . ."

He fell silent and stared down at his white knuckles.

"And . . . ?" Annika said.

"It said I should vacate my office before lunch. SOCOG doesn't intend to make use of my services anymore. Consequently, it's not necessary for me to be at the disposal of the organization. I'm free to seek employment elsewhere. My severance packet will be paid out on 27 December."

"How much?"

"Five annual salaries."

"Poor you," Annika said tartly.

"I know—it's horrible," Evert Danielsson said. "And while I sat there reading the letter, a guy from the service department came in. He didn't even knock, just stepped right in. He said he'd come for my keys."

"But you had until lunch to clear out?"

"The car keys, they took my car from me!"

He bent over the table and started crying. Annika looked at the top of his head. His hair looked a bit stiff, as if he blow-dried it and used hairspray. She noticed it was thinning at the top.

"You can always use some of your severance pay and buy yourself a car," Annika suggested. As she said it, she realized it was pointless. You can't tell someone whose pet has just died that he should get a new one.

The man blew his nose and cleared his throat. "I see no reason to remain loyal. Christina is dead. I can't harm her."

Annika picked up her pen and pad from the bag.

"What was it you wanted to tell me about?"

Evert Danielsson gave her a tired look.

"I know everything about Christina," he said. "She was never the obvious candidate to head SOCOG or even the campaign to get the Games for Stockholm. There were other people, mainly men, who were considered more suitable."

"How did you get to know Christina?"

"She started in banking; you probably knew that already. I got to know her about eleven years ago when I was head of administration at the bank where she was the deputy managing director. Christina was pretty much hated by the rank and file; she was seen as hard as nails and unfair. The first was true, but not the latter. Christina always acted consistently; she would never carpet anybody who didn't deserve it. Though she did like public executions, which meant people were scared of not making the grade. It's possible it had a positive effect on profits, but it was devastating for the working atmosphere at the bank. The union was talking about staging a vote of no confidence in her; such things are not common in the banking business, I'll tell you that. But Christina put a stop to that. The union representatives behind the move resigned and left the bank the same day. I don't know how she managed to get rid of them, but there were no more calls for a vote."

A waiter brought coffee for Annika and gave Evert Danielsson a refill. Annika thanked him. She thought she recognized his face from a commercial for a credit card. She had a good memory for faces, so she was probably right. The TV companies in the building often used extras close at hand.

"How could she keep her job if people detested her that much?" Annika asked when the coffee man had gone.

"I've wondered about that too. Christina had been at her job for almost ten years when I got there. During that time they had changed managing director more than once, but Christina's name never came up. She was unassailable where she was, but she didn't get any higher."

"Why not?" Annika wondered.

"Don't know. The glass ceiling, perhaps. The board may have been afraid of what she might do if given more power. They must have seen what stuff she was made of." Evert Danielsson put a lump of sugar in his cup and Annika waited while he stirred his coffee.

"In the end, I think Christina understood she wasn't going to get any further. When the City of Stockholm decided to apply for the Olympic Summer Games, she made sure the bank went in as one of the main sponsors. I think she had her plan all laid out already then."

"Which was . . . ?"

"Taking over the Games. She became deeply involved in the preparations. After some maneuvering, she was granted leave of absence from the bank and took over the application work as acting Olympic head. Her appointment wasn't particularly remarkable, even though she was an unknown entity in a semi-important position. The job paid poorly, much less than she got at the bank. That's why most of the business highfliers weren't interested in it. Nor was it an assignment that would propel you to the top after. Maybe you remember the initial disapproval of people and all the debates at the time? The Olympic Games weren't particularly popular with a lot of people. It was really Christina who turned public opinion around."

"Everyone says she did a fantastic job," Annika interjected.

"Oh, yes," Evert Danielsson said, pulling a wry face. "She was very skilled at lobbying and at hiding the cost of such exercises under various budgets. The swing in Swedish opinion concerning the Olympics is the most expensive PR campaign ever mounted in this country."

"I've never read anything about that," Annika said, unconvinced.

"Of course not. Christina would never have allowed facts like that to come out."

Annika made some notes and contemplated the information.

"When did you enter the picture?"

Evert Danielsson smiled. "You're wondering whether I can bear this out, and just how dirty *my* hands are? They're not clean. I stayed on at the bank when Christina transferred to the Olympic campaign and was given some of her tasks. They were mostly minor matters of an administrative nature. My job at the Secretariat came about through chance."

He leaned back in his chair, seeming more at ease.

"Once Christina had landed the Games, the situation changed dramatically. The post as MD of SOCOG became a lot more prestigious. Everyone agreed it should go to a competent person with extensive experience from the private sector."

"There were several possibles, weren't there? All men," Annika said.

"Yes, but mainly one man who at the time was director-general of one of our largest government departments."

Annika searched her memory and saw the man's pleasant face.

"Right—he pulled out for personal reasons and was appointed Governor of Stockholm County instead, is that right?"

Evert Danielsson gave a smile. "Yes, exactly. Those 'personal reasons' were a bill from a Berlin brothel, which ended up on my desk just after Stockholm was given the Games."

Annika looked up in surprise. The former head of the Secretariat was happy now.

"I don't know exactly how she did it, but Christina learned that this man had taken several colleagues to a brothel at the time of a Socialist convention in Germany. She dug out the credit card bill, which was paid for with taxpayers' money, and that was it for him."

"How? And how did you get hold of it?"

Evert Danielsson pushed aside his cup and leaned forward over the table.

"Once the Games were in the bag, Christina was supposed to return to her job at the bank. The Swedish IOC saw to it that her mail was forwarded to us again. Since I already had been dealing with some of her stuff, it seemed natural for me to take care of the bills that came in."

"Did you really have the authority to open her mail?" Annika asked in a silky voice.

The smile stiffened on the man's face.

"I'm not pretending I'm snow white," he retorted. "I forwarded the original bill to Christina without any comment, but I made sure to make a photocopy of it. The day after, the prospective MD of SOCOG announced that it wasn't his intention to accept the post. Moreover, he recommended that Christina Furhage get the job. And that's what happened."

"Where do you enter the picture?"

Evert Danielsson leaned back and sighed.

"By then I was thoroughly fed up with my job at the

bank. The management had clearly shown what they thought of me by leaving me to deal with Christina's menial tasks. There was no future for me there. So I showed Christina the copy of that bill and said I wanted a job at the Secretariat, a good job. It only took a month before I started my duties as head of the Secretariat."

Annika bowed her head and contemplated the new information. It was possible. If the director-general had visited a brothel with some other men after an international Socialist convention, it wasn't only his head on the block. The other people involved would be influential social democrats, and their careers would be at stake as well. They could have been local or national politicians, high civil servants, or union officials. Whoever they were, they would have a lot to lose from being exposed. They could be fired or prosecuted for fraud or breach of trust. The families of these men would suffer, and their marriages would be ruined. For the director-general, it would have been an easy choice between relinquishing the Olympic job or having everything blown sky-high.

"Do you still have your copy of that bill?" Annika asked.

Evert Danielsson shrugged. "Sorry. I had to give it to Christina in exchange for getting the job."

Annika contemplated the man in front of her. Perhaps he was telling the truth. The story made sense and did not give a particularly flattering picture of himself. Then she suddenly remembered seeing the director-general recently in some picture, his nice, smiling face next to Christina Furhage's.

"Isn't the director-general on the board?" she said.

Evert Danielsson nodded. "Yes, but he's the Stockholm County Governor nowadays."

Annika felt ill at ease. Evert Danielsson could be out for revenge. He could be trying to con her. For Christina, as he himself had said, it didn't matter anymore. But he could still do harm to the members of the board that had fired him. She decided to continue the conversation and see where it took them.

"How did Christina perform in the job?" she asked.

"Brilliantly, of course. She knew all the stratagems. She was well in with some of the weightiest IOC members. I don't know exactly how she did it, but she had a serious hold on several of them. Sex, money, or drugs. Maybe all of them. Christina never left a single thing to chance."

Annika took notes, trying to keep a straight face.

"Earlier you hinted that she had many enemies."

Evert Danielsson let out a short, dry laugh.

"Oh, yes," he said. "I can think of a whole series of people, starting from her time at the bank and onwards. People who'd like to see her dead and cut up to pieces. Any man who tried being macho in her presence she'd humiliate to the point of him breaking down in public. Sometimes I think she got a kick from it."

"Didn't she like men?"

"She didn't like people at all, but she preferred women. At least in bed."

Annika blinked. "What makes you think that?"

"She had a relationship with Helena Starke. I can stake my life on it."

"But you don't know for sure?"

The man looked at Annika.

"You can tell when people are sexually involved. They move into each other's personal space, they stand a bit too close, their hands touch at work. Little things, but decisive."

"But she didn't like all women?"

"Not at all. She hated coquettish women. She would pull them to pieces, scrap everything they did, and bully them into resigning. Sometimes I think she enjoyed firing people in public. One of the nastiest ones was this young woman, Beata Ekesjö. In front of a whole group of people . . ."

Annika's eyes were now wide open.

"Really. So what did Ekesjö think of Christina?"

"She hated her. Absolutely and utterly," Evert Danielsson said, and Annika felt the hair on her neck rising. Now she knew the man was lying. Only yesterday Beata Ekesjö had told her how much she admired Christina Furhage. Christina was her role model and her death had left her brokenhearted. There was no doubt about that. Evert Danielsson had shot himself in the foot. He couldn't know that Annika knew who Beata Ekesjö was.

It was half past eleven and the restaurant was beginning to fill up with lunch guests. Evert Danielsson fidgeted and looked around. People from the Secretariat would come here for lunch. He obviously wasn't keen on being seen talking to a journalist. Annika decided to go for the last, decisive questions.

"So who do you think killed Christina, and why?"

Evert Danielsson licked his lips and grabbed the table-top again.

"I don't know who could've done it. I really haven't the faintest idea. But it must have been someone who hated her. You don't blow up half a stadium unless you're seriously angry."

"Are you aware of any links between Christina Furhage and Stefan Bjurling?"

Evert Danielsson looked nonplussed.

"Who is Stefan Bjurling?"

"The second victim. He worked for one of your sub-contractors, Building&Plumbing."

"Oh, Building&Plumbing is one of our best subcon-tractors. They've had a finger in more or less every building project that SOCOG has been involved in over the past seven years. Was it one of their guys that died?"

"Don't you read the papers?" Annika wondered. "He was a foreman, thirty-nine years old. Ash-blond hair, sturdy guy . . ."

"Oh, him," Evert Danielsson said. "Yes, I know who he is, Steffe. He is . . . *was* a real nasty piece of work."

"His workmates said he was a nice guy. A cheerful man."

Evert Danielsson gave a laugh. "The things people will say about the dead!"

"Is there a connection between him and Christina Furhage?" Annika persisted.

The former head of the Secretariat pursed his lips and gave it some thought. His eyes traveled over a group of people entering the restaurant. He momentarily stiffened but then relaxed again. No one he knew.

"Yes, there is, actually. I mean, not so much of a connection. Probably more of a coincidence," he said.

Annika waited, not turning a hair.

"Christina sat next to Stefan at that big Christmas dinner last week. They sat there talking until long after people had left their tables."

"Was that at the Basque restaurant?"

"No, that was the Secretariat's Christmas dinner. This was at the big Olympic do for all the functionaries, voluntary workers, and subcontractors' employees . . . We won't be throwing a party like that again until after the Games are over."

"So Christina Furhage and Stefan Bjurling knew one another?" Annika said in surprise.

Evert Danielsson's expression suddenly darkened. He remembered that he no longer could say "we" and that he probably wouldn't be attending any more Olympic parties.

"Well, it seemed like it. They sat there talking most of the evening. But I really think I have to . . ."

"How come Stefan Bjurling was seated next to the MD?" Annika asked rapidly. "Why wasn't she sitting next to the chairman of the board or some other big shot?"

Evert Danielsson gave her an annoyed look. "They weren't there. This was a party for the foot soldiers. It was very grand, though. Christina chose the place: *Blå Hallen*, the banqueting hall at the Stockholm City Hall."

He stood up, pushing at the chair with his legs.

"What do you think they talked about?"

"I haven't got the faintest idea. Look, I really have to go now."

Annika got to her feet, too, collected her stuff, and shook hands with the ex-head of the Olympic Secretariat.

"Give me a call if there's anything you want to add," she said.

He nodded and hurried out of the restaurant.

Instead of taking a right by the exit, Annika went down one floor to Anne Snapphane's office. Anne was on Christmas leave, Annika was told. Nice for her. The receptionist called a taxi for Annika.

While the car drove toward the paper, she was sorting through the information in her head. She couldn't tell the police about this; her sources were protected by law. But she could use Evert Danielsson's statement to formulate questions, including some that involved him.

Lena heard Sigrid, the daily help, singing in the kitchen while putting yesterday's dirty dishes in the dishwasher. Sigrid was a woman of about fifty whose husband had left her when the daughters had grown up and Sigrid had grown too big. She did the cleaning, washing-up, shopping, laundry, and cooking in the Furhage-Milander household. It was a full-time job. She had been doing it for close to two years now. Mother had welcomed the recession: Before they had had problems finding people and making them stay. In recent years, people had begun thinking twice about leaving a job. To tell the truth, all the nondisclosure agreements and threats of lawsuits that Mother forced them to sign may have had a cooling effect on their willingness to be employed. But Sigrid seemed to be happy and never had she been happier than during the last few days. She seemed to like being at the center of things, of being able to move freely in the world-famous murder victim's home. She would be cursing the nondisclosure agreement now, because Sigrid probably would open her heart to the media if she had a chance. She had cried to great effect off and on, but they were the kind of tears people had shed over Princess Diana. Lena recognized them. Because Sigrid had hardly met her mother since the papers had been signed, although she had been cleaning the toilet and washing her dirty underwear for nearly two years. Maybe that gave a certain feeling of intimacy.

Sigrid had bought both the evening papers and left them on the table in the hallway. Lena took them into the library where her poor father lay sleeping on the couch with his mouth open. She sat down in her armchair and put her feet on the antique table beside it. Both the tabloids were full of the new Bomber murder, but there were a few things about her mother's death, too. She couldn't help reading the details about the explosives, which had now been analyzed. Maybe the psychologist at the hospital had been wrong in not classifying her as a pyromaniac. She knew that she liked fire and everything connected with explosions and fires. Things like fire engines, fire extinguishers, hydrants, and gas masks also got her excited. Oh, well, she'd been declared fit and wasn't going to tell the doctors their diagnosis might be wrong after all.

She leafed through one paper and continued with the other. Before the center pages, she saw a spread and she felt like she'd been hit in the stomach. Her mother was looking up at her from the paper with smiling eyes. Under the picture it said in big letters, "THE IDEAL WOMAN." Lena threw the paper down and screamed out, a howl that cut through the light stillness of the Art-Nouveau apartment. Poor Daddy woke up and looked about him in a daze, saliva hanging from the corner of his mouth. She rushed to her feet, threw the table at the door, and grabbed the bookcase nearest to her. The whole section fell over, books and wood crashing with a deafening noise to the floor, crushing the TV and the stereo.

"Lena!"

She heard her father's distressed call through the red haze of her hatred and stopped short.

"Lena, Lena, what are you doing?"

Bertil Milander opened his arms to his daughter, his look of dejection making the young woman's own desperation spill over.

"Oh Daddy!" she exclaimed and flung herself into his arms.

Sigrid quietly closed the door on father and daughter and went to get garbage bags, a broom, and the vacuum cleaner.

When Annika returned to the newsroom, she walked straight into Patrik and Eva-Britt Qvist. They were on their way to the canteen, and Annika decided to go with them. She saw that this annoyed the secretary, who no doubt had been looking forward to ragging on her to Patrik. The canteen, the Three Crowns, was always referred to as the Seven Rats after a mythical health and safety check. Now it was so full that there barely would be room for the rats.

"You wrote some really good copy last night," Annika

said to Patrik as she picked up an orange plastic tray at the self-service counter.

"Do you think? Thanks!" he said and glowed.

"You managed to make the analysis seem interesting. Even when it wasn't. You must have found someone really good to tell you about different types of dynamite."

"I found him in the yellow pages, under 'explosives.' He was amazing! Do you know what he did? He set off three test charges over the phone so I could hear the difference between different makes."

Annika laughed, Eva-Britt didn't.

Special of the day was herring salad followed by ham or boiled fish. Annika took a cheeseburger with French fries. The only available seats were over in the cafeteria, among the smokers. Consequently, they ate quickly without talking and decided to have coffee up in the office and talk through the day's work.

On the way up, they bumped into Nils Langeby. He was back after taking the time off he'd earned the past weekend. He came to attention when he saw Annika and the others.

"Well, are we going to have a meeting today or not?" he said imperiously.

"Yes, in fifteen minutes, in my office," Annika informed him.

"Just as well, because I think we're being far too lax with these meetings nowadays," Langeby said. Annika pretended not to hear but walked toward the ladies' room. She really had to bite her tongue with him. Annika thought he was being unreasonably bitter, mean, and stupid. But he was part of the desk she was head of, and she knew it was her responsibility to see to it that things ran smoothly. He was trying to provoke her into making mistakes, and she was not going to give him that satisfaction. Jerk.

Nils Langeby had already made himself comfortable on the couch in her room when she returned from the ladies' room. She was annoyed that he'd entered her office when she wasn't there but decided not to show it. He was ridiculously early for the meeting as well.

"Where are Patrik and Eva-Britt?" she asked, as if everyone turned up ten minutes early.

"That's your job. You're the boss here, not me."

She went outside and asked Patrik and Eva-Britt to come in and then walked over to the news editor Ingvar Johansson and asked him to join them. On the way back, she grabbed a cup of coffee.

"Didn't you bring one for me?" Nils Langeby said reproachfully when she entered her room.

Breathe calmly now, she thought and sat down behind her desk.

"No," she said. "I didn't know you wanted coffee. But you have time to get some if you hurry."

He didn't budge. The others came in and took their seats.

"Okay," Annika began, "four things: One. The hunt for the Bomber. The police are sure to have some leads now. We have to try and crack that one today. Anybody have a good idea?"

She left it open, letting her gaze sweep over the people in the room: Patrik cudgelling his brains, Ingvar Johansson showing a skeptical indifference, Eva-Britt Qvist and Nils Langeby just waiting for her to expose a weak spot.

"I can do some digging," Patrik said.

"What were the police saying last night?" Annika wondered. "Did you get the feeling they're looking for a link between the two victims?"

"Yes, absolutely," Patrik replied. "It could be anything, maybe the Games themselves, but something makes me think they have more. They seem focused and aren't saying a word. Perhaps they're about to arrest someone."

"We have to keep the pressure up there," Annika said. "It's not enough to monitor the police radio and rely on the tipsters; we have to try and work out if they're about to make an arrest for ourselves. A picture of the Bomber getting into a police car would be an international scoop."

"I'll see if I can ferret something out," Patrik said.

"Good, I'll make some calls, too. Two: I know of one link already. The victims knew each other. They sat next to each other at a Christmas dinner last week."

"Christ!" Patrik exclaimed. "That's hot stuff!"

Ingvar Johansson woke up. "What if there are some photos!" he exclaimed. "Incredible! Imagine the picture: the victims kissing each other under the mistletoe, and the headline, 'Now They Are Both Dead.' "

"I can look into the pictures," Annika said. "There could be other links between them. I met Evert Danielsson this morning, and when I described Stefan Bjurling, he knew who he was. 'Steffe,' he called him. Christina Furhage could have known him too, before the party."

"Why were you meeting Danielsson?" Johansson wanted to know.

"He wanted to talk," Annika said.

"About what?" Ingvar Johansson said, and Annika realized she had her back to the wall somewhat. She would have to say something, or she'd end up in the same mess as at the Six Session last Monday, and she didn't want that, especially with Nils Langeby and Eva-Britt Qvist present.

"He said he thought Christina Furhage was a lesbian," was therefore what she said. "He thought that she'd been having an affair with Helena Starke, a woman at the Secretariat, but he had no evidence. It was just a feeling, he said."

No one said anything.

"Three: Did Bjurling receive any threats? Anyone heard anything? No? Okay, I'll check it out myself. And lastly, four: What happens next? The security, the Games, will they finish building in time, are the police monitoring any terrorist organizations, etc. Are you doing that out at the newsdesk?"

Ingvar Johansson sighed. "No, there are hardly any reporters in today. They've all started their Christmas holidays."

"Nils, can you look into that?" Annika said. What was put as a question was really an instruction.

"How long are the rest of us going to have to sit and listen to this?" Nils Langeby said.

"What do you mean?" Annika said, straightening up.

"Are we just going to sit here like schoolchildren while you ram assignments down our throats? And where the hell is the analysis, the reflection, the commentary? Everything that used to distinguish *Kvällspressen?*"

For a moment Annika deliberated on what to say. Should she nail Langeby to the wall? With Langeby's expertise in self-justification, that would take at least an hour, and she felt with her whole body that she didn't have the energy for it.

"Oh, for God's sake. Why don't you take care of that," she said instead and got up. "Anything else?"

Ingvar Johansson and Patrik left first, Eva-Britt Qvist and Nils Langeby followed. But Langeby stopped in the doorway and turned round.

"I think it's a damned shame how this desk has gone to the dogs. We don't turn out anything but crap these days."

Annika went up to him and took hold of the door.

"I don't have time for this right now," she said tensely. "Just go."

"It's pathetic that a manager can't have a simple discussion about our work."

He walked away slowly, provocatively. He was goading her.

"I don't know what to do with that man," Annika said to herself. "Next time he starts whinging, I'll kick his fucking teeth in."

She closed the door to get some space to think. She looked up Building&Plumbing in the phone directory and dialed a cellphone number some way down the list. As she had guessed, it was for the general manager of the firm, a man standing somewhere at a building site.

"Yes, I was at the Christmas party," he said.

"You didn't bring a camera, by any chance?" Annika asked.

"Camera? No, I didn't. Why?"

"Did anyone else bring one? Someone who took pictures at the party?"

"What? It's over there, behind the scaffolding . . . Pictures—yes, I think so. Why do you want to know?"

"Do you know if Stefan Bjurling had a camera?"

The man went quiet, all you could hear was the droning noise of a lorry unloading. When the man returned, his voice had changed.

"Listen, lady, where did you say you're calling from?"

"I told you, *Kvällspressen*. I'm Annika Be . . ."

He switched off.

Annika put the phone down and started thinking. Who was the most likely person to have taken a picture of Stefan Bjurling together with the world-famous Games supremo? She took a few deep breaths and then dialed the number of Eva Bjurling. The woman sounded tired but composed when she answered. Annika did the usual commiseration bit, but the woman interrupted her.

"What do you want?"

"I was wondering whether you or your husband knew the MD of SOCOG, Christina Furhage? Personally," Annika said.

The woman thought about it.

"Well, not me, I know that," she said. "But Steffe was sure to have met her; he did talk about her now and then."

Annika switched on her tape recorder.

"What did he say?"

The woman sighed.

"I don't know. He would talk about her, saying she was a tough bitch and stuff like that. I don't remember . . ."

"But you didn't get the impression they knew each other well?"

"No, I wouldn't say that. What makes you think that?"

"I was just wondering. They sat next to each other at the Christmas party last week."

"Did they? Steffe didn't say anything about that. He said it was a pretty boring party."

"Did he bring a camera to the party?"

"Steffe? No way; he thought cameras were a waste of time."

Annika hesitated for a couple of seconds and then decided to ask what was actually on her mind.

"You have to forgive me for asking this, but how come you sound so calm and collected?"

The woman gave another sigh. "Of course I'm sad, but Steffe was no angel," she said. "It was hard work being married to him. I filed for divorce twice but rescinded both times. I couldn't get rid of him. He always came back, never gave up."

The scenario sounded familiar. Annika knew exactly what her follow-up question should be:

"Forgive me, but did he hit you?"

The woman hesitated for a moment.

"He was convicted of assault and battery once. The court issued a restraining order, which he constantly violated. In the end, I'd had enough and took him back," the woman said calmly.

"Did you believe he'd change?"

"He'd stopped making such promises; we were way past that stage. But he did get better after that. This last year it wasn't too bad."

"Did you ever go to a women's shelter?"

Annika put the question quite matter-of-factly; she'd uttered it hundreds of times over the years. Eva Bjurling paused but for some reason decided to answer this too.

"A couple of times, but it was so hard on the kids. They couldn't go to daycare and school like they were used to. It all got too complicated."

Annika waited in silence.

"You're wondering why I'm not brokenhearted, aren't you?" Eva Bjurling said. "Of course I am sad but mostly for the kids' sake. They loved their dad, but it'll be better for them now he's gone. He hit the bottle pretty seriously from time to time. So, there you have it . . ."

They both remained silent for a moment.

"I don't want to disturb you any longer," Annika said. "Thanks for being honest. It's important to know about these things."

Suddenly the woman remembered who she was talking to.

"Are you going to write about this? Most people I know really don't know anything about this."

"No," Annika said. "I won't write about it, but it's important for me to know; it may help me to prevent it happening again."

They ended the call there and Annika switched off the tape recorder. She sat staring into the air for a while. Wifebeating was everywhere, she'd learned that over the years. She had written many long series of articles about women and the violence they're subjected to. While she let her thoughts run freely on the subject, she had a sudden realization. There was another common denominator between the two victims: People who didn't know them very well had paid warm tribute to both of them. Both had later turned out to be real bastards, unless Evert Danielsson really was lying about Christina.

She heaved a sigh and switched on her Mac. It was best to write everything down while it was still fresh in her mind. While the computer was booting up, she picked up the pad from her bag. She couldn't make Evert Danielsson out. One minute he seemed professional and competent, the next he was crying because they'd taken his precious company car away from him. Were men of power really that sensitive and naive? Yes, probably. Men of power aren't very different from other people. If they lose their jobs or something else that matters to them, they'll have a crisis. A hard-pressed person in a crisis situation isn't rational, regardless of what his job title is.

She had almost finished writing up all her notes when the phone rang.

"You told me to phone if something you wrote was wrong," someone said.

It was the voice of a young woman. Annika couldn't place it.

"Yes, absolutely," she said, trying to sound neutral. "What can I do for you?"

"You said so when you were here last Sunday. That I could call you if there were any mistakes in the paper. Now you've really gone too far."

It was Lena Milander. Annika's eyes grew wide.

"What do you mean?"

"Surely you read your own paper. There's a huge picture of my mother there, and then you've written 'THE

IDEAL WOMAN' underneath it. What do you know about that?"

"What do you think we should write?" Annika asked.

"Nothing," Lena Milander said. "You should leave her alone. She hasn't even been buried yet."

"As far as we're aware your mother *was* an ideal woman," Annika said. "How could we know otherwise unless someone tells us?"

"Why do you have to write anything at all?"

"Your mother was a person in the public eye. She had chosen to be one. The image is of her own making; if no one tells us differently, it's the only one we've got."

Lena Milander was silent for a moment, then she said:

"Meet me at the Pelikan in South Island in half an hour. Afterwards you will promise me never to write trash like this again."

She hung up, and Annika looked with surprise at the receiver. She quickly saved the notes from her meeting with Evert Danielsson onto a disk, erased it from the hard drive, picked up her bag and coat, and left.

Anders Schyman was in his office, going over the circulation figures for the past weekend. He was happy; this was how it was supposed to look. Last Saturday, the rival tabloid had sold more copies than *Kvällspressen*, as it usually did. But Sunday there had been a break in the trend. For the first time in a year, *Kvällspressen* had won the circulation war, even though the rival had a bigger and more lavish Sunday supplement. It was the news-gathering work about the bombing of the Stockholm Olympic arena that had paid off, and the determining factor had been the first-page story. In other words, Annika's discovery that Christina Furhage had received death threats.

There was a knock. Eva-Britt Qvist was standing in the doorway.

"Come in," the editor-in-chief said, signaling her to sit down on the chair on the other side of his desk.

The crime-desk secretary smiled briefly, adjusted her skirt, and cleared her throat.

"Well, there's something I feel I have to talk to you about."

"Please, go ahead," Anders Schyman said, leaning back in his chair. He clasped his hands behind his neck and observed Eva-Britt Qvist behind half-closed eyelids. Something unpleasant was coming, he was sure of it.

"I think the atmosphere at the crime desk has deteriorated lately," the secretary said. "There's no real pleasure in the work anymore. I've been here for a long time, and I don't think I should have to accept this."

"No, you shouldn't," Anders Schyman agreed. "Can you give me an example of something that makes the situation so bad?"

The secretary fidgeted and gave it some thought.

"Right . . . Well, it felt bad to be ordered in harsh words to come in to work in the middle of baking, and this just before Christmas. There has to be some flexibility."

"Were you ordered in while you were baking?" Schyman asked.

"Yes, by Annika Bengtzon."

"Was it in connection with the Bomber?"

"Yes, she's so incredibly inflexible."

"So you don't think it's appropriate that you work overtime when everybody else is?" he said calmly. "Tragedies on this scale fortunately don't occur that often in this country."

The woman's cheeks turned a pale pink and she chose to go on the offensive:

"Annika Bengtzon can't behave herself! Do you know what she said after lunch today? Well, she said she'd kick Nils Langeby's teeth in!"

Anders Schyman found it hard to keep a straight face.

"Really," he said. "Did she say that to him?"

"No, she didn't say it *to* anyone, more to herself, but I actually heard it. I really think it was unnecessary. You shouldn't talk like that at work."

The editor leaned forward and placed his hands almost at the opposite edges of the desk.

"You're quite right, Eva-Britt, it was an unsuitable thing to say. But do you know what I find a lot worse? People who come running to their boss like children, telling tales about their colleagues."

Eva-Britt Qvist first turned white as a sheet, then red as a lobster. Anders Schyman didn't let go of the woman with his gaze. She looked down at her lap, looked up, looked down again, and then stood up and went out. She would probably spend the next fifteen minutes crying in the ladies' room.

The editor leaned back and sighed. He had thought the weekly quota of nursery squabbles had been filled, but he'd clearly been wrong.

Annika jumped out of the taxi on Blekingegatan and for a moment puzzled the rich little miss's choice of restaurant. The Pelikan was a classic beer hall with "character," good home cooking, and a very high sound level later in the evening. At this time of the day, it was still pretty quiet, as people sat talking over beer and sandwiches. Lena Milander had just arrived; she'd chosen a table by the far wall and sat facing the room, dragging hard on a rolled-up cigarette. She fit in perfectly, with her short hair, black clothes, and somber expression. She could easily be a regular. The waitress came up to take their order and said:

"The usual, Lena?" She *was* a regular.

Annika had coffee and a ham-and-cheese sandwich, Lena a beer and a meat hash. The young woman stubbed out the cigarette halfway through, looked at Annika, and gave a wry smile.

"No, I don't really smoke, but I like lighting up," she said, watching Annika closely.

"I know you're a bit of a firebug," Annika said and blew on her coffee. "That children's home in Botkyrka."

Lena's face remained blank.

"How long are you going to go on lying about my mother?"

"For as long as we don't know any better," Annika said.

Lena lit her cigarette again and blew the smoke in Annika's face. Annika didn't blink.

"So, have you bought any Christmas gifts yet?" she said, picking a tobacco flake from her tongue.

"Some. Have you bought any for Olof?"

Lena's gaze hardened while she took a deep drag on her cigarette.

"Your brother, I mean," Annika went on. "Let's start with him, shall we?"

"We have no contact with each other," Lena said and stared out through the window.

Annika felt that familiar thrill travel along her spine again—Olof was alive!

"Why don't you have any contact?" she said as dead-pan as she could manage.

"We never did. Mother didn't want it."

Annika picked up a pad and pen from her bag and the copy of the family photograph where Olof was two years old. She put it on the table in front of Lena. She looked at it for a long time.

"I've never seen this one," she said. "Where did you find it?"

"In the morning paper's archive. You can have it if you like."

Lena shook her head. "No point, I'll only set fire to it."

Annika put it back in her bag.

"What is it you want to tell me about your mother?"

Lena fingered her cigarette.

"Everyone's writing about how fantastic she was. In your paper today, she was little short of a saint. In actual fact, Mom was a tragic person. She failed in a whole lot of ways. She hid all her failures by threatening and deceiving people. I sometimes wonder whether there wasn't actually something wrong with her, she was so fucking vicious."

The young woman fell silent and looked out through the window again. It was getting dark already. The snow didn't ever seem to be ceasing.

"Could you explain that a bit?" Annika said guardedly.

"Well, take Olle, for example," Lena resumed. "I didn't even know he existed until Gran told me. I was eleven then."

Annika took notes and waited in silence.

"Grandad died when Mom was little. Gran sent her up to live with some relatives in the far north. She grew up there. The relatives weren't very fond of her, but Gran paid them. When she was twelve, she was sent to a boarding school, where she lived until she married Carl. That's the old man in the photograph. He was nearly forty years older than Mom but from a good family. That was important to Gran. She arranged the whole thing."

Lena started rolling another cigarette. She was quite clumsy about it, spilling tobacco on her untouched food.

"Mom was barely twenty when Olle was born, and dirty old Carl liked to show off his new family. But then his company went bust and the money ran out. The penniless child bride lost her charm, so the swine dumped Mom and Olle and married some loaded old bag instead."

"Dorotea Adelcrona," Annika said, and Lena nodded.

"Dorotea was the widow of some old timber magnate outside the city of Sundsvall. She was swimming in money, and Carl managed it well. The old cow died after only a year, and Carl became the richest widower in Norrland. He instituted a grand scholarship for some kind of idiotic achievement in the timber industry."

Annika nodded. "Right. It's still awarded every year."

"Anyway, Mother didn't get a cent. Socially, she was given the cold shoulder, of course. A destitute, divorced single mother wasn't exactly the flavor of the month with high society in the 1950s. She'd done some sort of book-keeping course at the boarding school, so she moved to Malmö and got a job as private secretary for some direc-tor in the scrap metal industry. She placed Olle with an old couple in Tungelsta, outside Stockholm."

Annika looked up from her notes.

"She gave him up?"

"Yep. He was five years old. I don't know if she ever saw him again."

"But why?" Annika said, somewhat shocked. The mere thought of giving up her own son made her feel sick.

"He was difficult, that's what she said. But the real reason was of course that she wanted to work and not have a kid weighing her down. She was getting a career, remember?"

"Yes, and she certainly succeeded," Annika muttered.

"I think she had a really tough time to begin with. Her first boss harassed her sexually and made her preg-nant, at least that's what she said. She went to Poland for an abortion and got really sick as a result. The doctors thought she'd never be able to have another child. She was sacked, of course, but got a new job at a bank in Skara. She kept at it, and eventually got a job at the head office in Stockholm. She climbed up the hierarchy, and somewhere along the way she met Dad. He fell madly in love with her. They married after a couple of years, and Dad started nagging her about having a child. Mom said no but stopped taking the pill to humor him. She knew she probably couldn't get pregnant again."

"But she did," Annika said.

Lena nodded.

"She was over forty. You can imagine how incredibly pissed off she was. Abortion was legal by then, but for once Dad stood his ground. He refused to agree to an abortion, threatening to leave her. She swallowed the bitter pill and had me."

The young woman made a face and drank some beer.

"Who told you all this?" Annika asked.

"My mother, of course. She never tried to hide what she thought about me. She always said she detested me. My first memory is of her pushing me away so that I fell over and hurt myself. Dad loved me but never dared be fully open with it. He was totally scared of her."

She thought this over for a while, and then continued: "I think most people were afraid of her. She terrified people. Everyone who ever came anywhere close to her had to sign an agreement of complete secrecy. They could never speak publicly about Christina without her permission."

"Is an agreement like that valid?" Annika wondered.

Lena Milander shrugged. "Didn't matter, people believed it and were frightened into shutting up."

"No wonder we haven't been able to find anything out," Annika said.

"Mom was afraid of only two people—me and Olle."

How sad, Annika thought.

"She was always worried about me setting fire to her," Lena said with a wry smile. "Ever since that day when I burned the parquet floor, she was on alert when it came to me and matches. She sent me to a treatment center for disturbed youths, but after I burned that down, I was allowed back home again. That's what happens to kids no one can cope with. When the social services can't manage any longer, the little bastards are sent back to their parents."

She lit her new, knobbly cigarette.

"Once I experimented with a homemade explosive charge in the garage. It went off early and sent the garage door flying, and I got shrapnel in my leg. Mom got it into her head that I was going to blow her up in the car, so after that she was hysterically afraid of car bombs."

She laughed without any mirth.

"How did you know how to make an explosive device?" Annika asked.

"There are plans on the Internet. It's not hard; do you want me to show you?"

"Thanks, that won't be necessary. But why was she afraid of Olof?"

"I don't know, actually, she never told me. All she said was that I should beware of Olle, that he was dangerous. He must have threatened her in some way or other."

"Have you ever met him?"

The woman shook her head, her eyes turning blank. She blew out the smoke and tapped off nonexisting ash against the edge of the plate.

"I don't know where he is," she said.

"But you think he's alive?"

Lena took a deep drag on the cigarette and looked at Annika.

"Why else should Mother have been so scared?" she said. "If Olle was dead, we wouldn't have had to have secret identities."

True, Annika thought. She hesitated for a moment but then asked an unpleasant question.

"Do you think your mother ever met anyone else that she may have fallen in love with?"

Lena shrugged. "I don't give a shit," she said. "But I

doubt it. Mom hated men. Sometimes I think she hated Dad as well."

Annika dropped the subject.

"As you see, she was hardly an 'ideal woman'," Lena said.

"No, she wasn't," Annika agreed.

"Will you ever write that again?"

"I hope we can avoid it," Annika said. "But to me it sounds as if your mother also was a victim."

"What do you mean?" Lena said, immediately wary.

"She was sent away, just like Olof."

"That was different. Gran actually couldn't take care of her, there was a war on, and Gran really loved her. Gran's great sorrow in life was that Christina couldn't grow up with her."

"Is your Gran alive?"

"No, she died last year. My mother actually went to the funeral, anything else would have looked bad, she said. But they were together on all holidays when Mom was little, and they always celebrated Mom's birthdays together."

"It sounds like you can forgive your gran but not your mother," Annika said.

"And when did you become a fucking psychologist?"

Annika held up her hands in an apologetic gesture. "Sorry."

Lena watched her warily.

"Okay," she said in the end, finishing her beer. "I'm going to stay here and get drunk. Do you want to join me, into the mist and down the river?"

Annika smiled wanly. "I'm afraid not," she said and started collecting her things. She put on her coat and scarf, hanging the bag over her shoulder. Then she stopped suddenly and said:

"Who do you think killed her?"

Lena's eyes narrowed. "All I know is, it wasn't me."

"Did she know a man named Stefan Bjurling?"

"The new victim? Haven't got a clue. I just want you to stop writing crap," Lena Milander said and demonstratively turned in the other direction.

Annika took the hint, went over to the waitress and paid for her and Lena's orders, and left the restaurant.

The woman walked inside the ultramodern entrance of *Kvällspressen*, trying to look like she belonged. She was dressed in a straight, half-length coat, alternating between navy and purple depending on the light; her hair was obscured by a brown beret. A small and elegant Chanel copy bag dangled from her left shoulder, and in her right hand she carried an oxblood red leather briefcase. She wore gloves. When the front doors slid shut behind her, she stopped for a moment, looking around. Her gaze landed on the glassed-in reception in the far left-hand corner. She adjusted the thin shoulder strap and headed over to it. Inside it sat a porter, Tore Brand, who had relieved the regular receptionist who'd gone for a cup of coffee and a smoke.

Tore Brand pushed the button that operated the opening mechanism of the glass panel when the woman reached the counter. He assumed an official look and said:

"Yes?"

The woman again adjusted the shoulder strap of her handbag and cleared her throat.

"I'm looking for one of the reporters, Annika Bengtzon is her name. She works at . . ."

"Yes, I know," Tore Brand interrupted. "She's not in."

The porter's finger was poised above the button, ready to close the panel. The woman fingered the handle of the briefcase.

"Oh, isn't she in . . . ? When will she be back?"

"You never can tell," Tore Brand said. "She's out on a job, and then you never know what could happen or how long it may take."

He leaned forward and said, in a confidential tone:

"This is a newspaper, you know."

The woman gave a nervous laugh.

"Thanks, I'm aware of that. But I would very much like to see Annika Bengtzon. I have something for her."

"Oh, what's that then?" the porter said curiously. "Is it something I can hold for her until she gets back?"

The woman took a step backwards.

"It's meant for Annika. She's the recipient. We spoke about it yesterday; it's quite important."

"If it's papers or anything like that, I can take care of it and make sure she gets them."

"Thanks, I think I'll just return later."

"You know, we get people bringing in whole cases of papers every day. Hard-done-by, insurance victims, and lunatics, but we listen to them all. Just give me the stuff and I'll deal with it."

The woman abruptly turned on her heel and hurried toward the door. Tore Brand closed the panel and realized he was dying for a smoke.

Annika elbowed her way past Christmas shoppers on Götgatan. She realized she was only a few blocks from Helena Starke's house. Instead of fighting against the torrent of people emerging from the subway station, she turned around and moved with it. She slipped and slid along Ringvägen—South Island was just as badly plowed as her own part of town. Her memory for numbers didn't let her down; she remembered the entry code for the street door. She took the elevator up, and this time Helena Starke answered the door on the first signal.

"You don't give up, do you?" she said when she opened the door.

"I'd just like to ask a few questions," Annika said benignly.

Helena Starke groaned loudly.

"What is it with you? What the hell do you want from me?"

"Please, not out here in the hallway . . ."

"I don't care, I'm leaving anyway."

She yelled out the last words so the old women in the building would hear; now they'd have something to gossip about.

Annika looked over the woman's shoulder. It did look like she was packing her things. Helena Starke sighed.

"Well, come on in, but be quick about it. I'm leaving tonight."

Annika decided to be upfront.

"I know you lied to me about the boy, Olof, but I don't care about that. I'm simply here to find out if it's true you had a relationship with Christina Furhage."

"If I did—is that any of your fucking business?" Helena Starke said calmly.

"No, except I'm trying to make sense of the whole thing. So, did you?"

Helena Starke sighed again.

"And if I were to confirm it, it would end up on the front pages all over the country tomorrow, right?"

"Of course not," Annika said. "Christina's sexual preference had nothing to do with her public functions."

"All right," Helena Starke said, almost amused. "I confirm it. Happy?"

Annika lost the thread for a moment.

"So what are you going to ask me now?" Helena Starke said acidly. "How we did it when we fucked? Did we use dildos? Did Christina shout when she came?"

Annika cast down her eyes. She felt like a fool. This really was none of her business.

"I'm sorry," she said. "I didn't mean to intrude."

"You must say that a lot. It's your job," Starke said. "Do you want anything else?"

"Did you know Stefan Bjurling?" Annika said, and looked up again.

"A real asshole," Starke said. "If anyone deserved a pack of dynamite in the kidneys it was him."

"Did Christina know him?"

"She knew who he was."

Annika closed the door, which had been open all along.

"Please, can you tell me what Christina really was like . . ."

"Christ, the papers have been packed with stories about what she was like!"

"I mean the real Christina, not the official one."

Helena Starke leaned against the doorpost of the living room, looking with interest at Annika.

"Why are you so curious?"

Annika breathed in through her nose. The place really had a stale smell.

"Every time I talk to someone who knew Christina, my picture of her changes. I think you were the only one who was really close to her."

"You're wrong there," Helena Starke said. She turned around and sat down on the couch in the small living room. Annika followed her without being invited.

"So who *did* know her?"

"No one," Helena said. "Not even she herself. Sometimes she was afraid of who she was, or rather of who she had become. Christina carried some pretty terrifying demons inside her."

Annika watched the woman's partly turned-away face. The light from the hallway fell on her neck and clean profile—Helena Starke was actually strikingly beautiful. Further away in the room, the darkness loomed; outside the traffic was thundering past.

"What demons?"

Helena Starke gave up a sigh.

"Her life was hell, from childhood onward. She was extremely intelligent, but that was never taken into account. People just messed her around in all possible ways; she dealt with it by becoming cold and unapproachable."

"What do you mean by people messing her around?"

"She did some pioneering work as a female executive in the private sector, in the banking business, in board rooms. People constantly tried to break her, but they never succeeded."

"The question is whether they didn't in the end," Annika said. "You can break inside, even if the surface is still intact."

Helena Starke didn't respond to that. She was staring unseeing into the darkness. After a while she raised her hand to her eyes, wiping something away.

"Did people know that you . . . were together?"

Helena Starke shook her head.

"No. Not a single person. I'm sure people talked, but no one ever asked us straight out. Christina was very nervous about it becoming known. She changed drivers every eight weeks to make sure they wouldn't see a connection in her coming here so often."

"Why was she so afraid? There are lots of people in the public eye who are open about their sexuality nowadays."

"It wasn't only that," Helena Starke said. "Any relationships between people at the Olympic Secretariat were prohibited. Christina herself had made that rule. If our relationship were to have become public, I wouldn't have been the only one who would have had to go. She wouldn't have been able to stay on as MD if she'd broken one of her most important rules herself."

Annika let the words sink in. Here was yet another thing Christina Furhage had been afraid of. She looked at Helena Starke's profile and saw the paradox of it all. Christina Furhage had risked everything she had ever worked for on account of this woman.

"She was here that last night, wasn't she?"

Helena Starke nodded.

"We took a taxi. Christina must have paid cash. I don't quite remember, but she usually did. I was out of it, but I remember that Christina was really mad at me. She didn't like it when I drank and smoked. We made rather rough love, and I passed out. She was gone when I woke up."

She fell silent and turned those last words over in her mind.

"Christina was dead by the time I woke up."

"Do you remember when she left here?"

The woman in the dark sighed.

"No idea, but the police said she received a call on her cellphone at 2:53. She had answered it and talked for a couple of minutes. That must have been after we'd finished having sex, because Christina never could talk on the phone while we were at it . . ."

She turned to face Annika with a wry smile.

"It must be difficult not to be able to be open about how you feel . . ." Annika said.

Helena Starke shrugged.

"When I fell in love with Christina, I knew what to expect. It wasn't easy to get her to let herself go. It took more than a year."

She gave a little laugh.

"Christina was incredibly inexperienced. It was as if she'd never enjoyed sex before, but once she discovered how much fun it was, she couldn't get enough. I've never had such a fantastic lover."

Annika felt uneasy; this was none of her business. She didn't want to picture this beautiful forty-year-old making love to an ice-cold, sixty-plus woman. She shook herself to get rid of the feeling.

"Thanks for telling me," was all she said.

Helena Starke didn't reply. Annika turned around and walked toward the door.

"By the way, where are you moving to?" she asked.

"Los Angeles," Helena Starke replied.

"Isn't that a bit sudden?"

Helena Starke looked around the doorpost and fixed her with her eyes.

"It wasn't me who blew them up," she said.

Annika returned to the newsroom just in time to catch the 16:45 *Eko*. They led with a scoop, at least by *Eko* standards: They had gotten their hands on the government bill on regional issues that would be introduced to Parliament at the end of January. The following item was more interesting. The *Eko* had gotten hold of a preliminary lab report on the explosives used in Stefan Bjurling's murder. The ingredients were probably the same as those at the Olympic arena: a high-density mixture of nitroglycerine and nitroglycol, but the dimension and size of the charge were different. According to the news program, the explosive probably consisted of paper-wrapped cartridges of the smallest size, with a diameter of somewhere between 22 and 29 millimeters. The police were not willing to comment on the information.

Patrik will have to deal with this, Annika thought, making a note on her pad.

There was nothing more on the news that affected her work, so she switched off the radio and started making some calls. The builders who had worked together with Stefan Bjurling should be home by now. She opened the paper at the page with her own story, looked at the caption below the photo of the men, and then called information. Some of the men had common names like Sven Andersson, which would be difficult to find, but five names were unusual enough to save her calling fifty people, asking if she'd found the right person. She got lucky on the fourth call.

"Yes, I had my camera with me," said the plumber Herman Ösel.

"You didn't take any pictures of Christina Furhage, by any chance?"

"I certainly did."

Annika's heart started beating faster.

"Did you take any of Stefan Bjurling?"

"Not of him alone, but I think he's in one of the pictures I took of Christina."

This isn't happening, what incredible luck, Annika thought.

"You don't know yet, do you?" she asked.

"No, I haven't developed the film yet. I'm planning to take a few snaps of the grandchildren over Christmas . . ."

"Herman, we can help you develop your film; we'll naturally give you a new roll in exchange. If there should be a photo on your roll that we might be interested in printing, would you consider selling it to us?"

The plumber didn't quite follow.

"You'd buy my film?" he said dubiously.

"No, the film is yours, you'll get it back. But we might be interested in buying the rights to one of your pictures. That's how it usually works when we buy pictures from freelance photographers, which is what you'd be in this case."

"Well, I don't know . . ."

Annika drew a soundless deep breath and decided to educate him.

"This is the scenario . . ." she began. "At *Kvällspressen* we believe it's crucial that the Bomber, who has murdered Christina Furhage and Stefan Bjurling, is apprehended and put in jail. It's important both to Christina's and Stefan's families, to their colleagues, and to the whole country—even the whole world. The Games are being jeopardized. The best way to spread information and rouse public opinion is by the mass media doing their bit, which for *Kvällspressen* means writing about the victims and the police work. We work partly in conjunction with the police and the public prosecutor, partly independently. This involves talking to the colleagues of the victims. That's why I'm asking you if we could publish a picture of Christina and Stefan together, if there is such a one on your roll of film."

Her throat was parched after the lecture, but it seemed to have the desired effect.

"Oh, well, in that case I suppose it's all right. But how do we do it? The last mail collection has been out here."

"Where do you live?" Annika asked.

"In Vallentuna, north of town."

"Herman, I'll ask one of my colleagues to drive over to your house and pick up that film."

"But there are still several shots left . . ."

"You'll get a new film from us, for free. Tomorrow morning you'll get the film back, developed and all. If we find a picture that we want to publish, we'll pay you 930 kronor, which is the going rate. In that case our picture editor will call you tomorrow to arrange the payment. Does that sound okay?"

"Nine hundred and thirty kronor? For one picture?"

"Yes, that's the going rate."

"Why the hell didn't I become a photographer? Of course you can come and pick up my film! When will you be here?"

Annika took down the address and some simple directions and then finished the call. She picked up a roll of film at the picture desk and went out to Tore Brand at the porters' desk to ask if one of the drivers could go out to Vallentuna. "No problem," said Tore.

"By the way, someone was asking for you earlier today," he said as Annika was just about to leave.

"Oh—who?"

"She didn't say. She wanted to give you something."

"What was it?"

"She didn't say that either. Said she'd come back later."

Annika smiled, groaning inwardly. They really should learn to take a message properly. Any day now it could be something important.

She walked past Patrik's desk on the way back to her office, but he was out. She'd have to call him on his cellphone to check up with him before the Six Session. As she walked past Eva-Britt Qvist's desk, the phone started ringing in her office. She ran over and answered. It was Thomas.

"When are you coming home?"

"I don't know, late, I think. Maybe around nine."

"I have to get back to work, we have a meeting at six."

Annika felt herself getting angry.

"Six o'clock? But I'm working. I have a meeting at six, too! Why didn't you call earlier?"

Thomas sounded calm, but Annika could hear the anger was building up in him, too.

"The *Eko* ran some stuff about the government's

regional bill this afternoon. It came as a complete bomb-shell at the Association of Local Authorities. Politicians from the advisory committee are on their way here now and I have to be there. You understand that, don't you?"

Annika closed her eyes and breathed. Shit, shit, she'd have to go home now.

"We agreed that I was going to work Monday and Wednesday and you Tuesday and Thursday," she said. "I've stuck to my part of the deal. My job is just as impor-tant as yours."

Thomas climbed down. Now he was appealing to her.

"Please, honey. I know, you're right. But I *have* to go back, you've got to understand that. This is a panic meet-ing; it won't take long. I've made dinner already, all you have to do is come home and eat with the kids and I'll come back straight after the meeting. We should be done by eight, there isn't really much to be said. You can go back to work when I come back."

She sighed and closed her eyes, pressing one hand against her forehead.

"Okay. I'll go right now."

She went outside to tell Ingvar Johansson about Herman Ösel's photo, but the news editor wasn't at his desk. Picture Pelle was on the phone, so she waved her hand in front of his face.

"What?" he said, putting the receiver against his shoulder, annoyed.

"Some pictures are on their way from Vallentuna of Christina Furhage and Stefan Bjurling together. Develop the film and make prints of all negs. I have to go, but I'll be back by eight. Okay?"

Picture Pelle nodded and resumed his conversation.

She didn't bother to call for a taxi but took one from the stand in the street below. She felt the stress like a lump in her stomach. It grew until she had difficulty breathing. This was certainly not what she needed right now.

Back at home, the children rushed toward her with kisses and drawings. Thomas gave her a quick kiss on his way out. He took the taxi she'd arrived in.

"Hey, listen, let me take my coat off. Calm down . . ."

Ellen and Kalle were stopped short by the irritated note in her voice. She leaned down and hugged them just a little bit too hard and walked over to the phone. She called Ingvar Johansson, but he'd gone into the Six Session. She groaned out loud. Now she wouldn't have time to tell the others what her desk had been doing all day. Oh, well, she'd have to talk to Spike later.

The food was on the table, and the kids had eaten already. She sat down and tried to eat a chicken leg, but the food just grew in her mouth until she was forced to spit it all out. She had a few mouthfuls of rice and then threw the rest away. She usually didn't manage to eat at all when she was this stressed.

"You have to eat," Kalle said reproachfully.

She placed the kids in front of the TV, closed the door to the living room, and called Patrik.

"The Tiger phoned," the reporter howled. "He's furious."

"Why?" Annika asked.

"Believe it or not, he's on his honeymoon on Tenerife—Playa de las Americas. He left last Thursday and will be coming home tomorrow. He says the cops knew very well that he was there; they'd checked all departures from Arlanda and found his name. The Spanish police picked him up and held him for questioning a whole afternoon. It made him miss a barbecue and the free pool-side drink. Sad, isn't it . . . ?"

Annika smiled wanly.

"Will you write something on that?"

"Sure."

"Did you hear the *Eko* item about the lab report on the explosives?"

"Yes, I'm sorting that out as we speak. Ulf Olsson and I are in an explosives depot, blowing shit up. Did you know the explosives look like sausages?"

Dear Patrik! He was so enthusiastic. Whatever the situation. He always found his own angle.

"Did you get anywhere with the police hunt?"

"Nope, they're not saying a word. But I think they're closing in on someone."

"We have to get some kind of confirmation. I'll try to get something out of them tonight," Annika said.

"We have to get out of here now or we'll get a headache, our blaster friend is telling us. Talk to you later."

The children's programs must have ended. The kids had started squabbling over a comic book. She went in to them and switched over to TV2 for the local news.

"Can we do a jigsaw, Mom?"

They sat down on the floor with a wooden jigsaw puzzle of twenty-five pieces depicting the storybook characters Alfons and Milla in their treehouse. They stayed there until the familiar tune of the local *ABC* news started up at ten past seven. She sent the children out to brush their teeth while she checked out what *ABC* had put together. They had been to Sätra Hall and got in the judges' room. The footage wasn't particularly dramatic, since there didn't seem to have been much blast damage to the room itself. All traces of poor Steffe had been thoroughly scrubbed away. They said nothing about an arrest being at hand. She went out into the bathroom and helped the children with their teeth while *ABC* proceeded with a report on Christmas sales.

"Put your pajamas on and then we'll read a story. And don't forget the fluoride tablets!"

She left them to bicker in their room while watching the headlines of *Rapport*. They went to town on the regional bill, nothing she needed to watch. She read a story to the children and tucked them in, but they were being difficult and did not intend to go to sleep.

"It's Christmas soon and all children have to be good, or Santa Claus won't come," she said menacingly, feeling bad for threatening her kids.

But it did the trick, and soon they were asleep. She called Thomas at work and on his cellphone, but naturally he didn't answer either. She started up the old PC in the bedroom and quickly wrote down the main points of her conversation with Helena Starke from memory. As she saved the document onto a disk, she was becoming increasingly anxious. Where the hell was Thomas?

Just after half past eight he arrived.

"Thanks, honey," he panted as he stepped inside the front door.

"Did you tell the taxi to wait?" she asked more brusquely than she intended.

"Shit! No, I forgot."

She ran down the stairs to catch the taxi, but of course it was already gone. She walked down to the square, but there were no cars at the taxi stand. She walked past the pharmacy and toward Kungsholmsgatan where there was another stand. There was one single car from some suburban company. She walked into the newsroom at five to nine. The place was deserted and quiet. Ingvar Johansson had gone home ages ago, and the night people had all gone to the canteen. She went into her room and started making calls.

"This is getting tedious," said her contact.

"Don't be difficult," she said wearily. "I've been on the go for fourteen hours, and I'm getting fed up. You have the measure of me, and you know where I stand. Come on now—truce?"

The police officer at the other end clicked his tongue a couple of times.

"You're not the only one who's been at it since seven this morning."

"You've got a fix on him, haven't you?"

"What makes you think that?"

"You usually stick to your working hours, especially when a big holiday is coming up. You've got something in the pipeline."

"Of course, we always do. This is a big case, of course we're working late."

Annika groaned out loud. "For Christ's sake . . ."

"We couldn't leak any information about being close to apprehending the Bomber. You must understand that. Then he'll get clean away."

"But you're closing in on him?"

"I didn't say that."

"But are you?"

The man didn't reply.

"How much can I write?" Annika asked cautiously.

"Not one line, it could wreck the whole thing."

"When are you moving in?"

The police officer was quiet for a couple of seconds, then said:

"As soon as we locate him."

"Locate?"

"He's disappeared."

The hair on Annika's neck rose.

"So you know who it is?"

"We think we do, yes."

"Christ," Annika whispered. "How long have you known?"

"We've had our suspicions for a couple of days, but

now we're certain enough to want to bring the person in for questioning."

"Would you let us be there?"

"At the arrest? I find that hard to imagine. We haven't a clue where the person is."

"Are there many of you out looking?"

"No, we haven't put out a wide alert yet. We want to check the places we know about first."

"When will you put out an alert?"

"Don't know."

Annika racked her brains. What could she write without using this?

"I know what you're thinking," the police officer said, "and you may as well give up wondering. Think of it as a test. I've trusted you with some information. Think very carefully before you use it."

The call was over and Annika sat in her office with a pounding heart. She might be the only reporter to know about this, and she couldn't do a thing with it.

She walked out into the newsroom to calm down and have a word with Spike. The first thing she laid her eyes on was a dummy of the next day's front page. It said: "CHRISTINA FURHAGE LESBIAN—Her Lover Talks About Their Last Hours Together."

Annika felt the whole room turn around. It can't be, she thought. Christ, where did they get this? With tunnel vision, she walked up to the easel where the layout was fastened, pulled it down, and threw it down on the desk in front of Spike.

"What the hell is this?" she demanded to know.

"Tomorrow's biggest story," the night editor said indifferently.

"We can't print this," Annika said, unable to keep her voice under control. "It has nothing to do with anything. Christina Furhage never spoke publicly about her sexuality. We have no right to expose her like this. She didn't want to talk about it when she was alive, and we have no right to do it now she's dead."

The night editor straightened up, clasped his hands behind his head, and leaned back so that his chair nearly tipped over.

"It's nothing to be ashamed of, liking girls—I do, too," he leered. He looked over his shoulder to get support from the sub-editors around the desk.

Annika forced herself to be businesslike.

"She was married and had a daughter. Could you look her family in the eye tomorrow if you print this?"

"She was a public person."

"That's got fuck all to do with it!" Annika said, unable to curb her outrage. "The woman has been murdered! And who the hell wrote the fucking story?"

The night editor laboriously got to his feet. He was riled now.

"Nisse has dug up some good stuff. He's got confirmation from a named source that she was a dyke. She had a relationship with that woman Starke . . ."

"That's my material!" Annika raved. "I mentioned it as a rumor at our lunch meeting. Who's the named source?"

The night editor went up to Annika and said, inches away from her face:

"I don't give a fuck where it came from," he hissed. "Nisse has written the best piece of tomorrow's paper. If you knew about it, why then didn't you write something? Isn't it time you dried out behind your ears?"

Annika felt the words sink in. They landed in her midriff and added to the lump in her gut, making her lungs too small. She couldn't breathe. She forced herself to ignore the attack on her person and to focus on the journalistic part of the argument. Was she right? Perhaps Christina Furhage's sexual preference really was a scoop they should publish? She pushed the thought away from her.

"Who Christina Furhage slept with is neither here nor there," she said softly. "What *is* interesting is who killed her. Another interesting aspect is what effect it will have on the Olympic Games, on sports, and on Sweden's standing in the world. It's also important to sort out why she was killed, who the killer is, and what motivated him. I don't give a shit who she fucked, unless it's got something to do with her death. And neither should you."

The night editor breathed in so forcefully through his nose that he sounded like a fan.

"Do you know what, Miss Crime Editor? You are so totally wrong. You should have made sure your feet were big enough before you stepped into those shoes. Nils Langeby is right, you obviously can't handle your job. Can't you see how pathetic you are?"

The lump of stress in her stomach exploded. She felt as if she had broken into pieces. All sounds disappeared and she saw flashes before her eyes. To her own surprise, she discovered that she was still standing up, registering things with her eyes and still breathing. She turned on her heel and walked over to her office, focusing on crossing the newsroom floor with the other reporters' eyes like darts in her back. She reached her office and closed the door. She slumped down on the floor inside the door, her entire body shaking. I'm not dying, I'm not dying, I'm not dying, she thought. It'll pass, it'll pass, it'll pass . . . She wasn't getting any air and tried desperately to breathe; the air wasn't reaching her lungs and she took another breath, yet another one, and in the end her arms started cramping. She realized she was hyperventilating and had too much oxygen in her blood; she got to her feet and staggered over to the desk, pulled out a plastic bag from the bottom drawer, and started breathing into it. She conjured up Thomas's voice: *Nice and easy, nice and easy, everything'll be all right, my friend, just breathe, you're not falling to pieces, my sweet little Annie, nice and easy, nice and easy . . .*

The shaking subsided and she sat down in the chair. She wanted to cry but swallowed it and called Anders Schyman's home number. His wife answered and Annika tried to sound normal.

"He's at the management Christmas dinner," Mrs. Schyman said.

Annika called the switchboard and asked them to put her through to the banqueting room. She could hear that she wasn't being coherent anymore, that she barely managed to make herself understood. After a long interval of murmuring and rattling, she heard the voice of Anders Schyman.

"I'm sorry . . . Forgive me for disturbing you during dinner," she said quietly.

"I'm sure you have good reason to," Anders Schyman said shortly.

People were talking and laughing in the background.

"I'm also sorry I didn't make the Six Session tonight, we had a crisis at home . . ."

She broke out crying, uncontrollably and loud.

"What's happened? Is it something with the children?" he said with alarm.

She collected herself.

"No, no, nothing like that, but I have to ask—at the meeting, did you discuss what Spike has put on tomorrow's front page, that Christina Furhage was a lesbian?"

For several seconds, Annika only heard the background chatter and laughter.

"That what?" Anders Schyman finally said.

She put her hand on her chest and forced herself to breathe calmly.

" 'Her lover tells all,' according to the headline."

"Jesus Christ! I'm coming in," the editor-in-chief said and hung up.

She put the phone down, leaned over the desk, and started to cry. The mascara dripped onto her notes, and her whole body was shaking. I can't take it anymore, I can't, I'm dying, she thought. She realized she'd fallen down on the job. Now she'd really fucked it up. The sound of her despair would escape through the door and across the newsroom floor. Everyone would see that she wasn't up to it, it had been a mistake to promote her; she was a washout. This realization didn't help. She just couldn't stop crying. The stress and exhaustion had finally taken over her whole body. She couldn't stop shaking and crying.

After a time, she felt a hand on her shoulder and heard a soothing voice somewhere above her.

"Annika, it's all right. Whatever has caused this, we can sort it out. Do you hear me, Annika?"

She held her breath and raised her head; she felt a flashing pain at the light. It was Anders Schyman.

"I'm sorry . . ." she said, trying to wipe the mascara off with her hands. "Sorry . . ."

"Here, take my handkerchief. Sit up straight and wipe your nose while I fetch a glass of water."

The editor disappeared through the door, and Annika mechanically did as she had been told. Anders Schyman returned with a plastic cup of cold water, closing the door behind him.

"Have some of this, and then tell me what's happened."

"Did you talk to Spike about the headline?"

"I'll deal with that later. It's not so important. I am worried about you. Why are you so upset?"

She started crying again, this time softly and quietly. The editor waited in silence.

"I guess it's mostly because I'm tired and worn out,"

she said when she had collected herself. "And then Spike said all those things you only hear in your worst nightmares—about me being a useless idiot who wasn't up to the job and stuff like that . . ."

She leaned back in the chair; she'd said it now. Strangely, it had made her calm down. "He has absolutely zero confidence in me as a manager, that's obvious. And he's probably not the only one."

"That's possible," Anders Schyman said, "but immaterial. What matters is that I have confidence in you, and I am absolutely convinced that you are the right person for your job."

She drew a deep breath. "I want to quit."

"You can't," he said.

"I'm resigning," she said.

"I won't accept your resignation."

"I want to go right now, tonight."

"Impossible, I'm afraid. I intend to promote you."

She stared at her boss.

"Why?" she asked in amazement.

"I wasn't going to tell you yet, but sometimes your hand is forced. I have big plans for you, Annika. I might as well tell you about them now, before you decide to leave the company for good."

She stared at Anders Schyman in disbelief.

"This paper is facing big changes," the editor began. "I don't think any of the employees can imagine just how big. We have to adapt to completely new markets, the IT world and increased competition from the free papers. We have to concentrate on our journalism. We have to have senior editors competent in all these areas. People like that don't grow on trees. We can either sit around hoping for them to appear, or we can see to it that the people we most believe in are adapted to the new conditions in advance."

Annika listened wide-eyed.

"I'll be working for ten years longer at the most, Annika, maybe only five. There'll have to be people ready to take over after me. I'm not saying it'll be you, but you are one of three people I consider who might. There's a whole pack of things you need to learn before then, and controlling your temper is one of them. But right now you're the best candidate for my job. You're creative and quick-witted. I've never seen the like, actually. You take responsibility and conflict with equal aplomb. You're structured, competent, and full of initiative. I'm not going to let some idiot night editor drive you away, I hope you realize that. You're not the one who's leaving, the idiots are."

The potential future editor blinked in astonishment.

"So I would appreciate it if you could delay handing in your resignation until the new year," Schyman went on. "There are a couple of people in the newsroom who want to harm you, and it's hard to defend yourself against that. Leave it to me. We'll talk again when this Bomber crisis has calmed down a bit. I'd like you to think about what further training might be good for you. We need to make a plan for which different posts you should cover. It's important you learn the trade at all levels of the newsroom. You also need to have a grasp of the technical and administrative side of the company. You have to win acceptance and respect everywhere, that is imperative. And you will, if we do this the right way."

Annika just sat there gaping. She couldn't believe what she was hearing.

"You've really thought this through," she said in amazement.

"This isn't an offer to become editor-in-chief; it's a call for you to get started on your training and get the experience you need to be taken into consideration when the time comes. And I don't want this to go any further, excepting your husband. What do you say?"

Annika shook herself.

"Thank you."

Anders Schyman smiled. "Why don't you go on holiday now and come back after New Year's? You must have a mountain of overtime by now."

"I was going to work tomorrow morning, and I don't want to change that just because Spike was an asshole. I hope to have my picture of Christina Furhage clear by then."

"Anything we can use?"

She mournfully shook her head.

"I really don't know. We need to talk about it; it's a tragic story."

"All the more interesting. We'll talk about it later."

Anders Schyman got up and left the room. Annika was left sitting at her desk, an enormous feeling of peace inside her. That's how easy it was to feel okay again, all it took to erase despair as black as night. Setting the record straight, and it was as if the humiliation in the newsroom had never occurred.

She put her coat on and left through the back door, grabbed a taxi from the stand, and went home.

Thomas was asleep; she washed off the remnants of her mascara, brushed her teeth, and crept into bed next to her husband. It wasn't until there, in the dark, with the ceiling floating somewhere above her in the dark, that she remembered what the police had hinted to her earlier that night:

They knew who the Bomber was, and they were about to move in on him.

# EVIL

**M**y intuition warned me of its existence and power early on. Reason, surrounding me on all sides in the form of adults, was trying to tear this certainty out of me. "That's just make-believe," they would say. "That's not how it is in real life, and anyway, it's always the forces of good that win out." I knew this was a lie because I had heard the story of Hansel and Gretel. There, evil prevailed everywhere, even though the author insisted it was all part of a grander design. Evil forced the little children out into the woods, evil fatted Hans up and heated the oven, but Gretel turned out to be the most evil of them all, for she was the one who actually committed murder.

Stories of that kind never scared me. You don't fear the entity that you're familiar with. This gave me an advantage over the world around me.

Experiences later on in life naturally showed me I had been right. In our country, we've made the fatal mistake of abolishing evil. It doesn't exist officially. Sweden is a state governed by law; understanding and logic have taken the place of evil. That made it possible for evil to move underground, and there, *in the dark, it thrived more than ever. It fed on envy and suppressed hatred, became impervious, and with time grew so dark that it became invisible. But I recognized it. Anyone who has once known its being can smell it out, wherever it lies hidden.*

*A person who has learned from Gretel knows how to deal with evil. Like cures like, that's the only way. I saw evil in the malicious faces at my workplace, in the eyes of the members of the board, in the taut smiles of my colleagues—and I would smile back. The seven-headed monster was nowhere to be seen; it hid behind union talks and in supposedly objective discussions. But I knew and played along. They couldn't fool me. I held up a mirror, and their powers were reflected.*

*But I saw it make other advances in society. I noted how the violence against several of my employees was ignored by police and prosecutors. A woman in my office reported her ex-husband some twenty times, and every time the police classified it as a "domestic incident." The social services appointed a mediator, but I knew it was futile. I could smell the stench of evil, and I knew her time was up. The woman would die because no one took evil seriously. "He didn't mean any harm; he really only wanted to see the children," I once heard the mediator say. I told my secretary to shut the door because people's inability to act vexes me.*

*In the end, the woman had her throat slit with a bread knife and those around her reacted with surprise and dismay. They looked for an explanation but overlooked the most obvious one.*

*Evil escaped yet another time.*

# THURSDAY 23 DECEMBER

The apartment was empty when Annika woke up. It was half past eight and the sun shone in through the bedroom window. She got up and found a big note on the fridge door, held up with Santa Claus magnets:

*"Thanks for being there.*

*Kisses from your husband.*

*P.S. I'll take the kids to daycare. Your turn to pick up."*

She made herself a cheese sandwich while leafing through the morning papers. They were also making a great deal of the government regional bill, and they had started their Christmas material, a historical retrospective of Christmas through the ages and stuff like that. There was nothing new on the Bomber. She had a quick shower, then microwaved a cup of water and added some instant coffee, which she drank while getting dressed. She took the bus to the old entrance and took the back stairs up to the newsroom. She didn't want to see anyone until she'd seen what had been published on Christina Furhage's sexuality.

There wasn't a single smutty line about Christina Furhage or Helena Starke in the entire paper. Annika switched on her computer and entered the so-called Historical server. You could read discarded copy there for up to twenty-four hours afterwards.

Nils Langeby had indeed written a piece titled "Christina Furhage—Lesbian." The copy had been discarded at 22:50 last night. Annika clicked to open it and skimmed through it. What she saw made her feel faint. The named source who supposedly had confirmed that Christina Furhage was a lesbian was a woman at the Olympic Secretariat whom Annika had never heard of. She said: "Well, of course we wondered. Christina always wanted to work with Helena Starke, and a lot of us found that peculiar. Everyone knew that Helena Starke is one of those . . . Some people even thought they were an item." The reporter then quoted a couple of anonymous sources saying they'd seen the two women together out on the town.

At the end was a quote from Helena Starke herself: "The last time I saw Christina was at the restaurant last Friday night. We left at the same time. We each went home to our respective houses."

That was it. No wonder Schyman had pulled the story.

Annika read on and was hit by an unpleasant thought: How the hell did Nils Langeby get hold of Helena Starke's unlisted phone number, if indeed he had talked to her?

She looked in the newsroom electronic contacts book and saw that she had made a mistake when inputting the woman's number. She had put it in the common book, instead of in her private one. Without a moment's hesitation, she lifted the receiver and dialed Helena's number to apologize. She got the phone company's automated response: "The number has been disconnected. The customer has not registered a forwarding number." Helena Starke must have left the country.

Annika sighed and went through what had been printed. They had chosen to lead with something completely different from the Bomber story: a celebrity telling all about his incurable condition. One of the anchors on the public service television sports desk suffered from gluten intolerance; he was allergic to flour and recounted how his life had changed since he was diagnosed with the ailment a year before. It was okay for a lead on a day like this, the day before Christmas Eve. Anne Snapphane would fall on it.

Herman Ösel's snapshot of Christina Furhage and Stefan Bjurling was lousy, but it worked. The two murder victims were sitting next to each other in a dark room. The flash had given Christina red-eye and her teeth shone white. Stefan Bjurling was pulling some kind of a face. The photo was blurred but was spread over pages six and seven with Patrik's piece about the police hunt directly underneath. The headline was the one Ingvar Johansson had coined: "Now They're Both Dead." Patrik's story on the explosives was on page eight. She would tell him he'd done a good job when she next saw him.

Annika leafed through the rival, which had opted for a lead about the economy: "Do Your Tax Returns Now— Save Thousands." You could always lead with stuff like that at the end of December because there would always be one tax law or another changing at the turn of the year. Annika couldn't be bothered to read the advice. It never concerned the likes of herself, people who neither saved in share funds, nor owned houses or drove a company car to work. She knew this kind of material sold well but believed you should use it sparingly.

She fished out the disk from her bag on which Christina Furhage's lover really told all about their last hours and put it in the drawer together with the rest of her sensitive material. She called her contact, but he didn't answer. He had to sleep some time. In a fit of restlessness, she walked out to the newsroom, and noted that Berit wasn't there yet. She asked the picture desk to call Herman Ösel to arrange his payment, fetched coffee, and said good morning to Eva-Britt Qvist.

"So what was the fuss about yesterday?" the secretary asked with poorly disguised glee.

"Fuss?" Annika said, pretending to search her mind. "What do you mean?"

"Here in the newsroom. You and Spike?"

"Oh, you mean Spike's bullshit front page on Christina Furhage as a lesbian? Well, I don't know what happened, but Anders Schyman must have stopped it. Poor Spike, talk about a loser," Annika said and walked into her office. She couldn't resist it.

She drank her coffee and started outlining the day's work. The police might pick up the Bomber today, and most likely they would not announce it over the radio. So they had to rely on sources other than the tipsters. She would have to talk to Berit and Ingvar Johansson about that. Personally, she was going to try to put the pieces of Christina Furhage's past together. She would try to find her son Olof.

She closed her notebook and went on the Internet. When she had time, she did her own search with the phone company on the Net. It took longer, but it was probably more secure and more reliable. Directory enquiries would sometimes miss obvious things. She did a national search for Olof Furhage, the computer searched and sorted, and she got a hit as clear as a bell.

There was only one in all of Sweden, and he lived in Tungelsta, south of Stockholm.

"Bingo!" Annika said.

Christina Furhage had placed her five-year-old son in Tungelsta, almost forty years before, and a man with that same name lived there now. She wondered whether to call him first but decided to go on an outing instead. She needed to get away from the newsroom.

At the same moment, there was a knock on the door. It was the editor; he was holding a large jug of water and he looked terrible.

"What's happened?" Annika said anxiously.

"Migraine," Anders Schyman said curtly. "I had a glass of red wine with the venison last night, so I only have myself to blame. But how are *you* today?"

He closed the door behind him.

"I'm fine, thanks," Annika said. "I can see why you pulled the story about Christina's lesbian escapades."

"It wasn't difficult: The story had nothing to substantiate it."

"Did Spike say how he felt he could go to press with it?" Annika asked.

The editor sat down on Annika's desk.

"He hadn't read the story, only heard Nils Langeby's description of it. When I asked Langeby to see his copy, it was settled. He had nothing substantial, and even if he had had something, we couldn't have published it. It would have been different if Christina herself had made her love affair known publicly, but to write about a dead person's intimate secrets is the worst way to intrude on her private life. She can't answer back. Spike understood that when I explained it to him."

Annika bowed her head, noting that her reflex response had been the correct one. She wondered what the editor's "explaining" consisted of.

"It was true," she said.

"What was?"

"They had a relationship, but no one knew about it. Helena Starke has been absolutely devastated. She seems to have left for the U.S., by the way."

"Really?" said the editor. "What else have you found out that we can't print?"

"Christina hated her children and scared the shit out of the people around her. Stefan Bjurling was a drunk and wife-beater."

"Shit, is that all? And we can't use it. Okay. So what are you up to today?"

"I'm off to talk to a guy, and then I'm going to check something with my contact."

Anders Schyman raised an eyebrow.

"Something we might read about in tomorrow's paper?"

"I hope we might," she said and smiled.

"What did your husband think of our plans for the future?"

"I haven't talked to him yet."

The editor got up and left the room. Annika packed her pad and pen and noted that the battery of the cellphone was running low. She packed a fully charged one to be on the safe side.

"I'm going out for a while," she said to Eva-Britt, who was barely visible behind the piles of post.

She picked up the keys from the porters for a car without the newspaper's logo on it and went down to the car park. It was a glorious sunny winter day. The snow was almost knee-deep and covered the city the way it does on postcards. Nice. With a white Christmas, now the kids can go sledding in the park, she thought.

Annika turned on the car radio and switched to one of the commercial stations and took the West Circular to the

Årsta Bypass. They were playing an old Supremes song. Annika sang along at the top of her voice while the car rushed along toward Huddinge Way. She drove over the Örby Link to Nynäs Way. All the time they played songs she could sing along to. She screeched and laughed straight up into the ceiling of the car. Everything was white and crystal-clear, and soon she'd be off for a week, *and* she was going to be the editor-in-chief! Well, maybe not, but she would be training, and the management had faith in her. She'd suffer setbacks over time, but that came with the territory: That was a fact of life. She turned up the volume when Simon and Garfunkel started singing.

Tungelsta is a garden city about thirty-five kilometers south of Stockholm, a little oasis after the concrete desert of Västerhaninge. Work had begun on the suburb just before the First World War. Today there was nothing much distinguishing it from other residential areas of that era, with one exception: All of the gardens had greenhouses, or remnants of greenhouses. Some were beautiful, others just jagged skeletons.

Annika arrived in mid-morning. Old men shoveling snow gave her a friendly wave as she drove past. Olof Furhage lived in Älvvägen. Annika had to stop at the local pizzeria and ask for directions. An old man who'd been a postman in Tungelsta all of his adult life gave her an animated account of the old district; he knew exactly were Olle Furhage lived:

"Blue house with a big greenhouse," he informed her.

She drove across the railway and saw the place from far off. The greenhouse was by the road: further up toward the woods stood an old blue house. Annika parked on the front lawn, stopping in the middle of an ABBA tune, grabbed her bag, and stepped out of the car. She had put the phone on the front seat so she would hear it if it rang. Seeing it lying there, Annika couldn't be bothered to take it with her. She looked at the house. It was an old-fashioned semidetached house. From the windows and front she guessed it was built in the 1930s. The mansard roof was tiled with red shingles. It was a cozy and well-kept little house.

She started walking toward it when she heard a voice behind her.

"Can I help you with anything?"

It was a man in his forties, with medium-length brown hair and clear blue eyes. He was wearing a knitted woollen sweater and a pair of soil-covered jeans.

"Yes, thank you, you can. I'm looking for an Olof Furhage," Annika said and held out her hand.

The man took her hand and smiled. "You've come to the right place. I'm Olof Furhage."

Annika smiled back. This could be tricky.

"I'm from *Kvällspressen*," she said. "I was wondering if I could ask you some rather personal questions?"

The man gave a laugh. "Oh, well, that's direct. What sort of questions would those be?"

"I'm looking for the Olof Furhage who's the son of the late MD of SOCOG, Christina Furhage," she said calmly. "Would that be you?"

The man looked down on the ground for a moment, then looked up and pushed his hair back.

"Yes," he said, "that's me."

They stood in silence for a few seconds. The strong sunlight was harsh on their eyes. Annika felt the chill rise up through her thin soles.

"I don't want to be forward," she said, "but in the last few days I've spoken to a lot of people who were around Christina Furhage. It's important for me to speak to you too."

"Why have you been talking to people?" the man said guardedly but not unpleasantly.

"Your mother was a well-known figure, and her death has had worldwide repercussions. But despite her prominent position, she was virtually anonymous as a private person. This has prompted us into speaking to the people closest to her."

"But why? She wanted to be anonymous. Couldn't you respect that?"

The man was no fool; that much was clear.

"Naturally," Annika said. "It's out of respect for her family and her own wish to remain anonymous that I'm doing this. Since we don't know anything about her, there's a real risk of our making fundamental errors in writing about her, mistakes that could hurt her family. Unfortunately, this has already happened. Yesterday we ran an article where your mother was described as an ideal woman. That made your sister Lena extremely unhappy. She called me yesterday, I met her, and we had a long talk. I wanted to make sure we didn't overstep the mark the same way with you."

The man looked at her in wonder.

"You make it sound like you are doing me a favor."

Annika didn't know whether she should smile or be serious. The man saw her puzzlement and laughed.

"It's okay," he said, "I'll talk to you. Do you want a cup of coffee, or are you in a hurry?"

"Both," Annika said, returning the laugh.

"Would you like to have a look at my greenhouse first?"

"I'd love to," Annika said, hoping it would be warmer in there.

It was. The air was warm and smelled of soil and damp. The greenhouse was old-fashioned, and big, at least fifty yards long and ten yards wide. The ground was covered with enormous dark green plastic sheets. Two parallel paths ran alongside the wall.

"I grow organic tomatoes," Olof Furhage said.

"In December, too," Annika remarked.

The man laughed again; laughter seemed to come easily to him.

"No, not at the moment. I lifted the plants in October. You let the soil rest over the winter. In organic farming, it's vital to keep the greenhouse and soil free of bacteria and fungus diseases. Present-day farmers often use rock wool or peat, but I stick to soil. Come here, I'll show you."

He walked down the path and stopped at the far end. There was a big metal device on the outside.

"This is a steam-boiler," Olof Furhage said. "Through the pipes that enter here I pipe in steam, which goes down into the soil and warms it up. That kills off the fungus. I've had it on in the morning, which is why it's so warm in here."

Annika watched with great interest. There are so many things one doesn't know.

"So when will there be some tomatoes?" she asked politely.

"You shouldn't rush tomatoes; the plants become weak and unstable. I start toward the end of February, and by October the plants are up to eighteen feet tall."

Annika looked around the greenhouse.

"How? The ceiling isn't high enough."

Olof Furhage gave another laugh.

"Do you see that wire up there? When the plant reaches that, you bend it over the wire. About two feet from the ground is another wire. That has the same function: You bend the plant around it and it starts growing upwards again."

"That's clever," Annika said.

"How about that coffee now?"

They left the greenhouse and walked toward the house.

"You grew up here in Tungelsta, didn't you?" she asked.

The man nodded and held the door open for her.

"Please take your shoes off. Yes, I grew up nearby, in Kvarnvägen. Hello, sweetheart, is everything okay?"

The last few words he called toward the interior of the house, and a girl's voice could be heard from upstairs.

"Fine, Dad, but I'm stuck. Can you help me?"

"Sure, in a little while. I've got a visitor."

Olof Furhage pulled off his heavy boots.

"She's been down with the flu. She was really sick. I bought her a new computer game on CD-ROM to comfort her. Please come in, this way . . ."

A little face appeared on the stairs to the upper floor.

"Hello," the girl said. "My name's Alice."

She was nine or ten years old.

"My name's Annika."

Alice disappeared back to her computer game.

"She lives with me every other week, and her sister Petra has moved in here for good. Petra's fourteen," Olof Furhage said, while pouring water into the coffeemaker.

"You're divorced?" Annika said, sitting down at the kitchen table.

"Yes, a couple of years now. Milk and sugar?"

"Neither, thanks."

Olof Furhage prepared the coffee, laid the table, and sat down opposite Annika. It was a cozy kitchen, with a wooden floor, paneled kitchen cupboards, a checked red-and-white tablecloth, and an electric Star of Bethlehem in the window. There was a splendid view of the greenhouse from the window.

"How much do you know?" he asked.

Annika took out her pad and pen from the bag.

"Do you mind if I take notes? I know that your father

was Carl Furhage and that Christina left you with a couple in Tungelsta when you were five years old. I also know that you contacted Christina a few years ago and that she was terrified of you."

Olof Furhage laughed again but this time a sad laughter.

"Yes, poor Christina, I could never understand why she was so horror-struck," he said. "I wrote a letter to her just after my divorce, mostly because I was feeling so incredibly low. I wrote and asked her all those questions I'd always had and never got an answer to. Why she gave me up, if she'd ever loved me, why she'd never come to visit me, why she wouldn't let Gustav and Elna adopt me . . . But she never replied."

"So you went to see her?"

The man sighed. "Yes, I took to driving over to Tyresö, sitting outside her house during the weeks when the girls were at their mother's. I wanted to see what she looked like, where she lived, how she lived . . . She'd become well-known by then. With the Olympics, she was in the papers every week."

The coffeemaker spluttered, Olof Furhage got to his feet, fetched the pot, and put it on the table.

"I'll let it percolate a bit longer," he said. He took out a plate with a sponge cake from the refrigerator. "One night she came home alone. It was in the spring, I remember that. She was heading for the front door when I stepped out of the car and walked up to her. When I said who I was, she looked as if she was going to faint. She stared at me as if I were a ghost. I asked her why she hadn't answered my letter, but she didn't reply. When I started asking the questions that I'd asked in the letter, she turned around and walked toward the front door, still not saying a word. I was furious and started screaming at her. 'Bloody bitch!' I screamed. 'Couldn't you at least give me a minute of your time,' or something like that. She started running and stumbled on the steps in front of the door. I ran after her and grabbed her, turning her around and shouting 'Look at me!' or something . . ."

He dropped his head, as if the memory hurt him.

"Didn't she say anything?" Annika asked.

"Yes, two words: 'Go away!' Then she went inside, locked the door, and phoned the police. They picked me up, here in this kitchen, that same evening."

He poured out coffee and put one sugar in his cup.

"Have you ever had any contact with her?"

"Not since she left me with Gustav and Elna. I remember the evening when we went there clearly. We went in a taxi, Mom and I; it felt like a long journey. I was happy. She had made it into an adventure, a fun outing."

"Did you like your mother?" Annika queried.

"Of course I did. I loved her. She was my mother, she read stories and sang to me, often gave me hugs, and said evening prayers with me every night. She was slim and bright, like an angel."

He fell silent and looked down at the table.

"When we arrived at Gustav and Elna's, we had dinner, pork sausages and mashed turnips. I remember it to this day. I didn't like it, but Mom said I had to finish it. Then she took me out in the hallway and said that I had to stay with Gustav and Elna because she had to go away. I was hysterical. I suppose I was a bit of a momma's boy. Gustav held me while Mom grabbed her things and rushed out. I think she was crying, but my memory could be deceiving me."

He had some coffee.

"I lay shaking all through the night, screaming and crying when I could muster the strength. Though things got better as the days passed. Elna and Gustav were both over fifty and had no children of their own. You could justifiably say that they spoiled me. They came to love me more than anything else in the world. You couldn't have had better parents. They're both dead now."

"Did you ever see your mother again?"

"Yes, once, when I was thirteen. Gustav and Elna had written to her, saying they wanted to adopt me. I remember I sent along a letter and a drawing as well. She came one evening, asking us to leave her alone. I recognized her immediately, even though I hadn't seen her since I was a small child. She said that adoption was out of the question, and she didn't want any more letters or drawings in the future."

Annika was speechless.

"I was devastated, of course, what kid wouldn't be? She remarried soon after coming here, perhaps that was why she was so uptight."

"Why wouldn't she let your foster parents adopt you?"

"I've wondered about that," Olof Furhage said, pouring out more coffee for Annika and himself. "I was about to inherit an awful lot of money. Carl Furhage had no other children apart from me, and after the death of his third wife he was wealthy—maybe you knew that? Yes, well, then you also know that he instituted a generous scholarship with most of his money. I received my statutory share of the inheritance, and Mother held that in trust. And she did that with a vengeance. There was hardly anything left by the time I came of age."

Annika could hardly believe her ears.

"Are you serious?"

Olof Furhage sighed.

"Yes, I'm afraid so. There was enough left to buy this house and a new car. The money came in handy, since I was at college and had just met Karin. We moved in and started doing the place up; it was barely fit to live in when we came here. Karin let me keep the house when we divorced. We had what you could call an amicable settlement."

"But you should have sued your mother!" Annika said indignantly.

"I couldn't be bothered, quite frankly," Olof said and smiled. "I didn't want anything to do with her. But when my marriage broke up, the bubble of my childhood came to the surface and burst. I tried to blame my failure on myself and my background. That's the reason I contacted her again. And it didn't make matters any better, as you might understand."

Alice came into the kitchen. She was dressed in pink pajamas and a dressing gown, holding a Barbie doll in her arms. She gave Annika a quick, shy glance and then crept up in her father's lap.

"How are you?" Olof Furhage asked and kissed the child's head. "Did you cough a lot today?"

The girl shook her head and buried her face in her father's knitted sweater.

"You're beginning to feel better, aren't you?"

She took a slice of cake and ran into the living room. Soon they could hear the theme music of the *Pink Panther* through the open door.

"I'm glad she'll be well enough to join in on Christmas Eve," Olof said and helped himself to another slice of cake. "Petra baked it. Try it, it's not bad!"

Annika had a slice: It was good.

"Alice came here last Friday after school and fell ill in the evening. I called the doctor at midnight; by then she ran a temperature of over a hundred and three. I sat there with a boiling hot kid in my arms until after three in the morning, when the doctor finally arrived. So when the police came on Saturday afternoon, I had an airtight alibi."

She nodded; she'd already figured that herself. They sat in silence for a while, listening to the doings of the Pink Panther.

"Well, I have to be getting back now," Annika said. "Thank you so much for making time to speak to me."

Olof Furhage smiled.

"It was nothing. A tomato grower isn't too busy during the winter."

"Do you live off your tomatoes?"

The man laughed. "Hardly! I barely break even. Making a business growing greenhouse vegetables is practically impossible. Even people who grow tomatoes further south, with subsidies, a warm climate, and cheap labor can barely make ends meet. I do it because I enjoy doing it. It doesn't cost me anything more than the commitment and the effort, and then I do it for the environment."

"So what do you do for a living?"

"I do research at the Royal Institute of Technology—waste product technology."

"Composts and stuff like that?"

He smiled. "Among other things."

"Will you become a professor?"

"Probably never. One of the two existing professorships has recently been filled, and the other one is up north, in Luleå, and I wouldn't want to move, for the girls' sake. And things might work out between me and Karin in the end. Petra is with her now, but we're spending Christmas together, all four of us. Who knows?"

Annika smiled, a smile that came from somewhere deep inside her.

Anders Schyman sat in his office, elbows on the desk, his head in his hands. The pain was out of this world. He had migraine attacks a couple of times a year and always when he started unwinding after a stressful period. And last night he had made the mistake of drinking red wine. Sometimes he could but not just before going on holiday. Now he was feeling sick, not only because of the headache, but because of what lay ahead of him. He was about to do something he'd never done before, and it wasn't going to be pleasant. He'd been on the phone for half of the morning, first with the MD and then the company lawyer. The longer the conversations went on, the worse his headache had become. He sighed and put his hands among the piles of paper on the desk. His eyes were bloodshot and his hair tousled. He stared into space for a moment, then reached out for his pills and a glass of water. He popped out yet another Distalgesic—now he would definitely not be driving home.

There was a knock and Nils Langeby popped his head around the door.

"You wanted to see me?" he said expectantly.

"Oh, yes, come in," Anders Schyman said, laboriously getting to his feet. He walked around his desk and indicated that the reporter should sit on one of the couches. Nils Langeby sat down in the middle of the largest couch, stretching himself out ostentatiously. He seemed nervous, and anxious to hide the fact. He was looking quizzically at the coffee table in front of him, as if expecting a cup of coffee and a Danish pastry. Anders Schyman took a seat in an armchair directly facing him.

"I wanted to talk to you, Nils, because I have an offer to make you . . ."

The reporter sat up, a light appearing at the back of his eyes. He thought he was going to be promoted, that he'd get some form of recognition. The editor noted this and felt like a bastard.

"Yes . . . ?" Nils Langeby said when his boss didn't continue.

"I was wondering what your attitude would be toward working for the paper on a freelance basis in future?"

There, he'd said it. It sounded like a normal question, posed in a completely regular tone of voice. The editor made an effort to look calm and collected.

Nils Langeby was at a loss.

"Freelance? But . . . why? Freelance . . . how . . . ? I'm on the permanent staff!"

The editor got up from the armchair and walked over to his desk to get the glass of water.

"Yes, of course, I know that, Nils. You've been an employee with the paper for quite a few years, and you could remain here for another ten or twelve years until retirement. I'm offering you a more autonomous way of working during your last active years."

Nils Langeby's gaze was wandering.

"What are you saying?" he said. He'd dropped his cheek; his mouth was a large black hole. Schyman sighed and went back and sat down in the armchair with his glass of water.

"I'm asking you if you'd be interested in a freelance contract with the paper. Very favorable. We'd help you set up your own business, maybe a company, and then you'd work for us on a less regulated basis."

The reporter gaped and blinked a couple of times. He reminded Schyman of a fish out of water.

"What the . . ." he said. "What the hell is this?"

"Exactly what I'm telling you," the editor said wearily. "An offer of a different form of employment. You've never thought of moving on?"

Nils Langeby closed his mouth and pulled in his legs under the couch. As the realization of the enormity of what he was hearing sank in, he turned his gaze toward the office building on the other side of the street. He clenched his teeth and swallowed.

"We could help you find an office in town. We'll guarantee you an income of five contracted days a month, that's 12,500 kronor plus contributions and holiday pay. You will of course continue to cover your own particular areas, crime in schools and . . ."

"It's that bloody cunt, isn't it?" Nils Langeby said hoarsely.

"Pardon . . . ?" Schyman said, dropping part of his calm demeanor.

Langeby turned his gaze to the editor, who all but recoiled at the hatred he saw in it.

"That cunt, that whore, that bitch—she's behind all this, isn't she?"

"What are you talking about?" Schyman said, noticing he'd raised his voice.

The reporter clenched his fists and breathed raggedly through his nose.

"Damn, damn, damn! The fucking cunt wants me fired!"

"I haven't said a word about firing you . . ." Schyman began.

"Bullshit!" Langeby shouted and got up so abruptly that his big stomach swayed. His face had turned scarlet, and his fists were clenching and unclenching.

"Please sit down," Schyman said in a quiet, cold voice. "Don't make this more unpleasant than it already is."

"Unpleasant?" Langeby bawled, and Schyman, too, got to his feet. He took two strides up to Langeby and put his face close to his.

"Sit down, man, and let me finish talking," he hissed.

Langeby didn't do as he was told but walked over to the window and stood staring out. It was clear and cold, and the sun was shining over the Russian Embassy.

"Who are you referring to? Your boss, Nils? Annika Bengtzon?"

Langeby let out a short, rueful laugh.

"My boss. Christ, yes! It's her I'm referring to. She's the most incompetent cunt I've ever come across. She's clueless! She knows nothing! She's making enemies all over the newsroom. Ask Eva-Britt Qvist. She shouts and goes on at people. No one can understand why she got the job in the first place. She has no authority and no sub-editing experience."

"Sub-editing experience?" Anders Schyman said. "What's that got to do with it?"

"And everybody knows about the guy who died, just so you know. She never talks about it, but everybody knows."

The editor breathed in, his nostrils flaring.

"If you're alluding to the episode that occurred before Annika Bengtzon got on the permanent staff, you know that the court established that it was an accident. It's rather low of you to bring that up here," he said icily.

Nils Langeby didn't answer but rocked to and fro on his feet, fighting back the tears. Schyman decided to put in the knife and twist it.

"I find it remarkable you speak this way about your boss," he said. "The fact is that attacks of that kind could result in a formal written warning."

Nils Langeby didn't show any reaction, only kept on rocking over by the window.

"We have to discuss your performance, Nils. Your so-called article last night was a near disaster. That in itself wouldn't give cause for a warning, but recently you've been displaying a shocking lack of judgement. Your piece last Sunday about the police suspecting that the first bomb might have been a terrorist act—you haven't been able to identify a single one of your sources."

"I don't have to divulge my sources," Langeby said in a strained voice.

"Yes, to me you do. I'm the editor-in-chief of this paper. If you're wrong, I'm the one who has to carry the can. You know that."

Langeby went on rocking.

"I haven't contacted the union yet," Schyman said, "I wanted to talk to you first. We can do this whichever way you want to: with or without the union, with or without a conflict. It's up to you."

The reporter shrugged his shoulders but didn't reply.

"You can go on standing there, or you can sit down so I can explain how we can sort this out."

Langeby ceased rocking to and fro, hesitating for a moment, but then slowly turned around. Schyman saw that he'd been crying. They both sat down again.

"I don't want to humiliate you," the editor said in a low voice. "I want this to be carried out in as dignified a manner as possible."

"You can't fire me," Nils Langeby sniveled.

"Yes, I can," Schyman said. "It would cost us about three years' pay in the industrial tribunal, maybe four. It would be a damned ugly and nasty affair with mud-slinging and accusations that neither you, nor the paper would have anything to gain from. You'd probably never get another job. The paper would look like a harsh and unforgiving employer, but that wouldn't matter much. It could even be good for our reputation. We'd be able to give good reasons for letting you go. You would immediately, today, receive a written warning, which we would cite. We would maintain that you are sabo-taging our publication, harassing and thwarting your immediate superior with invectives and four-letter words. We would produce evidence of your incompe-tence and poor judgement. All we have to do is refer to what has happened during the last few days and then count the number of articles of yours that are in the archives. How many have you written the last ten years? Thirty? Thirty-five? That's three and a half articles per year, Langeby."

"You said, you said only last Saturday that I would be going on writing front-page copy for *Kvällspressen* for many years to come yet. Was that just bullshit?"

Anders Schyman sighed.

"No, not at all. That's why I'm offering you the opportunity to continue working for the paper, albeit in a different situation. We'll fix you up with a company and an office, and we'll buy five days of your time every month for five years. The going rate for a freelance reporter is two and a half thousand kronor per day, plus holiday pay and pension contributions. That will give you half of your current salary for five years, while at the same time you can work as much as you like for anyone else."

Langeby wiped off the snot with the back of his hand and stared down at the carpet. After some time he said:

"What if I find another job?"

"Then we'll pay out the money as a severance packet, 169,500 a year or 508,500 for three years. That's the most we can offer."

"You said five years!" Langeby said, suddenly irate.

"Yes, but that's when you're producing copy for us. This freelance contract isn't a golden handshake. We expect you to continue working for us, under different conditions."

Again, Langeby turned his gaze to the carpet. Schyman waited for a while, then moved on to the next stage: to lessen his humiliation somewhat.

"I can see you're not happy here anymore, Nils. You haven't quite adapted to the new culture. I feel bad about you being unhappy. This is a highly advantageous way for you to build a foundation for a new career as a self-employed reporter. You don't like working for Annika Bengtzon, and I'm sorry about that. But Annika is staying; I have big plans for her. I don't agree with your assessment of her. She loses her temper sometimes, but that will soften with time. She's been under a lot of pressure lately, largely because of you, Nils. I'd like to keep you both, and I think a contract of this nature would be the best solution for all involved . . ."

"508,000 is just two years' salary," Nils Langeby said.

"Yes, two full annual salaries, three if you work part time. You'll get that without any argument. No one need even know about the money. You'll just make it known that you're moving on in your career and are starting up as a freelancer. The paper will be sorry about losing such an experienced member of the staff but will be grateful for your continued contributions as a stringer . . ."

Nils Langeby looked up at the editor-in-chief with an expression of loathing.

"Damn you," he said. "What an oily, false fucking serpent you are . . . Damn you . . ."

Without saying another word, Nils Langeby got up and walked out the door. He slammed it loudly behind him and Anders Schyman heard his steps disappear among the steps of the other people in the newsroom.

The editor went over to his desk and drank another glass of water. The headache had abated somewhat with the last pill, but it was still pounding like a red heart inside his forehead. He heaved a deep sigh. This was going better than he'd hoped. Had he already won the battle? One thing was sure: Nils Langeby had to go. He was going to be thrown out of the newsroom and not be allowed to set foot there ever again. Unfortunately, he would never go of his own accord. He could hang around and poison the air for another twelve years.

Schyman sat down in his chair behind the desk and looked out over the Embassy enclosure. Some children were trying to sled down the muddy hill on the front.

This morning the MD had given the go-ahead for the editor to juggle a few items in the budget to make money available to buy out Nils Langeby with up to four salaries. It would be cheaper than paying him twelve, which the company would have to do if he stayed on. If Nils Langeby had the bare minimum of intelligence—which, granted, he didn't—he'd accept the offer. If he didn't, the other, more protracted measures were at hand. He could, for example, be transferred to the proof-reading section. This would naturally mean union involvement and a big fuss, but the union wouldn't be able to stop it. They could never show that the paper had made any formal mistake. As a reporter, you're assumed to be qualified for proofreading, so that shouldn't be a problem.

The union wouldn't have much to make a noise about anyway. Anders Schyman had simply made the reporter an offer. People were often offered severance packages in the trade, even if it hadn't happened many times at this particular paper. All the union could do was to support its member during negotiations and make sure he got as good a deal as possible.

And should all hell break loose, one of the in-house lawyers, an expert in employment law, was preparing a really nasty case before the industrial tribunal. Then the union's central ombudsman would enter as the other party and appear for Nils Langeby in court, but the paper couldn't lose. Schyman's only objective was to get rid of the fucker, and he intended to succeed.

The editor took another sip of water, lifted the

receiver, and asked Eva-Britt Qvist to come in. He'd given Spike one hell of a tongue-lashing the night before, so there wouldn't be any further hassle from him. He might as well deal with them all at a stroke.

The call from the tipster Leif came to the newsdesk at 11:47 A.M., only three minutes after the event. Berit took the call.

"The central Stockholm sorting office has been blown up. There are at least four casualties," the tipster said and hung up. Before the information had even registered in Berit's brain, Leif had already dialed the next paper. You had to be first, or there'd be no money.

Berit didn't put the receiver down; she just quickly pressed the cradle down and phoned the police central control room.

"Has there been an explosion at the sorting office?" she quickly asked.

"We have no information as yet," an extremely stressed police officer replied.

"But has there?" Berit insisted.

"Looks like it," he said.

They hung up, and Berit threw the remains of her sandwich in the trash.

At 12:00 P.M. *Radio Stockholm* was the first to report on the explosion.

Annika left Tungelsta with a peculiar sense of warmth in her soul. The human psyche did, after all, have a remarkable ability to self-heal. She waved to Olof Furhage and Alice as she turned into Älvvägen and drove away toward Allévägen, cruising at a leisurely pace in the pleasant neighborhood toward the main road. She could picture herself living here. She drove past the villages Krigslida, Glasberga, and Norrskogen over toward

Västerhaninge Junction and the motorway into Stockholm.

She put the car in the right lane and picked up the phone that she had left on the passenger seat. "Missed call" the display said; she pressed for "show number" and noted that the switchboard of the paper had tried to reach her. She sighed lightly and put the phone back down. She was very happy Christmas was so near.

She switched on the radio and sang along to Alphaville's "Forever Young."

Just after the exit to Dalarö, the phone rang. She swore and turned down the radio, pushed the earpiece into her ear, and pressed "answer."

"Is that Annika Bengtzon? Hello, this is Beata Ekesjö. We met last Tuesday at Sätra Hall and then I called you in the evening . . ."

Annika groaned to herself, of course—the loony project manager. "Hello," Annika said, overtaking a Russian container truck.

"I was wondering if you've got time for a chat?"

"Not really," Annika said and steered back into the right-hand lane.

"It's quite important," Beata Ekesjö said.

Annika sighed.

"What's it about?"

"I think I know who killed Christina Furhage."

Annika nearly drove into the ditch.

"You do? How could you know that?"

"I've found something."

Annika's brain had really got going now.

"What?"

"I can't say."

"Have you told the police?"

"No, I wanted to show you first."

"Me? Why?"

"Because you've been writing about it."

Annika slowed down in order to be able to think and was immediately overtaken by the Russian truck. The snow whirled around her on the road.

"It's not me investigating the murder, but the Krim," she said.

"You don't want to write about me?"

The woman was obviously intent on appearing in the paper.

Annika considered the pros and cons. On the one hand, the woman was eccentric and probably didn't know a thing, and she just wanted to get home. On the other hand, you don't hang up if someone calls and offers you the solution to a murder.

"Tell me what you've discovered and I'll tell you whether I'll write about it or not."

It was hard work driving in the snow whipped up by the Russian truck, so Annika overtook it once more.

"I can show you."

Annika groaned quietly and looked at her watch: a quarter to one.

"All right, where is it?"

"Out here, at the Olympic arena."

She was just driving past Trångsund, and Annika realized she would practically be driving past Victoria Stadium on her way back to the newspaper.

"Okay, I can be there in fifteen minutes."

"Great," Beata said. "I'll meet you on the forecourt below . . ."

The phone emitted three short tones and the call was interrupted. The battery was dead. Annika started digging for the other battery at the bottom of her bag but gave up when she veered into the outside lane by mistake. The phone would have to wait until she got out of the car. Instead she turned up the radio again and to her delight heard that they'd just started spinning Gloria Gaynor's old hit "I Will Survive."

There were already several news reporters and photographers outside the sorting office when Berit and Johan Henriksson arrived. Berit squinted up at the futuristic building; the sun was glittering on the glass and chrome.

"Our Bomber is reinventing himself," she said. "He hasn't done letter bombs before."

Henriksson loaded his cameras while they climbed the steps to the main entrance. The other reporters were waiting inside in the bright entrance hall. Berit looked around as she stepped inside. It was a typical 1980s building: marble, escalators, and ceilings reaching for the sky.

"Is anyone from *Kvällspressen* here?" a man over by the elevators asked.

Berit and Henriksson looked at each other in surprise.

"Yes, over here," Berit said.

"Could you come with me, please?" the man said.

The cordons had been lifted and the approach plowed, so Annika could drive all the way up to the steps below the stadium. She looked around. The sunlight was so strong she had to squint, but she couldn't see a soul anywhere near. She stayed in the car, leaving the engine running, while she listened to Dusty Springfield in "I Only Wanna Be with You." She jumped when there was a knock on the window right by her ear.

"Hiya! My God, you scared me there," Annika said when she opened the door.

Beata Ekesjö smiled.

"Don't worry," she said.

Annika switched off the engine and put her cellphone in the bag.

"You can't park here," Beata Ekesjö said. "You'll get a ticket."

"But I'm not staying long," Annika protested.

"No, but we've got to walk a bit. The fine is 700 kronor here."

"So where should I park?"

Beata pointed. "There, the other side of the footbridge. I'll wait here for you."

Annika started the car again. Why do I let people push me around? she mused as she drove back the way she had come and parked among the other cars next to the new housing development. Oh, well, she could do with a couple of minutes' walk in the sunshine, that didn't happen every day. The main thing was not to be late picking up the kids from daycare. Annika took out the phone and changed batteries. There was a beep when she put the new one in, and "message received" appeared on the display. She pressed "c" to remove the message and called the daycare center. They closed at five, an hour earlier than usual but still later than she'd counted on. She breathed out and started walking across the footbridge.

Beata was still smiling, her breath a white cloud around her head.

"What was it you wanted to show me?" Annika said, hearing how gruff she sounded.

Beata continued smiling.

"I've found something really odd over here," she said, pointing. "It won't take long."

Annika gave a quiet sigh and started walking. Beata followed behind.

At the same moment as Berit and Henriksson stepped inside the elevator at Stockholm Klara sorting office, the

Chief District Prosecutor Kjell Lindström called the *Kvällspressen* newsdesk. He asked to speak to the editor-in-chief and was connected to his secretary.

"I'm afraid he's gone to lunch," the secretary said when she saw Schyman wave his hands in a dismissive gesture. "Can I take a message? I see . . . One moment please, and I'll see if I can get hold of him . . ."

Schyman's migraine just wouldn't go. More than anything he just wanted to lie down in a blacked-out room and sleep. He had, despite the headache, achieved something constructive during the morning. His talk with Eva-Britt Qvist had gone surprisingly well. The crime-desk secretary had said she thought Annika Bengtzon was a very promising manager whom she would give all her support; she wanted to join forces to make the crime desk function under Annika's leadership.

"It's a prosecutor and he's very persistent," the secretary said, emphasizing "very."

Anders Schyman sighed and picked up the phone.

"So, the law is still at it this close to Christmas," he said. "Though you've got it the wrong way around, it's we who should be hounding you . . ."

"I'm calling about the explosive charge that has gone off at the Stockholm Klara sorting office," Kjell Lindström broke in.

"Yes, we've got a team on its way . . ."

"I know, we're talking to them now. The bomb was meant for one of your employees. A reporter by the name of Annika Bengtzon. She must be given protection immediately."

The words penetrated Anders Schyman's brain through a haze of Distalgesic. "Annika Bengtzon?"

"The envelope was addressed to her and was set off by mistake in the terminal. We believe it was sent by the same person who's behind the explosions at the Olympic stadium and Sätra Hall."

Anders Schyman felt his legs give way under him. He sat down on his secretary's desk. "My God . . ."

"Where is Annika Bengtzon now? Is she in the newsroom?"

"No, I don't think so. She went out this morning to interview someone. I haven't seen her since."

"Man or woman?"

"What? Who she was interviewing? Man, I think. Why?"

"It's extremely important that Annika Bengtzon is found and given twenty-four-hour protection straight away. She shouldn't go home or to her workplace until the person in question has been apprehended."

"How do you know the bomb was for Annika?"

"It was addressed to her in a registered letter. We're looking into the details right now. But most importantly, Annika Bengtzon has to get protection immediately. A patrol is on its way over to you; they should be with you any minute. They'll see to it she's taken to a safe house. Does she have a family?"

Anders Schyman closed his eyes and passed his hand over his face. This can't be happening, he thought, feeling all the blood draining from his brain.

"Yes, a husband and two small children."

"Are they in a daycare center? Which one? Who might know? Where does her husband work? Can you get hold of him?"

Anders Schyman promised to take care of Annika's family. He gave the police Annika's cellphone number and begged them to hurry.

They walked away from Sickla Canal and past a small cluster of trees near the arena. The small pine trees had been torn by the explosion, one lay with its roots in the air, the branches of the others splayed in all directions. The snow was a foot deep and got into Annika's shoes.

"Is it far?" she asked.

"Not very," Beata said.

They plodded on through the snow; Annika was beginning to get annoyed. The training facility loomed large above them, and Annika glimpsed the uppermost floors of the media building further ahead.

"How do you get up when there are no steps?" she said and looked at the ten-foot-high concrete wall that supported the track.

Beata came up and stood beside her. "We're not going up there. Just follow the wall."

She pointed ahead and Annika plodded on. She could feel the stress creeping into her veins: She had to write a story on the police closing in on the Bomber, and she still hadn't wrapped the children's Christmas gifts. Oh, well, she'd have to do that after they go to bed tonight. Beata's discovery might be just the thing to get the police talking.

"Do you see how the wall disappears over there?" Beata said behind her. "You can get underneath the arena there, that's where we're heading."

Annika shivered; it was cold here where the wall blocked out the sun. She could hear her own breathing and the traffic on the South Bypass behind her; apart from that it was completely silent. At least she knew where they were going now.

The police patrol was made up of two policemen in uniform and two plain-clothes detectives. Anders Schyman received them in his office.

"Two bomb patrols with dogs are on their way," one of the detectives said. "There's a real risk that there are more bombs, possibly here at the paper. The premises have to be evacuated and searched straight away."

"Is that necessary? We haven't received any threats," Anders Schyman said.

The detective gave him a serious look. "Of course. She hasn't issued any warnings the other times."

"She?" Schyman said.

The other detective stepped forward. "Yes, we believe the Bomber may be a woman."

Anders Schyman looked from one man to the other. "What makes you think that?"

"We can't tell you that yet."

"She's disappeared," the first detective said, changing subjects. "And we haven't been able to locate Annika Bengtzon. Do you have any idea where she might be?"

Anders Schyman shook his head, his mouth parched. "No, all she said was that she was meeting someone for an interview."

"Who?"

"She didn't say. A man, she said."

"Does she drive her own car?"

"I don't think so."

The two detectives exchanged glances—this man didn't know a whole lot.

"Right, we've got to find out what car she's in, get a description of it, and circulate that to all units. Let's get moving with the evacuation of the building."

"Up there the competitors will be warming up before the events," Beata said when they were standing under the arena. It was gloomy, almost dark, in here under the concrete roof. Annika looked out through the long, low opening. On the other side stood the Olympic Village, the white houses sparkling in the sunlight. The windows glittered and gleamed; they were all absolutely new.

Replacing the blasted windows had been given priority. There was a risk of the water pipes in the uninhabited block freezing and bursting.

"The competitors have to be able to reach the stadium quickly," Beata said. "This area is open to the public to avoid them having to queue for the main entrance. We've built this underground passage, leading from the training facility and up to the stadium."

Annika turned around and looked into the gloom. "Where?" she said, bewildered.

Beata smiled. "We didn't exactly put up a large sign," she said. "If we had, the public could have found it. Over there in the corner. Come on, I'll show you."

They walked further in under the roof, Annika blinking to get accustomed to the darkness.

"Here it is," Beata said.

Annika stood in front of a gray iron door, hardly noticeable in the gloom. A large iron bar lay across the door. It looked like it would be a door to a refuse room or something similar. Next to the iron door was a small box, which Beata opened. Annika saw her take out a card from her coat pocket and pull it through a swipe machine.

"Do you have an entry card to this place?" Annika said with surprise.

"Everyone does," Beata said and removed the bar.

"What are you doing?" Annika asked.

"Opening the door," Beata said and pulled the iron door open. The hinges didn't make a sound. Inside the darkness was complete.

"But can you do that, aren't the alarms primed?" Annika said, feeling an uneasiness creep up on her.

"No, the alarms won't go off during the day. They're hard at it upstairs, repairing the arena. Come inside, and I'll show you something strange. Hang on, I'll just switch on the light."

Beata turned a big switch next to the exit and a row of fluorescents flickered on. The passage had concrete walls, and the floor was covered with yellow linoleum. The ceiling height was around seven feet. The passage stretched straight ahead for about twenty yards and then veered to the left and disappeared up toward the Olympic stadium. Annika took a deep breath and started walking. She turned around and saw Beata pull the door to.

"Regulations say it mustn't be left open," Beata said and smiled again.

Annika returned the smile, turned around, and continued walking down the passage. Should she be doing this?

"Is it up here?" she asked.

"Yes, just around the bend."

Annika felt her blood pumping. In spite of herself, she thought this was exciting. She walked quickly and heard the echo of her heels in the tunnel. Further along, around the bend a pile of trash appeared.

"There's something there!" she said and turned around to Beata.

"That's what I wanted to show you. It's really curious."

Annika secured her bag on her shoulder and jogged up to the pile. It was a mattress, two simple garden stools, a folding table, and a cooler. Annika walked up to the things and studied them.

"Someone's been sleeping here," she said, and just then she spotted the box with the dynamite. It was small and white and the name "Minex" was printed on the side. She gasped, and at the same instant felt something being thrown around her neck. Her hands flew up to her neck, but she couldn't grab hold of the rope. She tried screaming, but the noose was already too tight. She started pulling and tugging, tried to run. She fell to the floor, desperately trying to crawl out of the noose, but that only caused it to be pulled even tighter.

The last thing she saw before everything went black was Beata fading in and out of focus, the rope in her hands, hovering over her, the concrete ceiling above her head.

The evacuation of the newspaper offices was comparatively fast and smooth. The fire alarm was turned on and in nine minutes the whole building was vacated. The last man to leave was the news editor, Ingvar Johansson, who said he had more important things to do than practice the fire drill. Only when the editor-in-chief had bawled at him down the phone did he leave his post, under protest.

The staff was relatively calm. They knew nothing of the bomb being targeted at one of their colleagues and were treated to coffee and sandwiches in the canteen of an adjoining office block. Meanwhile, the police bomb squad searched all the areas belonging to the paper. Anders Schyman suddenly realized that his migraine had disappeared, the blood vessels had contracted, and the pain was gone. He was sitting with his secretary and the chief telephone operator in an office behind the kitchen in the adjacent building. Getting hold of Annika's husband had turned out to be easier said than done. The switchboard at the Association of Local Authorities had closed at one o'clock and no one at the paper had Thomas's direct number. Nor did they have his cellphone number. None of the services, neither Telia, Comviq, nor Europolitan had the right Thomas Samuelsson among their subscribers. Nor did Anders Schyman know which daycare center they had their children in. His secretary was phoning around to all the daycare centers in District 3 on Kungsholmen, asking for the Bengtzon children. What she didn't know was that the daycare center didn't give out information about Annika's children to anyone. They weren't even on the telephone lists that were handed out among the other parents. After the articles on the Paradise foundation, Annika had received death threats, and since then both she and Thomas were careful to whom they handed out their address. The daycare staff were in agreement, so when Schyman's secretary called, they calmly said that Annika's children weren't in their group. Immediately, the manager called Annika on her cellphone, but there was no reply.

Anders Schyman had the metallic taste of fear in his mouth. He told the chief telephone operator to phone all possible extensions at the Association of Local Authorities. First the number to the switchboard, and then -01, -02, and so on until she got hold of someone who could reach Thomas. The police already had a patrol waiting outside Annika's house. After that the editor didn't know what to do next but went out to the detectives to hear how things were progressing.

"So far we haven't found anything. We'll be done in half an hour," the officer in charge announced.

Anders Schyman went back to help his secretary phone daycare centers on Kungsholmen.

Annika slowly came to. She heard someone groaning loudly and eventually realized it was herself. When she opened her eyes, she was immediately gripped by uncontrollable panic. She'd gone blind. She screamed like a madwoman, opening her eyes as wide as she could in the darkness. Her terror increased when all she heard was a high piping croak. Then she noticed that the torn noise echoed in the dark, bouncing and returning like horror-stricken birds against a window, and remembered the underground tunnel beneath the Olympic stadium.

She stopped screaming and listened to her own panicky breathing for a minute. She had to be in the tunnel. She focused on feeling her own body, making sure all the parts were still there and functioning. She first lifted her head. It hurt, but it wasn't damaged. She realized she was lying on something relatively soft, probably the mattress she had seen before . . .

"Beata . . . ," she whispered.

She lay still, breathing in the darkness. Beata had put her here, had done something to her, that's how it was. Beata had thrown a rope around her neck, and now she had left. Did Beata think she was dead?

Annika noticed that one of her arms hurt, the one that was wedged in underneath her. When she tried lifting it, she realized she couldn't move it. Her arms were tied. She was lying on her side with her arms tied behind her back. She tried lifting her legs: same thing. They were tied up, and not only to each other, but they were fastened to the wall next to her. When she moved her legs, she noticed something else: While she'd been unconscious, her bladder and bowel had emptied. The urine was cold and the excrement was sticky. She started to cry. What had she done? Why was this happening to her? She cried so hard she was shaking, the tunnel was cold, her crying seeped through the chill and into the darkness. She was rocking slowly on the mattress, back and forth, back and forth, back and forth.

I don't want to, she thought. Don't want to, don't want to, don't want to . . .

Anders Schyman was back in his office, staring out at the dark facade of the Russian Embassy. They hadn't found any bombs at the newspaper offices. The sun had set behind the former tsardom's flag, leaving the sky a glowing red for a few, short minutes. The staff were back in

their seats, and still no one but himself, his secretary, and
the telephone operator knew that the bomb had been
addressed to Annika. Anders Schyman had been quickly
briefed. All the police knew so far was that the Bomber
was a ruthless bungler.

The letter containing the explosive charge had arrived
at the Stockholm Klara sorting office at 18:50 on
Wednesday evening. It had been sent as a registered
letter from Stockholm 17, the post office in
Rosenlundsgatan on South Island, at 16:53. Since the
letter was sent registered, it didn't go with the regular
mail but was sent in a separate shipment that would
leave the terminal a bit later.

The brown padded envelope hadn't attracted any
particular attention. Stockholm Klara is Sweden's largest
sorting office, situated on Klarabergsviadukten in central Stockholm. The terminal building is eight floors
high and occupies a whole block between the City Bus
Terminal, City Hall, and the Central Station. One and a
half million letters and parcels pass through there every
day.

Having arrived at one of the terminal's four loading
platforms, the envelope had ended up at the Special
Delivery Section on the fourth floor. The staff working
with various kinds of valuable items have received special security training. Since *Kvällspressen* has its own
postcode, the receipt was sent out to the paper's ordinary
postbox. This postbox is emptied several times a day and
its contents delivered at the newsroom in Marieberg. At
the terminal, the paper has several letters giving power
of attorney, enabling the various porters to collect registered letters and parcels on behalf of other employees.
Whatever registered and insured items there are, they
would usually be picked up once a day, early in the afternoon.

On Thursday morning, there had been a number of registered letters in the morning delivery, since it was the time of year for Christmas gifts. The receipt for the letter addressed to Annika Bengtzon therefore ended up in a pile of other receipts in the porters' folder.

The explosion had occurred when Tore Brand was standing in the sorting office reception, waiting to pick up these special deliveries. One of the employees at the Special Delivery Section had slipped and dropped the letter. The envelope didn't fall more than half a meter, back into the same crate where it had been lying overnight, but it was enough for the device to go off. Four people were hurt, three seriously. The person who had been standing the closest, the man who dropped the envelope, was in a critical condition.

Anders Schyman bit his nail. There was a knock on his door, and one of the detectives entered without waiting for a reply.

"We can't get hold of Thomas Samuelsson either," the detective said. "We've been to his office. He wasn't there. They thought he might have gone somewhere for the day, some meeting with a local politician. We've tried his cellphone, but there's no reply."

"Have you found Annika or the car?" Schyman asked.

The detective shook his head.

The editor turned around and stared out at the embassy roof. Dear God, don't let her be dead.

Suddenly her sight returned. The light came on with a clicking sound, the lamps flickering to life. Annika was dazzled and for a moment couldn't see anything. She heard the clatter of heels in the passage and rolled up into a ball, shutting her eyes tight. The steps came closer, stopping right next to her ear.

"Are you awake?" a voice above her said.

Annika opened her eyes and blinked. She saw the floor and the tip of a pair of leather boots.

"Good. We've got work to do."

Someone pulled at her so she ended up with her back against the concrete wall and her legs pulled up, bent at the knees and jutting out to the side. It was very uncomfortable.

Beata Ekesjö leaned over her and smelled the air.

"Did you shit yourself? That's disgusting!"

Annika didn't respond. She just stared into the opposite wall and whimpered.

"Let's get you sorted out," Beata said, grabbing Annika by the armpits. Pushing and lifting, she forced Annika to sit tilted forward with her head by her knees.

"It worked all right the last time," Beata said. "It's good when you get used to doing something, don't you think?"

Annika didn't hear what the woman was saying. She was lost in a deep pit of fear, which killed off any brain activity. She didn't even notice the stench from her own shit. She cried quietly while Beata was busying herself with something next to her, humming some old popular song. Annika tried to speak but was unable to.

"Don't try to talk yet," Beata said. "The rope squashed your vocal cords a bit. Here we go!"

Beata stood up next to Annika. She was holding a roll of masking tape in one hand and what looked like a pack of red candles in the other.

"This is Minex. Twenty paper-wrapped cartridges, 22 x 200mm, at 100 grams each. Two kilos. That's enough, I noticed with Stefan. He broke in two."

Annika understood what the woman was saying. She realized what was about to happen and leaned over to throw up. She vomited so hard her whole body was shaking and bile was coming up.

"What a mess you're making!" Beata exclaimed disapprovingly. "I should have you clean up after yourself."

Annika panted and felt the bile dripping from her mouth. I'm dying, she thought. I can't believe this is happening. Why had she followed this woman down here? It's never like this in the films.

"What the hell did you expect?" Annika croaked.

"See, your voice is returning," Beata said cheerfully. "That's good, because I'd like to ask you a few questions."

"Fuck you, you maniac," Annika said. "I'm not talking to you."

Beata didn't reply but leaned over and pushed something onto Annika's back, just underneath the ribs. Annika reflected, breathed in, smelled damp and explosives.

"Dynamite?" she asked.

"Yep. I'm fastening it to your back with masking tape."

Beata wound the tape around Annika's body and embraced her a couple of times. Annika felt this might be a chance for her to escape, but she didn't know how to. Her hands were still tied behind her back and the feet were fixed to a metal frame in the wall.

"There, that's it," Beata said and got to her feet. "The explosives are quite safe, but the detonator can be a bit unstable, so we'll have to be careful. Do you see this wire here? This is what I use to detonate the charge. I'm pulling it to over here, and do you see this? It's a battery from an ordinary flashlight. It's enough to set off the detonator. Amazing, isn't it?"

Annika watched the thin, yellow and green wire winding toward the small folding table. She realized that she didn't know the first thing about explosives; she couldn't say whether Beata was bluffing or telling the truth. At the murder of Christina, she had used a whole car battery. Why, if a flashlight battery was enough?

"I'm sorry it had to be like this," Beata said. "If you'd only stayed in the office yesterday afternoon we could have avoided all this. It would have been better for everyone concerned. Completion should take place in its proper place, and in your case that means the newsroom at *Kvällspressen*. Instead the bomb went off at the sorting office, and I'm not very happy about that at all."

Annika stared at the woman—she really was insane.

"What do you mean? Has there been another explosion?"

The Bomber let out a sigh.

"Well, I didn't bring you here for fun. We'll just have to do it this way instead. I'm going to leave you now for a while. If I were you, I'd try to get some rest. But don't lie on your back, and don't try to pull the chain from the wall. Sudden movements could trigger the charge."

"Why?" Annika asked.

Beata looked at her with complete indifference for a few seconds. "See you in a couple of hours," she said and started walking toward the training facility on her clattering heels. Annika heard her steps disappear beyond the bend and then the light was gone again.

Annika carefully turned around, away from the vomit, and infinitely slowly lay down on her left side. She lay with her back toward the wall and stared into the darkness, hardly daring to breathe. Another explosion—had anyone died? Was the bomb meant for her? How the hell was she going to get out of this alive?

Lots of people were working on the stadium, Beata had said. That should be at the other end of the passage. If she screamed loud enough they might hear her.

"Help!" Annika cried as loud as she could, but her vocal cords were still damaged. She waited for a while and shouted again. She realized her cries wouldn't reach out.

She put her head down and felt panic creeping up on her. She thought she could hear the patter of animals around her but realized that it was only the sound of the chains around her feet. If only Beata had left the light on, she could have tried to get rid of them.

"Help!" she screamed again, this time with even less effect.

Don't panic, don't panic, don't panic . . .

"Help!!"

She was breathing hard and fast. Don't breathe too quickly, you'll only start cramping up. Nice and calm now, hold your breath, one-two-three-four, breathe, hold your breath, one-two-three-four, you're doing fine. Just take it easy, you'll be all right, everything can be sorted out . . .

Suddenly the first digital notes of Mozart's 40th Symphony sounded in the dark. Annika stopped hyperventilating from sheer astonishment. Her cellphone! It was working down here! God bless the cellphone! She got up on her heels. The sound was muffled and came from over on her right side. The music played on, bar after bar. She was the only one in town who used this particular signal: number 18 on the Nokia 3110. Cautiously, she started crawling toward the sound as the melody started from the beginning. She knew she was running out of time, soon the answering service would pick up the call. And then she ran out of chain—she couldn't reach her bag.

The telephone went dead. Annika was breathing loudly in the dark. She remained propped on her knees, thinking. Then she carefully moved back to the mattress; it was warmer and softer there.

"Everything'll be all right," she told herself. "As long as she isn't here, I'm all right. A bit uncomfortable, perhaps, but as long as I move around cautiously, I'm all right. I'll be fine."

She lay down and sang to herself, like an incantation, Gloria's old hit: "First I was afraid, I was petrified . . ."

Then she cried quietly, into the dark.

Thomas was walking away from the Central Station with long strides when his phone rang. He got hold of it in his coat pocket just before the answering service picked up the call.

"We told you we close at five today," one of the male staff at the daycare center said. "Will you be here soon?"

The traffic on Vasagatan was so loud that Thomas could barely hear himself think. He stepped aside and stopped in a shop's doorway, asking what was up.

"Are you on your way, or what?" the man said.

Thomas was shocked by the anger that hit him in his midriff. Christ, Annika! He'd let her sleep this morning, had taken the kids to the daycare center, and was coming back home on time—despite the leak on the regional bill—and she couldn't even pick up her own children on time.

"I'm so sorry. I'll be there in five minutes," he said and switched off.

Furious, he marched off toward Kungsbron. He turned the corner at Burger King, nearly bumped into a stroller loaded with Christmas gifts, and hurried up past the Oscar Theater. A group of men stood outside the jazz club Fashing. Thomas had to step out in the street to get past them.

This is what he got for being so understanding and equal-handed. His children were left waiting at a municipal institution the day before Christmas Eve because his wife, who was supposed to pick them up, let her work come before her family.

They'd been through this before. He could hear her voice through the city's noise.

"My work is important to me," she used to say.

"More important than the children?" he'd shouted once. Her face had turned pale and she'd said, 'of course not,' but he'd barely believed her. They'd had a couple of furious arguments on the issue, especially once, when his parents had invited them to celebrate Midsummer at their summer house. There had been a murder somewhere and naturally she was going to abandon all plans and take off.

"I'm not doing it just because I enjoy it," she had said. "I *do* enjoy going off on a job, but I'll also get a whole week's extra holiday out of them if I take on this assignment."

"You never think of the children," he'd fumed, and then she'd gone all cold and stand-offish.

"That's completely unfair," she'd said. "This will give me a whole week's extra holiday to be with them. They won't miss me for a second out on the island; there'll be loads of people there. You'll be there, gran and grandad, and all their cousins . . ."

"You're so damn selfish," he'd said to her.

She had been absolutely calm when she'd replied:

"No, it's you who are selfish. You want me to be there to show your parents what a nice family you have and to prove I'm not always working. I know your mother thinks I do. And she believes the children spend far too much time at the daycare center. Don't contradict me. I've heard her say it myself."

"Your work always comes before your family," he'd blurted out, intending to hurt her.

She had given him a disgusted look, and then said:

"Who stayed at home for two years with the kids? Who stays at home when they're ill? Who drops them at the daycare center every day, and who picks them up most of the time?"

She'd walked right up to face him.

"Yes, Thomas, you're absolutely right. I *am* going to put my work before my family this time. For once I'm going to do just that, and you'll just have to lump it."

Then she'd turned on her heel and walked out the door taking not so much as a toothbrush with her.

The Midsummer weekend had of course been ruined. For him, not the kids. They didn't miss Annika for a second, just as she'd predicted. Instead they were overjoyed when they returned home and found Mommy waiting at home with freshly baked buns and presents. In retrospect, he had to admit she was right. She didn't often put her work before her family, only sometimes, just like he did. But that hadn't stopped him from being furious. And the past two months everything had revolved around the paper. Being a manager wasn't good for her: The others tore into her and she just wasn't prepared for it.

He'd seen another sign of her not feeling well: She wasn't eating. Once, covering a mass murder, she was away for eight days and came back having lost ten pounds. It took her five months to put them back on. The company doctor had warned her about the risks associated with being underweight. She took it as praise and proudly told all her friends on the phone. All the same, she still got it in her head to go on a diet now and then.

He turned off Fleminggatan and took the steps down past the restaurant Klara Sjö, along the canal, approaching the daycare center the back way. The children were waiting inside the door, dressed and ready to go. They were tired and hollow-eyed; Ellen was holding her blue teddy in her arms.

"Mommy's picking us up today," Kalle said dismissively. "Where's Mommy?"

The nursery teacher who had stayed behind with the children was really annoyed.

"I'll never be able to get compensation for these fifteen minutes."

"I'm incredibly sorry," Thomas said, noticing how out of breath he was. "I don't understand where Annika's disappeared to."

He hurried away with the kids, and after a quick run, they managed to get on the 40 bus outside the lunch restaurant Pousette å Vis.

"You shouldn't run for the bus," the driver said irritably. "How are we going to teach children that if their parents do it?"

Thomas almost punched the idiot in the mouth. He held up his travel pass and shoved the kids toward the back of the bus. Ellen fell over and started to cry. I'm losing my mind, Thomas thought to himself. They had to stand up, jostling with Christmas shoppers, dogs, and strollers. Then they nearly didn't get off at their stop. He groaned out loud when he pushed the street door open, and as he was stamping the snow off his shoes, he heard someone speak his name.

He looked up in surprise and saw two uniformed police officers walk toward him.

"You must be Thomas Samuelsson. I'm afraid we're going to have to ask you and the children to come with us."

Thomas stared at them.

"We've been trying to get hold of you all afternoon. Haven't any of our messages reached you? Or any from the paper?"

"Where are we going, Daddy?" Kalle asked and took Thomas's hand. All at once Thomas realized something was terribly wrong. Annika! Christ!

"Annika. What's happened? Is she . . . ?"

"We don't know where your wife is. She disappeared this morning. The officers in charge of the investigation will tell you more. If you'd be so kind as to come with us . . ."

"Why?"

"Your apartment may be booby-trapped."

Thomas bent down and picked up both the children, one on each arm.

"Let's get away from here," he said in a stifled voice.

The Six Session at the paper was the most tense in many years. Anders Schyman felt panic lurking just beneath the surface. His instinct told him they shouldn't be publishing a paper; they should be out looking for Annika, giving support to her family, hunting for the Bomber—anything.

"We're going to sell one hell of a lot of papers," Ingvar Johansson said as he entered the room. He didn't sound smug or triumphant; it was more a sad statement of fact. But Anders Schyman went through the roof.

"How dare you?" the editor-in-chief shouted and grabbed Ingvar Johansson so violently that the news editor dropped his mug, spilling hot coffee down his leg. Ingvar Johansson didn't even feel the burn, he was so shocked. He had never seen Anders Schyman lose his cool like this. The editor-in-chief breathed in the other man's face for a few moments, then got a grip on himself.

"I'm sorry," he said, let go of the man, and turned away. "I'm not quite myself. I'm sorry."

Jansson enterered the room last, as always, but without his usual cheerful remarks. The night editor was pale and subdued. This was going to be the hardest paper he'd put together his whole career, he knew that.

"Okay," Schyman began, looking at the handful of

men around the table: Picture Pelle, Jansson, and Ingvar
Johansson. The soft-news and sports people had all gone
home. "How do we do this?"

For a few seconds, a tense silence filled the room.
Everyone sat with his head bent down. The chair Annika
normally occupied seemed to grow until it occupied the
entire room. Anders Schyman turned to face the night
outside the window.

Ingvar Johansson broke the silence and began talking,
quietly and focused. "I suppose what we have so far
must be called embryonic. There are several editorial
decisions involved in this . . ."

Unsure of himself, he leafed through his papers. The
situation felt both absurd and unreal. It was rare that the
people in this room were personally affected by the business they were dealing with. Now the discussion was
about one of them. And he'd just been half-strangled by
the editor-in-chief. As Ingvar Johansson started going
through the items on his list and giving an account of
what he'd done up to that point, they did at least find a
sort of strength in their routine. They couldn't get away
from it; the best they could do was to go on with their
work as well as they were able.

So this is what it's like to be the colleague of a victim,
Anders Schyman mused and stared out the window. It
might be a good idea to remember this feeling.

"First, there's the bomb at the Klara sorting office,"
Ingvar Johansson said. "We need one story about the victims. The man who was most badly injured died an hour
ago. The others are in a stable condition. The authorities
will be releasing their names during the night, and we're
counting on getting passport photos of them. Then
there's the damage to the building . . ."

"Leave the families alone," Schyman said.

"Sorry?" Ingvar Johansson said.

"The injured post office workers—leave their families alone."

"We haven't even got their names yet," Ingvar Johansson replied.

Schyman turned around to face the table. Distractedly, he pulled his hand through his hair, causing it to stand straight up. "Okay," he mumbled. "Sorry—go on."

Johansson took a few breaths, braced himself, and then continued: "We've actually been inside the damaged room at Klara. I've no idea how he did it, but Henriksson managed to get in and shoot a whole roll. Normally, the room isn't open even to regular staff; it's full of special delivery mail. But we've got the pictures."

"And to that we can add something on the responsibility," Schyman said, slowly walking around in the room. "What's the responsibility of the post office in a case like this? How thoroughly should they be checking the mail? It's the classic compromise between the integrity of the general public and the safety of their employees. We'll have to talk to the director general of the post office, the union, and the cabinet minister whose portfolio it falls within."

The editor stopped by the window, looking out at the dark night outside. He listened to the sighing of the ventilation system, searching for the sound of the traffic far below in the street. He couldn't hear it. Ingvar Johansson and Jansson took notes. After a while, the editor continued his run-through.

"There's the question of how we're affected by this at the paper, as the bomb was addressed to our crime editor. We'll have to give an account of that, the whole course of events, from when Tore Brand went to collect the parcel at lunchtime to the police attempts to trace the package."

"Annika has disappeared," Ingvar Johansson said in a low voice. "We have to face that now, and we have to write about it, don't we?"

Anders Schyman turned around. Ingvar Johansson looked uncertain.

"The question is whether we should say anything at all about the bomb being targeted at us," the news editor said. "We could end up with a flood of letter bombs, any number of copycats starting to kidnap our reporters or phone in bomb threats . . ."

"We can't think of it in that way," Schyman replied. "If we did, we wouldn't be able to cover anything that happened to anyone. We have to give an account of everything that has occurred, including anything involving ourselves and our crime editor. What I will do, though, is talk over with Thomas, Annika's husband, what we should write about her personal life."

"Has he been told?" Jansson asked, and Anders Schyman nodded.

"The police finally got hold of him around half past five. He'd been out of town, in Falun, all day and hadn't had his phone switched on. He had no idea what Annika was up to today."

"So we'll do a story on Annika having disappeared," Jansson said.

Schyman nodded and turned away again.

"We'll outline her work, but we have to be very careful with any details about her private life," Johansson said. "The next story will cover the police theories on why Annika was . . . targeted."

"*Do* they know why?" Picture Pelle asked, and the news editor shook his head.

"There is no connection between her and the other victims. They never met. Their hypothesis is that Annika has been digging around and found out something she shouldn't have. She's been leading the news from the first moment on this story. The motive has to be somewhere there. She simply knew too much."

The men fell silent, listening to each other's breathing.

"Not necessarily," Schyman said. "This lunatic just isn't rational. She could have sent off the bomb for reasons incomprehensible to anyone but herself."

The other men all looked up simultaneously. The editor-in-chief gave a sigh. "Yes, the police think it's a woman. I think we should print that. Annika thought this morning that the police had pinpointed her, but they hadn't told her who it was. Let's write that the police are searching for a suspect, a woman, whom they haven't been able to locate."

Anders Schyman sat down at the table and hid his face in his hands. "What the hell do we do if the Bomber has her? What if she's killed?"

No one replied. Somewhere out in the newsroom, *Aktuellt* came on. They could hear the voice of the anchor through the plasterboard walls.

"We'll have to do a recap of the bombings so far," Jansson said, stepping in. "Someone will have to pump the police for information on how they fixed on this particular woman. There are bound to be details there that we should . . ."

He fell silent. Suddenly, it wasn't so obvious what was relevant or not. The horizon had been shifted, the benchmark moved. All frames of reference were distorted; the focus was upside down.

"We'll have to handle this the normal way, as far as it's possible," Anders Schyman said. "Do what you usually do. I'll stay here tonight. What pictures do we have for this?"

The picture editor began to speak. "We haven't got that many pictures of Annika, but there is one from last summer, when we took pictures for the portrait gallery of employees. That could work."

"Isn't there one of her at work?"

Jansson snapped his fingers. "There is one of her in Panmunjom, in the demilitarized zone between North and South Korea, where she's standing next to the American president. She went there on a grant and got a place in a press delegation before the four-party talks in Washington last autumn, remember? She happened to step off the coach at the same moment as the president got out of his limo, and AP took a picture of the two of them standing right next to each other . . ."

"We'll use that," Schyman said.

"I've picked out some archive pictures of the damaged stadium, Sätra Hall, Furhage, and the builder, Bjurling," Picture Pelle added.

"Right," Schyman said, "what goes on the front page?"

Everyone waited in silence, letting the editor say it out loud.

"A portrait of Annika, preferably one where she looks happy. She's the news. The bomb was meant for her, and now she's disappeared. Only we know that. I think we should do it logically and chronologically: on pages six and seven, the bombing of Stockholm Klara sorting office; eight–nine, the new victims; ten–eleven, our reporter is missing; twelve–thirteen, the Bomber is a woman, the police have her pinned down; fourteen–fifteen, a recap of the bombings, an examination of mail security versus personal integrity; the center spread, the piece about Annika and her work, the picture from the DMZ . . ."

He fell silent and stood up, feeling nauseated at vocalizing his own decisions. Once again he went up to the window and looked out over the dark embassy building. By rights, they shouldn't be doing this. By rights, the paper shouldn't be published at all. By rights, they should let all coverage of the Bomber be. He felt like a monster.

The others quickly ran through the rest of the paper. No one said a word when they left the room.

Annika was shivering. It was cold in the passage; she thought the temperature to be somewhere around forty. Luckily, she'd put on long underwear that morning since she'd planned on walking home after work. At least she wouldn't freeze to death. But her socks were damp after the trudge through the snow and they chilled her feet. She tried wiggling her toes to keep warm. Her movements were cautious; she didn't dare move her feet too much or the explosive charge on her back might go off. At irregular intervals, she shifted position to rest different parts of her body. If she lay on her side, one of her arms was jammed; if she lay on her stomach, her neck hurt; her legs became numb if she tried kneeling or crouching. She cried from time to time, but the more time that passed, the more collected her thoughts became.

She wasn't dead yet. Panic subsided and her reasoning returned. She considered ways of escaping. That she could physically get away and run was not a realistic option. Attracting the attention of the builders up at the arena was out of the question; Beata had probably been lying when she'd said they were working up there. Why would they start the restoration on the day before Christmas? And for that matter, Annika hadn't seen a single car or person anywhere near the stadium. If the builders really had started work, there would have been various vehicles parked near the stadium, and she hadn't seen a single one. Anyway, they would have gone home a long time ago: It must be evening by now. Or even night. That meant they would have started looking for her. She started crying again when she realized that no one had picked up the kids from the nursery. She knew how pissed off the staff could get; it had happened to

Thomas about a year ago. The children would be sitting there, waiting to go home and dress the Christmas tree, and she wouldn't come. Maybe she'd never come home again. Maybe she'd never get to see them grow up. Ellen would probably not even remember her. Kalle might have vague memories of his mother, especially if looking at the photographs from last summer in the cottage. She started crying uncontrollably; it was all so horribly unfair.

The tears subsided after a while; she had no more energy for crying. She mustn't start thinking about death, then it would be guaranteed to happen, a self-fulfilling prophecy. She *was* going to get through this. She would be home for the Christmas Disney show at three o'clock tomorrow afternoon. She hadn't reached the end of the line yet. The bomber clearly had plans for her, otherwise she'd have been dead already, she was positive of that. Furthermore, the newspaper and Thomas would have sounded the alarm about her disappearance, and the police would start looking for her car. It was, however, lawfully and discreetly parked among a whole row of other cars, half a mile from the arena. And who would think of coming down here? No one had done so far. They would have discovered this hideout. How could the police have missed it? The entrance from the stadium must be well hidden.

The phone rang at regular intervals. She'd searched for a stick or something that she could use to pull her bag closer but had found nothing. Her range was less than ten feet in any direction and judging by the sound, her phone must be at least ten yards away. Oh, well, at least it meant they were trying to get hold of her.

She had no real grasp of what time it was or how long she'd been lying in the passage. It had been just before half past one when she walked inside, but she had no idea of how long she'd been unconscious. Neither could she judge for how long she had been panicking, but it must have been at least five hours since she got a grip of herself. That would mean it was at least half past six now, but it could be considerably later, nearer half past eight or nine. She was both hungry and thirsty and had pissed herself again—nothing much to worry about. Her excrement had started to harden and was itching. It was disgusting. This must be what it's like for children to wear a diaper. Except they get them changed.

Suddenly she was struck by another thought: What if Beata didn't come back? No one would think of coming down here during the Christmas holidays. A person could survive without water only a couple of days. Come Boxing Day and it would all be over. She started crying again, quietly with exhaustion. The Bomber *would* return. She had a reason for holding Annika captive down here.

She shifted positions again. She had to try and think clearly. She'd met Beata Ekesjö before. She had to start from what she knew about her as a person. During their short conversation in Sätra Hall, Beata had displayed strong emotion. She had been grieving sincerely for something, whatever that may have been, and she'd been eager to talk about it. Annika could use that. The question was how. She had no idea of how to behave in a situation where you were being held captive by a lunatic. She had heard somewhere that there were courses on that kind of thing, or had she read it? Or seen it on TV? Yes, that's it, on TV!

In an episode of *Cagney & Lacey*, one of the female cops had been taken prisoner by a madman. Cagney, or maybe it was Lacey, had attended a course on how to behave in a hostage situation. She had told him everything about herself and her children, about her dreams and her love—anything to awaken empathy in the kidnapper. If she were talkative and friendly enough, it made it harder for the kidnapper to kill her.

Annika shifted again, this time getting up on her knees. That stuff might work on a normal person, but the Bomber was crazy. She had already blown several people to pieces. That thing about children and empathy might not stir Beata; she hadn't shown much pity toward children and families this far. She'd have to think of something else but using the lesson learned from Cagney: to establish some form of communication with your kidnapper.

What had Beata said? That Annika had misinterpreted her state of mind? Was that really why she was here? She'd better read the Bomber's mood more accurately from now on. She would listen closely to what the woman said and try to be as responsive as she possibly could.

That's what she would do. She would try to establish a communication with the Bomber, pretending to understand and agree with her. She would under no circumstances contradict her but just go with her flow. She had a plan at least.

She lay down on her right side on the mattress, facing the concrete wall, determined to get some rest. She wasn't afraid of the dark, the blackness enveloping her held no danger for her. Soon she felt that familiar tug in her body, and a short while after she was asleep.

# DEATH

The school I attended was a wooden building with three floors. As we got older, we moved higher up. Once every year, in the spring, the entire school had a fire drill. In those days, old school buildings were dry as dust and burned down in minutes—there was no room for either negligence or anyone crying off.

There was a boy in my class who suffered from epilepsy. I forget his name. For some reason he couldn't hold his hands above his head. Nevertheless, he took part in the fire drill the year after the end of the war. I remember the day clearly. The sun was shining, a cold and pale light, and there was a hard and gusting wind. I hate heights—I always have—and was numb with fear as I stepped out on the fire escape. The world over by the river looked like it was about to keel over, and I gripped the railings. Infinitely slowly, I turned around and stared into the red wooden wall of the school building. I held on to each rung of the fire escape with the same desperate grip. When I finally reached the ground, I was completely exhausted. My legs were shaking, and I just stood there trying to compose *myself while my classmates started walking back toward our classroom. That's when I raised my eyes and saw the epileptic boy slowly climbing down the ladder. He had just reached the last landing when I heard him say: "I can't go on any further." He lay down, turning his face against the wall, and died, right before our eyes.*

*The ambulance came and picked him up. I had never seen one before. I stood next to the back doors when they lifted him inside on a stretcher. He looked as he usually did, only a bit paler, his eyes were closed, and his lips blue. His arms shook a bit when the stretcher was put in its place inside the large car, and a last breeze ruffled his blond curls before the door shut.*

*I can still recall my wonder at the fact that I felt no dread. I had seen a dead person, no older than myself, and I wasn't affected by it. He was neither repugnant nor tragic, only still.*

*Afterwards, I have often wondered what makes a person alive. Our minds are really nothing but a neurotransmitter and some electricity. The fact that I to this day still think about the epileptic boy actually lends him continued existence. He's present here in this dimension that we call reality, not by virtue of his own neurotransmitter, but because of mine.*

*The question is whether there aren't worse ways of harming people than killing them. Sometimes I suspect that I myself have crushed people, much as the teacher had by forcing that boy out onto the fire escape.*

*So the ultimate question in that case is whether I need absolution and, if so, from whom?*

# FRIDAY 24 DECEMBER

Thomas sat by the window, looking out across the water. It was a cold and clear evening. The water had frozen over and lay like a black mirror far below. The grayish brown facade of the Royal Palace was illuminated and stood like stage scenery against the wintery sky. On the bridge below, the taxis glided past toward the restaurant and Gamla Stans Bryggeri bar. He could just make out the line outside Café Opera.

He was in the living room of the corner suite on the fifth floor of the Grand Hotel. The suite was as big as an ordinary one-bedroom apartment, with a hallway, living room, bedroom, and a huge bathroom. The police had brought him here. They regarded the Grand Hotel as a suitable place for accommodating people under threat. Royalty and other heads of state often stayed here. The hotel staff were used to dealing with difficult situations. Naturally, Thomas wasn't registered under his own name. Two bodyguards had been posted in the adjoining suite.

An hour ago, the police had informed him that there were no explosive charges in the apartment on Hantverkargatan. But they would have to stay away all the same, until the Bomber had been apprehended. Anders Schyman had decided that Thomas and the children could spend Christmas at the hotel at the paper's expense, if need be. Thomas let go of the view outside and let his gaze travel across the dark room. He wished that Annika could have been there, that they could have enjoyed the luxury together. The furnishings were shiny and expensive looking, the green pile carpet as thick as a mattress. He stood up and walked in to the children in the bedroom next door. They were deep asleep, breathing softly, tired out after the adventure of going on a mini-holiday. They had had a bath in the beautiful bathroom, splashing all over the floor. Thomas hadn't even bothered to mop up after them. They'd had meatballs and creamed potatoes, brought up by room service. Kalle had thought the creamed potatoes were yucky; he was used to Annika's instant mash. Thomas didn't like it when Annika cooked sausages and mash for dinner—once he'd called it pig feed. Thinking about their stupid argument over it, he started crying, something he rarely did.

The police had found no trace of Annika. It was as if she'd vanished off the face of the earth. The car she'd been driving was also gone. The woman who they suspected was the Bomber hadn't been seen in her home since the police became suspicious of her, which was on Tuesday night. They'd circulated an alert for her. The police hadn't said what her name was, only that she'd been a building project manager at the Olympic stadium in Hammarby Dock.

Lost, he paced the thick carpet. He forced himself to sit down in front of the TV. As anticipated, it had seventy digital channels and a bunch of in-house movie channels, but Thomas couldn't settle down to watch anything. Instead he went out into the bathroom and spread the bath towels on the floor. He washed his face in ice-cold water and brushed his teeth with the complimentary toothbrush. The thick towels soaked up the water beneath his feet. He left the bathroom, undressed on the way to the bedroom, and threw his clothes in a heap on a chair in the hallway, then went in to his children. Thomas stood watching them for a moment. As usual, Kalle had spread out his arms and legs so that he occupied most of the double bed. Ellen lay curled up among the pillows at the top. One of the bodyguards had gone to a department store and bought two pairs of pajamas and some Game Boys. Thomas gathered up Kalle's limbs and tucked him in, then walked around to the other side of the bed and nestled down next to Ellen. Carefully, he put his arm under the girl's head and pulled her close. The little girl stirred in her sleep, and put her thumb in her mouth. Thomas didn't bother to pull it out; instead he breathed in the fragrance of the girl, letting his tears run free.

Work in the newsroom was performed with maximum concentration and in great silence. The noise level had been reduced considerably some years ago when the newspaper was computerized, but never before had it been this quiet. They were all sitting around the desk where the paper was produced during the night. Jansson was continuously on the phone, as usual, only quieter and mumbling more than ever. Anders Schyman had installed himself in the chair where the lead writer would sit during the day. He did very little, mostly just sat staring into thin air or talking quietly on the phone. Berit and Janet Ullberg usually worked at their desks in the far corner of the newsroom, but now they sat writing by the night reporters' desk so they could follow what was going on. Patrik Nilsson was also there; Ingvar Johansson had called him in the afternoon. The reporter had been on his flight to Jönköping, and of course he had answered the call.

"It's forbidden to have your cellphone on during the flight," Ingvar Johansson told him.

"I know that!" Patrik screamed with obvious delight. "I just wanted to check if it's true that the plane will crash if you have it on."

"So is it?" Ingvar Johansson asked sarcastically.

"Not yet, but if it does, you'll have a major scoop for tomorrow! '*Kvällspressen* Reporter in Plane Crash Drama—Read His Last Words.' "

He shrieked with laughter and Ingvar Johansson rolled his eyes.

"I think we'll hold that, we already have one reporter at the center of a bomb drama. When can you get back?" Johansson filled him in.

Patrik hadn't even stepped off the plane but returned with it to Stockholm. He'd arrived at the newspaper at five in the afternoon. Now he was writing copy for the story of the police hunt for the Bomber. Anders Schyman was secretly watching him. He marveled at the young man's speed and commitment; there was something quite improbable about him. His only flaw was his undisguised delight in accidents, murder, and various other tragedies. But with a bit of experience that would no doubt tone itself down. With time, he would become a very good tabloid journalist.

Schyman stood up to get some more coffee. He felt slightly sick with all the coffee he'd drunk already, but he needed to remain awake. He turned his back on the people in the newsroom and slowly walked toward the

row of windows on the other side of the Sunday supplement desk. He stood watching the apartment block next
to the newspaper offices. The lights were still on in several windows, even though it was past midnight. People
were up watching the thriller on TV3, drinking glogg.
Others were wrapping the last of their Christmas gifts.
On several balconies, there were Christmas trees, the
lights glimmering in the windows.

Schyman had talked to the police several times during
the night. He'd become the link between the newsroom
and the Krim people. When Annika hadn't showed up at
the daycare center by 5 P.M., they began dealing with it as
a missing person case. After talking to Thomas, the police
command regarded it as out of the question that Annika
had disappeared of her own free will. Her disappearance had during the evening been classified as
abduction.

Earlier, the police had banned them from calling
Annika's cellphone. Schyman had asked why but got no
reply. He had, however, passed on the order to the
others, and as far as he knew, no one had tried to phone
her since.

The staff were shaken and upset. Berit and Janet
Ullberg had been crying. It's strange, Anders Schyman
thought; we write about these things every day, using
people's suffering to spice things up. Yet we're wholly
unprepared when hit by it ourselves. He walked off to
get another mug of coffee.

Annika was wakened by a cold wind rushing through
the passage. She immediately knew what that meant.
The iron door under the arena had been opened. The
Bomber was returning. Fear made her curl up in a little
ball on the mattress; she lay still, breathing raggedly as
the strip lights flickered on.

Her instincts were whispering: Be calm, listen to the woman, find out what she wants, do as she tells you, try to win her confidence.

The sound of clattering heels approached; Annika sat up.

"Look at that, you're awake. Good," Beata said and walked over to the folding table. She began unpacking various food items from a 7-Eleven plastic bag. She lined them up around the flashlight battery and the timer. Annika could make out some cans of Coke, Evian water, some sandwiches, and a chocolate bar.

"Do you like Fazer Blue? It's my favorite," Beata said.

"Mine, too, actually," Annika said, trying to keep her voice steady. She didn't like chocolate and had never tried Fazer Blue.

Beata folded up the plastic bag and put it in her coat pocket.

"We have some work to do," she said, sitting down on one of the stools.

Annika tried to smile. "Oh, what are we doing?"

Beata looked at her for a couple of seconds. "We're finally going to get the truth out."

Annika tried to follow the woman's reasoning but failed. Fear was making her mouth dry and parched. "What truth?"

Beata walked around the table and picked something up. When she straightened up, Annika saw that she was holding a noose, the one she'd put around her neck earlier. She felt her pulse quicken but forced herself to look at Beata with a steady gaze.

"Don't worry," the Bomber said, smiling. She approached the mattress with the long rope in her hands. Annika felt her breathing speed up; she couldn't control her feelings of panic.

"Relax, I'm just going to put this back around your neck," Beata said, laughing lightly. "You're so jumpy!"

Annika forced a smile. The noose was around her neck, the rope hanging like a tie on her chest. Beata held onto the end of the rope.

"That's it. Now I'm going to walk around you . . . I told you to relax!"

Out of the corner of her eye, Annika saw the woman disappear behind her back, still with the rope in her hand.

"I'm going to release your hands, but don't try anything. If you do, I'll tighten the rope for good."

Annika breathed and racked her brains. She realized there was nothing she could do. Her feet were chained to the wall, she had the noose around her neck, and the explosives on her back. It took Beata close to five minutes to untie the rope around Annika's hands.

"Phew, that was tight," she panted when she'd finished. Annika's fingers immediately started tingling as the blood started flowing again. Carefully, she moved her hands back and forth, wincing at the look of them. The skin on her wrists was chafed and raw, either from the rope, the wall, or the floor. Two of the knuckles on her left hand were bleeding.

"Get up," Beata ordered.

Using the wall to support herself, Annika did as she was told.

"Kick the mattress to the side," Beata said, and Annika obeyed. The dried-up vomit disappeared under the foam rubber. While doing this, Annika spotted her bag. It lay some twenty feet away, toward the training arena exit.

Still with the rope in her hand, the Bomber walked backwards to the table. She put the battery and the timer on the floor, keeping her eyes on Annika. Then she gripped the table and pulled it closer. The scraping sound of the table legs against the floor echoed in the passage. When the table was right in front of Annika, Beata backed away again and picked up a stool.

"Sit down."

Annika pulled the stool closer and gingerly sat down. Her stomach turned when she saw the food on the table.

"Have something to eat," Beata said.

Annika started pulling off the plastic seal on the water bottle. "Do you want some?" she asked Beata.

"I'll have a Coke later; you drink," Beata said, and Annika drank. She had a small ham and cheese baguette and forced herself to chew properly. Having eaten half, she couldn't continue, she couldn't get any more down.

"Finished?" Beata asked, and Annika smiled.

"Yes, thanks, that was really nice."

"I'm glad you liked it," Beata said, pleased. She sat down on the other stool. On one side of her was the parcel with Minex, on the other was a brown box, the flaps open.

"Time to begin," she said and smiled.

Annika returned the smile. "Can I ask you something?" she asked.

"Of course," Beata replied.

"Why am I here?"

Beata's smile died at once. "You really don't understand?"

Annika took a deep breath. "No. What I do understand is that I must have made you very angry. I really didn't mean to, and I apologize," she said.

Beata chewed on her upper lip. "Not only did you lie, you wrote in the paper that I was devastated by the death of that creep. On top of that you humiliated me publicly, twisting my words to get a better story. You wouldn't listen to me and my truth, but you listened to the guys."

"I'm sorry I misread your frame of mind," Annika said, as calmly as she could. "I didn't want to quote you saying things you might regret later. You were obviously shaken, and you were crying a lot."

"Yes, I was despairing of the evil of people, that bastards like Stefan Bjurling were allowed to live. Why should fate use me to end the misery? Why should everything always be up to me, eh?"

Annika decided to wait and listen. Beata continued chewing on her lip.

"You lied and spread a false picture of that bastard," she went on after awhile. "You wrote that he was nice and funny and that his workmates liked him. You let them talk, but not me. Why didn't you write what I said?"

Annika felt increasingly confused, but she made an effort to sound calm and friendly. "What did you say that you think I should have written?"

"The truth. That it was a shame that Christina and Stefan had to die. That it was their own fault and how wrong it was that I had to do it. I don't enjoy doing this, if that's what you think."

Annika braced herself to play along. "No, of course I don't think that. I know how you're sometimes forced to do things you'd rather not."

"What do you mean by that?"

"I had to get rid of someone once, I know the feeling." Annika looked up. "But we're not here to talk about me now. This is about you and your truth."

Beata observed her in silence for a while. "Maybe you're wondering why you're not dead yet. Because first you're going to write down my story. It will be published in *Kvällspressen*, and it will be given as much space as Christina Furhage's death was."

Annika nodded and smiled mechanically.

"I'll show you what I've got," Beata said and pulled something out of the box next to her. It was a laptop computer.

"Christina's Powerbook!" Annika gasped.

"Yes, she was very fond of this. It's fully charged."

Beata got to her feet and walked over to Annika with the computer in her right hand. It looked heavy, her hand was shaking slightly.

"Here you are. Switch it on."

Annika took the laptop. It was a basic Macintosh Powerbook, with a rechargeable battery, a disk slot, and a port for the mouse. She opened the lid and switched on the machine. It hummed to life and started loading the programs. There were only a few, among them Microsoft Word. After a few seconds, the desktop appeared. The desktop pattern was a sunset in pink, blue, and purple. There were three icons on the desktop: the hard disk itself, the Word icon, and a file marked "Me." Annika double-clicked on the Word icon and the 6.0 version started up.

"Right, I'm ready to begin," Annika said. Her fingers were frozen stiff and aching; she squeezed them discreetly under the table.

"Good. I want this to be as good as is possible."

"Okay, sure," Annika said and prepared to start writing.

"I want you to write what I tell you, in my own words, so it'll be my story."

"Naturally," Annika said.

"Though I want you to touch it up so it's neat and easy to read and is stylistically good."

Annika looked up at the other woman. "Beata, trust me. I do this every day. Shall we begin?"

The Bomber straightened up on her stool.

"Evil is everywhere. It's devouring people from within. Its apostles on earth are finding their way into the heart of humanity, stoning it to death. The battle is leaving bloodstained remnants in space because Fate is resisting. One knight is fighting on the side of Truth, a human of flesh and blood . . ."

"Forgive me for interrupting," Annika said, "but this feels a bit muddled. The reader won't be able to follow."

Beata looked at her with surprise. "Why not?"

Annika knew that she had to choose her words very carefully. "Many people haven't thought as far and gained the same insights as you have," she said. "They won't understand, and then the whole piece is pointless. The idea is for them to get closer to truth, right?"

"Yes, of course," Beata said. It was her turn to be confused.

"Maybe we should wait a bit before we bring in Fate and Evil, and instead do it in a more chronological order. It will make it easier for the reader to take in the truth later on. Okay?"

Beata nodded eagerly.

"I thought maybe I could ask you a few questions, and you can answer whichever ones you want."

"Okay," Beata agreed.

"Can you tell me a bit about your childhood?"

"Why?"

"It'll make the readers picture you as a child and that way they'll identify with you."

"I see. So what should I tell you?"

"Anything you like," Annika said. "Where you grew up, who your parents were, if you had any sisters or brothers, pets, special toys, how you did at school, all those things . . ."

Beata looked at her for a long time. Annika could see in her eyes that her thoughts were far away. She started talking, and Annika put her words into a readable story.

"I grew up in Djursholm. My parents were both doctors. Are both doctors, in fact. They're both still working and still live in the house with the iron gate I grew up in. I had an older brother and a younger sister. My childhood was relatively happy. My mother worked part time as a child psychologist, and my father had a private practice. We had nannies taking care of us—male ones, too. This was in the '70s and my parents were into equality between men and women and open to new ideas.

"I developed an interest in houses early on. We had a playhouse in the garden; my sister and her friends used to lock me inside it. During my long afternoons in the dusk, we started talking to each other, my little house and I. The nannies knew that I'd get stuck in the playhouse, so they'd always come and open the door after a while. Sometimes they'd scold my sister, but I didn't care."

Beata fell silent and Annika stopped writing. She breathed on her hands; it really was cold. "Can you tell me a bit about being a teenager?" she asked. "What happened to your sister and brother?"

The Bomber continued:

"My brother became a doctor, just like our parents, and my sister qualified as a physiotherapist. She married Nasse, a childhood friend, and doesn't have to work. They live with their children in a house in Täby.

"I broke the family pattern a bit because I studied to be an architect. My parents were skeptical. They thought I'd be more suited to be a preschool teacher or occupational therapist. But they didn't try to stop me; they are modern people, after all. I went to the Royal Institute of Technology and finished among the best graduates.

"Why did I choose to work with houses? I love buildings! They speak to you in such an immediate and straightforward way. I love traveling, only to talk to houses in new places—their form, their windows, colors, and luster. I get excited by courtyards sexually. I have thrills up and down my spine when I'm on a train traveling through the suburbs of a city, seeing laundry hung out to dry across the railway line, leaning balconies . . . I never look straight ahead of me when I'm out walking, always upwards. I have bumped into traffic signs and phone boxes all over the city because I've been studying house facades. I'm simply interested in buildings. I wanted to work with my greatest passion.

"I spent many years learning to draw buildings. But when I graduated, I realized that I had made the wrong choice. Houses on paper don't speak to you; a sketched house is only a template for the real thing. So I went back to the university after only half a year at work and did a degree in constructional engineering. That took several years. When I finished, they were recruiting people for the municipal partnership building the new Olympic stadium in Hammarby Dock. I got a job, and that's how I first came to meet Christina Furhage."

Again, Beata fell silent. Annika waited a long time for her to continue.

"Do you want to read it?" she asked in the end, but Beata shook her head.

"I know you'll make it sound good. I'll read it later, when you've finished." She sniffed and then continued:

"Of course, I knew who she was already. I'd seen her in the paper lots of times, ever since the campaign to get the Olympics to Stockholm was mounted, which she won and was appointed MD of the entire project.

"Where did I live during that time? Oh, yes, where I still am now, in an absolutely adorable little house by Skinnarviksparken on South Island. Are you familiar with the area around Yttersta Tvärgränd? The house is listed, so I've had to renovate it very gently. My home is important to me, the house I live and breathe in. We talk to each other every day, my house and I; exchanging experiences and wisdom. Do I need to point out that I'm the novice out of the two of us? My house has stood on the hill since the end of the eighteenth century, so in our conversations, I'm usually the one listening and learning. Christina Furhage visited me once. It felt good that my house got to know her a bit; it helped me later on in my difficult decision."

The woman again fell silent.

"Tell me about your work."

"Is that really relevant?" Beata asked with surprise.

No, not one bit, but it'll buy me time, Annika thought to herself.

"Yes, of course," she said. "A lot of people work. They will want to know what your job was like, what was on your mind when you were doing it, things like that . . ."

Beata straightened up. "Oh, yes, I can see that," she said.

Self-centered little shit, Annika thought to herself and managed a smile.

"I don't know how versed you are in the building trade. Maybe you don't know how the process of procurement is carried out? Actually, it doesn't really matter in this case, since the building of Victoria Stadium was so special that no general rules applied.

"Stockholm was chosen to host the Summer Olympic Games under the leadership of Christina Furhage, you know that. The decision wasn't a straightforward one. She really had to fight for her post.

"Christina really was amazing. She pushed the Olympic suits around something wonderful! We women really enjoyed having a boss like that. Not that I met her very often, but since she kept an eye on every single detail in the entire organization, I did run in to her now and then.

"I admired her a lot. When she came around, everyone pulled their socks up and did their best. She had that effect on people. What she didn't know about the Olympic planning and the building of the arena wasn't worth knowing.

"Anyway, I was employed by Arena Bygg AB. As I was both an architect and a constructional engineer, I was given several major administrative assignments straight away. I took part in negotiations, made construction drawings and calculations, visited subcontractors, and drew up contracts—a kind of general factotum in a semi-important position.

"The actual construction of Victoria Stadium was supposed to begin five years before the Games. Christina herself appointed me project manager. I remember clearly the day she asked me. I'd been called to her office, a grandiose place next door to Rosenbad with a view over the Stockholm Canal. She asked what I had been doing so far and if I was happy. I didn't think I'd done very well and stuttered a bit—my hands were all clammy. She was so impressive behind her polished desk: tall, yet slim; sharp, yet beautiful. She asked me whether I was willing to take responsibility for the building of the Olympic stadium in Hammarby Dock. My head was spinning when she uttered the words. I wanted to shout 'Oh yes!' but just nodded and said it would be a challenge. An exciting responsibility I felt ready to shoulder. She quickly added that I would have several managers and other people above me, and at the top, her. But she needed someone on site who was responsible for the operation, someone who would see to it that it ran according to schedule, that we weren't over budget, and that deliveries of building material arrived in the right place at the right time. I would of course have a team of foremen under me with responsibility for specific sections where they led the work. These foremen would be reporting to me, so that I in my turn could do my job and report to Christina and the board.

" 'I need loyalty,' Christina said and leaned toward me. 'I need your unwavering conviction that what I do is right. That's a prerequisite for anyone taking this job. Can I trust you?'

"I remember her radiance at that precise moment, how she brought me into her light, filling me with her strength and power. I wanted to scream 'YES!' but instead I just nodded. Because I knew what had happened—she had included me in her circle. She had made me her crown princess. I was chosen."

Beata started crying. She bent her head and her whole body was shaking. The rope lay by her feet, her hands holding the battery and the fuse in a desperate grip. I hope her tears don't short-circuit the battery so the charge is set off, Annika thought.

"I'm sorry," Beata said and wiped her nose on the sleeve of her coat. "This is hard for me."

Annika didn't say anything.

"It was a big responsibility, but it wasn't really a difficult job. First there was the clearing, the blasting, the
excavating, and subsequent filling in and moulding.
Then the builders and carpenters would arrive. It all
had to be done in four years. The arena was to be ready
for trial competitions a year ahead of the Games.

"It went all right at first. The workers drove their
machines around and did what they were supposed to
be doing. I had my office in one of the sheds down by
the canal. Maybe you saw them when you came to have
a look? No?

"Anyway, I did my job, talking to the coordinators
down in the pit, making sure they carried out their
tasks. The men who did the actual work weren't very
talkative, but at least they listened to me when I gave
them directions.

"Once a month, I went to Christina's office and told
her how the work was coming on. She always received
me with warmth and interest. After every meeting, I
felt as if she knew beforehand what I was going to tell
her and that she just wanted to check up on my loyalty.
I always left her office with a churning feeling in the pit
of my stomach and a peculiar sense of exhilaration. I
was still in her circle, the power was mine, but I would
have to continue fighting for it.

"I really loved my work. Sometimes, in the evening,
I would stay behind after the men had gone home. On
my own, I would climb around among the remains of
the old Hammarby ski slope, imagining the finished
arena: the enormous stands, the 75,000 spectator seats
in green, the sweep of the arched openwork steel roof.
I would caress the construction drawings. I even put up
a large-scale picture of the model on the wall in my
office. From the very beginning, I talked to the stadium.
Just like a newborn baby, it didn't answer, but I'm sure

it listened. I observed every detail in its development, like a breastfeeding mother marveling at the progress in her child.

"The problems started when the foundation was laid and the carpenters arrived. Several hundred men were going to perform the work I was responsible for. They were supervised by thirty-five team leaders, all men between forty and fifty-five. At this point, my workload quadrupled. On my advice, three supervisors were hired who were to share the responsibility with me, all men.

"I don't know where it all went wrong. I continued working in the same way as I had been the first years, trying to be clear and straightforward and direct. We stayed within budget and on schedule as well. Building materials arrived on time and at the right place, and work was progressing and meeting the quality requirements. I tried to be cheerful and friendly, taking pains to treat the men with respect. I can't quite say when the first signals that something was wrong started appearing, but it didn't take long. Conversations that stopped, faces I wasn't meant to see, condescending smiles, cold eyes. I organized information and update meetings, which I found constructive myself, but my message wasn't getting through. In the end, the foremen stopped coming. I'd go outside to get them, but they would just look at me and say they were busy. Naturally, it made me feel like a fool. The few who did show up questioned everything I said. They said I had ordered the material in the wrong sequence, at the wrong place, and anyway the entire batch was useless as they'd already ordered another load. Of course, that angered me, and I asked on what authority they ignored my orders and took it upon themselves to make decisions in this way. They answered me in a condescending tone: that if this project ever was to be finished on time, it needed people who knew what they were doing. I remember the feeling when I heard those words; it was as if something broke inside me. The men got up and left, contempt in their eyes. The three supervisors immediately under me stopped just outside and talked to the foremen. I heard them giving *my* orders and forwarding exactly the information I had on the paper in my hand—now they listened. They could take my orders if given by someone else. It wasn't my work, my judgement, or my knowledge they found faults with: It was me as a person.

"After the meeting, I summoned the three supervisors and said that we needed to work out our next step. I wanted the four of us together to put the organization to rights and take command of the employees in order for work to continue in the direction we'd decided on. They sat down around my desk, one on each side and one directly in front of me.

" 'You can't handle this job,' the first one said.

" 'Don't you see you're making a complete fool of yourself around the whole site?' asked one of his companions.

" 'Frankly, you're a joke,' the third one said. 'You've no authority, no command, and no competence.'

"I just stared at them. I couldn't believe what they were saying was true. I knew they were wrong. But once they'd got going, nothing could stop them.

" 'All you can do is swing your hips,' said number one.

" 'You're demanding too much of the men,' said number two. 'It's obvious. You must see it.'

" 'They're going to freeze you out completely,' number three said. 'You were hired on the wrong grounds and with the wrong background.'

"I remember looking at them, seeing their faces change. They all lost their features and became white and vague. I couldn't get any air; I thought I was going to suffocate. I got up and left the room. I'm afraid it didn't come over as particularly dignified."

The woman sniveled with her head bent down. Annika glanced at her with aversion. "So what?" she wanted to say. "It's like that for everybody," but she didn't say anything, and Beata continued her story:

"That night in bed, my house talked to me; words of comfort whispered through the rose-patterned wallpaper. The next day, I couldn't bear to go to work. I was paralyzed with fear, tied to my bed with it. Christina saved me. She called me at home and asked me to come to work the following morning. She had some important information that concerned everyone at the building site.

"I went to the shed the next morning in a state of peace. We had been asked to come to the North Stand at eleven o'clock. The three supervisors didn't speak to me, but I smiled at them so that they'd understand. Christina would soon be there.

"I waited for everyone to be present before I went out. I made sure I'd walk out on the stand the same time as Christina. In her light, clear voice, she said she was there to inform us of a change in management at the Olympic stadium. I felt her warmth and smiled.

" 'Beata Ekesjö will leave as project manager and be replaced by the three supervisors immediately under her,' Christina said. 'I have full confidence in her successors and hope that work will progress as successfully as it has so far.'

"It was as if the sky had turned a flashing white. The light changed and the people froze to ice.

"On that day, the realization of what I had to do was born, but I hadn't yet formulated the goal to myself. I left the North Stand while the people were still listening to Christina's charismatic voice. Inside the shed, I had my bag with gym clothes, as I'd planned to go to the gym straight after work. I emptied the bag of its contents in my locker and brought the bag with me around to the back of the sheds. That's where the explosives bins stood, about a hundred yards apart—there are rules about how close they can stand because of the risk of detonation. One set of cartridges fits perfectly inside a gym bag; it's almost as if they're made for each other. It got really heavy, fifty pounds with the bag. But that's about the weight of a normal suitcase. You can carry it a short distance, especially if you work out in a gym three times a week . . ."

"Hang on," Annika said. "Aren't explosives usually guarded by all kinds of safety regulations? How could you just walk in and pick up a load of explosives?"

Beata gave her a look of pity. "Annika, I was the boss at that site. I had keys to all the locks. And I fixed the ledger so the stuff wouldn't be missed. Don't interrupt me."

"In the first box were fifteen cartridges wrapped in pink plastic. I put the box in the trunk of my car and drove home. With great care I carried my treasure into the house. That night I caressed it with my hands. There were metal clips at both ends; the plastic felt cool to the touch. My weapons both looked and felt like sausages that have been in the fridge. They were quite soft; in the evening I would sit and bend them this way and that. Yes, just like sausages, only heavier."

Beata laughed at the memory. Annika felt sick, from tiredness but also from the other woman's absolute madness.

"Can we take a break?" Annika wondered. "I'd like to have a Coke."

The Bomber looked up at her. "Well, a short break. We have to finish tonight."

Annika felt herself stop cold.

"They didn't know what to do with me. My contract was for the construction of the Olympic stadium and the Village. They'd have to pay me a lot to get rid of me, and they didn't want to do that. Besides, I knew the job, so it would be stupid of them to pay for losing expertise that they needed. In the end, they made me site engineer for the construction of the technical facilities building right next to the stadium; an ordinary ten-floor building built to house cables, control rooms, and offices. Do I need to tell you that this structure felt mute and dead compared with my stadium? An empty concrete shell with no contours or shape—and it never learned to speak.

"There already was a building manager there. His name was Kurt and he regularly drank large quantities of alcohol. He hated me from the very first moment, claiming I was there to spy on him. Already on my first day at the site, his features disappeared. I couldn't see him.

"The site was one big mess. Everything was delayed and they were badly over budget. I started clearing up behind Kurt without his noticing it. On the occasions he caught me making any form of decision, he had a go at me. But after I got there, he didn't do a stroke of work. Often he didn't even show up. The first time that happened I reported it, but it made him so furious that I never did it again.

"In addition, I was now supposed to be site foreman, something I'd never been before. It got difficult.
The concrete often shifted colors, and sometimes I
would float, weightless, about three inches above the
floor. The men changed, both shape and substance.
When they asked me to order more visual angles and
wondered where the eye measure was, I was dumb-
founded. I knew they were poking fun at me. But I
couldn't defend myself. I tried being flexible and strong
at the same time. I talked to the building, but it refused
to answer. Once again I was taking care of timetables
and estimates, moving around on the site, but the glass
cage around me was impenetrable. But we finished on
time, and only marginally over budget.

"Christina was coming out to perform the inauguration. I remember the fervor and pride I felt on that
day. I'd done it, I'd bounced back, I hadn't given up. I'd
made sure the technical facilities building was ready in
time for the trial competitions. I detested the building
itself, but I had done my duty. Christina knew this,
Christina would see it, Christina would understand
that I was worthy of a place in the light again. She
would see me for who I was and put me back in my
rightful place, by her side, as her attendant, her crown
princess.

"I dressed with care on the day: blouse, well-ironed
trousers, and loafers. This time I was among the first to
arrive; I wanted to make sure of a place near the
entrance.

"I hadn't seen Christina for a long time, only
glimpsed her at a distance once when she came to
inspect the building of the stadium. It wasn't going
very well, I'd heard. It was uncertain whether they'd
finish on time. Now, here she was, shining brighter and
with clearer features than I'd remembered. She said

nice things about the Olympic Games and our proud Olympic Village, praising the workers and those responsible for making the work run so smoothly. So she wanted to call the project manager forward, the person who had made sure that the building was ready on time, and what a great building it was too. And she called out Kurt's name. She applauded, everyone applauded, and Kurt went up to Christina, smiling, taking her hand, she putting her hand on his arm, their mouths laughing, but there was no sound. The bastards, the bastards . . .

"That night I went to the explosives storage and picked up the second box of dynamite and a bag of electric detonators. This box was full of little paper-wrapped cartridges of a hundred grams apiece, little pink and purple paper tubes that looked like peppermint rock. It's some of those that you have on your back now. The box contained two hundred and fifty of them; even though I've used quite a few, there are still a lot left."

She sat in silence for a while. Annika took the opportunity to rest her head in her hands. The tunnel was completely quiet; there was only a low hum from the strip lights under the ceiling. They've stopped calling, Annika thought. Have they stopped looking for me already?

Beata resumed her story and Annika stretched her back.

"During the last year, I've been off sick quite a lot. I'm formally stationed in the pool of project managers that go around inspecting and completing details at the various training arenas. The last two months I've been working at Sätra Hall. You see the demotion I've been subject to— from the proudest of all buildings to thrashing out technicalities at the oldest training facilities. I never have time to establish any communication with my workplaces nowadays. The buildings taunt me, just as the men do. Stefan Bjurling was worst of all. He was a foreman with the subcontractor responsible for Sätra Hall. There was always a sneer on his face when I tried to talk to him. He never listened to me. He called me 'pet' and ignored everything I said. The only occasions he did refer to me were when the men asked him where they should put trash and lumber. 'Give it to little pet,' he'd say. He laughed at me, and the beautiful hall joined in. The sound was unbearable."

Beata fell silent and didn't say anything for so long that Annika started fidgeting. Her muscles ached with weariness, and on top of that she now had a bad headache. Her arms felt like lead—that paralyzing feeling that would come creeping after half past three in the morning. She recognized it from the night shifts.

She thought of her children, where they were, if they missed her. I wonder if Thomas will find the Christmas gifts? I never got to tell him I hid them in the big closet, she thought.

She looked at Beata. The woman was sitting with her head in her hands. Annika carefully turned her head and looked furtively at the bag behind her. If only she could get hold of the phone, then she could call and tell them where she was! The signal went through, even though they were in an underground tunnel. She'd be free in fifteen minutes. Easier said than done. As long as she was tied up and as long as Beata was still here. If only Beata would get her the bag and put her fingers in her ears while she made the call . . .

She gasped—suddenly she remembered a story she had written two years before. It was a beautiful late winter day, and people were out walking on the ice-covered waters around Stockholm . . .

"Are you dreaming?" Beata said.

Annika started and smiled. "No, not at all. I'm looking forward to hearing the rest," she said.

"A couple of weeks ago, Christina arranged a big party in *Blå Hallen*, the banqueting hall at City Hall. It was the last big party before the Games, and everyone was invited. I was really looking forward to the night. City Hall is one of my best friends. I often go up in the tower, climbing the steps, letting the stone walls dance under my hands, feeling the draught from the small apertures in the walls. I rest on the top landing. Together we share the view and the wind. It's over-poweringly erotic.

"I arrived much too early. I soon realized I was far too dressed up. But I didn't mind. City Hall was my partner and I was well looked after. Christina was coming, and I was hoping that the forgiving atmosphere in the building would straighten out all misunderstandings. I moved around among the people, had a glass of wine, and talked to the building.

"When the murmur in the hall rose to an excited buzz, I knew Christina had arrived. She was received like the queen she was. I got up on a chair in order to see it properly. It's hard to explain, but Christina had a sort of light about her, an aura that made her look like she was always in a spotlight. It was fantastic—*she* was fantastic. Everyone greeted her, and she nodded and smiled. She had a word for everyone. Shaking hands like an American president on an election campaign. I was standing quite far back in the hall, but she was slowly working herself over my way. I jumped down from the chair and lost sight of her, since I'm so short.

But suddenly she was standing there in front of me, beautiful and glowing in her light. I felt myself beginning to smile, from ear to ear, I think I even had tears in my eyes.

" 'Welcome, Christina,' I said, holding out my hand. 'I'm so glad you're here.'

" 'Thank you,' she said. 'Have we met?'

"Her eyes met mine and her mouth was smiling. I saw she was smiling, but the smile was contorting and her face died. She had no teeth. There were maggots in her mouth and her eye sockets were empty. She smiled, breathing death and sewage. I felt myself recoiling. She didn't recognize me. She didn't know who I was. She didn't know her crown princess. She spoke, and her voice came from an abyss, dull and raucous like a tape being played too slowly.

" 'Shall we move on?' Christina boomed, the maggots crawling out of her head, and I knew then I had to kill her. You understand that, don't you? Surely you must understand? That she couldn't be allowed to live? She was a monster, a fallen angel with a halo. Evil had devoured her, corrupting her inside and out. My house was right; she was evil incarnate. I hadn't seen that, the others hadn't seen it, all they saw was what I'd seen: her successful exterior, her luminous aura, and her bleached hair. But I'd seen it, Annika; I discovered her true self. She'd shown herself to me as the monster she was, reeking of poison and rotten blood . . ."

Annika felt the nausea growing inside her. It was almost unbearable. Beata opened a can of Coke, drinking it in small, careful sips.

"One should really drink Diet Coke, for the calories, but I can't stand the taste. What do you think?" she asked Annika.

Annika swallowed. "You're absolutely right," she said.

Beata smiled a bit.

"My decision helped me survive the evening because the nightmare wasn't over. Do you know who she chose for her Prince, her partner at table? Of course you know that, you had a picture of them together. All of a sudden everything fell into place. I knew what the purpose of my cold treasures at home was. It was all revealed to me. The big box was meant for Christina, the smaller cartridges for those who walked in her footsteps.

"My plan was simple. I would follow Christina around. Sometimes I got it into my head that she knew I was there. She would look around anxiously before she hurried into her big car, always with the laptop under her arm. I used to wonder what she wrote on it, if she wrote anything about me or maybe about Helena Starke. I knew she often went to Helena Starke's house. I would wait outside and see her leave early in the morning. I understood they were lovers. I knew it would be fatal for Christina if this got out. That made it simple, at least theoretically. Certain things get very messy when you put them into practice, don't you think?

"Anyway, last Friday night when I saw Christina and Helena leave the Secretariat's Christmas party, I knew the time had come. I went home and picked up my big treasure. It was heavy, and I put it next to me on the front seat. On the floor in the front was a car battery that I'd bought at a gas station in Västberga. The timer I got from IKEA. People use them in their holiday cottages to fool burglars.

"I parked over where your car is now. The bag was heavy, but I'm stronger than I look. I was a bit nervous.

I didn't know how much time I had, and I had to finish the preparations before Christina left Helena's house. Luckily, it all went quite quickly. I carried the bag up to the entrance around the back, switched off the alarms, and unlocked the doors. I nearly got into trouble there; a man saw me enter—he was on his way to that horrible club. If I'd still been the project manager, I'd never have allowed such an establishment right next to the stadium.

"That night, the arena was absolutely stunning. It shone at me in the moonlight. I put the box on the North Stand. The lettering gleamed all white in the dark: 'Minex 50 x 550, 24kg, 15 p.c.s. 1,600g.' I put the masking tape next to the box. It would be so easy to prime the charge, all I had to do was put the metal piece into one of the sausages and pull the fuse over toward the main entrance. There I put the battery and set the timer in the way I'd practised. Where did I practise? In a gravel pit outside Rimbo, in the Lohärad parish. The bus only runs twice a day, but I've had plenty of time to wait. I've only set off small charges, one peppermint rock at a time; they'll last me a long time yet.

"When I'd finished my preparations, I went and unlocked the main entrance, but I left the building via this passage. The entrance here from the stadium is at the bottom of the basement, deep under the main entrance. You can go down with the main elevator, but I used the stairs. Then I walked quickly over to Ringvägen; I was afraid I'd be too late. But I wasn't, on the contrary. I had to wait for a long time in a doorway on the other side of the street. When Christina stepped out, I dialed her number from my cellphone. They can't trace me, because I used a pay-as-you-go card. They couldn't trace the call to your car yesterday either; I still had time left on the card.

"It was easy to persuade Christina to come to the stadium. I told her I knew everything about her and Helena, that I had photographs of it all, and that I'd give the negatives to Hans Bjällra, the chairman of the board, if she didn't come and talk to me. Bjällra hates Christina. Everyone at the Secretariat knows that. He would pounce on the first opportunity to humiliate her. So, Christina came, but she must have been in two minds about it. She came walking across the footbridge from South Island, fuming. It took her quite a while. For a while I thought she wasn't going to show up.

"I was waiting inside the entryway, hiding among the shadows behind the statues. My blood was boiling. The whole building was exulting. My stadium was behind me; it would stand by me. I wanted to do this properly. Christina was going to die in the place where she had broken me. She was going to be torn to pieces on the Victoria Stadium North Stand because I had been. When she entered, I was going to hit her on the head with a hammer, the builder's classic tool. Then I'd move her to the stand, prime the charge, and with my snakes of pink plastic coiled around her body, I would tell her why she was here. I was going to reveal to her that I'd seen her monster. My superiority would shine like a star in the night. Christina would ask my forgiveness, and the explosion would be the consummation of our relationship."

Beata paused for a moment to drink some Coke. Annika felt like she was about to faint.

"Unfortunately, that's not how it happened," Beata said quietly. "But the truth has to be told. I'm not trying to be a hero. I know that there'll be people who'll think I've done wrong. That's why it's important not to lie. You have to write it as it really was. Not glamorize it."

Annika nodded sincerely.

"Everything went wrong. Hitting Christina with a hammer didn't knock her out; it only made her mad as hell. She started screaming like a madwoman that I was an incompetent lunatic and that I should leave her alone. I kept hitting her with my hammer. One blow hit her on the mouth and some of her teeth flew out. She screamed and screamed, and I hit and hit. The hammer was dancing on her face. There's a lot of blood in a person's eyes. I didn't know that. In the end she fell down, and it wasn't a pretty sight. She went on screaming, and to make sure she wouldn't get up again, I smashed her kneecaps in. I didn't enjoy it. It was hard work and difficult to do. You understand that, don't you? She wouldn't stop screaming, so I hit her on the throat. When I tried dragging her up to the stand, she scratched my hands. I had to hit her on the elbows and the fingers, too. Then I started the long climb up on the stand, up to the place where she'd stood that day she crushed me. I started sweating. She was quite heavy, and she wouldn't stop moaning. By the time I reached my treasure, my arms were shaking. I put her between the seats and started tying the explosives to her with the masking tape.

"But Christina didn't understand it was time to give up. Her role was to be the audience. She squirmed like the worm she was, and got out on the steps next to her. She started rolling down the stands, screaming all the while. I started losing control of my work; it was terrible. I went and got hold of her and hit her on the back a few times. I don't know if I broke it. In the end, she was lying still enough for me to tie the sausages on her. Fifteen in all. There was no time for forgiveness or reflection. I just pushed the metal piece into one of the sausages and ran over to the battery. The timer was set for five minutes, but I turned it down to three. Christina was still whimpering; she didn't sound human. She sounded like the monster she was. I stood at the entrance, listening to her song of death. When only thirty seconds remained, she managed to get two of the charges loose, despite her smashed-up limbs. That shows her strength, don't you think? Unfortunately, I couldn't stay to the end. I missed her last seconds because I had to take cover in my cave. I was halfway down the stairs when the shockwave hit me. I was amazed. I think I'd underestimated the power of the explosive. The damage was enormous. The whole North Stand was destroyed. That wasn't my intention, you understand that, don't you? I didn't want to damage the stadium. What had happened was none of the building's doing . . ."

Annika felt her tears rolling. She had never written anything so appalling in her life. She was close to passing out. She'd been sitting on the stool for several hours. Her legs ached so badly she wanted to scream out. The charge on her back was heavy. She was so tired she just wanted to lie down, even if it meant setting off the charge and dying.

"Why are you crying?" Beata said suspiciously.

Annika breathed for a second before she replied: "Because it got so difficult for you. Why couldn't she have let you do it the right way?"

Beata nodded and also wiped away a tear. "I know," she said. "Life's never fair."

"It was easier with Stefan. That went more or less according to my plans. I made him responsible for finishing off the judges' changing rooms before the Christmas holidays. The choice of location was simple. That's where I first met Stefan and where he told me that the workers in Sätra Hall would all freeze me out.

I knew he would do the work himself. Stefan played the horses and took every opportunity to put in some overtime. He saw to it that he was the only one left at the site, and then he bumped up his hours on his time sheet. This must have been going on for years. No one ever checked up on him since he was a foreman. Besides, he was a fast worker when he wanted to be and pretty sloppy, too.

"Last Monday, I went to work as usual. Everyone was talking about the blowing up of Christina Furhage, but no one said anything to me. I hadn't expected them to either.

"In the evening, I stayed on in the office with my papers. When the hall was quiet, I took a stroll and saw that Stefan Bjurling was working in the changing rooms at the far end. I went to my locker and got out my gym bag. Inside it were my treasures: the peppermint rocks, the yellow and green wires, the masking tape, and the small timer. This time I didn't bring a hammer; it had been far too messy. Instead I'd bought a rope, the kind you use for children's swings and similar. The rope around your neck is from the same roll. While Stefan was drilling into the far wall, I walked in, put the rope around his neck and pulled. Hard. This time I was more determined. I would not tolerate any screaming or fighting. Stefan Bjurling dropped the drill and tumbled backwards. I was ready for it and used his fall to pull the noose even tighter. He lost consciousness and I struggled to get him onto the chair standing nearby. I tied him to it and dressed him for his funeral. Peppermint rocks, fuse, timer, and flashlight battery. I fastened it all to his back and waited patiently for him to come around.

"He didn't say anything, but I saw that his eyelids were twitching. I explained to him what was going to happen and why. The reign of Evil on Earth was coming to an end. He was going to die because he was a monster. I explained to him that more people would go his way. I have many more treasures in my box. Then I set the timer for five minutes and walked back to my office. On my way, I made sure that all doors were unlocked. The Bomber would have had no problem getting inside the building. I pretended to be shocked by the explosion when I called the police. I lied to them and said someone else had done what was really my work. They took me to South Hospital and escorted me into the Accident and Emergency Department. They said they wanted to interview me the following day. I decided to go on lying for the time being. The time wasn't yet ripe for the truth. It is now.

"The doctors examined me, I assured them I was just fine, and then I walked through the city, past Yttersta Tvärgränd and home. I realized it was time for me to leave my house for good. That night I slept in it for the last time. It was a brief and composed leavetaking. I already knew then that I would never return. My wanderings will end elsewhere.

"Early Tuesday morning, I went to work to collect my last belongings. When I entered Sätra Hall, I was met by the instant and unfair censure of the building. I was overcome with a deep and heavy sadness, so I hid in a room where the building couldn't see me. In vain, naturally, because that's when you found me."

Annika felt she couldn't write any more. She put her hands on her lap and bowed her head.

"What is it?" Beata asked.

"I'm so tired," Annika said. "Can I stand up and move my legs? They've fallen asleep."

Beata looked at her in silence for a moment. "All right, then, but don't you try anything.

Annika slowly stood up; she had to lean against the wall not to fall over. She stretched and bent her legs as well as she could with the rattling chains. She glanced furtively at her feet and saw that Beata had used two small padlocks to fasten the chains. If only she could get hold of the keys somehow, she could get loose. It looked hopeless. She didn't even know where the keys were.

"Don't think you can get away," Beata said.

Annika looked up with feigned surprise. "Of course not," she said. "We haven't finished our work yet."

She moved the stool away from the table a bit to get more room for her legs.

"There's not much left now," Beata said.

She studied Annika, and Annika realized that she didn't know what to think.

"Do you want to read it?" she said and turned the computer so that the screen was facing Beata.

The woman didn't reply.

"It would be good if you could read it through to make sure I've got everything right. And you should size up my tone of voice. I haven't quoted you directly all the time, but have made your story a bit more literary," Annika said.

Beata studied Annika closely, then she walked up to the table and moved it closer to her.

"Could I rest for a while?" Annika wondered, and Beata nodded.

Annika lay down and turned her back to the Bomber. She needed to think about her next move.

Two years before, a man in his sixties had disappeared on the ice in the Stockholm archipelago. It was a sunny and warm late-winter day. The man had gone out walking and lost his way. For three days and nights the coast guard and the police had searched for him. Annika had been in the helicopter that finally saved him.

Suddenly, she knew exactly what she had to do.

Thomas got up from the bed. He wouldn't be able to get any more sleep. He went to the bathroom and peed. He went over to the living room window and stood staring at the Royal Palace again. The traffic had died down. The floodlit facades on the majestic neighboring buildings, the glimmering streetlights, the depth of the black water—the view really was stunning. Yet he felt he couldn't stand it for another second. He felt as if he'd lost Annika right here in this room. It was here that he'd realized that she might be gone forever.

He rubbed his dry, red eyes and heaved a deep sigh. He'd made up his mind. As soon as the children woke up, they'd leave the hotel and go to his parents' home in Vaxholm. They would spend Christmas with them instead. He had to experience what life without Annika might look like. He had to prepare, or he'd go to pieces. He tried to imagine how he'd react if they told him that she was dead. He couldn't. The only thing that would remain would be a bottomless black hole. He'd have to go on, for the children, for Annika. They would have pictures of Mommy everywhere. They would often talk about her and celebrate her birthdays . . .

He turned away from the window and began crying again.

"Why are you sad, Daddy?"

Kalle was standing in the bedroom door. Thomas quickly composed himself.

"I'm sad because Mommy isn't here. I miss her, that's all."

"Grown-ups get sad too sometimes," Kalle said.

Thomas went up to the boy and took him in his arms.

"Yes, and we cry when things are hard. But do you know what? You should get some more sleep. Do you know what day it is today?"

"Christmas!" the boy shouted.

"Shh, you'll wake up Ellen. Yes, it's Christmas, and Santa will come tonight. You'll have to be awake for that, so hurry back to bed now."

"I have to go to the toilet first," Kalle said, struggling free from Thomas's arms.

When the boy returned from the bathroom, he asked: "Why isn't Mommy coming?"

"She'll be here later," Thomas said without a moment's hesitation.

"It's Disney on TV today, and Mommy loves to watch that on Christmas Eve. Will she be back to watch it?"

"I'm sure she will," Thomas said and kissed the boy on his head. "Off you go to bed!"

Tucking the boy in under the fluffy duvet, his eyes landed on the clock-radio next to the bed. The digital red numbers colored the corner of the pillowcase pink. They were showing 5:49.

"This is good," Beata said contentedly. "It's exactly as I wanted it."

Annika had fallen into a light doze but immediately sat up when the Bomber started talking.

"I'm glad you think so. I've done my best."

"Yes, you really have. That's the nice thing about professionals," Beata said and smiled.

Annika returned the smile, and they sat smiling at each other until Annika decided it was time to implement her plan.

"Do you know what day it is today?" she said, still smiling.

"Christmas Eve, of course," Beata said and laughed. "Of course I know that!"

"Yes, but the time leading up to Christmas always flies past. I hardly ever manage to buy all the gifts in time. But do you know what—I've got something for you, Beata."

The woman instantly became suspicious. "You couldn't have bought a present for me. You don't know me."

Annika was smiling so hard that her jaws were beginning to ache.

"I do now. I bought the present for a friend, a woman who deserves it. But I think you deserve it more."

Beata didn't believe her. "Why would you give me a present? I'm the Bomber."

"It's not for the Bomber," Annika said in a steady voice. "It's for Beata, a girl who's had a really shitty time. I think you need a nice Christmas gift after all you've been through."

Her words were upsetting Beata's calculations, Annika could see that. The woman's gaze was wandering, and she was twiddling the fuse with her fingers.

"When did you buy it?" she asked uncertainly.

"The other day. It's very nice."

"Where is it, then?"

"In my bag. It's at the bottom, underneath my sanitary towels."

Beata winced, just as Annika had gambled she would. Beata was squeamish about her female functions. She was really rolling the dice.

"It's a beautiful little parcel," Annika said. "If you get the bag, I'll give you your Christmas gift."

Beata didn't buy that, Annika immediately saw.

"Don't try anything," she said menacingly and got to her feet.

Annika sighed. "I'm not the one walking around with

dynamite in my bag. There's nothing in that bag except for a pad, some pens, a packet of sanitary towels, and a present for you. Get it and see for yourself!"

Annika held her breath; she was taking a big risk. Beata hesitated for a moment.

"I don't want to rummage through your bag," she said.

Annika took a deep breath. "What a pity. The present would have looked nice on you."

That made Beata's mind up. She put the battery and the fuse on the floor and picked up the end of the rope tied around Annika's neck.

"If you try anything, I'll pull."

Annika put her hands in the air and smiled. Beata walked backwards to the place where the bag had landed more than sixteen hours ago. She picked up both the handles with one hand, holding the rope in the other. She slowly walked up to Annika.

"I'll be standing here all the time," she said and dropped the bag in Annika's lap.

Annika's heart was pounding so hard her head was echoing. Her whole body was shaking; this was her only chance. She smiled up at Beata, hoping her pulse wasn't visible on her temples. Then she looked down at Beata's legs. She was still holding on to the handles of the bag. Slowly, she put her hand into the bag and found the parcel right away, the little box with the garnet brooch for Anne Snapphane. She quickly started feeling among the things inside the bag.

"What are you doing?" Beata said, snatching the bag away from her.

"I'm sorry," Annika said, barely making out her own voice for the thundering noise of her beating heart. "I can't find it. Let me try again."

Beata hesitated for several seconds. Annika's brain had stopped working. She mustn't plead because that would be the end of it. She had to play on Beata's curiosity.

"I don't want to tell you what it is beforehand; that would spoil the surprise. But I think you'll like it," Annika said.

The woman held out the bag once more, and Annika took a deep breath. She firmly pushed her arm down, felt the parcel, and right next to it the phone. Dear God, she thought, please let the hands-free kit be connected! Her upper lip was covered in sweat. The battery side was turned up, good, or Beata might see the green display light up. She'd done this a thousand times without giving it a thought. She fumbled for the different buttons, found the big oval one, and pressed it lightly. Then she moved her finger an inch down to the right, found the number one button, pressed that, and moved her finger back to the big one for a third push.

"There we are. I've got it," Annika said, moving her hand to the package nearby. Her arm was shaking when she lifted it out, but Beata didn't notice. All the Bomber saw was the gold wrapping paper and the blue ribbon gleaming in the harsh light. There was no sound from the bag. The hands-free kit was connected. Beata backed away and put the bag next to the dynamite box. Annika desperately needed air and forced herself to soundlessly take deep, gulping breaths. "Menu-1-Menu," she had pressed; "Phone book-Newsdesk-Dial."

"Can I open it now?" Beata said, full of expectation.

Annika couldn't speak. She just nodded.

Jansson had sent off the last page to the printers. He was always a little tired the first night of his shift, but now he felt totally paralyzed. He usually had breakfast in the cafeteria, a cheese roll and big mug of tea, but he wouldn't have any today. He'd just stood up and was putting on his jacket when his phone rang. Jansson groaned loudly and considered not even checking the display to see who it was. I'd better, he thought, it could be the printers. Sometimes the color files weren't transferred properly and the yellow plate would be missing. He reached out for the phone and saw the familiar number. At the same moment, every single hair on his body stood on end.

"It's Annika!" he bellowed. "Annika is phoning on my extension!"

Anders Schyman, Patrik, Berit, and Janet Ullberg all turned toward him from where they were standing at the picture desk.

"There's a call from Annika's cellphone!" he roared. He was staring wide-eyed at his telephone.

"Then pick it up, for God's sake, pick it up!" Schyman shouted back and started running across the floor.

Jansson took a deep breath and picked up the phone.

"Annika! Annika, is that you?"

There was nothing but a crackle and hum.

"Hello! Annika!"

The others had reached Jansson's desk and were standing around him.

"Hello? Hello! Are you there?"

"Give it to me," Schyman said.

Jansson handed the phone to the editor. Schyman put the receiver to his ear and plugged the other with a finger. He heard static and buzzing, and a rising and falling noise which could be voices.

"She must be alive," he whispered, handing the phone back to Jansson. "Don't hang up." He walked into his office and phoned the police.

"It's beautiful! Absolutely beautiful."

Beata really sounded overwhelmed. Annika felt a renewed energy.

"It's old, almost antique," she said. "Real garnets and gold on top of silver. It's the kind of thing I would like to have myself. Those are the best gifts, don't you think?"

The woman didn't reply, just stared at the brooch.

"I've always been fond of jewelry," Annika said. "When I was a little girl, I saved up money for years to buy a heart of white gold with a wreath of diamonds. I had seen it in a catalog from the jeweler's shop in town, one of those mailings they do before Christmas. When I finally had saved enough to buy it, I'd outgrown it all and bought a set of skis instead . . ."

"Thank you so much," the Bomber said in a hushed voice.

"My pleasure," Annika said. "My grandmother had a similar brooch, maybe that's why I decided on it."

Beata undid the top buttons of her coat and pinned the brooch to her sweater.

"This could be the breakthrough we need," the cop on the phone told Schyman. "You can hang up now; the call has gone through. We'll fix the rest together with the service provider now."

"What are you going to do?" Schyman asked.

"We'll contact the central operations office of the service provider, Comviq, out in Kista. They may be able to trace the call."

"Can I come with you?" Schyman quickly asked.

The policeman wavered only briefly. "I don't see why not," he said.

Schyman hurried back to the newsroom.

"The police are tracing the call, so you can hang up now," he called out, putting his coat on.

"Do you think it'll do any harm if we keep listening?" asked Berit, who was now sitting with the phone against her ear.

"I don't know. I'll call if that's the case. Don't anyone leave. I need you all to stay right here."

He took the stairs down to the entrance and noticed his legs were shaking from weariness. It wouldn't be a good idea to drive now, he thought, and ran over to the taxi stand.

It was still dark outside and the road out to Kista was deserted. They drove fast and met only a few other cars along the way, the taxi driver saluting those from his own firm with his left hand. They reached Borgarfjordsgatan, and while Schyman was paying the taxi with his company card, a car drove up next to them and stopped. A man got out and came over to Schyman. He asked Schyman who he was and introduced himself as a police officer.

"If we're lucky we might be able to track her down this way," the policeman said.

His face was white with exhaustion and there was a rigid line round his mouth. Suddenly Anders Schyman thought he knew who this man must be.

"Do you know Annika?" the editor asked.

The policeman drew a deep breath and looked askance at Schyman.

"Sort of," he said.

At that moment, a sleepy security guard appeared and let them into the building housing the head offices of both Comviq and Tele2. He led them through a series of long passages and corridors until they eventually stepped into a room filled by enormous TV screens. Anders Schyman gave a whistle.

"Looks like in an American spy movie, doesn't it?" a man approaching them said.

The editor nodded and said hello to the man. "Or the control room at a nuclear power station," Schyman said.

"I'm a systems technician here. Welcome. Please come this way," the man said and showed them to the center of the room.

Anders Schyman slowly followed the cop and the technician. The room was packed with computers; projectors made the walls serve as gigantic computer screens.

"From here we control the entire Comviq network," the technician began. "There are two of us working the night shift. The search you want to do is a very simple one. I only had to execute one single command from my terminal and the search is underway."

He indicated his workstation. Anders Schyman had no idea what he was looking at.

"It'll take up to fifteen minutes, even though I limited the search to start at 5 A.M. It's been going about ten minutes now. Let's have a look and see if we've got anything . . ."

He turned to a computer and clicked on the keyboard. "Nope, nothing yet," he said.

"Fifteen minutes, isn't that very long?" Anders Schyman said, noticing how dry his mouth was.

The technician regarded him steadily. "Fifteen minutes is quick. It's Christmas Eve morning, and there's very little traffic right now. That's why I think the search will be fast."

As he said that, a row of data appeared on the screen. He turned his back to Schyman and the cop and sat on his chair. He clattered away on his keyboard for a couple of minutes, then gave a sigh. "I can't find it. Are you sure the call came from her cellphone?"

Schyman's pulse quickened. They couldn't screw it up. He felt confusion mount within him. Did these people even know what had happened? Did they know how important it was?

"Our night editor would know her number in his sleep. They were still sitting around listening to the static from her phone when I left the newspaper," he said and licked his lips.

"Ah, that explains it," the technician said and executed another command. The data disappeared from the screen and it went black.

"All we can do now is wait," he said and turned to face Schyman and the policeman again.

"What do you mean?" Schyman queried, hearing himself sound upset.

"If the call is still going on, we haven't received any information yet. The data is stored internally in the phone for thirty minutes," he said and got up from the chair. "After thirty minutes, the telephone creates a bill, which it then sends here to us. Among that data, we can find A numbers and B numbers, base station and cell."

Anders Schyman looked at the flickering screens and felt ever more confused. Exhaustion was pounding his brain; he felt he was in the middle of a surreal nightmare.

"Please explain that," the cop asked.

"According to your information, the call from Annika Bengtzon reached the newsdesk of *Kvällspressen* just after 6 A.M., right? If the line hasn't been broken, the first data pertaining to the call will reach us just after six thirty, which is soon."

"I don't understand," Schyman said. "How can you tell where she is from her cellphone?"

"This is how it works," the technician said obligingly. "Cellphones work just like radio transmitters and receivers. The signals are transmitted via a number of base stations, that is telephone masts, up and down the country. Each base station has various cells that pick up signals from different places in different directions. All cellphones that are switched on connect with the exchange every four hours. We ran the first search on Annika Bengtzon's telephone number already last night."

"You did?" Schyman said with surprise. "Can you do that on anyone, just like that?"

"Of course not," the technician replied calmly. "Any kind of search like this one has to be authorized by a court order."

He walked over to another screen and typed something on the keyboard. Then he went to a printer and waited for the printout.

"Anyway, the last call from Annika's phone, apart from the ongoing one, was connected at 13:09 yesterday afternoon," he said, studying the sheet. "It was for the daycare center on 38B Scheelegatan in Kungsholmen."

He put the computer printout on his lap. "The signal from Annika's cellphone has been connected via a station in Nacka."

The plain-clothes policeman took over: "The call has been confirmed by the manager of the daycare center. Annika didn't sound strange or at all pressured. She was relieved when she heard they were open until five o'clock. This means she was still moving around freely at 1 P.M., and she was somewhere east of Danvikstull."

The technician went back to reading the printout. "The next signal from her phone went through at 17:09. As I said before, a phone that is switched on connects with the provider's exchange every four hours."

Schyman barely had the energy to listen to the technician. He sank down on an empty swivel chair and rubbed his fingers against his temples.

"There's an internal clock in every telephone that begins the countdown every time it's switched on," the technician continued. "After four hours, the countdown is complete. Then a signal is transmitted that tells the system where the phone is located. Since the signals have been coming through during the night, Annika must have had her cellphone switched on. As far as we can see, she hasn't moved during the night."

Schyman felt his body tense. "So you know where she is?" he said in a strained voice.

"We know that her phone is somewhere near Stockholm city center," the technician said. "We can only see which area it is, and that means the central city districts and the nearby suburbs."

"So she could be somewhere nearby?"

"Yes, her cellphone has not been moved outside of this area during the night."

"Is that why you told us not to phone her?"

The policeman stepped forward. "Yes, and for other reasons. If someone is with her and hears the phone ring, they might switch it off, and then we couldn't tell if she were moved."

"If she is in the same place as the cellphone . . ." Schyman pointed out.

"Hasn't it been fifteen minutes yet?" the policeman asked.

"Not quite," the technician replied.

They turned their attention to the screen and waited. Schyman had to go to the toilet and left the room for a few minutes. As he emptied his bladder, he noticed that his legs were shaking.

Nothing had happened when he returned to the room.

"Nacka," Schyman said absently. "What on earth was she doing there?"

"Here we go," the technician said. "Right, there it is. The A number is for Annika Bengtzon's cellphone, the B number is for the *Kvällspressen* switchboard."

"Can you tell where she is?" the policeman asked tensely.

"Yes, I've got a code here. One moment . . ."

The technician tapped on his keyboard and Schyman felt cold.

"527 D," the technician said doubtfully.

"What?" the policeman said. "What's the matter?"

"We never usually have more than three cells at each base station: A, B, and C. There are more here, and that's very unusual. D cells are usually special ones."

"Where is it?" the policeman asked.

"One moment," the technician said, as he quickly got to his feet and walked over to another terminal.

"What are you doing?" Schyman asked.

"We have more than a thousand masts around Sweden; you can't remember them all," he said apologetically. "Here it is, base station 527 in Hammarby Dock."

Anders Schyman felt his head spin and a strange chill on his neck. Christ, that's the Olympic Village!

The technician had another look. "Cell D is in the tunnel between Victoria Stadium and Training Arena A."

The policeman's face turned even whiter. "What tunnel?"

The technician looked at them gravely. "I'm afraid I can't tell you that, only that there is a tunnel somewhere under the stadium."

"Are you positive?"

"The call was transmitted via a cell that sits in the actual tunnel. A cell usually covers a larger area, but the reception is quite limited in tunnels. We have one cell covering only the South Tunnel, for example."

"So she's in a tunnel under the Olympic Village?" the policeman asked.

"Her phone is, at least. I can guarantee you that," the technician replied.

The policeman was already halfway out of the room.

"Thank you," Anders Schyman said, squeezing the technician's hand between both his own.

Then he hurried after the cop.

Annika had dozed off when she suddenly felt Beata tinkering with something on her back.

"What are you doing?" Annika asked.

"You go on sleeping. I'm just checking that the charge is okay. We're getting nearer the time now."

Annika felt like someone had poured a bucket of ice-cold water over her. All her nerves contracted in a hard knot somewhere in her midriff. She tried to speak, but couldn't. Instead she began shaking all over.

"What's with you?" Beata said. "Don't tell me you'll start acting like Christina. You know I don't like it to be messy."

Annika breathed rapidly and with her mouth slightly open. Calm down, talk to her, come on, talk to her, buy time.

"I was wondering . . . I just wanted to know . . . what will you do with my story?" she managed to squeeze out.

"It'll be published in *Kvällspressen*, as big as when Christina Furhage died," Beata said complacently. "It's a good piece."

Annika braced herself.

"I don't think that's going to be possible," she said.

Beata interrupted what she was doing.

"Why not?"

"How will they get hold of the text? You don't have a modem here."

"I'll just send the whole computer to the paper."

"My editor won't know I wrote it. It doesn't say that anywhere. It's written in the first person. In its present shape, it just looks like a long letter to the editor."

Beata stood her ground. "They'll publish it."

"Why should they? My editor doesn't know who you are. He might not understand how important it is that this piece is published. And who's going to tell him when I'm . . . gone?"

That gave her something to think about, Annika thought as the woman went back to her stool and sat down.

"You're right," she said. "You must write an introduction to the article and tell them exactly how to go about its publication."

Maybe that would buy her a little time. But perhaps she'd been wrong to play so much into the woman's hands. What if it had made everything even worse? But then she dismissed the thought. It couldn't really be much worse. Christina had fought her, and she'd had her face smashed in. If she had to die, it was better to be writing on a computer than to be tortured.

She sat up, her whole body aching. The floor was tottering beneath her feet, and she noticed she had difficulty judging the distance.

"Okay," she said. "Give me the computer and we'll finish this off."

Beata pushed the table back.

"Say that you've written it and that they must publish the piece in its entirety."

Annika wrote. She knew she had to buy more time. If she'd succeeded with the phone, the police ought to be somewhere nearby now. She didn't know how accurately the cellphone would pinpoint her, but the man out on the ice two years ago had been located immediately. He had been beyond all hope; his family had already begun to make arrangements for a memorial service when he phoned his son on his cellphone. The old man had been completely exhausted and very confused. He had had no idea where he was. He couldn't describe any landmarks. It's all white, was all he could say. Not a particularly distinctive feature in Sweden in the winter.

Still the man had been rescued within an hour. With the help of the phone operator, the police had narrowed down his whereabouts to within a radius of six hundred meters, and they'd found the man inside that circle. And the operator had been able to determine that from the signal of the cellphone.

"By the way," Annika said, "how did you get inside the stadium?"

"Nothing to it," Beata said in a superior manner. "I had both a card and the code."

"How come? It's been a couple of years since you worked on the arena."

Beata got to her feet. "I've already told you that," she said stridently. "I worked in the pool and visited every paltry little hall that was connected to the Games. We had access to the central office where all entry cards and codes are kept. We had to sign for them and hand them back after we were done, of course, but I managed to take a few. I wanted to be able to visit the buildings that spoke nicely to me. The Olympic stadium and I have always gotten along very well. I've always kept a card to this place."

"And the code?"

Beata sighed. "I'm good with computers," she said. "The codes for the arena are changed every month, and the changes are recorded in a special computer file that you have to have a password to enter. They never changed the password."

She smiled a lopsided smile. Annika started writing again. She had to think of other questions to ask.

"What are you writing?"

Annika looked up. "I'm explaining the importance of

making this story as big as the death of Christina Furhage," she said cheerfully.

"You're lying!" Beata cried, and Annika jumped.

"What do you mean?"

"They couldn't make as many pages as when Christina died." Beata suddenly looked wild. "You know it was *you* who started calling me 'The Bomber'? Can you imagine how much I hate that name? Can you?! You were the worst of all of them. You always wrote that bullshit on the front page. I hate you!"

Beata's eyes were on fire, and Annika realized that she had nothing to say.

"You came in the room where I had been overcome by sorrow," Beata said, slowly approaching Annika. "You saw me in my misery and yet you didn't help me. You listened to the others but not to me. It's been like that my whole life. No one has heard me call out. No one but my houses. But that's finished now. I'll get you all!"

The woman reached out for the rope hanging from Annika's neck.

"No!" Annika cried out.

Her cry made Beata stop momentarily in her tracks. Then she grabbed the rope and pulled it as tight as she could, but Annika had been prepared. She got both her hands in between the rope and her neck. The Bomber tugged again and Annika fell off her stool. She managed to twist her body so that she fell on her side and not on the charge.

"You're going to die now, you bitch!" Beata screamed, and in the same instant Annika noticed there was something wrong with the echo. Next she felt a cold draught on the floor.

"Help!" she cried out as loud as she could.

"Stop screaming!" Beata roared and pulled again at

the rope. She pulled Annika further out onto the floor, grazing her face on the concrete.

"I'm here, around the corner!" Annika cried, and right then Beata must have caught sight of them. She dropped the rope, turned around, and searched along the wall with her eyes. Annika knew what she was looking for. As if in slow motion, she saw Beata start for the battery and the fuse. The shot was fired a fraction of a second later. It ripped open a crater high up on Beata's back, pushing her violently forward. Another shot rang out. Annika instinctively turned her back to the wall, away from the gunfire.

"No!" she screamed. "Don't shoot, for Christ's sake! You might hit the charge!"

As the echo of the last shot died down, she saw smoke and dust in the air. Beata lay still a few yards away from her. The silence was complete. All she could hear was a high-frequency ringing in her ears from the shots. Suddenly, she felt that someone was standing next to her. She looked up at a pale, plain-clothes policeman stooped over her with his weapon drawn.

"You!" she said with surprise.

The man looked at her anxiously and loosened the noose around her neck. "Yes, me," he said. "How are you? Are you okay?"

It was her secret source, her "deep throat." She smiled wanly and felt him pull the rope over her head. To her surprise, she burst into a flood of tears.

The policeman picked up his radio and called out his number. "We need two ambulances," he said, looking up and down the passageway.

"I'm okay," Annika whispered.

"Hurry, we've got a gunshot injury," he called out on the radio.

"I've got an explosive charge on my back."

The man lowered his radio.

"What did you say?"

"There's an explosive charge on my back here. Have a look."

She turned around and the policeman saw the pack of dynamite on her back.

"Oh, my God, don't move," he said.

"It's all right," Annika said, wiping her cheeks with the back of her hand. "It's been there all night without going off."

"Evacuate the tunnel!" he shouted back toward the door. "Hold the ambulance people! We've got a charge here!"

The man leaned over her, and Annika closed her eyes. She could hear there were more people nearby, steps and voices.

"Take it easy, Annika, we'll sort it out," the policeman said.

Beata groaned where she lay on the floor.

"Make sure she doesn't get hold of the fuse," Annika said in a low voice.

The man got to his feet and followed the fuse with his eyes. Then he took a few steps, grabbed the yellow and green wire, and pulled it to him.

"There we are," he said to Annika. "Let's see what you've got here."

"It's Minex," Annika said. "Small, like peppermint rock."

"Yes," the policeman replied. "What else do you know?"

"It's approximately four pounds, and the firing switch could be unstable."

"Shit! I'm not very good with these things," he said.

Annika heard sirens far away. "Are they coming here?"

"Right again. Lucky you're still alive."

"It wasn't easy," Annika said, sniffling.

"Keep very still now . . ."

He studied the charge with great concentration for a few seconds. Then he grabbed the fuse, at the top of the charge, and pulled it out. Nothing happened.

"Thank God," he mumbled. "It was as easy as I thought."

"What?" Annika asked.

"This is an everyday charge, the kind you use at building sites. It wasn't booby-trapped. All you have to do to disarm it is to pull the metal piece away from the cartridge."

"You're joking," Annika said in disbelief. "I could have pulled it out myself, when she wasn't here?"

"More or less."

"So why the hell have I been sitting here all night?" she said, furious with herself.

"Annika, Annika, there was a noose around your neck as well. That could have killed you just as effectively. And were your hands free? You've got some nasty bruises, by the way. And if she had as much as let the fuse touch the battery it would have been the end, both for her and you."

"There's a timer as well."

"Hang on, let me get this off your back. What the hell has she fastened it with?"

"Masking tape."

"Okay. There's no wiring inside the tape? Good, I'll just rip it off . . . There, it's gone now."

Annika felt the weight lift from her back. She leaned back against the wall and pulled the tape from her stomach.

"You couldn't have gotten far anyway, the policeman said, pointing at the chains. "Do you know where the keys are?"

Annika shook her head and pointed at Beata. "She must have them on her somewhere."

The policeman picked up his radio and called out that the others could come in; the charge was disarmed.

"There's more dynamite over there," Annika said, pointing.

"Good, we'll take care of it.

He picked up the taped-up cartridges and put them among the others and then went up to Beata. The woman lay on her stomach, completely still, with blood running out of a hole in her shoulder. The policeman felt her pulse and lifted her eyelids.

"Will she live?" Annika asked.

"Who gives a damn?" he answered.

Annika heard herself say: "I do."

Two paramedics appeared in the tunnel, wheeling a stretcher between them. The policeman helped them lift Beata onto it. On his instruction, one of the paramedics went through her pockets and found two padlock keys.

"I'll do it," Annika said, and the policeman handed them over to her.

The paramedics checked Beata's vital signs while Annika unlocked the chains. She stood up on shaky legs and watched the men pushing Beata toward the exit of the tunnel. The woman's eyelids fluttered and she caught sight of Annika. It seemed as if she tried to say something, but her voice didn't carry.

Annika followed the stretcher with her eyes while it disappeared around the corner. Policemen and civilians were standing in the passageway. Speech was filling the air, voices rising and falling. She blocked her ears: She was near collapse.

"Do you need help?" her source said.

She sighed and felt that her tears were near. "I want to go home," was all she said.

"You have to go to the hospital for a check-up," he said.

"No," Annika said firmly, thinking of her soiled trousers. "I want to go past Hantverkargatan first. Where's Thomas? And the kids? Are they there?"

"Come on, I'll help you out. Everyone's fine. We're looking after them."

The man grabbed her around the waist and led her toward the exit. Annika realized something was missing.

"Hang on, my bag," she said, stopping. "I want my bag and the Powerbook."

The man said something to a uniformed policeman and someone handed Annika her bag.

"Is this your computer?" the policeman asked her.

Annika hesitated.

"Do I need to answer that right now?"

"No, it can wait. Let's get you home first."

They were approaching the exit and Annika glimpsed a wall of people in the dark outside the arena. Instinctively, she drew back.

"It's just police and medical personnel out there," the man next to her said.

At the same moment that she put her foot on the ground outside, a flash went off right in her face. For a second, she was blinded and heard herself cry out. The contours returned and she caught sight of the camera and the photographer. In two bounds, she reached him and decked him with a straight right.

"You bastard!" she screamed.

"Christ, Annika, what are you doing?" the photographer yelped.

It was Henriksson.

She asked the police to stop at a corner shop near her house and buy her some conditioner. Then she walked the two floors up to her apartment, unlocked the front door, and stepped inside the quiet hallway. It felt like another time, as if several years had gone by since she was here last. She pulled off all her clothes and dropped them on the floor. She took a towel from the toilet next door and wiped her stomach and bottom. She marched straight into the shower and spent a long time in there. She knew that Thomas was at the Grand Hotel. They'd come home when the children woke up.

She put on clean clothes. All the used ones, including the shoes and the coat, she put in a big black trash bag. She picked up the trash bag and went and threw it in the communal refuse room.

Now there was only one thing she had to do before she could lie down and sleep. She switched on Christina's computer; the battery was nearly dead. She got a disk and downloaded her own piece to it. She hesitated for a moment, but then she clicked on Christina's file, marked "Me."

There were seven documents, seven chapters that all began with one single word: Existence, Love, Humanity, Happiness, Lies, Evil, and Death.

Annika opened the first one and started reading.

She had spoken to everyone around Christina Furhage: her family, her lover, her colleagues, everyone who knew her. They had all contributed to the image of the Olympic supremo that Annika had formed in her mind.

At last, Christina was speaking for herself.

# EPILOGUE

Late in June, exactly six months after the last explosion, Beata Ekesjö was convicted by the Stockholm City Court of three counts of murder, four counts of attempted murder, arson, the destruction of civic buildings, endangering the lives of the public, unlawful abduction, theft, and driving without a license. She did not utter one word during the trial.

Beata Ekesjö was sectioned under the Mental Health Act to indefinite detention in a secure unit, subject to Home Office conditions. The sentence was not appealed, and it came into effect three weeks later.

Hardly anyone noticed, but all through the five-week-long trial the defendant wore the same piece of jewelry. It was a cheap, old garnet brooch in gold and silver.

The story of how the constructional engineer Beata Ekesjö became the serial killer called "The Bomber" was never published.

## AUTHOR'S NOTE

This is a work of fiction. All similarities between the characters in the novel and any real living persons are entirely accidental.

The newspaper *Kvällspressen* doesn't exist. It has traits of various existing media companies but is wholly a product of the author's imagination.

All the places that the characters in the novel visit have, however, been rendered as they are or would have looked. This includes Victoria Olympic Stadium and the Olympic Village.